Mrs. Kaputnik's
Pool Hall and Matzo Ball
Emporium

Rona Arato

Tundra Books

Published in Canada by Tundra Books,
75 Sherbourne Street, Toronto, Ontario M5A 2P9

Published in the United States by Tundra Books of Northern New York,
P.O. Box 1030, Plattsburgh, New York 12901

Library of Congress Control Number: 2009928987

Library and Archives Canada Cataloguing in Publication

Arato, Rona
    Mrs. Kaputnik's pool hall and matzo ball
emporium / Rona Arato.

ISBN 978-0-88776-967-2

    I. Title.

PS8601.R35M78 2010   jC813'.6   C2009-902986-3

We acknowledge the financial support of the Government of Canada through the
Book Publishing Industry Development Program (BPIDP) and that of the Government
of Ontario through the Ontario Media Development Corporation's Ontario Book
Initiative. We further acknowledge the support of the Canada Council for the Arts and
the Ontario Arts Council for our publishing program.

ONTARIO ARTS COUNCIL
CONSEIL DES ARTS DE L'ONTARIO

Design by Leah Springate

Printed and bound in Canada

1 2 3 4 5 6   15 14 13 12 11 10

For Alise, Debbie, and Daniel,
who grew up listening to stories about Snigger

———

Acknowledgments

I want to thank my publisher, Kathy Lowinger, for her faith in Mrs. Kaputnik and her wonderful comments and insights, and my editor, Lauren Bailey, for her fabulous suggestions, encouragement, and hard work. And to my children, Alise, Debbie, and Daniel, and my husband, Paul, thanks for pushing me to write down the stories that you so patiently listened to over and over and can now share with our new generation.

None of the animals is so wise as the dragon....
– LU DIAN, Chinese scholar (AD 1042-1102)

CHAPTER I

A Mysterious Egg

Shoshi Kapustin clapped her hands over her ears to shut out the pitying voices.

"Those poor darlings. Abandoned by such a selfish father. Mark my words: He has a new family in America. My cousin went to New York and never sent for his wife and children either."

The village women were gossiping while waiting to draw water from the well, and, as usual, her family was their favorite subject. "You think you know everything, you miserable *yentas*," Shoshi said. When it was her turn, she lowered her bucket so hard it slammed the surface of the water.

"Such manners," sniffed the baker's wife. "But then, look at her with that blazing hair and a temper to match. And a mother who lets her children run wild like animals."

Shoshi felt a sharp finger poke her back. "Hurry child," the rabbi's wife barked. "Passover starts in six hours, and we *all* need water."

Shoshi whirled around, and her braids slapped her face like fiery whips. "My father *will* send for us. And when he does, we will join him in America and pick gold from the streets." She grasped the rope-handled bucket with both hands and marched down the village street, searching the crowd for her mother.

Mama would reassure her that Papa still loved them. Holding the bucket carefully, Shoshi walked past the ramshackle wooden buildings lining the muddy street. She peered into the butcher shop, with its thick carpet of chicken feathers, but her mother wasn't there. She scanned the crowd of women buying Passover matzos in the bakery, but her mother wasn't one of them. Shoshi found her standing at a table in front of the synagogue, selling the last of her meager supply of fresh eggs.

Her mother's head was covered in a black scarf, which hid all but a few strands of dark hair threaded with silver. Her eyes crinkled as she smiled at Shoshi, and she opened her arms. Shoshi plunked down the bucket and rushed in for a soothing hug.

"Mama, the baker's wife says that Papa will never send for us."

"That woman has razor for a tongue. May it cut her words to pieces so they can't do any harm." Ruth

Kapustin stroked her daughter's head. "I've told you over and over. Papa went to America because his brother, Mendel – may he grow like an onion with his head in the ground – borrowed our passage money and used it to open a restaurant. Papa works in the restaurant to make back the money for our steamship tickets."

"Why hasn't he written for five years? The baker's wife says . . ."

"*Shoshile,* gossip is a disease. Do not catch it. Listen to *me.* Your father would never abandon us." She stood and pointed to the synagogue. "Papa carved the Star of David over the synagogue door."

Shoshi looked at the star that her father, Vrod's best carpenter, had carved on the day she was born. As always, she searched for the rose carved at the base. She recalled her mother telling her that Papa had put the rose there because that was what her real name, Shoshanna, meant in Hebrew. The same rose was in the amber charms that he had carved for her and for her younger brother, Moshe.

"Would such a man forget his family?" said Mama. "Besides, if I didn't believe that we are going to America, would I pay good money to Feivel for us to learn English?" She pointed to a tall man in a floppy black coat and wide-brimmed hat, who had just joined them.

"You call that pittance you pay me good money?" Feivel laughed. "Fortunately, my wonderful students make the endeavor worthwhile."

"Thank you." Shoshi blushed.

"In English, Shoshi, talk to me in English, not in Yiddish," said Feivel.

"Yes, Shoshi, speak English. It will take me longer to learn, but if you and your brother speak it, that will help me. Now, Shoshi, please, take the water home."

"Yes, Mama." Shoshi started for home, and Feivel fell into step beside her.

"So, Shoshi," he said, taking the bucket, "do you and Moshe speak English when I'm not with you?"

"Yes. We are getting better every day," Shoshi replied. "I can read almost every word of the American newspapers you give us and so can Moshe."

"Ah, but do you understand what you read?"

"Not everything. But I'm trying. Please thank your American relatives for sending them to us," said Shoshi. "Feivel, when you studied at the university in Kiev, what books did you read?"

Feivel smiled wistfully. "I read many books by great writers like William Shakespeare and Charles Dickens. And, I read *Tom Sawyer* by the American author Mark Twain. It is difficult to understand, but I like it because it is about children, like you and your brother."

"Why did you leave Kiev?"

Feivel rubbed his thumb and forefinger together. "Money. I earned my tuition by working as a tutor for the wife and children of an English professor. I lived in their house and taught them Russian. They helped me improve my English. When the family returned to England, I couldn't find another position in Kiev. There was no work for me in my village, so when your rabbi invited me, I came to Vrod to teach the children Hebrew and mathematics. And English," he added with a smile.

They had reached the Kapustin house. Little more than a stack of boards, it tipped to one side, as if a strong wind could knock it over. Shoshi took the bucket from Feivel. "I'm glad you're here."

"I am too. Happy Passover, Shoshi."

"Happy Passover to you, too." Shoshi opened the door and stepped into the cramped room she shared with her mother and ten-year-old brother, Moshe. She found him hunched over the wooden table in front of the brick oven. Steam misted the air from a large pot of water bubbling on the stove. Mama was making the matzo balls that were her annual contribution to Aunt Rachel's Passover seder.

Her brother looked up at her with a sly look, which usually meant he was about to drop a frog down her dress.

"Moshe, what have you been up to?" Shoshi asked.

"I got Mama a present for Passover." He showed her a dirt-encrusted egg on the table.

"What is it?"

"An egg."

"I can see that. But what kind of egg is it? *Ychh.*" Shoshi wrinkled her nose. "It stinks. Mama won't use it."

"It's only dirty on the outside. Mama said this morning that she only kept three eggs for us, so when the peddler offered to trade one of his. . . ."

"What peddler?"

"A man I met in the woods."

"*Moshe* Kaputstin, you went to the forest? You know we're not supposed to go there. It's too dangerous. There are wolves and bears . . . and *dybbuk*s."

"I don't believe in dybbuks. Mama says they're old wives' tales made up by stupid people who have nothing better to talk about. Besides, have you forgotten Papa's stories? Our forest is enchanted. It's called the Amber Forest because it has magic trees."

"You don't believe in dybbuks, but you believe the forest is enchanted?" Shoshi rolled her eyes. "Papa didn't say the forest was magic, he said the trees in the forest *give* magic. Amber comes from the sap of the trees." She pulled out her necklace. "He made us these for good luck."

Moshe pulled his own amber charm from beneath his shirt. "I know. That's why I'm not afraid to go into the forest. Besides, I was only there to gather wood for the stove."

Shoshi looked around. "So, where is the wood?"

Her brother's face turned red. "I sold it."

"Sold it? Who did you sell it to?"

"I sold it to the peddler for that egg."

"You traded good firewood for *that*?" said Shoshi. "*Oy*, Mama is going to kill you. Besides, you shouldn't ever be in the woods. Even if you don't believe in dybbuks, there are still wolves and bears. And the czar's soldiers."

Moshe looked out the narrow slit that was the house's only window toward the Amber Forest. "But Shoshi, the woods are beautiful. The trees are tall, and you can hear the birds sing."

"Oh, Moshe, you'll be the death of me," Shoshi said. "Did you bring home *any* wood?"

Moshe sighed. "No."

She clucked her tongue. "I can't believe you gave the peddler our good wood for that egg."

"That egg is special."

"Says who?"

"The peddler."

"Of course. He wanted to get rid of it, so what else would he say?"

"He said that when it cracks open, there will be enough egg inside for the whole week of Passover."

Before her brother could reply, the door flew open and a man in a dark hooded cloak burst into the house.

"Where is it? WHERE IS IT?" The man crossed the small room in three giant steps. Spying the egg, he moved toward it, but Moshe grabbed it quickly. "I should not have given it to you."

As the man lunged for the egg, his hood fell back, revealing a bony face with deep lines that ran from his prominent nose to his razor-thin mouth. His right eye was sky blue, while his left eye was black as mud. His smile was wavy as a snake.

"You didn't give it to me; I bought it," said Moshe.

The man dug into the pocket of his cloak and pulled out a gold coin. "Then I shall buy it back."

"Moshe, I think that coin is real gold. Give him the egg."

"Why did you sell it to me?" Moshe asked the stranger.

"It was a mistake. I sold you the wrong egg. This one is not good." The snaky smile was still on his face. "I am willing to buy it back."

"Moshe, give it to him," Shoshi hissed.

"That egg is no good to you," the man said. "Only I know its secret and how to use it."

"Secret?" The children exchanged glances.

The man glared at them. Or at least that's what Shoshi supposed he was doing because his blue eye moved toward his nose, while his black eye shifted in the opposite direction. It made him look like the beggar, Mulke, when he was in one of his spells.

"Eggs are the source of life," the man said. "But this egg contains a destructive power. If you keep it, it will haunt your lives forever."

"Moshe, give it back!"

"No," Moshe said. "If this egg really is magic, we can use it to show everyone that the Kapustins are special."

"You foolish boy," the man snarled. He grabbed Moshe and reached for the egg, but it flew out of the boy's hand, bounced off the table, and rolled onto the floor. "Get out of my way," the man roared. "That egg is of no use to you!"

Shoshi stepped in front of him. "If you want it so badly, give us back our wood."

"Wood? That pile of sticks that I took from the boy? *Pfah!* It was rotten, so I threw it away."

"Go get it, and we'll give you the egg," said Shoshi.

"No, we won't," said Moshe. "He can't have the egg. If you want it so much, it must be *really* special."

"It is, but only to me." The peddler reached down to grab the egg, but it rolled across the floor and disappeared behind the oven.

The man started after it, then skidded to a stop. He pulled himself to his full height, straightened his cloak, and cupped a hand to his ear. "I hear thunder. They're coming."

"What do you hear?" Shoshi asked.

"Trouble. Beware." With a swirl of his cloak, the peddler stepped through the door and disappeared into the street.

"We have to get rid of that egg before Mama comes home." As Shoshi spoke, a loud *crrrraaaack* echoed throughout the house. The children jumped. The egg rolled out from behind the oven and bounced toward them. It stopped at Shoshi's feet and, with a sound like river ice breaking during spring thaw, cracked open.

"*Aaah!*" screamed Shoshi. "Moshe, what is it? The peddler was right, it is a dybbuk!"

CHAPTER 2

The Dybbuk

Shoshi and Moshe stared in horror at the animal emerging from its shell. It was dark-green with yellow eyes, wings, and a long spiky tail. It curled into a ball at Shoshi's feet and licked bits of eggshell from its skin with a forked red tongue.

"What is it?" said Shoshi.

"I don't know." Moshe bent down to get a closer look. "It's not a chicken, that's for sure."

Shoshi squatted beside her brother. "Look." She touched a wing. They were like flaps on both sides of its body. "Maybe it's a bird."

The animal lifted its head and flicked its tongue. Sparks flew out of its mouth.

"It's on fire!" Moshe studied the animal. "That's how it breathes." His fear turned to fascination. "It isn't a chicken, and it's certainly not a bird."

Shoshi knelt down and stroked the animal. It licked her hand. "It tickles," she laughed. "Look, Moshe. Its skin is as dimpled as the outside of Mama's matzo balls."

"Matzo balls! Uh, oh! I forgot about the matzo balls!" Moshe dashed across the room, grabbed the pot from the stove, and plunked it onto the dirt floor. "We're in trouble. All the water boiled out and they're like rocks."

"Mama really is going to kill you. She won't have anything to take to Aunt Rachel's for the seder. It's all because of you and this *thing*."

Everyone in Vrod knew Mrs. Kapustin was a terrible cook. While other women produced golden loaves of challah bread and sponge cakes so light, they would float on water, their mother's bread was like bricks and her cake could break a plate. But the matzo balls she made every Passover were soft as clouds.

The animal uncurled a whiplike tail, lifted its head, and breathed out a stream of sparks.

"Look, you scared it," Moshe said.

"I scared *it?*"

Moshe scooped the animal into his palm and lifted it in the air. "There, there, don't be afraid of Shoshi. She just likes to act mean, but I'm used to her. Soon, you will be too."

Shoshi giggled. "I guess it's cute. For a dybbuk."

"Snig, snig, snig, sniggerer, snigger."

"That's what we'll call you: Snigger," said Shoshi.

"*Snig, snig, snigger.*"

The animal jumped from Moshe's hands to the top of the oven. Stretching to its full length, it draped its claws over the edge. "*Snig, snig, snigger,*" it said, and, lowering its head, it promptly fell asleep.

"What will we tell Mama?" Shoshi asked. She grabbed a broom and began sweeping up the broken eggshell. "We can tell her it's our new pet . . . which you got by giving our firewood to a mysterious peddler."

"Leave out the mysterious part," Moshe said. "Mama trades with peddlers all the time." Snigger woke up, lifted his head, and snorted. His yellow eyes glowed like lamps. "See, he likes us. We'll tell Mama he's a firestarter and that he'll keep wolves and foxes away from the chickens. Trust me. She'll beg us to keep him."

"*Meshugana,* crazy children, that's what I have. Such a creature you bring into my house? And before Passover?"

"Beg us to keep him, huh?" Shoshi muttered.

"Leave it to me." Moshe tucked his thumbs under his suspenders. "Mama, Snigger is special. No one else in Vrod has a pet like him."

"And why would they? He's a . . . snake!" She screamed as Snigger wriggled across the floor. "I'm going to Aunt Rachel's to tell her we won't have matzo balls for the seder. About the monster, I won't say a word. But get rid of it before I get back!"

CHAPTER 3

Attack!

Sundown and Passover were an hour away. Shoshi swept the last bits of dust from the house into the street and shook out her apron. Moshe had gone to the well, and her mother was still at Aunt Rachel's. Snigger was hidden under the bed.

The thunder of horse's hoofs shattered the silence. COSSACKS! Moshe dashed into the house, his eyes wide with terror. "Sssssoldiers."

Shoshi ran outside and saw a dust cloud rolling up the street.

"Get back in the house." Mrs. Kapustin, back from Aunt Rachel's, grabbed her daughter, shoved her inside, and slammed the door shut. "It's a pogrom! Quick, hide behind the stove."

Before they could move, two bearded men burst into the room. They wore tall fur hats, dark-green tunics that were belted at the waist, and high black leather boots. Each carried a sword.

Moshe ran behind his mother and clutched her skirt.

"Shoshi, over here!" Mrs. Kapustin reached for her daughter, but one of the Cossacks grabbed Shoshi's braids, pulling her toward the door.

Shoshi struggled, but the man's grip was like iron. "Help me!" she called out. She tried to kick him, but her feet just scratched the surface of his boots.

"LET HER GO!" Mrs. Kapustin stretched her arms toward her daughter, while, at the same time, shielding her son.

"ROAR!" Shoshi ducked as a green body hurtled at her abductor's head. Sparks filled the air.

"Aaaagh!" The man dropped Shoshi and slapped at his burning beard. He ran to the water bucket and dunked his head. Snigger set fire to the seat of his pants. Then Snigger jumped on the other soldier, wrapping his tail around the man's neck.

"KILL THAT MONSTER," shouted the first Cossack, as he rolled on the floor. He leapt to his feet, lifted his sword, and brought it down with a *whoosh*. Instead of striking Snigger, however, he sliced his partner's ear. The man roared with pain. Enraged, the first Cossack aimed his sword at Shoshi and lunged, when something hard struck his temple, and he tripped and fell flat on his face. He got to his feet only to fall again as another matzo ball knocked him on the side of his head. His partner went after Moshe, but Shoshi tripped him.

Now Moshe, Shoshi, and Snigger worked together. Moshe tossed matzo balls in the air, and Snigger blasted them with his red-hot breath. Shoshi used her mother's rolling pin to bat the matzo balls at the man's head. The two men struggled to their feet and raced for the door.

"This place is cursed," cried the first Cossack.

"Let's get out of here," said the other.

With Snigger breathing fire at their heels, they ran into the street, jumped on their horses, and galloped out of town.

The commotion had attracted the other villagers, who poked their noses through the Kapustins' open door. The rabbi entered the house, and the villagers crammed in behind him.

"You have saved us," said the rabbi, peering over his glasses.

"Mama's matzo balls saved us," said Shoshi.

"Snigger saved us," said Moshe. He lifted the trembling animal and stroked its head. Snigger blew out a puff of sparks.

The crowd parted, and their aunt rushed through. "Ruth, Shoshanna, Moshe! Are you hurt?"

Shoshi was squashed against her aunt's chest. "No, Aunt Rachel."

"*Blug, glug, blah,*" said Moshe, as he, too, wriggled out of his aunt's grasp.

"How can you stand there, when your children were attacked?" Aunt Rachel said to Mrs. Kapustin.

"You want me to sit on the floor?" Mrs. Kapustin said.

"What is that thing?" Aunt Rachel demanded, as Snigger slithered across her feet.

"I'll tell you what it is. It's a dybbuk," the rabbi's wife announced. "May it leave our village in peace and haunt our enemies."

"Dybbuks are an old wives' tale. Educated people do not believe in such things," said Feivel.

"I did not go to university," said the rabbi's wife, "but I know a dybbuk when I see one."

"Well, whatever that thing is, it almost got us all killed," said the butcher. "I will take care of it." He waved his meat cleaver in the air.

"No!" said Shoshi. "Snigger is not evil. He saved us from a pogrom."

"That dybbuk brought the soldiers to our town in the first place. I say kill it!" said the butcher.

The rabbi raised a hand for silence and focused on the children. "Tell me, where did this *thing* come from?"

"Moshe bought him from a peddler," said Shoshi.

The rabbi's wife turned to the crowd and said, "I saw him. A man with burning eyes, like coals. Mark my words – he came from the other world, and this dybbuk he left behind is cursed."

The baker's wife wagged a finger in Moshe's face. "You have brought a plague upon us all."

"Stop it. Stop it." Mrs. Kapustin moved between the angry women and her children. "Feivel is right. There is no such thing as a dybbuk. This animal is not cursed."

"And how would you know," said the baker's wife. "You, a woman without a husband? A woman whose husband goes to America and disappears, rather than send for her?"

A babble of voices drowned out her words. The rabbi signaled for silence. "Enough!" he said. The air inside the tiny house was thick with the scent of singed hair, burnt food, and sweat. He pulled a handkerchief from his pocket and wiped his brow. He glowered at the villagers, who had all settled into silence. "Is this how we start the Passover, our holiday of freedom? By tearing each other apart?"

"Mama, Moshe, look!" Shoshi's voice quivered with excitement. She picked up a small pouch that was lying on the floor by the oven. "The Cossacks dropped this."

Mrs. Kapustin took the pouch, opened it, and peered inside. "Gold coins. There's enough for our passage to America."

The rabbi's wife leaned forward; her sharp nose sniffed like a dog searching out a bone. "They do not belong to you. They should go to the synagogue." She snatched the bag of coins from Mrs. Kapustin's hand.

The baker's wife shook her head, her chin wobbling like a mound of her husband's dough. "Those coins belong to all of us," she said.

"Give them back," said Shoshi. "They're ours."

"They belong to the people of Vrod," shouted the candlemaker.

"Yes," the other villagers echoed.

"They belong to the Kapustins," said Feivel. "So much money. . . ."

"Yes, so much money," echoed the rabbi's wife, who held the sack in the air. Her husband took the coins from her. Everyone stopped talking and listened to him.

"Mrs. Kapustin," he said, stroking his beard. "You and your children wish to go to America?"

"Of course. We want to go to America to be with my husband in New York." She shot a venomous look at the baker's wife.

"Your bravery has defeated the Cossacks and saved us from a pogrom. So, by rights, this money should be yours."

A babble of protest erupted from the crowd.

"That's not fair!" whined the baker's wife.

The rabbi's wife started to speak, but her husband silenced her with a look.

"They may have saved us, Rabbi, but who knows what they have unleashed on our town," said the butcher.

As if on cue, Snigger breathed out a cloud of fiery sparks.

Everyone began shouting. The rabbi handed Mrs. Kapustin the pouch. "Use this money to take your family to America." Then to the villagers he said, "The sun is leaving the sky. Go home to your tables. It is time to begin our Passover seders. Mrs. Kapustin, you and your family should go to America in peace. And," he added, casting a doleful eye at Snigger, "take that *monster* with you."

CHAPTER 4

By Ship to America

It took two weeks for the Kapustins to travel by train from Vrod to Hamburg, Germany, where they were to board a ship to America. The trip from Vrod had been exhausting. They had sat cramped together on hard wooden benches as the train rumbled through Russia, Poland, and Germany. They breathed air sooty with coal dust from the engine, and the potbellied stove that heated the passenger car added more soot. The stove's embers mixed with sparks from Snigger's breath, so no one suspected that they were hiding him.

Most of the time, Snigger slept in a basket tucked under a blanket. Whenever he woke up, the kids fed him pieces of bread, dried salami, and boiled potatoes that their mother had packed for the journey. They changed trains several times, and during each stop, the family got off and stretched their legs. When they could get away from the other passengers, Shoshi and Moshe took Snigger out of the basket so that he could stretch too.

At last, the Kapustins were in Germany, waiting to board the ship to America. Shoshi was so excited, she could barely stand still. She had never seen a ship before. Occasionally, small boats floated through Vrod on their way downriver, but they were little more than flats of logs tied together. Not like the rusted hulk of a steamship looming before her. She saw rows of round windows punched into its sides, smokestacks belching black ash, and towering masts scraping against gray clouds that blanketed the sky.

"How can the ship float if it's so big?" asked Shoshi.

"It floats because that's how it's built," Moshe answered. "You're a girl, so you don't understand such things."

"I know as much as you do. What I don't know is how we are going to stand being cooped up for six weeks."

"You are lucky. The first time I sailed to America, it took three months," said a man with a bushy beard and eyebrows to match. He spoke to the children in Yiddish. "There weren't any steamships in those days. They used sails, and if a storm came up . . ." He shook his head. "You only shouldn't know from being so sick."

"You've been to America?" Moshe asked.

"Many times."

"How many?"

The man held up nine fingers.

"Why do you come back here?"

"To sell. That's what I do. I go to America to buy, and then I come back to Europe to sell."

Before they could ask him what it was he bought and sold, the man pulled a piece of paper from his coat pocket. "This is a picture of the Statue of Liberty, the lady with a lamp, in New York Harbor. Keep it, keep it," he said, when Shoshi handed it back. "You should have this beautiful lady with you, so you will recognize her and know you are in America."

"I guess we're lucky that we're sailing on a steamship. I couldn't stand being on a ship for three months," Moshe said. He bent down and lifted a corner of the blanket that covered Snigger's basket. "*Brrrr,* it's cold. We need your fiery breath to warm us, Snigger."

Snigger snorted, and smoke seeped through the slats.

"What do we have here?" The man peered over Moshe's shoulder.

"We don't know what he is, but he saved our lives."

"Oh, my." The man took a step back. "I can't believe you have a dragon. I saw one of these once in China. Oh, my!"

"What is a dragon?" Moshe asked.

"A dangerous fire-breathing creature. Where did you get him?"

"He hatched from an egg," said Shoshi.

"Well, if I were you, I'd be very careful," said the man. "I don't think the captain will take kindly to having a dragon on board his ship," he said, before disappearing into the crowd.

Shoshi petted Snigger and replaced the blanket.

Their mother returned. "Have you two been up to something?"

"No, Mama." Shoshi smiled sweetly. "We're just happy about the trip."

"Yes," said Moshe. "We're excited to go to America." Their mother's expression softened. But when she saw the smoke coming from Snigger, she jumped.

"*Oy,* that *animal* is smoking again. We should leave him here."

"Mama!" Shoshi glared at her mother. "Snigger saved our lives."

"Yes, yes," their mother sighed.

"Mama," Moshe asked. "How will we find Papa when we get to America?"

"We will ask Uncle Mendel," answered Mrs. Kapustin.

"What if Uncle Mendel doesn't know?"

"Then we will find out for ourselves and tell Uncle Mendel what it is he doesn't know."

Waaah ahhhh!! The ship's horn blasted.

"Come." Their mother motioned them toward the gangplank. "Think how surprised and happy Uncle Mendel will be to see us."

But would he be happy to have three strangers and a *dragon* land on his doorstep? Shoshi and Moshe exchanged worried looks.

On the dock, everyone picked up their parcels, gathered their children, and formed lines, while an officer barked orders through a cone-shaped tube. Moshe held Snigger's basket, and, together, the Kapustins inched their way toward the gangplank. The first- and second-class passengers had boarded hours before. The Kapustins saw women in their fancy dresses with rows of gleaming buttons and flouncy ruffles and men in dark suits, starched white shirts, and silk tophats. These passengers looked so different from the noisy crowd of men, women, and children in fraying coats and worn shoes who were speaking a dozen different languages as they straggled onto the ship.

"Mama," Shoshi asked, as they inched forward in the line. "What if Uncle Mendel doesn't have room for us?"

"We're family. If he has to, he will stretch the walls," Mrs. Kapustin said.

Stretch the walls? The man who took her father's money and never answered their letters? Shoshi doubted he would even open the door.

"*Ohhhh,* I didn't know I could feel this awful." Shoshi held her head in her hands and leaned over the ship's railing. The water below was choppy.

Moshe checked on Snigger. The dragon was curled up in a tight ball, his tail wrapped around his body.

"Look, at his wings, Shoshi. They're growing fast. Do you think he'll be able to fly?"

"Fly?" Shoshi thought about this. "He's so scared of the top bunk that he shivers whenever he's up there. All he wants to do is eat. Last night, he gobbled a string of sausages from Mrs. Finklestein's bag. She screamed so loud, I can't believe you didn't wake up." Two red spots flared up on Shoshi's pale cheeks. "I hate this ship. It's crowded and hot downstairs in steerage. You can't see anything with that one dim light, and the slop bucket stinks and keeps overflowing. People are always sick. The woman in the bunk beneath ours said her husband died before his ship reached America. Maybe Papa died too, and they threw him overboard."

"Don't be stupid. Of course, Papa got there. He sent us a letter."

"Stop talking. We only have one hour a day to be on deck. We should use this time for exercise," Mrs. Kapustin said. Her black skirt swished as her body swayed each time the ship pitched and tossed. "*Aaaah,* what is that?" Two scaly green feet stuck out from beneath her daughter's skirt.

"Shoshi, Snigger is out of his basket," Moshe said.

Shoshi jumped as Snigger darted through her legs in an attempt to run across the deck. "*Snig, snig, snigger, snigger.*" He exhaled a stream of fire.

"I told you to keep him hidden." Mrs. Kapustin

slapped a spark off her skirt. "We will be thrown off the ship and into the middle of the ocean."

"I'm sorry, Mama. It's just that he's getting too frisky to hide. He's a baby, and he wants to play."

"Play, *shmay*," said Mrs. Kapustin. "Mrs. Finklestein is telling everyone that a sea monster ate her sausages. Of course, no one believes her, but now they'll see the monster for themselves."

"Don't worry, Snigger, we'll protect you." Shoshi bent down and patted the animal's head. A pink tongue flicked against her cheek. "See, Mama, he's a pet. Like a kitten." She set him back in the basket.

"Kittens don't set things on fire when they sneeze," Mrs. Kapustin said. "And they don't grow so fast." It was true; Snigger was almost too big for the basket.

Mrs. Finklestein stormed on deck. Her round face was purple with anger, and her chest heaved like the ocean waves. "There they are, the thieves, the *gonifs* who stole my food!"

"We didn't touch your rotten sausages," Shoshi said.

"Aiiiiieeee, a dybbuk!" Mrs. Finklestein covered her face with her hands. "I knew it. An evil spirit is haunting the ship."

"Yes, it is a dybbuk." Mrs. Kapustin put an arm around the terrified woman and pushed her gently away from Snigger's basket. "And once a dybbuk steals your food, it gets a taste for it. Next, it will come back for you!"

"You don't fool me." Mrs. Finklestein shook a finger in their mother's face. "I know gonifs when I see them. I hear that the immigration authorities don't let in thieves."

Mrs. Kapustin laughed. "If *you* can get into America, so can *we.*"

"Ha! A family like you, America doesn't need."

"And what does America need?"

Mrs. Finklestein puffed up like a seagull fluffing its feathers. "Solid people like me. I've got family in America, who have been there for fifteen years and are waiting for me."

"I'll bet they're holding their breaths," Moshe muttered.

His mother shot him an angry look. "We have family in America too. My husband's brother has a restaurant on Hester Street in New York."

Three boys wearing caps pulled low on their foreheads and sporting wicked smiles approached them. "We want to see the monster," the tallest boy demanded in Yiddish.

"There is no monster," Moshe said. He pulled the blanket firmly around Snigger's basket and stood in front of it.

"Mrs. Finklestein says there's a monster, so show us." He jabbed a finger at Moshe's midsection.

"Fight! Fight!" the boy's friends shouted.

"Put these gonifs out to sea in a lifeboat," said Mrs. Finklestein.

"No fights, no lifeboats," said Mrs. Kapustin.

A blast of hot air seared Moshe's back. "Ouch!"

"*Shhh!*" Shoshi kicked him.

"FIRE!" screamed an old woman in a red kerchief, who was standing behind the boys. "Something is burning!"

"It's nothing." Mrs. Kapustin put a hand on Moshe's forehead. "The child has a fever."

"People with fever don't catch on fire. What kind of craziness is this?" said Mrs. Finklestein. "You people are no-goodniks!"

"Call the captain," screamed the old woman.

"*I* will call the captain," said Mrs. Finklestein.

Suddenly, Snigger darted out of the basket. The crowd was so busy arguing that they didn't even notice him. As Shoshi watched, he flapped his wings, and, for a moment, she thought he was going to fly. Instead, he pulled his wings close and raced up the deck.

Moshe and Shoshi crept away from the crowd to follow him. Legs and tail flying, he disappeared around a corner in a blur of green.

"Where should we look now?" Shoshi asked. They had climbed from one level of the ship to the next without sighting a cinder or a single green scale. There were so many places for him to hide: in storerooms, closets, and long narrow corridors with hundreds of doors. They had reached the upper deck in the area reserved for the first-class passengers. "We're not allowed up here."

"Act as if you belong," said Moshe.

Shoshi looked down at her brown wool dress that was stained and wrinkled from the trip and her cracked leather boots. She sighed. "Maybe this wasn't such a good idea. Let's go back."

"Not without Snigger," said her brother. "You know we have to find him before someone else does." He slid his finger across his throat.

Shoshi shivered. She thought how lucky they were that it had started to rain. The passengers, who would normally be out enjoying the ocean sunset, had retired to their cabins. The deck was narrow and slippery. She and Moshe stopped at a window and peeked into a large room filled with gleaming wooden tables and ornate, shaded lamps. A group of men played cards and drank golden liquid from balloon-shaped glasses. No sign of Snigger. They moved further along the deck and looked into another room. Ladies in silk dresses sipped from tiny teacups and talked softly. Each wore a plumed hat. Their heads tilted together like a flock of birds.

"I hope we find him soon." Shoshi studied the wind-whipped ocean. The ship swayed, and they struggled to keep their balance.

Moshe grabbed Shoshi's hand. Carefully, they made

their way along the deck, poking their noses into door-ways, peering around corners, even lifting the covers on the lifeboats. No Snigger. They walked into a large room and gasped.

"I've never seen anything like this," said Shoshi. The room had plush red carpets, a grand staircase with carved wooden handrails, and an enormous ball of glittering lights was suspended from the ceiling. They crossed the room, weaving between round tables set with crisp white linen, crystal glassware, and gleaming silver. Through a door at the end of the sprawling room, they entered a kitchen, where a dozen cooks were busy chopping vegetables, stirring the contents of steaming pots, and rolling out dough.

Shoshi looked around the room. Three enormous stoves were covered with gleaming iron pots. Long counters groaned under oval platters piled with roasted meats, potatoes, and vegetables, and the yeasty aroma of freshly baked bread perfumed the air. The sight of so much food after a diet of bland soup, salami, and hard bread made her mouth water and her knees go weak.

"Hey! What are you ragamuffins doing in my clean kitchen?" shouted a man in a tall white hat and starched apron.

The man spoke in English. Shoshi listened carefully to understand him. He glared at them, twirling the end of his thin mustache around his finger. The other cooks stopped what they were doing and stared.

"How did you get in here?" snarled the man. "You are not allowed out of the steerage compartment." He grabbed a carving knife and waved it in their faces.

"We are lost," said Shoshi.

"LOST!" He ran his thumb along the knife's edge. "I think you are here to steal my food."

"What did he say?" Moshe asked his sister.

"He thinks we want to steal his food," she whispered.

"He sounds like Mrs. Finklestein."

"Oh, no, sir," Shoshi said in halting English. "We are very lost. We were looking for our–".

Moshe cut her off. "–For our mother."

"I am busy preparing a meal for important people, and I do not want to be disturbed by the likes of you," the man said to Moshe and Shoshi. "Go back where you belong, or I will call the captain to lock you up in the ship's jail."

"Let's go." Moshe grabbed his sister's hand and yanked her into the hallway. "Where do we go now?"

"Down is good. All the best folks are down in the boiler room. Step ye here and see."

"Who is that?" asked Shoshi.

"I don't know."

"Hee, hee, hee."

The kids spun around and found themselves face-to-face with a short stocky man in a blue-and-white striped shirt, dark-blue pants that belled out at the bottom, and a soiled white sailor's cap. A wide grin split the copper beard covering the lower half of his face. He leaned against the wall, muscled arms folded across his chest.

"Ye wouldn't, by any chance, be lookin' for a green animal about yea big?" said the man.

"We were just taking a walk," said Shoshi.

"Yes. A walk," said Moshe.

"Aye, 'tis a pity, then. Because it is just such an animal that I've hidden in me boiler room, and I fear the poor thing is hungerin' to see its owners. 'Tis droppin' these." He held up a green scale. "Like he is hopeful that someone will find them and fetch 'im."

Shoshi and Moshe exchanged glances.

"So, if it's not yer animal that I'm hidin' in me place, I'll just be gittin' back to see if the poor thing is needin' some food or other creature comforts."

"Wait," Shoshi yelled. "Please, take us with you."

He turned and cocked an eyebrow. "And why would ye be wantin' that? If it t'aint yer animal, that is?" He crooked his finger.

Silently, they followed him down a stairwell to the bottom of the ship. The air had become hotter. They followed the man down a narrow passageway and into a room where four men, who were dressed in the same striped shirt and dark-blue pants, shoveled loads of shiny black coal into the bellies of four glowing furnaces. The men stopped, turned, and stared, their eyes white dots in soot-blackened faces.

"Hey, Salty, your guest is getting restless," said a stout man.

Snigger was huddled beside a boiler, his breath lighting up the steamy air. As Shoshi ran forward, the dragon roared a fiery greeting, quivering with excitement as his tail clanked against the side of the boiler.

"Snig, snig, snigger." He hiccupped and rubbed his head against Shoshi's skirt.

"How long has he been here?" Moshe asked.

"Well, Salty found him racing through the halls. Didn't ya, Salty?" said the man.

"That I did." Salty wiped his brow with his sleeve. "Saw the rumpus about the sausages, and then this monster 'ere, 'e comes chargin' down the stairs like a cannonball. *Well,* I tells meself, *this can only mean trouble.* Them fancy folks won't stand for anythin' rufflin' their fine feathers. So I figure I'd better keep 'im down with us. What's a little more smoke in this stinkin' hole, huh, boys?"

The men nodded and laughed.

"Well, it certainly is hot down here," said Shoshi, brushing limp red curls off her forehead.

"I'm Moshe, and this is my sister, Shoshi." Moshe held out his hand. "Is your name really Salty?"

"On this ship it is."

"What about off the ship?" Shoshi asked.

Salty's face darkened. "Off the ship, I don't have a name." He turned back to his crew. "What're ye lookin' at? Think this crate'll run itself? Back to work with ye."

To the children, he said, "Bring that monster and come with me." He led Moshe, Shoshi, and Snigger to the back of the room. Salty and the kids sat around a small metal table. Snigger curled up on Shoshi's lap, while she rubbed his head.

"How come you two speak English?"

"We had a tutor back in Vrod, our village. Mama paid him to teach us all English before we left for America."

"Smart woman, yer mama." Salty pointed at Snigger. "This thing is a dragon, ain't it? Saw a picture of one in a book once. Ne'er seen the real thing before, though."

"Moshe got him from a peddler that he met in the forest near our home," said Shoshi.

The man scratched his head. "Forests are full o' dragon eggs. Come in with the Mongols from China, they did, and been there for hundreds o' years. Most o' them ne'er hatch. Lucky yours did – or maybe not."

"How do you know all that?" Shoshi asked Salty.

Salty scratched his beard. "Been around. 'Ere, there, everywhere. You'll never get 'im through immigration. Officers on Ellis Island are tough. Yer gonna need a plan, that's fer sure."

Moshe and Shoshi had thought they could put him in a basket and carry him ashore as baggage. But that was before Snigger started growing. It was one thing to hide a baby animal, but it was quite another to deal with a rapidly growing, fire-breathing dragon. It would take more than wishes to sneak him into the *Goldene Medina*.

They still had two days before the ship docked in New York. They decided it was best to keep Snigger down in the boiler room with Salty. "Down 'ere," he said, "Snigger will be just one more overheated boiler pumping out hot air." He laughed at his own joke. Shoshi and Moshe smiled reluctantly. They hated to leave Snigger "down below," but it was just until the ship docked.

CHAPTER 5

America at Last

The whistle blast jolted Shoshi from a deep sleep. Her mother and brother were already out of bed and dressed for the day. Excited voices in different languages filled the steerage compartment.

Shoshi sat up and peered through the damp shirts and stockings dangling from the upper bunk. "What's going on? Why is everyone so excited?"

Her mother pulled down the drying clothes. "Get dressed," she said, handing Shoshi a pair of stockings. "We're almost in America. Get up! Such a lazy bones. Because of you, we will be the last people on deck." She pulled her leather purse out of her skirt and snapped it open. The last of the Cossacks' coins gleamed. She sighed with satisfaction. The money would start them off in America.

Shoshi pulled on the stockings, shivering as the damp cloth crawled over her skin. She slipped into her dress, wrapped a shawl around her shoulders, tied her hair back with a kerchief, and pulled on her boots. By the time she reached the deck, the ship was passing a small island with a giant statue of a woman holding a torch high over her head. She recognized the Statue of Liberty from the postcard the man had given them in Hamburg. Tear-streaked faces turned to it, as people pointed, shouted, and laughed.

Ferryboats chugged between the New York shore and an island that was dominated by a large redbrick building. "That must be Ellis Island, where we go through immigration," said Moshe.

As she faced New York Harbor, Shoshi saw people on its dock carrying bundles from the ships to wagons that were waiting to take the goods into the city. She thought of the man who had given them the postcard. Did he carry such bundles on his journeys to and from America? She wondered if each package had beautiful fabrics or strange food from distant lands. There were so many wondrous experiences ahead in America that she could hardly wait to get off the ship. Soon, they would find Papa and be a family again – Mama, Papa, Moshe, herself, and . . . Snigger? Her insides curled up like a fist. "Moshe, we haven't seen Salty for two days. We have to get Snigger off the ship and through Ellis Island."

Their mother appeared, her face flushed. "So what are you two up to now? Where is that monster of yours?"

"How much time do we have before we leave the ship?" asked Shoshi.

"Four hours. The first- and second-class passengers get off first. Then it's our turn."

Mrs. Finklestein appeared at Mrs. Kapustin's elbow. "You, in America? HA!"

"We will be drinking tea in America while you are still fighting with the authorities to let you in," said Mrs. Kapustin.

"God should help thieves? HA!" Mrs. Finklestein spat. "HA!"

"Don't you worry about us, Mrs. Finklestein." Mrs. Kapustin waved her fist under the other woman's nose. "My family will get into America. I only hope we see *you* there as well."

Shoshi and Moshe left the two women and walked to the far side of the deck. Shoshi smiled slyly at her brother. "Moshe, I know how we are going to smuggle Snigger into America."

As he listened to her plan, Moshe's expression changed from annoyance to excitement. "I hate to admit it, but at times, you can be very smart – for a girl."

"Girl, *schmurl*," Shoshi snapped. "Come. We're wasting time. Let's find Salty and Snigger."

CHAPTER 6

Ellis Island

Shoshi shivered as needles of icy spray stung her cheeks. The ferry that had taken them from New York Harbor across the Hudson River to Ellis Island was little more than an open barge. The wind whistled across its deck and cut through her clothes like a knife. "I hope they let us off soon," she said through chattering teeth. "Where is Salty?"

"He said that he'd find us. We're next," Moshe said.

"I heard that once you're in that building, they put hooks into your eyes," said a boy who was standing next to Moshe.

"Hooks? For what?"

"To see if you have a disease."

Moshe was about to ask what disease, when a guard ordered everyone off the ferry.

The passengers lugged their baggage and shuffled

forward in a line that stretched from the boat into the building. Inside, each person was given a numbered tag. "What is this?" Mrs. Kapustin asked, as the officer pinned one to her clothing.

"It is an identification tag," he said.

Although Mrs. Kapustin could speak some English, it was hard for her to understand the guard's rapid American accent, so Shoshi translated his words as much as she could.

"He thinks we don't know who we are?" Mrs. Kapustin said to her daughter.

"Already you are causing trouble?" Mrs. Finklestein called out.

"Do whatever the guards tell you," Mrs. Kapustin instructed her children. "Don't make them notice us."

Shoshi clutched her amber necklace. She hoped Papa was right and that it would bring good luck.

They entered a room where they were told to leave their valises and bundles on shelves. They climbed a steep flight of stairs until they reached a long hall with tables on either side. A doctor stood behind each table and checked immigrants – looking inside their mouths, tapping their chests, and examining their skin for open sores. Anyone who coughed, wheezed, or sneezed was taken aside for further inspection. Shoshi breathed a sigh of relief to see that each doctor had a translator. Her mother would be fine. The room was filled with many voices speaking all at once in dozens of languages.

"What did that boy on the boat tell you?" Shoshi asked her brother, while they waited their turn.

"That the doctors will put needles in our eyes."

"Needles!" Shoshi cried. "No one is going to put a needle in my eye!"

"Quiet," her mother ordered. "Whatever *they* have to do, *they* will do, and whatever *we* have to do to get into America, *we* will do."

Shoshi sulked. She was tired from the long delay to get off the ship and the ferry ride, and now they had to wait to be inspected. Suddenly, she wanted to be back in Vrod, safe in her own home. But had they been safe? She remembered the Cossacks.

The inspections continued. So far, the Kapustins had passed all the tests. They were healthy and had answered the inspector's questions. They moved into another line and continued to wait.

"Here it comes. The dreaded eye inspection," said a man in front of them. Sure enough, a doctor was checking people in line with a curved needle that peeled back their eyelids.

"They are looking for a disease called trachoma," the man explained in Yiddish. "It is a terrible affliction that can cause blindness. It is very contagious, and if you have it, you cannot get into America."

"How do they know if you have it?" Moshe asked.

"When they lift the lid, the underside is red. But there are other things that can keep you out, too," he continued. "Like if they think you are crazy. Crazy people they don't want in America."

Shoshi had noticed that some of the immigrants were marked with blue chalk; others had letters of the alphabet written on their cards.

"Each letter is a disease," said the man. "*B* is for back problems, *Ct* means trachoma, *E* is for eyes, and *P* means you have physical or mental problems."

"How do you know?" asked Shoshi.

"My sister came here last year. She sent me a letter about it."

Shoshi shuddered. She hoped that her family would be spared the letters. If they didn't get into America, they would never find Papa. And what would happen to Snigger? Which reminded her – where was he?

It was her family's turn for the eye exam. Shoshi clenched her fists, trying not to scream as the hook lifted first one eyelid, then the other. Then it was Moshe's turn, and, finally, their mother's. As the doctor waved them forward, Shoshi sighed with relief. Had her father passed the needle test? Of course, he had. So, where was he now?

They were directed into the main section of the building called the Registry Room. An arched ceiling soared above their heads, and pale sunlight filtered through the many tall windows. The great hall was divided into lines and passages by metal railings that stretched the length of the room.

To fill the time, Shoshi studied the people around her. On her right, a Gypsy family waited with stoic patience. The women wore long scarves tied *babushka* style under their chins or draped over their heads and across their shoulders. The men's heads were bare, unlike orthodox Jewish men who kept their heads covered at all times. Small girls in brightly colored dresses clutched their mothers' skirts, while boys in embroidered jackets and baggy pants seemed overwhelmed by the dizzying crowd.

On her left were two dark-skinned women, elegant in white long-sleeved dresses; bits of cloth twisted into elaborate hats were wrapped around their hair. Beside them, a weary mother in a bright checkered dress and matching babushka scolded her two daughters in rapid Russian. How could one country take in so many people? No one ever immigrated to Vrod. Except for the occasional rabbi or teacher, everyone who lived in Vrod was born there.

Their line moved forward. Men in starched white collars and dark-blue jackets stood behind tall desks, interviewing each immigrant in turn. She heard questions translated into different languages by the assistants. At last, it was the Kapustins' turn.

"What is your family name?" the inspector asked. A young woman standing beside him was translating his question into Yiddish, when a commotion broke out in the next aisle.

Mrs. Finklestein was at the front of her line. "Look,

look," she shouted. A man in a blue-and-white striped shirt pushed a wooden cart filled with coal through the aisles. The cart was so big, it kept bumping into people. Mrs. Finklestein grabbed the arm of the inspector. Her grip was so hard that his pen dripped black ink onto his white shirt.

"Stop attacking me, you crazy woman," he shouted. He turned to the translator. "Tell her to stand still and answer my questions."

Mrs. Finklestein jumped up and down. Her chest heaved, her wig flopped, and her big gold watch swung back and forth like a pendulum. "There is a monster," she babbled. "There is a monster under the coal in that wagon."

"Hee, hee, hee." The man's laughter rang through the hall. Shoshi stood on her tiptoes. Salty rushed toward the door, but the cart bumped into a pillar and the top layer of coal spilled onto the floor.

"Uh-oh," Shoshi muttered, as smoke rose from the cart and the top of a soot-covered head with two yellow eyes popped up.

"That's it! The monster!" Mrs. Finklestein screamed.

"Be quiet," hollered the inspector. Then to the translator he said, "Please tell her to be quiet."

"That monster ate my sausages," Mrs. Finklestein continued.

"What is she saying?" the inspector asked the translator.

"That a monster ate her sausages."

"What monster?" asked the inspector. The translator shrugged.

"There is a monster in the coal!"

The inspector beckoned two doctors, who proceeded to push through the crowd.

"I tell you there is a monster in that cart," yelled Mrs. Finklestein.

"Are you insane, woman?" shouted the inspector. "Quiet down."

"What is she saying?" asked one of the doctors.

"Something about a monster in the coal," said the translator.

"You don't understand. It's not me. It's *them*. They're crazy! They're thieves, no goodniks, with monsters that steal people's food."

The doctors looked at each other and grabbed Mrs. Finklestein's arms.

"No, no, you don't understand," she said, as they lifted her into the air. "You won't get away with this," she shouted at the Kapustins. The men carried her from the room, kicking and screaming.

"*Oy.*" Mrs. Kapustin clapped a hand to her forehead. "If she keeps talking like that, we are finished, *KAPUT!*" They were now at the front of their line.

"Speak up. I can't hear you with all this noise. Is that your name? Kaput?" the translator asked.

"*Nicht.*" She shook her head.

"Kaput nicht." The inspector wrote something on a piece of paper. "Now, Mrs. Kaputnik, do you have anyone waiting for you in America?"

The translator repeated the question in Yiddish.

"My husband is in America."

"Good. And where will you live?"

She listened to the translator, then replied. "We will live with my husband's brother, who owns a restaurant on Hester Street."

"Hester Street. *Hmmm.*" The inspector tapped a finger against his cheek. "So, you have relatives waiting for you, you know the name of the street where you are going, and these people have a business." He stamped their paper, handed it to her, and moved on to the next family.

"We made it." Shoshi hugged her mother and her brother.

They joined Salty, who was leaning against the wheelbarrow, his hand on top of the coal pile.

A guard approached him. "Get that filthy cart out of here," he snarled.

"Jest makin' a delivery," said Salty.

"Deliveries are at the back of the building."

The coal shifted, and the top of Snigger's head appeared between the cracks. Salty pushed it down.

"*Ahh choo!*" Snigger sneezed.

Salty whipped out a handkerchief and wiped his nose. "Coal dust," he said, faking another sneeze.

"Out! Now!" ordered the guard.

"Let's go," said Salty. He lifted the handlebars of the wheelbarrow and headed for the exit. The family followed him out of the hall. They passed an office selling railroad tickets. Salty explained that people going west, to places like Chicago or California, bought their tickets there. "Ye don't need those because ye'll be goin' to Manhattan." He led them out of the building and across the grounds to the dock. He stopped in front of an empty ferryboat. The cart trembled as Snigger, black with coal dust, jumped out.

"Quick, get in the boat," Salty said.

Moshe ran after him. "Shoshi, help me!"

Shoshi dashed ahead and ran in front of the terrified beast. "Snigger!" She stamped her foot.

Snigger stopped and lowered his head. Shoshi rubbed his ears and led him onto the boat. As she and Moshe started to climb aboard, their mother issued a stream of questions in Yiddish. "What is going on? Who is this man? Why does he have your animal? Where is he taking us?"

"Mama, this is Salty," said Shoshi. "He saved Snigger on the ship and hid him in the boiler room."

"He's our friend, Mama," said Moshe.

Shoshi switched to English. "Salty, this is our mother."

"Happy to meet ye . . ." Salty looked at the paper that their mother held in her hand. ". . . Mrs. Kaputnik." Shoshi translated.

Mrs. Kapustin wearily shook the sailor's hand. "Mrs. Kaputnik? Who is Mrs. Kaputnik?" she asked. "This English is different from Feivel's teachings."

Judging by her confused look, Salty knew something was wrong. He pointed at her, then at the paper. "Ye are. See, for yer name, it says *Mrs. Kaputnik.* 'Tis what the inspector wrote." Shoshi translated his words. Mrs. Kapustin blanched.

"But that is not our name. The inspector will have to change it," Moshe piped up.

"Aye, that is impossible," Salty replied. "If it's on that paper, it's official. Ye've been admitted into the U-nited States of America as Kaputniks and Kaputniks ye will be. Welcome to America." Salty shook her hand again. He looked over his shoulders. "Now, we had better get off this island before they send us back where we came from. Into the boat, all of ye."

Salty started the engine, and the kids stumbled onto the deck. "Mama, come on," Shoshi said, noticing her mother's hesitation.

"How do I know this man isn't a pirate? How do I know he won't kill us all?"

Shoshi relayed her mother's concerns to Salty.

"Ma'am, if ye be wantin' to get to New York, ye'll need to trust me and get on this boat *now.*" Mrs. Kaputnik's gaze followed Salty's to a stocky guard marching in their direction.

"Mama, please come aboard," Shoshi begged.

Reluctantly, her mother climbed on board the small boat.

Salty gunned the engine, and the boat headed toward the New York shore.

"How did you keep this boat empty?" Moshe asked, as they steamed across the Hudson River.

"I put that up." Salty showed them a sign tacked on the side.

THIS BOAT IS RESERVED FOR VERY
SICK PEOPLE WITH CONTAGIOUS DISEASES.

His beard bobbed up and down with laughter. "And now, I'm going to get all of ye safely ashore. *Hee, hee hee.* New York City, ready or not, 'ere comes the Kaputnik family and Snigger, their fire-breathing dragon!"

CHAPTER 7

Welcome to New York

The boat ride from Ellis Island to New York took forty-five minutes, more than enough time for everyone to collect their thoughts and plan for their arrival.

Shoshi was enjoying the ride. On her right, the Statue of Liberty's torch glowed against a milky-white sky. Ahead of her, New York's buildings gleamed in the brilliant sunlight.

"We'll have to talk about what to do when we reach shore," said Salty. "Smugglin' this creature in is the easy part. Gettin' 'im through the streets of this city is somethin' else entirely. Now tell me, Mrs. Kaputnik, where exactly is it ye be goin'?"

"Say my right name."

"Ma'am, but Mrs. Kaputnik's yer name now," said Salty. "It's got a nice ring to it, don't 'cha think? Tell me, where ye be goin' once we dock in New York?"

"*Hmmm*, a new name for a new country," their mother said. She lifted her arms, waved at the Statue of Liberty, and in English said, "Mrs. America, I want you should meet Mrs. Kaputnik and Shoshanna and Moshe Kaputnik."

"Mrs. Kaputnik, me thinks ye'll do fine in America," said Salty.

Mrs. Kaputnik reverted to Yiddish. "Where *are* we going in New York?"

Shoshi was surprised. In all the years since Papa left, Shoshi had never seen her mother at a loss for action. If it was snowing and the cracked walls of their house leaked frigid air, she heated up the stove, sat in her rocking chair, and warmed them all with her stories. When they grew and couldn't afford new clothes, she altered their old ones until they fit perfectly and looked like new. If there wasn't enough food to make a meal, she pulled together scraps and invented a recipe. And hadn't she always bragged about Uncle Mendel's restaurant? How Papa had loaned him money to start it, and how they would all be welcome once they got to America? Why, then, was she unsure of herself now?

Mrs. Kaputnik straightened her shoulders, pulled the crumpled letter from her pocket, and showed it to Salty. In her halting English, she said. "Hester Street. See – famous restaurant."

Shoshi turned to Salty. "Salty, what did you mean

when you said you don't have a name on shore? Was your name changed at Ellis Island, too?"

Salty shook his head. "Salty is the only name ye need to know."

"Why were you afraid of the immigration officers catching you?"

"'Tis a long, sad story."

Clang! Clang! Snigger had smashed his head against the side of the boat, trying to dislodge a bucket that was stuck to his snout. *"Snig, snig,"* came his muffled cry.

"Blimey, the beast got 'is head stuck in the fire bucket." While Salty watched, Moshe grasped the bucket and held Snigger's neck in place, and Shoshi and Mrs. Kaputnik grabbed his tail.

Finally, the bucket flew off with a pop, sending Moshe skidding across the deck, landing with a thud against a wooden storage locker. He rubbed his head. "You sure are a load of trouble."

The dragon bounced up and down and back and forth, rocking the boat violently from side to side. He snorted a fireball into the air, sank to his knees, and meekly lowered his head against his paws.

"Aye, Mrs. Kaputnik, ye do have a problem. I don't think I'd be bringin' this 'ere thing with me to anyone I wanted to give me an' mine a home."

"What are we going to do? We can't abandon him." Shoshi crawled over to Snigger and wrapped her arms around his neck.

Moshe patted the dragon's side. "He's really not that bad. In fact, he's quite good. For a dragon."

"But still, 'e *is* a dragon – a wild beast that can't ever truly be tamed. Aye, 'tis a problem ye've got 'ere, no doubt about that."

It occurred to Shoshi that a baby dragon might be a lot of fun when it hatched in your house in Vrod, but here, on the threshold of America, a dragon was a problem. She exchanged glances with Moshe. Obviously, he was thinking the same thing. Maybe he *should* have given that dirty cracked egg back to the peddler. But if he had, Snigger wouldn't have been there to save them from the Cossacks. "We have to take Snigger with us," she said.

Salty sighed. "Leave 'im with me." When they protested, he stopped them. "Only 'til tomorrow. I'm goin' to dock at the East River. It's close to where ye want to go, and there be such a den of thieves down 'ere, one monster more or less will go unnoticed. Ye go find yer uncle and get yerselves settled."

Moshe looked at him in surprise. "How can you do that? What about your ship? Don't you have to go back tonight?"

"I've a few days shore leave while the ship gets repaired."

"I didn't know it was broken," said Shoshi.

"Funniest thing. Number one engine jammed right up 'bout the time we reached New York." Salty grinned.

He steered the boat through the harbor, bringing it to a stop at a sagging wooden pier.

"How will we find you?" Shoshi asked, as they gathered their bundles and prepared to leave the boat.

"Don't ye worry 'bout that none. I'll be findin' ye." Salty offered his hand to Mrs. Kaputnik, who rose shakily to her feet.

Again, Shoshi translated. Mrs. Kaputnik spoke slowly and carefully in English. "Look for us at the fanciest restaurant on Hester Street, and ask for the owner, Mendel Kapustin."

"Good-bye, Salty. Good-bye, Snigger." Shoshi hugged Salty and gingerly patted Snigger. Then she followed her mother and brother onto the dock.

Salty held on to Snigger and watched them go. Snigger roared, and for a moment, Salty could see the outline of the blaze of his breath. The fiery sparks cooled to ashes and drifted upriver on a puff of wind. The Kaputniks disappeared into the grimy air of the city. "Calm down, lad. It's jest you and me fer tonight, but ye'll be seein' 'em again tomorrow."

He led Snigger to the lifeboat, settled him inside, and covered him with a blanket. Then, Salty stretched out on the deck and drifted into an exhausted sleep, unaware of a cloaked figure that stood in the shadows watching with a sly, excited smile.

CHAPTER 8

This Is Family?

What to do now? New York was hot, vast, and confusing. As the Kaputniks lugged their bundles through street after unfamiliar street, Shoshi wondered if they would ever make sense of this place. Her mother, however, was forging ahead with the same determination she'd shown throughout their adventure. Every few feet, Mrs. Kaputnik stopped to question passersby. Some people replied to her in Yiddish; from others she got questioning looks, shrugs, and a few rude answers.

The family trudged along streets crammed with people and pushcarts, until they reached Hester Street. The street was lined with narrow buildings pressed close together. There were stores on the street level and what Shoshi assumed were living quarters above. People were everywhere, sitting on stoops; leaning out of windows; shouting to each other; and elbowing their way along the jammed sidewalks.

Shoshi's heart sank. This was America? The *Goldene Medina?* Such a hot, smelly place could not be the magic land she'd been hearing about all her life.

A man in a long black coat and skullcap pushed by Moshe with a wheelbarrow filled with fruit. He yelled strange words, and as he passed Moshe, the cart's wheels sprayed the boy's pants with mud. He set his bundle down and brushed at the stains with his hand. "Are we at Uncle Mendel's yet, Mama?"

"When we get there, I'll let you know," his mother said. Sighing, she stopped in front of an open doorway. "Wait. I will ask in here for directions." She went inside and caught her breath as foul air engulfed her. Immediately, she saw the source of the smell. A woman, frail and bent, her head covered with a scarf, was sitting on a low stool, plucking a chicken. Holding the bird's legs in one hand, she pulled out feathers with the other, humming softly under her breath and occasionally reaching down to pat a gray cat curled up at her feet.

"Good evening," Mrs. Kaputnik said in Yiddish.

"You want to buy a chicken?" the woman replied. She smiled a toothless grin.

Mrs. Kaputnik sighed with relief. "We have just arrived in New York, and I am looking for my husband's brother."

"You won't find him here," the woman cackled. She turned back to her plucking, and her swift fingers sent feathers flying through the air. The cat howled in protest, as a downy shower tickled its face.

Mrs. Kaputnik raised her voice. "Please, I am looking for Mendel Kapustin. He has an elegant restaurant on Hester Street. This *is* Hester Street?"

"This is Hester Street, but there are no elegant restaurants here." *Pluck. Pluck. Pluck.*

"Oh, but there is. I have a letter," Mrs. Kaputnik pulled the crumpled paper from her pocket. "Mendel Kapustin's Russian Soup and Tea Parlor."

Pluck. Pluck. Pluck. "That, you should excuse the expression, is not a restaurant, it is a pig sty!" She spat on the ground. "Two doors down," she said. She tossed the chicken into a metal pail by her side. "*Zol zein mit glick.* Good luck to you," she called out, as Mrs. Kaputnik backed away. She reached into a wooden crate, pulled out another chicken, grasped its legs, and started yanking out its feathers.

"Mama, I'm tired and hungry," Moshe whined.

"Me too, and this bundle is heavy," Shoshi said.

"Stop your *kvetching*, both of you. After such a long journey, we have only a few more steps and now you complain?" They stopped under a striped awning in front of a dirty window with the words Hester Street Russian Soup and Tea Parlor written in Yiddish and English. "See, we are already here. Look, we only arrived today, and now we will be guests in this most elegant establishment." Mrs. Kaputnik pressed her nose against the glass.

Elegant? Shoshi and Moshe exchanged puzzled glances. Elegance was the ship's first-class dining room, with its sparkling lights and crisp white table-cloths. Their mother's nose had rubbed a clear spot on the grimy windowpane. Through it, they saw a dark narrow room with a few small tables, soot-blackened walls, and a dirt-encrusted floor. This was Uncle Mendel's famous restaurant?

As they entered, their mother took one look at the dingy interior and screamed. A man walked out from behind a curtain at the back of the room. He had an enormous stomach that rolled over the edge of his stained white apron, and his thick brown beard waggled up and down as he walked. He rubbed his hands together and spoke in English, and then he switched to Yiddish. "Good day, good day. We are not yet open for supper, but if you are hungry, I can give you hot soup." He waved to a table covered with a greasy, food-spotted cloth.

"I should live so long that I eat your filthy soup. So this rat-infested hole is what you've done with my husband's money?"

"Husband?"

"You don't remember me? Your brother's wife? Your sister-in-law, Ruth?"

The man tilted his head, squinted, and looked her up and down. *"Aiieee."* He slapped his forehead. "Of course! But how would I recognize you? I thought you were in Russia. What a wonderful surprise. When did you arrive? Come." He pulled out a chair. "Sit, sit. Imagine my brother's family, here in *my* restaurant!"

"Thank you." She put an arm around each of her children. "This is your nephew, Moshe Kaputnik, and your niece, Shoshanna Kaputnik."

"Kaputnik?" He scratched his head and gave her a puzzled look. "What is this, *Kaputnik?*"

"It is our new American name," Mrs. Kaputnik said proudly. "From Ellis Island."

"What is this *mishigas?* You are KAPUSTIN!"

"In Russia, we were Kapustin. In America, we are Kaputnik. So, tell me. Where is my husband?"

"Which husband? Kapustin? Or Kaputnik?"

"I have only one husband!"

"I know. Saul Kapustin. So why are you calling yourself Kaputnik?"

"Where is he?" she demanded, ignoring his question. "What have you done with him?"

"What have I done with him?" said Mendel. "She thinks I have done something with my brother? What would I do? Boil him in a pot of soup?"

"It wouldn't surprise me."

"Enough with the insults," he said. "This is what I have to put up with? A Greenie fresh off the boat. First she was a Kapustin, and now she is a Kaputnik. She doesn't even know her own name, and she accuses me of harming my brother!"

"Mama," Moshe said. "I don't think Uncle Mendel killed Papa."

"Of course, he didn't kill him." Mrs. Kaputnik's face had turned the color of ripe beets. Drops of sweat dotted her forehead. "So, if he's alive, tell me. Where *is* he?"

"Please, calm down. If I knew where he was, I would tell you. Believe me, I have no idea."

"He came here to see you! From Russia! Five years ago!"

"He came." Uncle Mendel sighed. "But he was here for only three days. On the third morning, he went out to get a newspaper and, *poof,* he disappears."

"What do you mean, he disappeared?" Mrs. Kaputnik asked.

"Exactly that. He went out to buy a newspaper and never came back."

"You didn't look for him?"

"Of course, I looked – on the street and down by the river. I even asked around." Mendel threw up his hands. "What else could I do?"

"Mama," Shoshi interrupted, "we're hungry and tired. Where are we going to sleep?"

"Sleep?" Mrs. Kaputnik looked out at the street. "*Oy,* it's dark already." She turned to her brother-in-law. "So, are you going to take us home?"

"Of course, of course. Excuse my manners. You must be exhausted. Wait while I close the restaurant, and I will take you upstairs to meet my Sadie and my Bernie."

Uncle Mendel led them to the door. "This is a special occasion," he said, locking the door behind him. "My customers will understand if I close for one night."

"Customers?" Mrs. Kaputnik looked up and down the street. "You have customers?"

Uncle Mendel ignored her. "We live upstairs, above the restaurant." He pushed open another door, and they stepped into a dark hallway that smelled like chicken soup and boiled cabbage.

Shoshi reached for Moshe's hand, as they followed their uncle and mother up the stairs to the fifth floor. A tiny needle-thin woman opened the door. Her gray dress touched the tip of scuffed black shoes, and her head was covered by a stiff black wig. "What are you doing here when you should be in the restaurant?" she snapped. "I was coming down to help you serve the supper."

"Not tonight, Sadie. Tonight is special. Look, I have such good news," Uncle Mendel said, panting from the exertion of climbing the stairs. "It's my brother's family. They came all the way from Russia." He turned to Shoshi and Moshe. "This is your Aunt Sadie. Sadie, this is Ruth Kapus–"

His sister-in-law interrupted him. "Kaputnik. I am Ruth Kaputnik."

Sadie looked at her in confusion. "Kaputnik? Why aren't you a Kapustin like us?"

"In America, we are Kaputniks."

Sadie turned to her husband with a puzzled expression. "What is this *mishigas?*" she said.

"The authorities changed her name at Ellis Island," replied Uncle Mendel.

"We came to find my husband," Mrs. Kaputnik told him. "Our name is none of your business." She looked around the room. "What *is* your business is where you want us to sleep."

"Here?" said Aunt Sadie. "You can't sleep here! There is no room."

"No room? In such an elegant apartment, you cannot fit three more people?"

"Elegant? We have two rooms with a toilet outside in the hall! This is what we have."

"We call this a railroad flat because the rooms are in a line, like the railcars of a train," said Uncle Mendel. "This is the living room and this is the kitchen." He led them into a small room with a stove and a metal sink. Then he showed them the bedroom. It had a metal bed, a wooden clothes cupboard, and a metal trunk.

Shoshi's spirits plunged. This was the beautiful American apartment? This dark, cramped space, where they were obviously not welcome? No wonder Papa left. She wished her mother would find them another place to live. If only they had stayed with Salty and slept on the boat. She was reminded of Snigger. How would he and Salty ever find them in this dirty, crowded city?

They followed their mother back to the living room, where she poked her nose into corners, examining the few sticks of furniture: a wooden table, three wobbly chairs, and a red plush sofa that sagged in the middle. She peered out the front window. It led to a metal fire escape that looked down on the street. "Where do you sleep?" she asked her brother-in-law.

"In the bedroom."

"And your son?"

"Behind that," Uncle Mendel pointed to a curtain stretched across the end of the living room.

"Then we will sleep here." Mrs. Kaputnik dropped her bundle by the window and motioned the children to do the same.

Aunt Sadie huffed into the kitchen.

The door flew open and a chubby boy, with a batch of newspapers under his arm, bounded into the room.

"Am I late for supper? I still have papers to sell, but I didn't want to be late." He saw the Kaputniks. "Who are *they?*"

"Our family from Russia." Mr. Kapustin put his arm around the boy's beefy shoulders. "Bernie, I want you to meet your Aunt Ruth and your cousins, Shoshanna and Moshe."

Bernie scowled. "Are they going to stay with us?"

"Just until they get settled."

Looking none too pleased, Bernie threw his papers on the floor and stomped into the kitchen.

Moshe and Mrs. Kaputnik sat at the table, but Shoshi was so exhausted, she spread her cloak and lay down in the corner, her head in her arms. So this was the *Goldene Medina.* She closed her eyes to shut out the offensive surroundings. This was the wonderful land where her Papa had come, the new world where they were supposed to get rich and live in splendor to rival the czar. Forcing back tears, she tried to convince herself that they'd get Snigger back and that they'd soon find a place of their own and start looking for Papa. She drifted off to sleep and dreamed that she was being chased through a densely wooded forest by men shouting for her to stop so they could put hooks in her eyes. Suddenly, Moshe and Salty joined her and together they eluded the men, moving deeper into the forest and searching under every tree for dragon eggs.

CHAPTER 9

Hester Street

"**D**ragon eggs are everywhere. The forest is full o' them," Salty said. He laughed a high-pitched laugh that went soaring to the branches of the tallest tree. "Keep looking and ye'll find yerself a fine specimen." Shoshi and Moshe foraged under every tree but all they found were brown, spongy mushrooms.

"We'll never get Snigger back this way," Shoshi cried, sinking to the ground. "He's lost, Moshe. Lost. What are we going to do?"

"Shoshi, Shoshi, wake up." Moshe shook his sister's shoulder.

Shoshi sat up. "What is it? Did you find him? Did you find Snigger?"

"It's me. We're at Uncle Mendel's, and it's morning. Mama and Aunt Sadie are downstairs. Get dressed. Let's go join them."

Shoshi scrambled to her feet. She splashed her face

with water from a pitcher by the stove, straightened her rumpled clothes, and followed Moshe downstairs.

Hester Street was alive with color and motion. Children sat on stoops, skipped rope, and played hopscotch on the sidewalk. Women gossiped in doorways. Men in wide-brimmed hats and long black coats moved leisurely down the street, heads together, talking in rapid Yiddish. Handcarts and horse-drawn wagons filled with produce, household goods, and clothing clogged the street. Women with straw baskets slung over their arms picked over the contents and haggled with the grocers. Like on the ship, people spoke many languages intermingled with English words. They passed two children arguing, and one shouted "*Shaddap!*" Was that English? She spotted Aunt Sadie inspecting potatoes.

"Four cents a pound for potatoes? Such a robber! I paid Levinsky on Delancey Street three cents."

"So, go buy from Levinsky."

"Why should I buy from Levinsky? I'll give *you* the three cents."

The grocer looked down at Aunt Sadie and shook his head. "My price is my price. You want to pay three cents, go to Levinsky." He turned his back on her and went to help the next customer.

"*Hmmmph.*" Aunt Sadie flounced away, her empty basket slapping against her hip.

"Good morning, Aunt Sadie," Moshe called after her. She ignored them. The children exchanged glances.

"How will Salty ever find us with all this confusion?" Shoshi asked, as they walked up the street. "Look, Moshe." Shoshi stopped in front of a small brown monkey. The monkey wore a red coat and a matching hat. A man in a black hat, black-and-white striped shirt, a black bowtie, and red suspenders held the monkey's leash in one hand and cranked the handle of an organ with the other. The monkey danced up to them, tipped his hat, and held out a tin cup.

"Misha wants to say hello," said the man. "What are your names?"

"I'm Shoshi, and this is my brother, Moshe. Hello, Misha." Shoshi held out her hand. The monkey thrust his tin cup into it. "I'm sorry, I don't have any money," she said.

The organ-grinder laughed. "Next time, maybe. Good day." He ground out a song as they walked away.

Shoshi peered into vendors' pushcarts. In Vrod, market day was for eggs and chickens, potatoes, beets, and onions, and maybe a few pots and pans. Here, there were dozens of strange fruits and vegetables. There were pots, kettles, spoons, knives of every size, feather pillows, bolts of cloth, boys' pants, and men's hats and coats. Did people here really have so much money to spend? She stopped at a cart piled with bunches of curved yellow objects. "What are those?" she asked the owner.

"Bananas. Here, try it." He broke one off the bunch and held it out it to her.

Shoshi shook her head. "I'm sorry, we don't have any money."

"No, no. Eat it." He peeled back the waxy yellow cover and handed it to her. "It is good for you." She was ravenous. Shoshi broke the strange-looking fruit in two and handed half to Moshe. She bit into its pale yellow flesh. It slid across her tongue and a sweet taste filled her mouth.

Moshe popped his banana in his mouth. "*Ych*," he said, making a face. "It's slimy."

"Eat it anyway," Shoshi said. They thanked the push-cart owner and left. When they reached Uncle Mendel's restaurant, they stopped. Their mother and uncle stood in the doorway, engaged in a heated discussion.

"My husband sent you money to start this restaurant, and since you never paid it back, we are your partners."

Uncle Mendel stamped his foot. "My Sadie and I run this restaurant, and we do not need a partner."

"The way you run it, I'm surprised you haven't starved. Look at this place. Look at that window. It's filthy. What kind of food do you serve?"

Uncle Mendel was getting angrier by the minute. "How dare you come here from Russia, show up on my doorstep, and insult us," he sputtered.

"My children and I need a place to stay, and we are going to live and work with you." She pulled out her coin purse. "We have some money left so we can pay for our food."

Uncle Mendel eyed the purse. "How much is in there?"

Mrs. Kaputnik slipped it back into her skirt. "Enough. So, we have a bargain?"

An oily smile wreathed the man's face. "How can I say no? After all, we are family." He took her arm. "We will go inside and have a little schnapps to celebrate."

He winked, his gaze returning to the spot in Mrs. Kaputnik's dress where her purse bulged through the fabric. "Yes, I think this will work out fine."

"We must find Snigger before Salty goes back to his ship," said Shoshi. It was late afternoon, and she and Moshe were sitting on the metal fire escape outside the Kapustins' apartment. "Maybe we should go back to Salty's boat."

"Do you remember where it is?" Moshe asked.

"No. I guess we'd just get lost trying to find it."

"Look at all the people on the street. How will he find *us?*" Just then, they heard Bernie climb through the window onto the fire escape.

"So, Greenies, how do you like America?"

"What does it mean – Greenies?" Shoshi asked.

"It means newcomers. Just off the boat. Look at your clothes." He sneered at Moshe's worn pants and loose-fitting shirt. "You'll have to dress better than that if you want to be Americans." He stuck out his tongue before climbing back through the window.

"I hate it here," said Moshe. "I want to go home. I want Snigger. Maybe Salty took Snigger back to the ship, and we'll never see him again."

Shoshi looked out at the street. Every building had metal fire escapes just like the one they were sitting on, and many of them were draped with blankets or mattresses hung out to air. "There must be something we can do."

From the minute Salty and Snigger left the boat, Salty felt that someone was following him. It wasn't just his sailor's instinct of a wind at his back; it was a sense of foreboding that crackled through the air like summer lightning. Snigger was hidden on a pushcart that Salty had "rented" for the day from a friendly street vendor. The dragon was curled up under a canvas tarpaulin that was also covered by sacks of potatoes. If people noticed smoke seeping out from under the cover, they would think it was from the metal stove that was used to roast potatoes. Still, something wasn't quite right. Footsteps that almost, but not quite, matched his own echoed behind Salty.

Salty stopped walking. The footsteps behind him stopped too. He whirled around, but no one was there. "We'd better find Hester Street soon," Salty said. He had remained awake all night for fear that the dragon's hot breath would set the boat on fire. Then this morning, the beast had eaten all their food so that Salty's stomach now rumbled like a thunderstorm. And time was running short. His ship was sailing at daybreak tomorrow. But first, he had to return Snigger to his owners.

Grasping the cart's handles, he trundled down the street, then swerved to the left and entered an alley. He listened again. Nothing. Maybe whoever had been following him had given up. Or perhaps he'd imagined the whole thing. He breathed a sigh of relief and doubled his pace. His arms ached and the rumblings in his stomach were so fierce that he thought passersby must surely have heard them. "Hang in there, old feller," he told himself. Hoisting the cart, he gave it a mighty push forward, and then screeched to a stop. A hooded figure in a dark cloak was blocking his path.

"Give me the dragon," said the man in a gravelly voice.

"No' on yer life." Salty backed up. He swung the cart sideways and moved up the alley toward the street, but the black-robed figure jumped in front of him, blocking his exit.

"The animal is of no use to you," he hissed. The man reached into a pocket and pulled out a handful of coins. "I will pay you well."

"The animal is no' mine to sell," Salty said.

"Then I shall have to take it." The man drew nearer, and Salty saw the flash of a knife.

On the ship, Shoshi and Moshe had talked about their new family in America and wondered what they would be like. They thought it would be nice to have an aunt and uncle and a cousin. But Bernie wasn't the cousin they had wanted. Bernie was a bully. They'd been there less than a day, and already Bernie was pushing them around and taunting them unmercifully.

While their mother talked to Aunt Sadie, Bernie was given the task of showing Shoshi and Moshe around the neighborhood. He strutted and preened, and whenever they met other children, he raced ahead so that people wouldn't think they were together. Finally, he led them into a narrow alley that was filled with garbage. Laundry was hung on clotheslines that were suspended between the buildings. Thumbing his nose at them, he raced away.

"What do we do now?" Moshe asked.

"Find our way back, I guess," Shoshi said. "It can't be far. We'll just go back the way we came."

They started walking. The alley narrowed and the buildings crowded in on them. Overhead the laundry snapped like flags in the wind. A furry object darted over Shoshi's foot, and she screamed.

"It's only a cat," Moshe said. The cat slunk away through the garbage.

"Let's get out of here," said Shoshi. The buildings were so tall and close together that their shadows blackened the pavement. She turned a corner and led Moshe down another narrow alley, where they both stopped.

"Which way do we go now?" Moshe asked.

"I think it's that way." Shoshi headed toward a faint light where the buildings seemed to part in the distance. Moshe followed behind her. They heard a loud squeal, as one of the cats pounced on a mouse – or worse, a rat. Shoshi shuddered.

Finally, they emerged from the dark cavern of buildings. "What street is this?" Shoshi asked a woman. "Houston," the woman answered and continued on her way. "I think Hester Street is back there," Shoshi said. They resumed walking, only to find themselves back in another alleyway.

Bernie and a group of boys emerged from a doorway a few feet ahead of them. "Hey!" They yelled and waved their hands furiously to get their cousin's attention.

"Bernie, why did you run off? We can't find our way home," said Shoshi.

Bernie furrowed his brows. "It's not *your* home, Greenies."

His companions hooted, and one, a tall stringy boy with a cap pulled low over his forehead, slapped him on the back. "Who are your buddies?"

"They're not *my* buddies, Ziggy," Bernie said.

"Bernie, you brought us here. Now help us find our way home," said Moshe.

Dark-red spots dotted Bernie's round cheeks. "I *said*, it isn't *your* home."

"We don't like it either, but we're stuck there for now," said Shoshi.

"Not for long," said Bernie.

"Poor lost Greenies," Ziggy said. "Go back where you came from. You don't belong in America."

"We belong here as much as you do," Moshe shouted.

The boy took a step toward him and lifted his fists. In response, Moshe balled his hands into fists.

"Hey, look's like we've got a fighter here," said Ziggy. "I'm gonna teach your cousin a lesson."

Bernie stuffed his hands in his pockets and studied his shoes.

"Gotta show 'em who's boss in this neighborhood." Ziggy snapped his fingers, and his friends surrounded Moshe and Shoshi. Moshe pushed Shoshi behind him and faced Ziggy.

"I fought off a gang of Cossacks in Russia," said Moshe. "You don't scare me."

"Cossacks?" Ziggy flexed his muscles, then he punched Moshe in the stomach.

Moshe doubled over, gasping for breath. With his head lowered like a battering ram, he rushed toward Ziggy. Then Ziggy's friends jumped into the fight. The last thing Moshe heard before he was engulfed in a sea of squirming bodies was Shoshi screaming and Ziggy yelling for Bernie to join the fight. Moshe hit the ground and couldn't hear anything at all.

———

Salty looked up and down the street. No one paid him any attention. He wondered if he had been wise in promising to return the dragon to the Kaputniks. He had to think fast. The man was getting closer.

Moving swiftly, Salty upended the cart so the potato sacks fell at the man's feet. The impact jiggled Snigger loose and he tumbled out. Then, curling back onto himself, he knocked the cloaked man to the ground.

"Good boy, Snigger," Salty cheered.

The dragon grabbed the man's hood between his teeth. It fell back and Salty glimpsed one black eye and one blue eye. Sunlight danced off his dagger. "This doesn't need to be ugly. It's the dragon I want."

"Open fire, ye blasted dragon," Salty shouted. "Where's yer blazing breath when we need it?"

The man pointed the knife at Salty's heart. "Turn over the beast, and you won't be hurt."

Salty threw up his hands. "Take 'im. Hear that, Snigger?" he shouted. "This 'ere gent's come ter get yer."

A plume of smoke filled the air, as a fiery tongue knocked the knife from the attacker's hand.

Then, before Salty could stop him, Snigger reared up on his hind legs and raced down the alley.

Moshe didn't know what hit him. All at once, he was on the ground with a mound of boys piled on top of him. He struggled to break free of the tangle of bodies.

Shoshi pushed and pulled at the boys' legs and arms. He tried to call out to her, but he was submerged by blows again.

Shoshi looked frantically around the alley for help, but there were no adults in sight. Two boys stood guard, while the others joined in the fight. Shoshi thought of running to get her uncle, but she realized she didn't know which way to go. *Oh, if only Snigger were here,* she thought.

"ROAR!"

Yes, Snigger, yes!

"ROAR! ROAR!"

"Snigger! Over here," Shoshi yelled.

The dragon charged down the alley. When he reached them, he pulled one of the boys off of Moshe. Between his teeth, Snigger clutched the boy by the seat of his pants.

"Put me down, put me down." The boy's arms and legs beat the air.

Kerplunk! Snigger dropped him and reached for the next boy, who happened to be Bernie. *Kerplunk!* Bernie landed in a pile of garbage. Snigger pulled off another boy, and then Ziggy, dropping each of them on the trash heap.

"Snigger, I'm so happy to see you!" Shoshi opened her arms, and the dragon trotted into them.

"*Snig, snig, snigger,*" he hiccupped as Shoshi hugged him. It had been almost two days since the kids had seen Snigger, and he had doubled in size.

Moshe looked at him and whistled. "Snigger, what have you been eating?"

Ziggy struggled to his feet and approached them. Snigger bent down and stretched his neck so that Moshe and Shoshi could scramble onto his back. They held on tightly to his spikes.

"Hang on," Moshe panted.

Snigger bolted down the alleyway. They galloped along, careful to keep to the back alleys, until Snigger screeched around a corner and halted in the shadow of a doorway.

"You saved us again, Snigger," Moshe said. He and Shoshi slid off the dragon's back. Shoshi touched the dragon's wings. "If only you would learn to use these!"

Snigger's wings drooped. He lowered his head and snorted.

Shoshi stroked Snigger's neck. "Don't worry. You'll learn to fly one of these days. You're still a baby, after all." She turned to Moshe. "Did you see the look on those bullies' faces? I don't think they'll bother *us* again."

"Not if they want to stay in one piece," Moshe said, gingerly touching his eye. It had begun to swell. "Next time, Snigger, we'll be ready for them."

It was now evening, and the sun had dipped behind the buildings. Snigger reached the fifth-floor fire escape with Shoshi and Moshe right behind. "Don't let him go inside," Shoshi said, but she was too late.

Snigger's head poked through the open apartment window, and their aunt ran around the living room, screaming and flapping her arms. Her wig had slid over one eye, giving her the appearance of a frantic, half-blind alley cat.

Shoshi stooped down next to the dragon. "Snigger, stop scaring Aunt Sadie," she said, as her aunt's screams rolled through the open window.

At Aunt Sadie's screams, they looked up into the night and saw a large animal leaning over the railing, a fireball high above him in the air. The red cloud hovered, shining like a misplaced sun, and then slowly faded into showers of glowing sparks.

"What is that *thing?*" Aunt Sadie yelled.

"This is Snigger." Shoshi and Moshe pulled the dragon back from the railing. "Don't worry, he won't hurt you. He's our pet dragon."

"What is a dragon?"

"We bought him from a peddler, and he saved us from the Cossacks," said Moshe.

"He'll be very good," said Shoshi. "You won't even know he's in the apartment."

As if in agreement, Snigger shook his head, setting loose a fresh spray of sparks. One of them landed on Aunt Sadie's wig and flared up. Aunt Sadie shrieked again and slapped at her hairpiece. "Not in my house!" She shook her head so hard that the wig flew out the window. "*Aaaagh!* You're crazy if you think I would have such a demon living in my house! Better you should all go back to Russia!"

"Now why would they want to do that?" Someone in a striped shirt climbed up the fire escape. "Whew, I found ye. It was this beast's fireball that finally led me to ye."

"Salty!" Shoshi threw her arms around him.

"Who is *he?*" Aunt Sadie looked as if she were about to faint.

"He's our friend, Aunt Sadie," said Moshe. "He kept Snigger hidden for us so the captain wouldn't throw us off the ship."

Their aunt looked as if she wished he had, then abruptly turned on her heel and disappeared back through the window.

"Not very friendly, is she?" Salty grinned.

"I guess she doesn't like dragons," said Moshe.

"Or us. Salty, we were worried you wouldn't find us," said Shoshi.

"Snigger saved us again," said Moshe.

"Ye'd better keep an eye on 'im. There's people up to no good that want to get their 'ands on 'im. That's what I come ter tell yer."

"Oh, no!" said Shoshi.

"I 'ate to leave you alone in this big city, but I gotta get back to me ship."

"Will we ever see you again?" asked Moshe.

Salty stood and gazed out over the street. "That depends on which way the wind blows. Remember what I said. Be careful! Good-bye and good luck, Kaputniks."

CHAPTER 10

Betrayal

S hoshi rose quietly, careful not to disturb her sleeping mother and brother. She climbed out to the fire escape. Morning was breaking over the Lower East Side in a gentle wave, washing the street with a pale light that softened the grimy surfaces of the old buildings. A sway-backed horse, its pointy ears poking through holes in a straw hat, clopped by, pulling a milk wagon. A young boy trudged along the sidewalk, his back bent almost double under a thick pile of coats. From every doorway, men in work clothes spilled onto the street. Women and children swarmed around pushcarts. Shoshi thought of the sweet stickiness of the banana she'd tasted yesterday. What other wonders, she thought, might be hidden amongst the onions, potatoes, and cabbages on those carts? In Vrod, men worked and women gathered at the market to gossip and buy food. But Vrod was tiny compared to

New York. Salty said that New York was only one tiny corner of America. And Papa was lost somewhere in the immensity of this noise and bustle. "We'll never find him." Shoshi blinked to fight back tears.

The fire escape rattled, and two yellow eyes rose like twin moons over the edge. Snigger had escaped from the restaurant, where he had been banished to for the night. Together, they woke Moshe and her mother.

"Good morning, sleepyhead." Shoshi shook her brother's shoulder. "The whole world is awake while you waste your time in dreams."

Moshe groaned and rolled on his back. He brushed a lock of hair off his forehead, stretched, and stood.

"*Oy*, what time is it?" Mrs. Kaputnik asked.

"I don't know, Mama," Shoshi said. "But we're in America and that's wonderful!"

"We should wash up and go down for breakfast and . . . *ayeeee!*" Mrs. Kaputnik patted her pocket. "*Ayeeee!*"

"Mama, what's wrong?" said Shoshi.

"It's gone!"

"What's gone?"

Mrs. Kaputnik turned her pockets inside out. She tore back their blankets, peered under the rug, dug between the sofa cushions, and searched every inch of the room. She ran into the kitchen and then into the small bedroom at the back of the apartment.

"It's gone," she cried. "Our money is gone, all of it! When I went to sleep, my purse was here." She put her hand in her pocket. "*They* stole it! Those *gonifs*. Our money they took right from under my nose. Now they are laughing at us."

The restaurant door was open. No preparations had been made for the day's meals. The fire in the stove was out, and dishes encrusted with the remains of yesterday's food sat in a pile on the sink. A sheet of paper was left on one of the tables. Mrs. Kaputnik snatched it up. It was written in Yiddish. "They've gone!" she shouted, as she skimmed the note.

"Gone where?" said Shoshi.

In a shaky voice, Mrs. Kaputnik read the note out loud.

> "*You wanted the restaurant so now it is yours. We have taken your coins as payment. The apartment and furniture you can have for free. We are going to California to make our fortune.*"
>
> *Your loving relatives,*
> *Mendel, Sadie, and Bernie*

Mrs. Kaputnik sank onto a chair and buried her head in her hands. "Now we will never find your father."

Shoshi wrapped her arms around her mother. "Yes we will, Mama. We don't need Uncle Mendel and Aunt Sadie."

"Or Bernie," Moshe fingered his swollen eye. "Except to bash in his head."

Shoshi jumped to her feet. "Moshe, have you seen Snigger?"

In all the confusion, they had forgotten the dragon. Moshe ran to the door and peered out at the sidewalk. No Snigger. "We left him in the apartment. I'll get him." He came back a few minutes later with a stricken look on his face. "He's not there, either."

"Forget the dragon. We have more important things to worry about." Mrs. Kaputnik ran her finger over the tabletop and it came up black. "*Shmutz!* Never have I seen such a filthy–" *Clang! Clang!* They raced into the kitchen. Snigger was lighting the oven with his fiery breath.

"Snigger, stop that!" Mrs. Kaputnik stomped her foot. "Stop playing with the stove. You want to burn us down?"

"Wait, Mama! Let him light it." Shoshi watched Snigger's sparks ignite the gas flame. "Mama, food cooked by a dragon would be something special. Yes?"

"A dragon should cook our food? How would he know the recipes?"

"I don't mean prepare the food. I meant *cook* it – with his breath."

"*Hmmm,*" said her mother.

"That's a great idea," said Moshe.

Mrs. Kaputnik clapped her hands. "Don't just stand there. Get busy and clean up this place. Shoshi, you check the cupboards to see if there is anything to cook. Moshe, get the broom and start sweeping. And Snigger," she said, "don't scare away customers."

CHAPTER 11

How Can Anyone Live in New York?

"I don't know if I'm supposed to love New York or hate it." Shoshi swatted at a fly that had landed on the tip of her nose. Her hair stuck to her forehead in damp red streaks.

"Love it, I suppose," said Moshe. His face was pressed to the bars of the fire escape. His feet dangled over the edge. "Mama wanted to come here more than anything in the world, so it must be a good place." He cast a dubious eye on the street below. "Shoshi, do you miss trees and flowers and picking mushrooms in the forest?"

"Of course I do. And I miss the village. Remember how all the women went to market to buy food for *Shabbos* and gossiped around the well? Over here, it doesn't feel like the Sabbath," said Shoshi.

Moshe gave her a sharp look. "You called them mean old yentas who spread nasty gossip."

86

"But they were *our* yentas. We all went to synagogue together, and we brought each other soup whenever one of us was sick. Here, the relatives who were supposed to welcome us stole our money and disappeared. We don't know anyone else, and even if we did, it would never be the same. Sometimes I like it here, but other times I wish we'd stayed in Vrod."

"Me too. Shoshi, what does Papa look like?"

His sister scrunched up her face. "I think he's tall. Or maybe that's only because I was very little when he left. He has dark curly hair and a soft voice." Together, she and Moshe looked down into the street. "He always wore a black suit with a white shirt. And on holidays, he wore a big hat – like that." She pointed to a man bobbing through the crowd in a black hat. He stopped at a push-cart and bought two apples and put them in his shopping bag. He moved to the next pushcart and inspected the cans of vegetables. Shoshi clambered down the fire escape's ladder. Moshe followed her. When they reached the cart, the man had already moved on.

"Over there." Moshe grabbed her hand and pulled her across the street, where the man emerged from a store.

The man in the hat turned. Shoshi saw a wrinkled face, a silver beard, and two bright blue eyes.

"*Yiddishe kinder?*" he asked. "From where you have come?"

"Yes, we're Jewish. We're from Vrod. In Russia," Shoshi replied.

The man nodded. "Welcome to America." He smiled, exposing a mouthful of yellow teeth. *"Goot Shabbos."* He continued down the street. They watched his hat weave through the crowd.

Their first Sabbath dinner in America was eaten in the newly cleaned restaurant. With no money to shop, Mama had scraped together a meal from ingredients she'd found in the kitchen. An onion, two potatoes, and a handful of carrots became soup. Mama had discovered six eggs, flour, a container of yeast, and the remains of Passover matzo. From this, she had fashioned a small challah and a pot of matzo balls for the soup.

"Tomorrow we rest," said Mrs. Kaputnik. "The next day, we work."

"What will we do?" asked Moshe.

"Open the restaurant," she said. "But with what, I don't know." She placed a sugar cube between her teeth, lifted her glass of tea, and sipped.

Shoshi fed a handful of cubes to Snigger, who was curled in a spiky heap next to the table. He licked her fingers with his raspy tongue. "Mama, how much matzo is left?"

A crease dented Mrs. Kaputnik's brow. "This much," she said, placing her hand halfway between the table and the floor.

"That would make a lot of matzo balls, wouldn't it?"

"How can we open a restaurant serving only matzo balls?" her mother asked.

"Maybe the man with the vegetable pushcart will give us some vegetables for soup. We can pay him after we sell the matzo balls."

"Who would come to a restaurant to eat matzo balls?" asked Mrs. Kaputnik.

"Everybody," said Shoshi. "Once they learn the matzo balls are being cooked by a dragon."

CHAPTER 12

Mrs. Kaputnik's Restaurant

The next morning, Shoshi and Moshe helped their mother write a sign in English, which they pasted to the window of the restaurant.

MRS. KAPUTNIK'S MATZO BALL RESTAURANT.

By noon, the batter was made, the water was boiling, and three Kaputniks and a dragon waited for business. But no one wandered into the restaurant.

"Maybe we have to tell them we have a dragon cooking the food," said Moshe.

Shoshi made a face. "How? Stand outside and shout?"

"Why not? The pushcart owners do it, and they have lots of customers." Moshe tugged at his pants, which were getting shorter every day. Snigger wasn't the only one growing.

"You'll do no such thing," said Mrs. Kaputnik. "We will sit here and wait. If no one comes, tomorrow we will try again."

"Mama, we have to do something." Before she could answer, Shoshi grabbed Moshe by the hand and pulled him outside among the hordes of people. Suddenly conscious of her ragged appearance, Shoshi felt overwhelmed. She tried to smooth the wrinkles from her brown skirt and white blouse. "I don't think I can do this," she said.

"Remember when the Cossacks came? We were brave then," said Moshe. He took a deep breath and called out: "Matzo balls! Fresh and cooked by dragon fire!"

A few people gave them strange looks, but still no one stopped.

"We have a real fire-breathing dragon cooking soup inside," shouted Moshe.

"We don't have the soup yet," said Shoshi.

"Mama's making it. I got the carrots and greens from Mr. Schwartz's pushcart." He waved at a rotund man in a white apron, who waved back.

"Okay," Shoshi said. "Let me try." She cupped her hands over her mouth. "Come inside for soup and matzo balls!"

"My, my, my, that's no way to get people to listen. You have to get their attention first and then tell them what you're selling."

Shoshi looked up and saw a tall thin man with a waxed mustache that curled in twin spirals around his face. He wore a red-and-white striped jacket, with shiny buttons on the front and loops of gold braid on the shoulders. His striped pants were tucked into knee-high black boots. On top of his head sat a narrow stovepipe hat in the same red-and-white as his jacket.

"Excuse my lack of manners," the man said, bending low and sweeping the hat before him like a fan. "Allow me to introduce myself. I am Aloysius P. Thornswaddle. That's pronounced *Al-o-wish-us* with emphasis on *wish*." He clucked his tongue. "Oh, dear, you don't understand me."

"Yes, we do," said Shoshi.

"Now this *is* a surprise! Newly arrived children who speak English."

"We had a tutor in Vrod. That's our hometown in Russia," said Shoshi. "Mama wanted us to know English before we came to America."

"A wise woman, your mother."

"Where are you from?" asked Moshe.

"Romania. However, I consider myself a citizen of the world." He did a little dance, one long striped leg wrapped around the other until he looked like a barber pole. "And today, I am a circus barker who will help you sell your wares."

"What is a circus?" asked Shoshi. She didn't know whether to fear or embrace this bizarre person.

"A circus is a show with many people performing tricks. And animals – all kinds of animals."

"All kinds?" Shoshi nervously looked around for Snigger. Would this strange man want him for his circus?

"We are always looking for new talent. But come now. That is not why I stopped to talk to you. See this nose?" He tapped his sharp beak. "It's a nose for news. I can smell when someone has a story to tell. And you two want everyone to hear what you have to sell. Am I right?"

"We have a dragon in our restaurant," Moshe blurted.

"Moshe, be quiet!" Shoshi stamped on his foot.

"Ouch!"

"Children, children. Don't argue. You have a dragon? How extraordinary. A real, live fire-breathing dragon?"

"He cooks food with his breath," said Shoshi.

"And 'e's a great 'elp in a ship's boiler room. *Hee, hee, hee.*"

"Salty!" The children whirled around.

"I thought you went back to your ship," said Moshe.

"I did, but then the strangest thing 'appened. The second engine jammed up." He winked. "Jest wanted ter make sure you two and that beast of yers was alright." Suddenly he saw Mr. Thornswaddle. "Well, I'll be. If it t'ain't . . ."

"Aloysius P. Thornswaddle." Mr. Thornswaddle put a finger to his lips and shook his head.

Salty just stared at him.

"Do you two know each other?" asked Shoshi.

"Yes," said Salty.

"No," said Mr. Thornswaddle.

"We've met," said Salty.

"Well, briefly. On the ship," said Mr. Thornswaddle.

"Salty's ship?" asked Shoshi.

"Yes, when I came over from England."

"I thought you were from Romania," said Shoshi.

"Romania first, and then England." Mr. Thornswaddle pulled out a red-and-white striped handkerchief and wiped his brow. "As I said, I am a man of the world."

Salty shook his head. "The question is, what are ye doin' 'ere now?"

Mr. Thornswaddle's mustache ends twitched like twin snakes. "Waiting for these children to show me their, er, *dragon.*"

"His name is Snigger." Moshe folded his arms. "And he's *ours!*"

"Of *course* he's *yours,*" said Mr. Thornswaddle. "But what good is a dragon if no one knows about him? You want everyone to meet him, so they'll come to your restaurant. Wait." He rushed across the street and talked to the vegetable seller. He returned with a wooden crate. He set it on its end and jumped on top. "You are looking at a *Circus Barker Extraordinaire.*" He bent his body into a flourishing bow. "Watch and learn."

Salty held up his hand. "Before ye get started sellin' yer food or whatever it is ye're peddlin,' I'll say me good-byes." He turned to the children. "Ye'll be okay now 'cause yer in good hands."

"How do you know?" asked Moshe.

A slow smile spread across Salty's face. "Call it *sailor's intuition.* Take care 'o them," he said to Mr. Thornswaddle. As Salty passed his friend, he leaned in close and whispered in Aloysius's ear. "A determined stranger is after their dragon. Be careful!"

Salty walked up the crowded street and was gone. Mr. Thornswaddle stared after him. "Well, I'll be. Imagine that."

"Imagine what?" asked Shoshi.

"Er, nothing." He coughed into his handkerchief. "Now children," he said, regaining his composure, "as I was saying, you have to be a showman to sell people things they don't necessarily want. What is it your mother is cooking?"

"Matzo balls."

"What are they?"

"Balls of dough. Boiled," said Shoshi.

"Right, dumplings!" He stood on the crate and shouted: "Step right up, ladies and gentlemen, for the most original eating experience in these U-nit-ed States. Or anywhere in the world, for that matter." He turned to Shoshi. "What do you call them again?"

"Matzo balls," the children chorused.

"Yes. Marvelous, magical matzo balls! Mouthwatering morsels," Mr. Thornswaddle boomed through cupped hands. *"Matzo balls cooked by . . ."* he lowered his voice, *". . . dragon fire?* Oh dear, we can't broadcast that, now can we?"

"Why not?"

"We must protect the dragon." He raised his voice. "Come one, come all! Taste these delicious, um – dumplings, straight from Russia; never before eaten on this side of the ocean. But the supply is limited. First in; first served."

Mrs. Kaputnik appeared. "What is going on out here?"

"Mr. Thornswaddle is teaching us how to be barkers," said Shoshi.

"Barkers? *Dogs* bark. Not *my* children."

"Please, Madam, do not belittle our humble efforts. My sales technique has been used with great success at circuses and sideshows all over the world."

"Mr., my family is not a circus. We are respectable people trying to earn a living. Now, I will ask you please to mind your own business."

Again Mr. Thornswaddle gave a sweeping bow. "My business is helping people like you – new immigrants to this strange and wonderful land. Watch." He repeated his call. "Step right up, folks! Come to," he paused. "What is your name?"

"Kaputnik."

"Come to Mrs. Kaputnik's Matzo Ball Emporium, the most original restaurant on the Lower East Side of New York."

"What is an emporium?" asked Moshe.

"A place to buy very special things." He flashed a smile and wiggled the ends of his mustache.

"Mama, look!" Shoshi tugged at her mother's skirt. People were crowding through the restaurant door.

"Oh, my! Customers! And I haven't put the batter into the water. Shoshi, Moshe, come quick. We have to cook the matzo balls."

Shoshi winked at Mr. Thornswaddle. "Are you coming with us?"

"Of course," he answered. "I want to meet your dragon."

CHAPTER 13

Mrs. Kaputnik's Pool Hall and

Matzo Ball Emporium

"These matzo balls are like rocks. I eat this, I break my teeth!" The woman threw her matzo ball on the pile littering the floor and stomped out of the restaurant.

"That was the last customer," Mrs. Kaputnik sighed. "In Russia, my matzo balls were soft. Here they are hard. What is wrong?"

"Maybe we need to use more eggs," said Shoshi.

"More matzo meal?" suggested Moshe.

"It's the heat. The dragon made the water boil out," said Aloysius P. Thornswaddle.

"What do we do now?" Mrs. Kaputnik crumpled into a chair. "No food, no money, no business. We should have stayed in Russia."

Shoshi patted her shoulder. "But then we'd never find Papa. We'll think of something."

"Maybe we *should* publicize the dragon." Mr. Thornswaddle picked up a matzo ball. "The dragon will be a good draw for the restaurant. On the other hand, we do not want certain people to learn of its existence. They may take advantage of it," he explained to Mrs. Kaputnik.

"You want we should keep him a secret?" She pointed to Snigger, who had lumbered into the room and stretched out on the floor with his head in Shoshi's lap. "How do you hide such a monstrosity?"

"He's not monstrous," Shoshi protested. "He saved us, and so did these." She picked up a matzo ball. "These are good to throw. Like when we knocked out the Cossacks."

"There aren't any Cossacks in New York," said Mrs. Kaputnik.

"But we have to do something with these matzo balls," said Shoshi.

Mr. Thornswaddle jumped to his feet. "Do not despair," he said. "I will help you find a way." With a nod of his head and the *clackity-clack* of his shiny black boots, he left the restaurant.

"Good riddance," said Mrs. Kaputnik.

They picked up the matzo balls and put them in a large metal bucket. Then they mopped the floor and cleaned off the tables and the stove.

"Tomorrow we must find work," Mrs. Kaputnik announced. "Otherwise, we will starve."

Shoshi thought of the boy she'd seen, bent under his load of coats. "Somehow we've got to make the restaurant succeed."

Her mother gave her a severe look. "We must make money to live. Tonight we go upstairs to sleep. Tomorrow I shall think about what we must do to live in this country."

Life in America kept getting worse. First they got into a fight with Bernie and his friends, then they were robbed by their horrible Uncle Mendel and Aunt Sadie, now the restaurant was a failure, and there was still no sign of their father. Shoshi couldn't help but wonder what would happen next. As if on cue, her mother announced that they were taking in boarders.

"Boarders! I don't want to live with strangers," said Shoshi.

"Why not? We did it on the ship. Besides, it's what people do here to help pay the rent," said her mother.

"But what if our boarder is like Mrs. Finklestein?"

"Or worse," said Moshe. "And what about Snigger?"

"Snigger will stay in the restaurant." And that was the end of the conversation.

———

Shoshi and Moshe sat on the worn sofa, trying to look quiet and polite while their mother talked to a man with stooped shoulders, who wore wire-rimmed glasses.

"I'm a tailor so I will need a place to set up my sewing machine. I also play music, and I will need a place to put this." He held up a violin case.

Mrs. Kaputnik's brow furrowed. "This apartment is very small. The music will disturb the neighbors."

His expression turned soft and dreamy. "For music, there is always room." He had a quiet voice, and when he talked, his hands fluttered like birds. "My wife arrives tomorrow. I will bring her here from the ship." He handed Mrs. Kaputnik some money.

She accepted the coins. "Thank you, Mr. *Shlemiel*."

"Shmuel. A *Shlemiel* is a fool." He lifted his chin and his glasses slid down his nose.

"I'm sorry, Mr. Shmuel. It was a slip of the tongue. We are happy to have you. I will clear the back room for you and your wife." After he left, she joined her children on the couch.

Shoshi made a face. "I liked *Shlemiel* better."

"Is he going to sew clothes *here?*" asked Moshe.

"That's what he does. Maybe he will make you some new trousers." She eyed her son's ever-shortening pants.

"I don't want boarders," whined Shoshi.

"Shoshi! We need to live. Without Mr. Shlemiel and his wife, we will not have rent money. The landlord will throw us out into the street. Is that what you want?"

Shoshi and Moshe giggled.

"What? What is so funny?"

"You called him Shlemiel," Moshe said.

Their mother laughed. "We must be careful not to say that when he's here."

"Oh, Mama, why do they call America the *Goldene Medina?* There's no gold and everything is so difficult," said Shoshi.

Mrs. Kaputnik sighed. "Children, life is not always easy. But that does not mean we give up. Maybe somewhere, underneath all the *shmutz,* there is gold. And, if not, then we will simply have to make our own fortune."

With the boarder issue settled, Mrs. Kaputnik turned her attention to the restaurant. When they opened their door, the soup pot was full and a fresh batch of matzo balls was cooking on the stove.

While Shoshi helped in the restaurant, Moshe stood outside on his box, holding a bucket of matzo balls and calling to people just like Mr. Thornswaddle had shown him. Still, no one paid any attention.

"Mama's got to find something else to cook," Moshe plucked a matzo ball from the bucket. It was like stone.

"Mama's got to find *someone else* to cook," said Shoshi.

Ziggy walked by with a group of his friends. "Hey, look. It's the Greenies. Why are you standing on that box? To be taller?"

"I'm working, Ziggy. Go away," said Moshe.

"Working? What kind of work is standing on a box? Hey, maybe he'll dance for us, like Misha the monkey." Ziggy shook the wooden crate so hard that Moshe lost his balance and fell onto the sidewalk.

"Stop that, Ziggy! Go away." He struggled to his feet.

"Why? We're your friends. Hey, Greenie, what are these?" Ziggy picked up a matzo ball and tossed it in the air. "Catch." He threw it at Moshe, who caught it and threw it back to Ziggy.

"Wow, the Brooklyn Slobbers could use these."

"Who are the Brooklyn Slobbers?"

"They're a baseball team," said Ziggy.

"What's baseball?"

"What's baseball? Wow, you *are* a Greenie! Baseball is the best game in America. And the Brooklyn Slobbers are the worst team in the country. Their pitcher, Dingle Hinglehoffer, has never won a game against their arch-rivals, the New York Yoinkels."

"What does that have to do with matzo balls?"

"They make great baseballs." Ziggy pulled his arm back and hurled a matzo ball at a stack of cans mounted into a pyramid on a nearby pushcart. They crashed to the ground.

"You bunch of hoodlums!" The pushcart owner shook his fist. Ziggy stuck out his tongue, and he and his friends ran down the street.

Moshe glared after them. "I'm sorry, Mr. . . . ."

"Seltzer." He held up a bottle of water and squirted Moshe in the face. "Ha! That will cool you off. Clean up this mess."

Moshe picked up the cans and placed them back on the pushcart. Then he gathered the matzo balls. Back on the sidewalk, he felt a tug on his sleeve. It was a young boy. "Can I play, too?" he asked Moshe.

"Play what?"

"The can game."

A woman carrying a shopping basket stood behind him. "How many of those balls for a penny?"

Moshe looked at Mr. Seltzer.

"Five." Mr. Seltzer took her coin.

The boy grabbed five matzo balls and tossed them high, laughing as the cans tumbled to the ground. Mr. Seltzer re-stacked the pyramid. More children lined up, their mothers happy to turn over pennies to amuse their kids while they completed their errands.

"Here." Mr. Seltzer handed Moshe a stack of coins when the children were gone. "This is your share."

Moshe counted the money. Twenty-five cents. He looked up at Mr. Seltzer. "How many cans will this buy?"

Mr. Seltzer pursed his lips. "For anyone else, five. For you . . . ten. But you must set up your game somewhere else."

"I will." Moshe grinned. "Thank you."

Moshe ran into the restaurant. "Shoshi! Mama! this *is* the *Goldene Medina*. I made twenty-five cents just by letting people throw matzo balls at cans. Mr. Seltzer sold me ten cans of beans, and we can do that inside the restaurant. Play the game, I mean. So it won't matter if no one wants to eat your matzo balls."

His mother gave him a puzzled look. "Cans? Balls? What nonsense are you talking?"

Moshe explained.

Shoshi threw her arms around him. "Moshe, you are a genius!" She danced around the room. Snigger lumbered in from the kitchen. *Thump, thump, thump* went his tail in time to Shoshi's tapping feet.

"Well, well, well. Such revelry. And what has happened to cause this exuberant exhibit of mirth?" said a voice from the doorway.

"Mr. Thornswaddle!" The children ran to greet him.

"Yes, it is I, Aloysius P. Thornswaddle." He swept off his hat and bowed low. "At your service."

"Where did you go? I thought you'd left us," said Moshe.

He pressed his hands to his chest. "Ah, your words are arrows in my heart. Would I abandon such a delightful and loving family? Especially one with a magic mascot?" He glanced at Snigger. "I merely removed myself from the scene to allow my brain the time and space in which to come up with a solution to your predicament. And now I see you have developed the same conclusion by yourselves." He walked over to the pile of cans that Moshe had set up on a table near the window.

Moshe thumped his chest. "I made twenty-five cents from people throwing matzo balls at them."

"And you shall make even more." Mr. Thornswaddle snapped his fingers and two burly men entered, carrying a large green-surfaced table. He waved to the back of the room. "Set it over there."

"What is that thing?" Mrs. Kaputnik demanded.

"It's a pool table, my dear woman. Combine that with your matzo ball toss, and from now on this establishment will be known as," he held up a sign:

Mrs. Kaputnik's Pool Hall And Matzo Ball Emporium

"I shall replace your sign with this one to let people know that this is the most original restaurant and entertainment center in New York." Suddenly he became serious. He looked around, as if expecting ears to pop out of the walls. "A word of warning – in this neighborhood, it can be dangerous to be too successful."

"How can success be dangerous?" asked Mrs. Kaputnik.

"There are scoundrels who make their living by wresting money from hardworking shopkeepers."

"No one steals my money," said Mrs. Kaputnik.

"What about Uncle Mendel and Aunt Sadie?" asked Shoshi.

"That was different. They are family."

"I'm talking about gangsters who will try to take from you what is yours. I must warn you to be careful," said Mr. Thornswaddle. "Do not trust strangers, and if you ever hear the name Nick the Stick, run the other way. That is," he said with a stern glance at Mrs. Kaputnik, "if you want you and your children to remain safe."

CHAPTER 14

Who Needs Protection?

"If we have to have boarders, I'm glad they're the Shmuels," said Shoshi. It was the Sabbath and the restaurant was closed. She and Moshe were on the fire escape, waiting for Mama to call them inside for lunch.

The Shmuels had been in the flat for two weeks. Mrs. Shmuel was a small woman with a shy smile and brown hair, which she covered with a scarf. When her husband introduced her, his head snapped up, his shoulders un-slumped, and he glowed with pride. The couple took up residence in the bedroom, and, once Mrs. Shmuel had covered the bed with a handmade red-and-gold cover and matching cushions, the space looked warm and homey.

Every morning, Mrs. Kaputnik rolled up the mattress that she and the children slept on in the front room. Mr. Shmuel would then set up his sewing machine on a small table near the window. All day, he stitched shirts brought to him by a young boy, like the one Shoshi had seen on their first day in New York. Mrs. Shmuel took over the cooking in the restaurant, much to the relief of the Kaputniks and their customers.

"She really knows how to cook." Moshe sniffed the tantalizing aroma of roast chicken and potato pudding. "And she didn't scream like Aunt Sadie did when she saw Snigger."

Shoshi liked the Shmuels. It was just that the apartment was small and there was no place to be alone. In Vrod, she'd picked wildflowers in grassy fields, walked along the riverbank, and followed shady paths into the woods. Here, her only refuge was the fire escape.

It had rained that morning, and the air smelled fresh. With most stores closed for the Sabbath, Hester Street was quiet. Life was finally settling into a routine. Shoshi watched a man in a black coat and hat walking home from synagogue with his son.

It was July. In September, she and Moshe would start school, but for now, they could concentrate on the restaurant and the search for their father. Mr. Thornswaddle had shown them how to shoot matzo balls with long sticks called pool cues. His "barking" had attracted customers, and Mrs. Kaputnik's Pool Hall and Matzo Ball Emporium was always full of customers shooting pool, tossing matzo balls, and eating Mrs. Shmuel's cooking. But one thing still bothered

Shoshi. Mr. Thornswaddle seemed overly interested in Snigger. He had told them to keep Snigger inside to keep the dragon safe. But Shoshi thought about the whispered exchange that Thornswaddle had had with Salty before the sailor returned to his ship. If they did know each other, could their secret exchange have something to do with Snigger?

"Everything is going to work out, Snigger," she said, stroking the dragon's head. "Maybe you'll even learn to fly."

"*Snig, snig, snigger.*" The dragon opened a yellow eye, and then drifted back to his dragon dreams.

Aloysius P. Thornswaddle had been right. Matzo balls cooked by dragon fire were a curiosity, but those same matzo balls tossed against cans or hit with a pool cue were irresistible.

Once customers got over their fear of Snigger, he became everybody's pet. The Kaputniks' regular customers came to gawk, and a few children bravely reached out shaky hands to pet him.

With the increased business, Mrs. Kaputnik found it hard to produce the many batches of matzo balls that their customers now demanded. Since bakeries only made matzo at Passover, when it was traditional to eat it, she decided to bake it herself. Every night, she mixed dough out of water and flour, and then she flattened the dough with a studded rolling pin. The studs made lines in the matzo so it would dry crisp and thin and break into pieces. Mrs. Kaputnik baked it in the oven, and then ground the finished matzos into a fine meal, which she used for the matzo balls.

Mr. Thornswaddle was a regular visitor. When they asked about his circus, he brushed their questions aside, promising to show it to them someday. He did, however, produce a tattered poster of a man dressed in a black suit with a chalk white face and cherry nose. "A clown," he explained. What Mr. Thornswaddle seemed most interested in, however, was Snigger. At one point, Shoshi worried that he wanted him for his circus.

"Never you mind, little lady," he said, with his customary bow. "I would never harm a scale on your dragon's tail." Chuckling at his rhyme, Mr. Thornswaddle hoisted Shoshi on his shoulders and marched around the room. "Trust me. Snigger will remain right here in this restaurant where he belongs."

On his next visit, Mr. Thornswaddle brought a guest. "I want you to meet my friend Dingle Hinglehoffer."

Shoshi and Moshe had never seen anyone so tall. Dingle Hinglehoffer had blond hair that flopped into his eyes. He wore white-and-blue striped pants and a matching jersey with the words Brooklyn Slobbers on the front. An enormous leather glove covered his right hand.

"I know who you are," said Moshe. "You're the pitcher for the team that never wins."

Mr. Thornswaddle picked up a matzo ball and threw it at Dingle Hinglehoffer, who snatched it from the air with one deft movement.

"Wow!" said Moshe. "Can you do that again?"

"Not in here." Mrs. Kaputnik emerged from the kitchen shaking a finger. "Throwing at the cans, you can do. But only cans. And first, you pay." She held out her hand.

Mr. Thornswaddle laughed. "We won't break anything."

The men sat, and Moshe and Shoshi joined them.

"Two bowls of your delicious soup," Mr. Thornswaddle said. "Trust me, Hinglehoffer, you've never tasted anything quite like this." Mrs. Kaputnik bustled off to fill their order.

"Mr. Hinglehoffer, why are you dressed so funny? I've never seen anyone with such a big glove," said Shoshi.

"This is my baseball uniform," he answered.

"Dingle Hinglehoffer is the star pitcher for the Brooklyn Slobbers. The team, of which, I might add, *I* am the current *manager.*"

Shoshi planted her elbows on the table and cupped her chin in her hands. "Are the Brooklyn Slobbers part of your circus?"

"They are a sideline, a hobby, and . . ." Mr. Thornswaddle gulped air, " . . . the worst baseball team in these U-nite-ed States."

Dingle Hinglehoffer lowered his head. "Yes, it's true.

Our team is always in the cellar. That means we're at the bottom of the heap. And it's all because of that brute, Yicky Stickyfingers." He slapped the table.

"Yicky Stickyfingers?" said Moshe.

"He's the pitcher for our archrivals, the New York Yoinkles." He wound his arm around and around like a windmill. "When Stickyfingers pitches, we don't hit. When we don't hit, we don't score runs and we lose."

"That's terrible," said Shoshi. "Haven't you ever won a game?"

"Only once, against a high-school team from New Jersey." He pulled out an enormous handkerchief and blew his nose. "And even then, we only won by a single point."

"That's why I've brought him here," said Mr. Thornswaddle.

"We're not baseball players," said Moshe.

"We don't know *anything* about baseball," said Shoshi.

"That's easy. I'll teach you about baseball," said Dingle Hinglehoffer.

Mr. Thornswaddle snapped his fingers. "Better yet, we'll take them to a game at Nebbish Field. It's across the Williamsburg Bridge, in Brooklyn."

"But why did you bring him *here*?" asked Shoshi.

"I brought him for the matzo balls, of course." Mr. Thornswaddle grabbed one off the pool table and tossed it up and down. "They're perfect. Here, Dingle, try it. Hit those cans."

The pitcher took the matzo ball and stood facing the pile of cans. His arm spun around and around until *WHAM!* The ball smashed into the cans and sent them crashing to the floor. "Zowee!" cried Dingle.

"What did I tell you?" Mr. Thornswaddle placed his thumbs under his lapels and puffed out his chest. "These matzo balls are your answer. Pitch them, and the Slobbers will clobber the Yoinkles. Mark my words – by this time next month, the Brooklyn Slobbers will not only be champions, we will be legends!"

By August, the restaurant was busy enough that Mrs. Kaputnik told the children they could start looking for Papa. It was Monday morning, and they were cleaning the tables for the day's customers.

"Where will we look, Mama?" Moshe asked. "New York is soooo big." He spread his arms wide. "And how will we recognize him?"

His mother pulled a picture from her pocket. It was yellowed with age. "Look carefully and memorize his face. One day you will see it on the street, and you will say, 'Excuse me. You are Mr. Saul Kapustin from Vrod?' And when he turns to you and asks how you know, you will say, 'because we are your *kinderlach*, Moshe and Shoshi.'" Mrs. Kaputnik pulled out a handkerchief and dabbed at her eyes.

Shoshi thought of the man in the black hat, whom she and Moshe had followed on their first day.

A sudden hush filled the restaurant. A man stood in the doorway. The pool players put down their cues. The matzo ball tossers lowered their arms. Diners dropped spoons into their bowls, splashing soup onto their clothes.

The man walked over to Mrs. Kaputnik. He was short and muscular, with a hawkish nose and a small mouth. In spite of the heat, he wore a high-necked white shirt, gray suit, dark-gray hat, and he carried a brass-handled walking stick. "Who is the owner of this establishment?" he snapped.

"Children, go to the kitchen," Mrs. Kaputnik said.

"We want to stay, Mama," said Shoshi.

"Go!" She pushed them toward the door.

"We'd better hide Snigger," Moshe muttered.

Shoshi made sure Snigger was inside and closed the kitchen door, leaving it open a crack so they could hear what was going on.

Mrs. Kaputnik pulled herself up to her full height. "I own this restaurant," she said. "And who are you?"

"She doesn't know me?" The man looked around the restaurant, smiling as people avoided his gaze. "Igor." He snapped his fingers. His companion, a broad-shouldered man with a fleshy nose, closely set eyes, and ears that stuck out under his corduroy cap, handed him a card, which the man presented to Mrs. Kaputnik. "They call me Nick the Stick." He lifted his stick to expose a thin sharp knife, protruding from the bottom. "I carry this for protection. *Your* protection!"

"That's the man Mr. Thornswaddle warned us about," whispered Shoshi.

"He said if we saw him, we should run," said Moshe.

"*Shhhh*." Shoshi hushed him. "I want to hear what they're saying."

Mrs. Kaputnik, hands on hips and head thrust forward, looked like she was ready for a fight. "Thank you, Mr. Stick. But I don't need protection."

"Oh, but you do, Mrs. Kaputnik." He grabbed her arm, pulled her toward a table in the corner, and pushed her down into a chair. At once, the sound of voices and the clatter of utensils resumed. "Igor, explain to this lady why she needs my protection."

Igor leaned over the table, his eyes boring into Mrs. Kaputnik's face. "No one works in this neighborhood without Mr. Stick's protection. The way it works is this. You pay me, and Mr. Stick keeps bad things from happening to you."

"Is that so? And if I don't pay?"

"The last man who didn't give us his money disappeared."

Mrs. Kaputnik's face drained of color.

"He didn't care about our rules," said Igor.

"You, I trust, are smarter." Nick the Stick folded his hands on the table. "Now listen carefully. Every Friday afternoon at four o'clock, Igor will come to your restaurant. You will give him twenty-five dollars, and then you and your family and your business will be safe."

"Twenty-five dollars? But that is more than–"

"Trust me, Mrs. Kaputnik," said Nick the Stick. "Being under my protection is worth every penny. Come, Igor." Igor rushed forward and picked up his boss's walking stick from the chair. When he handed it to Nick, Mrs. Kaputnik spied a circle beneath the handle.

Afterwards, the more she thought about it, the more certain Mrs. Kaputnik was that what had looked like a circle was, in fact, a delicately carved wooden rose.

"Such an evil man. You should have let Snigger bite him," Mrs. Shmuel said, after the men had left. She wiped her hands on her apron.

The customers circled Mrs. Kaputnik. "Yes. Let Snigger's breath show him who needs protection," someone cried out.

"Those *gonifs*. Nobody can make an honest living without greasing their filthy palms." Mr. Seltzer shook his fist. "In the Old Country, we had the Cossacks. Here we have this, this . . . *stick person* stealing the food from inside our mouths."

"Stick, Cossack. His horse I didn't see." Mrs. Kaputnik leaned against a chair to steady herself. "Besides, if we keep our mouths shut, how can he take our food?" She held up a hand. "So tell me, Mr. Seltzer, how long has this *shnorer* been stealing?"

Mr. Seltzer scratched his head. "For as long as I can remember. If you want my advice, Mrs. Kaputnik, every Friday you pay him twenty-five dollars, like he says. We don't want something bad to happen to you or your children. Not like that poor *schnook* who vanished."

"Seltzer, do you remember the person who disappeared?" asked Mrs. Kaputnik.

"He wasn't here so long."

She pulled out her photo of her husband. "This, maybe, is the man?"

Mr. Seltzer studied the picture. "Maybe," he said.

"Let me see that," said a plump woman. She squinted and studied the photo. "Yes, yes, that's him. He was such a nice man."

Mrs. Kaputnik grasped the woman's arm. "Are you sure, Mrs. . . ."

"Sophie Schneider. That's definitely him. How do you know this man?" she asked.

Mrs. Kaputnik blinked back tears. "He is my husband."

A gasp erupted from the crowd.

"For this I came to America? To discover my Saul kidnapped by bandits?" Mrs. Kaputnik cried.

Shoshi and Moshe burst into the room. Moshe, red-faced and sweating, grabbed his mother's arm. "Mama, Mama, Snigger's gone."

Mrs. Kaputnik threw up her hands. "The dragon they're talking about. I wouldn't worry. Right now, he's probably outside scaring people."

"No, he's not. We looked. He's not anywhere," said Moshe. "Someone stole him."

CHAPTER 15

Our Dragon Is Missing

It seemed as if the whole neighborhood had gathered at Mrs. Kaputnik's restaurant to discuss Nick the Stick and his gang of thugs. Shoshi and Moshe sat in the corner, brooding about Snigger, while the adults voiced their complaints.

"Mr. Thornswaddle warned us to keep Snigger hidden," said Moshe.

"We did. He was in the kitchen. We saw him when we went in there."

"But then *you* wanted to hear what Nick the Stick had to say." He gave his sister an accusatory look.

"Don't blame me. You wanted to hear him as much as I did," she said. "Let's not fight. We've got to think of a way to find Snigger."

The talk in the restaurant was getting louder.

"He always terrorizes us with his threats," shouted Seltzer.

"I bake and they eat. Without paying me a penny," said Meyer the baker. He passed around a plate of warm bagels. "Stop that," he shouted, as Misha jumped up, grabbed a bagel, and scampered away. "Keep that crazy monkey on his leash," he said to the organ-grinder.

"Keep your bagels out of the way," said the organ-grinder.

"What are we going to do?" asked Mr. Seltzer.

"Feed the gangsters matzo balls," Shoshi said. "That will fix them."

Her mother gave her a stern look.

Shoshi sighed. With Snigger missing, their father kidnapped, and gangsters threatening their livelihood, nothing was funny. They had spent the afternoon combing the neighborhood, but to no avail. Snigger was gone.

"How do we find him?" said Shoshi.

"Maybe Mr. Thornswaddle can help us," said Moshe.

"Maybe Mr. Thornswaddle took him. We don't know where he is either." Shoshi reminded her brother.

All the adults seemed to be talking at once. Mr. Shmuel held up his hand for silence. "Please listen," he said in his soft voice. "If we all work together and organize, we can deal with this man."

"The tailor is right. We must be united and drive them away," said Mr. Seltzer.

"Are you a *jokenik?* If we organize, we won't live so long," said the organ-grinder.

"You'll live," said the baker. "Maybe without an arm or a leg . . ."

You think this is funny?" Seltzer growled. He and Meyer stood nose to nose, glaring at each other.

"Funny, *shmunny.* You want to fight? Save it for Mr. Stick."

Shoshi and Moshe left the adults to their argument. It was a hot, sticky night, and doorsteps were filled with people trying to escape the stifling tenements. Someone had taken the cap off a fire hydrant, and a group of children played in the water that gushed from its spout. They sat on an empty stoop. Shoshi fanned herself with her hand. Her clothes stuck to her body in wet, clammy layers, and her hair foamed around her head in a tangle of ginger curls. Moshe mopped his forehead with his handkerchief. "I don't think I like America. I want to go back to Vrod," he said.

Shoshi pictured trees and wildflowers in the fields and along the river of their village. She remembered their neighbors, all of whom she'd known her life whole life. But then she remembered the laws that said Jews could only live in the poor villages of the Pale. And she remembered the Cossacks, with their swords, stomping feet, and horses that trampled everything in their path. Here they had to deal with gangsters like Nick the Stick. Yet with all their troubles, she believed that

America was better than Russia. "We can't go back. America is our home," she said.

Music had begun to pour from the restaurant. The children rushed inside. To their astonishment, the arguing had stopped. Mr. Shmuel was playing his violin, the organ-grinder was grinding out a tune, and Mr. Seltzer was pumping an accordion. Tables had been pushed back, and people stood and clapped along to the rollicking notes. Two men linked arms and twirled around. Others joined in; men forming one circle, women another.

"I thought everyone was angry," Shoshi said.

"At Mr. Stick, they are angry, not with our neighbors." Mrs. Kaputnik smiled a rare smile, and Shoshi was filled with joy. Mama believed they were going to be all right in this new and puzzling land, and if Mama believed it, so should she.

Shoshi took her brother's hand and drew him into the circles of dancers. He joined the men and she danced with the women. Around and around they twirled until the room spun before their eyes. Shoshi dropped into a chair. Moshe plopped down beside her.

"We'll find Snigger," Shoshi said, as she gasped for breath.

"And Papa too?" Moshe pushed sweat-soaked hair from his forehead.

Shoshi hesitated. Who knew what those terrible men had done with their father. She raised her head and straightened her shoulders. "Yes, and Papa, too." Like her mother always said, if you are going to make a wish why not wish for the best? So that was what she would do – wish that soon they would all be together.

CHAPTER 16

Where Is Snigger?

"Snigger's missing!" Shoshi grabbed Aloysius P. Thornswaddle's hand. "He vanished yesterday, and we don't know where he's gone or how to find him. And those gangsters have our father. You can help us find them, can't you?"

Mr. Thornswaddle had come to check up on them. Now he knelt down and held her shoulders. "Slow down little lady. First, what is this about your dragon. When did you lose him?"

"We didn't lose him. He was stolen."

"And how do you know he was taken?"

Shoshi blinked back tears. "Snigger would never leave us."

Mr. Thornswaddle stroked his chin. "One never knows with dragons. Fickle animals they are. Is it possible he *flew* off?"

"Snigger doesn't fly," said Moshe.

Mr. Thornswaddle thought for a moment. "Not all dragons fly, you know. Only Western European dragons can fly. But those dragons are mean!"

"Snigger's not mean," said Shoshi.

"Eastern dragons from China don't fly at all, and they are much sweeter tempered than their western cousins."

"How do you know so much about dragons?" asked Shoshi.

"I am a man of the world. I pick up knowledge wherever I go. Your dragon could be from the east *or* the west. And that makes a big difference. Western dragons are fierce. They guard treasures. Eastern dragons are friendly. Is Snigger fierce or friendly?"

"Friendly," said Moshe. "Unless he's angry. Then he can be fierce."

Shoshi was losing patience. "Mr. Thornswaddle, Snigger *was* stolen. Someone took him. Maybe it was those gangsters."

They were interrupted by their mother. "It's time to open the restaurant."

"Mama," said Moshe. "Mr. Thornswaddle is going to help us find Snigger."

"That's good. And can he help us with this *Shtick* person?"

"Nick the Stick has been a problem for me too," said Mr. Thornswaddle. "Why, that perfidious piece of pestilence owns the New York Yoinkles."

"Mr. Thornswaddle, is there anyone you don't know?" asked Shoshi.

"Well, I don't know Mr. Theodore Roosevelt, the president of these U-ni-ted States. At least not yet," he added with a wink.

"What do you know about this Stick man?" asked Mrs. Kaputnik.

"I know that he runs all the rackets on the Lower East Side, and that he terrorizes people like you." He scowled. "And, that he has a secret weapon, his magic bat, which his team uses to win every baseball game."

Mrs. Kaputnik placed her hands against her temples, "He is the man who took my Saul."

Aloysius P. Thornswaddle looked frightened. "For now, I suggest you pay Mr. Stick his money, keep your children close, and leave the whereabouts of your husband to me."

It was Friday, and Nick the Stick's first payment was due. Mr. Thornswaddle had dropped by to assure them he was still looking for Snigger and their father.

"He talks a lot, your Mr. Thornswaddle," said Mrs. Kaputnik after Thornswaddle left. She and Shoshi were in the kitchen making matzo balls. "Better he should tell us how to stay in business if we must give all our money to Mr. Stick."

Shoshi took a broom from the corner and went into the restaurant's dining room. It was almost time to open. "Good morning," she said to Mrs. Shmuel, who was wiping down tables with Moshe.

"Good morning." Mrs. Shmuel smiled. She took the broom from Shoshi. "I will sweep. You fix the cans."

Shoshi relinquished the broom. She began to stack canned goods into a pyramid shape. As she worked, she thought about her mother's comments. Even though the restaurant's business had grown, there still wasn't enough money to pay Nick the Stick his twenty-five dollars. Life was looking bleak. No Papa, no Snigger, no money, and a gang of thugs beating at their door. How would they ever survive?

At precisely four o'clock, Igor appeared in the doorway. "Where is it?" He held out his hand.

Mrs. Kaputnik reached into her pocket and pulled out a handful of cash and coins. "Here, five dollars and twenty cents. This is all I have."

Igor snatched the money, counted it, and put it in his pocket.

"Where's the rest?"

"I hope next week."

"Nick won't like this."

"He doesn't like it, he can come himself."

Igor shot her a puzzled look. "Believe me, Mrs. Kaputnik, you do not want that. No one defies Nick the Stick."

"I have to get ready for *Shabbos*," Mrs. Kaputnik said.

Igor left the restaurant, but not before issuing a warning. "You haven't heard the last of this."

"I'm sure I haven't," Mrs. Kaputnik said after he'd gone. *What else can go wrong?* she thought.

On Sunday, Igor returned. He marched into the restaurant and waved the patrons out. He stood before Mrs. Kaputnik.

"Where's the money?" He held out his hand.

When she started to protest, Igor grabbed her arm and shoved her toward the desk where she kept her cash box. "Open it," he ordered.

Mrs. Kaputnik shot him a murderous look but did as she was told.

He pocketed the money. "Lady, this time you're gettin' away with a late payment. Next time, you ain't gonna be so lucky." Igor's eyes fell on Mrs. Kaputnik's picture of her husband, which she had tacked next to the box. "That guy should be a lesson for you. He didn't pay his debts and Nick took care of him. Remember to have the dough ready next Friday. We don't want nothin' bad happenin' to those nice kids of yours."

CHAPTER 17

How to Rescue a Dragon

Snigger's disappearance rocked the Kaputniks' world. Their sense of loss was overwhelming. Friends and loyal customers came into the store every day, asking about Snigger. The children were surprised by the neighborhood's interest and support. Instead of fearing Snigger, the people in their neighborhood had learned to embrace the dragon.

Mr. Thornswaddle, Moshe, and Shoshi sat at a table in the restaurant and discussed the problem over steaming glasses of tea. "Everyone who comes to this country from someplace else leaves the familiar behind. We learn to cope with strange customs, a new language, foods we've never tasted before. We miss our families and friends back home and feel trapped living in tenements."

"Even you, Mr. Thornswaddle?" Moshe asked. "I thought you were all settled in the new world."

"I speak English. I know my way around the city," said Mr. Thornswaddle. "But when I arrived, I was as green as unripe fruit. That's why newcomers are called Greenies. Immigrants take time to ripen. The people who arrived first have become Americans, and you remind them of what they used to be."

Shoshi thought about this. "We're starting school in September. Will that make us American?"

"My goodness, you've already begun. Your English is improving every day. You've helped your mother learn to speak better English. You see, becoming American is like assembling a giant puzzle. There are dozens of pieces: language, food, education, work, friends, and a neighborhood where you can walk down the street and see familiar faces. Once you know people, you don't want them to go away. That's why they miss Snigger."

"Mr. Thornswaddle, what does this have to do with finding Snigger?"

"Nothing, Shoshi. And everything. Nothing, because the people who took Snigger are obviously *not* Greenies. And everything, because your customers and neighbors will help you find him, if you let them. Snigger is a larger-than-life personality who makes people feel like they know him or want to know him."

"People like you?" Shoshi asked.

Mr. Thornswaddle beamed. "Like I was saying, Snigger has become neighborhood property, which is why the neighborhood wants to help you."

Soon people would be coming for their matzo balls; some to eat, but mostly to throw at stacks of cans or hit with sticks. Everything was so different than Shoshi had imagined. Was it better here or had they been better off in Vrod? They were safe from Cossacks but were threatened by crooks. They had new friends but no Papa. They owned the restaurant but shared their flat with boarders. America might not be the *Goldene Medina*, but it was definitely a land filled with possibilities, even if those possibilities were sometimes strange and frightening.

That evening, Ziggy paid them a visit. He'd brought his friend Noah, and the four of them gathered on the stoop outside the Kaputniks' building. "We've decided to let Moshe into our gang. You too," he said to Shoshi. "Even though you're a girl."

"Well, *thank you*." Shoshi stood, held out her skirt, and curtsied.

"You should be grateful," Noah informed her. "We don't like girls."

"I thought you hated both of us. You called us Greenies. What changed your mind?" Moshe asked Ziggy.

"We miss the dragon," Ziggy admitted. "So, we're gonna help you find him."

"Why should we trust you?" Shoshi said. "You tried to beat up Moshe."

"Aw, Bernie told us to do it. Anyway, you have to trust us now because you need us. First we'll find Snigger, and then we'll rescue your father."

Shoshi's jaw dropped. "What do you know about our papa?"

"We know lots about what goes on in the Lower East Side. Don't we, Noah?"

"Yeah." Noah smiled, exposing two missing front teeth.

"Aren't you a little old to lose your teeth?" asked Moshe.

"Didn't lose 'em. I had 'em knocked out." Noah held up his fists. "The other guy don't got any left."

Shoshi wondered what they were getting themselves into. She looked at Moshe, and he shrugged. "What choice do we have?"

"Okay," she said. "We'll work with you on one condition. We get Mr. Thornswaddle to help us."

"That barber pole?" Ziggy protested.

"He has a circus," said Moshe. "So he knows lots of tricks."

Ziggy scrunched his face into a thinking mask. "No adults," he said. "They talk too much. But us kids, we take a blood oath of silence." He pulled out a pocket-knife and pricked his thumb. The other three took the knife and did the same.

"Ouch!" said Shoshi.

"It's supposed to hurt, that's the point. Now we press our fingers together and we're bound by a blood oath. If any of us breaks the code of silence . . ." Ziggy ran a finger across his throat.

Shoshi shuddered.

"Now that we've sealed the pact, we need a plan," said Ziggy. They all huddled together. "It's about time you two learned what's what in this neighborhood. And who the real enemy is."

CHAPTER 18

Operation Dragon Search

For the next few days, Shoshi and Moshe spent all their free time learning their way around the Lower East Side with Ziggy and Noah. As they became more familiar with the neighborhood and their English improved, they felt less like outsiders. At mealtimes, they helped their mother in the restaurant. Evenings were spent on the street cooling off in the water from the fire hydrant; playing baseball with Ziggy, Noah, and the other neighborhood kids; and planning how to find Snigger and their father.

The street baseball games were their favorite pastime. They used broom handles for bats and hit matzo balls. Dingle Hinglehoffer dropped by occasionally, and the kids peppered him with questions about the game.

Life on Hester Street was good; but inside the restaurant, it was a different story. Every Thursday night,

Mrs. Kaputnik sat down with the money from the week's sales and set aside the twenty-five dollars for Nick the Stick. And every Friday, when Igor came to collect it, she asked him about her husband. What had happened to him? Where was he? Igor always feigned ignorance and smiled a creepy smile that made Mrs. Kaputnik's skin crawl. And each time, Shoshi and Moshe were more convinced that not only did he know, but that he was involved with their father's disappearance.

Another week went by, and Igor had paid his regular Friday visit. Shoshi and Moshe cleaned tables and swept the floor, avoiding their mother, who was in a foul mood. Shoshi didn't blame her, but she wished their mother wouldn't take her anger out on them.

One hot afternoon, Mr. Thornswaddle and Dingle Hinglehoffer appeared in the doorway.

"Fly ball." Dingle Hinglehoffer picked up a matzo ball and tossed it to Moshe. "Nice catch," he said, as Moshe snatched it from the air.

"Hello, Mr. Hinglehoffer," said Moshe. "Did you win your baseball game?"

Dingle Hinglehoffer folded his body into a chair. "Naw, we Slobbers can't get nowhere against those Yoinkles. Ya gotta have a special pitch. Somethin' the other team won't expect. Especially with a batter like Yicky Stickyfingers." He threw the ball in the air and caught it with one hand.

"What do you mean?" Moshe asked.

"Well, it's 'cause of Yicky's bats."

"No one can win against the special bats that he uses," said Hinglehoffer.

"What makes them special?" asked Moshe.

Dingle Hinglehoffer returned to his seat. "Only one man in New York makes them. He works for Nick the Stick. Some might even say he's Nick's slave."

Shoshi's ears perked up.

"Nick the Stick gets the people who owe him money to work for him. Some of them are never seen again. This man, though, is special. He's the one who makes Nick's walking sticks and the baseball bats."

"Mr. Hinglehoffer," Shoshi asked. "Do these bats have a rose carved into the wood?"

"Why yes, they do," he said, looking at her with surprise. "It's the same rose that he carves into Nick's walking sticks. How did you know that?"

"A lucky guess," Shoshi grinned.

"Good for you. Well, I'm off to Nebbish Field. Bye!"

As he walked up the street, a man in a black hooded cloak brushed past him. His hood fell back, revealing his eyes – the left one, blue; the right one, black.

"I wonder if Mr. Thornswaddle really has a circus," said Shoshi.

"Why would he lie about that?" asked her brother.

"I don't know." It was evening, and Shoshi and Moshe

were sitting on the fire escape. Strains of Mr. Shmuel's violin drifted through the open living-room window. Shoshi looked down into the street. As usual, it was crowded and noisy. She spotted their mother and Mrs. Shmuel on a stoop across the street, gossiping with a group of neighborhood women. Shoshi rested her head against the metal bars. "I don't know," she repeated, "but when he met Salty, he pretended he didn't know him."

A shrill whistle from the street caught their attention. Ziggy and Noah stood below them. "Come down."

The children clambered down the fire escape.

"What do you guys want?" asked Moshe.

"It's not what *we* want. It's what *you* want." Ziggy smiled slyly. He reached into the pocket of his overalls and pulled out a paper with a picture of a lion's head in the center of a blue circle that was surrounded by orange flames.

"What is that?" asked Moshe.

"A flyer for a circus," said Noah.

"And that, my friends," grinned Ziggy, "is where we'll find Snigger. Because . . ." he pointed to a picture of a man at the bottom of the flyer. "Look who it belongs to."

"Mr. Thornswaddle!" Shoshi exclaimed.

"See, I told you he owns a circus," said Moshe.

"Snigger will bring people into his circus, and that means money," said Ziggy. "Meet me here just before dawn. We're going on a dragon hunt."

CHAPTER 19

This Is a Circus?

It was still dark when Shoshi and Moshe slipped into the hallway, closed the door quietly behind them, and crept down the stairs. Ziggy and Noah were waiting for them on the street.

The children walked quickly and silently, so as not to attract any attention. At this early hour, there were few people out. A stray cat slinked through the shadows searching for food. A ragged man slept on a street corner, his arms wrapped around the tin can he used during the day to beg for coins.

Shoshi looked up. In Vrod, the sky would be an inky blanket spattered with stars, but here, only a few pinpoints of light poked through the smoky layer that covered the city.

"I'm worried about Snigger." Moshe slipped his hand into hers.

"Me too." Shoshi squeezed her brother's hand. "Don't worry," she said. "We'll find him."

The address on the flyer was a rubble-strewn lot by the docks on the East River. A large tent was set up in the middle.

"I remember this neighborhood," said Shoshi. "Salty brought us here the day we arrived in New York."

"Salty knows Mr. Thornswaddle, too. Shoshi, do you think they're in this together?"

"Salty doesn't need his help. He could have stolen Snigger when we left them together that first day."

"Maybe Snigger escaped. Remember, Snigger found *us* in the alley; we didn't find *him*," said Moshe.

"Mr. Thornswaddle warned us to keep Snigger inside so he'd be safe. Why would he do that if he wanted to steal him?" said Shoshi.

"To make it easier for *him* to steal Snigger," said Ziggy.

"Yeah," echoed Noah.

"I don't believe it," said Shoshi.

"You don't *want* to believe it, but it's true. Girls!" Ziggy shook his head.

They walked carefully to avoid piles of rotting garbage, rusty cans, and broken glass, and soon the children reached the tent. Shoshi poked her head inside the flap. "No one's here."

They entered. The tent was empty except for a cage in the corner. Moshe walked over to it. The cage was large

enough for a full-sized animal – a lion, tiger, or *a dragon.*
Several of the rusty bars were blackened, as if they'd been
burned, and the floor of the cage was lined with a thick
layer of straw. Moshe bent down to get a better view.
"See that dent in the straw? It's shaped like Snigger."

Shoshi knelt beside him. "It could have been another
animal."

"Well this animal had wings," said Ziggy. He poked
his finger at a triangular dent.

"So he *has* been here." Moshe looked around. "But
where is he now?"

"And where is Mr. Thornswaddle?" asked Shoshi.

"Aw, he probably took the dragon and ran off," said
Noah.

"I thought Mr. Thornswaddle was a circus barker
extraordinaire," said Noah. "This isn't much of a circus."

"It's definitely his circus." Ziggy pointed to a large
poster lying faceup on the ground. Aloysius P.
Thornswaddle's face smiled up at them.

"I don't understand any of this," said Shoshi.

Crack! Crack! The kids rushed outside just as a wagon
rattled past. The side of the wagon had an image of a
lion across it. They glimpsed the driver, who wore a tall
striped hat. As the wagon careened past, two yellow eyes
peered through the bars of the back window. The wagon
turned the corner and clattered out of sight.

"What do we do now?" asked Moshe.

"We should go home," said Shoshi.

The sky had lightened to a watery blue. A barge slid by on the river, its prow cutting a path through the water. The toot of a horn rang out across the waterfront. The children trudged along the street. Shopkeepers were opening up for the day's business. A man carried a carton of bananas into a fruit store. Shoshi recalled their first day in New York and the exotic taste of that strange fruit. They had come so far since then. But they still hadn't found their father, and now they had lost Snigger too.

"Whew!" She held her nose as they passed a fish market. "Good morning," Shoshi said to a man in a blood-spattered apron, who was prying open the lid of a barrel.

"Morning," he said. "Fresh catch today." He held out a large fish, its scales glinting in the sunlight. "Look at this beautiful flounder. You won't find better fish any-where." The children hurried by. "Tell your mothers to come to Moe's for fish," he called after them.

A man carrying a pole stacked with round pieces of bread stopped them.

"Bagels! Hot fresh bagels." The yeasty smell of freshly baked bread made Shoshi's stomach rumble.

"Thank you, but we don't have any money," she said.

"Have one anyway." He peeled one off the top and handed it to her. "Bagels! Hot fresh bagels," he called and continued up the street.

Shoshi broke the treat into four pieces and passed one to each boy. "*Mmmm,* this is good. Let's go.

Mama will be mad if she wakes up and finds that we aren't there."

A stout woman, who was hauling a pickle barrel to the sidewalk, overheard them. "What are you hoodlums doing out alone at this time of the morning?"

"Our mother sent us shopping, Ma'am." Shoshi turned to the others. "We'd better hurry." She walked in long strides and they followed. At the next corner, they paused to get their bearings.

"Look at that building," said Ziggy. "I think it's some kind of factory. There's lots of 'em down here."

With a shaky hand, Shoshi pointed to a line of flowers carved on the building's sign. "Moshe, look at those roses. They're like the ones Papa carved on the *shul* in Vrod."

Moshe scratched his head. "But how did they get here?"

"Papa must be inside the factory," answered Shoshi. "And if he is . . . it must be Nick the Stick's factory."

"Let's go inside and see," said Noah.

"Yeah," said Moshe.

"Whoa." Ziggy grabbed Moshe's arm. "You don't want to wander into Nick the Stick's place. Trust me."

"Ziggy's right," said Shoshi. "We have to figure out a plan first. Then, when we know what we're up against, we'll come back prepared." *But prepared for what?* Shoshi asked herself. What she did know was that she was the oldest, and she had to sound confident if she wanted the others to follow her lead. Moshe took his sister's hand, and, together, the four of them headed home.

Mrs. Kaputnik was waiting for them in front of the restaurant. "Where have you been?" she demanded.

"We went to find Snigger," said Moshe.

Mrs. Kaputnik was used to her children roaming freely when they were in Vrod, but here in New York, with Igor's threat hanging over their heads, she needed to keep them close. "Don't do that again!" she said, angrily. The children had never seen her this angry.

"But, Mama–" Shoshi began.

"I said no! You stay here, where I can keep an eye on you. You do not go off by yourselves. As for you two ruffians," she turned to Ziggy and Noah, "do not cause me more trouble than I already have. Get home to your families!"

"I feel like a prisoner," Moshe complained.

"Mama's afraid of Nick the Stick," Shoshi said. She refilled a saltshaker and set it back on one of the tables. "Everyone's afraid of him."

"Afraid? What are you afraid of?" boomed a familiar voice.

"Mr. Thornswaddle! What are you doing here?" said Shoshi. "And where is Snigger?"

Moshe dropped the broom. "Yeah, what did you do with him?"

"I don't have your dragon." Mr. Thornswaddle put his hands over his heart. "Do you really think I would steal your animal?"

"Where is your striped hat?" asked Shoshi.

"I lost it. That hat is as much a part of me as my head. But yesterday, I removed it for a moment and, *whoosh,* it was gone."

Shoshi and Moshe exchanged looks.

"We saw your hat this morning," said Moshe.

"Are you sure it was *my* hat? Where did you see it?"

"We saw it at your circus," said Shoshi. "Someone was driving *your* circus wagon and whoever it was had Snigger."

"I don't have a driver," said Mr. Thornswaddle. "Oh, my. Well, if we find my hat, we'll find your dragon. I, Aloysius P. Thornswaddle, do solemnly vow never to rest until the mystery of the dastardly demon who perpetrated this deed is solved."

Mrs. Kaputnik marched into the room. "In ten minutes, I open the door for customers. Save your mysteries for later."

CHAPTER 20

The Mystery Deepens

The following morning, Aloysius P. Thornswaddle and Dingle Hinglehoffer stopped by the restaurant. The baseball player looked tired. Dark circles rimmed his eyes, and his head hung low. Mr. Thornswaddle guided him to a chair and pushed him into it. "Our friend here has something to tell you," Thornswaddle said. The Kaputniks gathered round waiting for him to speak.

"I took your dragon," Dingle Hinglehoffer said.

"You have Snigger?" said Moshe. "Why did you take him?"

"And where is he?" asked Shoshi.

"I don't know," Hinglehoffer said sadly.

"If you took him, you should know," said Mrs. Kaputnik.

"Hear him out." Mr. Thornswaddle motioned for everyone to be seated.

Instead, Mrs. Kaputnik walked to the door, locked it, and turned the sign from open to closed. "Now, what is going on?"

Dingle Hinglehoffer sat up straight. "Could I have a cup of tea?"

"First, you talk." Mrs. Kaputnik said. She stared at Hinglehoffer from across the table. "Then you drink tea."

The baseball player cleared his throat and began. "We needed a mascot. The Yoinkels have their magic bats, so I thought we could use the dragon."

"Why didn't you just ask us?" said Shoshi.

"I was going to, but Mr. Thornswaddle wouldn't let me. He said Snigger was too valuable to use in a baseball game and that he had to be kept away from certain people."

"What people?" asked Mrs. Kaputnik.

"Nick the Stick," said Mr. Thornswaddle. "The man is more dangerous than any of you realize. If he gets hold of the dragon, he will use him to terrorize this neighborhood. No one will be safe. That is why I've warned you to keep Snigger hidden whenever Igor comes to collect his money."

"So who has Snigger now?" asked Shoshi.

"A man wearing a black cape," answered Dingle Hinglehoffer. "He stole him from the dugout. I ran out in time to see him put Snigger into a wagon. Then he took off with the dragon. This man had one blue eye and one black eye."

"Count Vladimeer!" said Mr. Thornswaddle.

"He's the peddler Moshe got Snigger's egg from in Vrod! What's he doing here in New York?" asked Shoshi.

"Well, we'll get to the bottom of this, don't you kids worry," said Thornswaddle.

"We saw the wagon! It must have been the count driving. He must have stolen your hat."

They were interrupted by a knock on the door. Mrs. Shmuel was standing outside with a line of people behind her. "I must open the restaurant," said Mrs. Kaputnik. "Shoshi, give the men their tea. We will talk tonight."

That evening, Shoshi and Moshe met with Ziggy and Noah on the tenement steps. It had rained earlier, and the hot, moist air was suffocating. "Does it ever cool off in this city?" said Shoshi.

"Wait until winter. You'll be begging for heat," said Ziggy.

"We get snowflakes as big as your mother's matzo balls," said Noah.

"In Russia, the snow covered our house," said Moshe. "We had to dig a tunnel to get out."

"Okay, okay. Enough," said Shoshi. "We have a problem to solve. I still don't trust Mr. Thornswaddle. He's hiding something. It might have to do with Snigger's disappearance. Maybe even with Papa's."

"But he's our friend," said Moshe.

"I told you not to trust grown-ups," said Ziggy.

"Okay. Let's say that Mr. Thornswaddle is our enemy too. What do we do?" asked Moshe.

"We have to go back to the building where we saw the roses on that sign. I have a feeling that once we get inside, we'll find everything we're looking for. Here's how we're gonna do it. . . ." said Shoshi.

CHAPTER 21

The Rescue

Two days later, the children set out to put Shoshi's plan into action. It was Saturday, so the restaurant was closed. After lunch, Mrs. Kaputnik took a nap, and Mr. and Mrs. Shmuel went for a walk. The children took the opportunity to go back to the warehouse.

"Where's Noah?" Moshe asked, as they walked down Hester Street.

"His aunt and uncle are visiting from the Bronx," said Ziggy.

"Well, that changes things," Shoshi said to the boys. "Now it's just the three of us, so we're going to have to be extra careful. We have to stick together at all times." The boys nodded. "Moshe, did you get the stuff from the kitchen?"

"Yup." Moshe patted his pocket.

"Good – let's hope we don't need them," said Shoshi. And the three of them headed for the docks.

"Well, here we are," said Ziggy, when they reached their destination. They looked at the river. Fishing boats were in the process of being unloaded. The boats reminded Shoshi of their voyage to America.

"There's the factory," said Shoshi.

"And here's how we get inside." Moshe pointed to a metal door in the sidewalk. He had seen others like it throughout the Lower East Side. They covered metal stairs leading from the sidewalk into cellars under the buildings.

Suddenly Shoshi stiffened. She grabbed Moshe's hand. "Look over there by that boat."

Moshe's eyes followed her gaze. "It's Salty!"

"And look who he's talking to."

"Igor. What is Salty doing with *him?* Uh-oh, they're coming this way."

The children ducked around the corner and shrank against the side of the building.

"This is the best shipment yet," they heard Igor say. "Nick will be pleased." He bent down and opened the metal door.

"'e better be. I stuck me neck out good this time. And I expect to be properly rewarded."

"You'll get your reward. Is everything ready?"

"Me men are waitin' to unload."

"Okay. Bring them in."

Salty whistled and two burly men appeared. Each carried an enormous wooden crate with the name of the steamship stenciled on the side.

"Where d'ya want this?" asked the first man.

"Down there," said Salty. He pointed to the door in the sidewalk.

The men disappeared through the door. Salty and Igor followed behind them. Minutes later, the men emerged. They went to the boat, picked up more boxes, and carried them down into the hole. They made three trips. On the last trip, Salty emerged with them. "We better get goin' before the cops get wind o' us," he said.

"That's the ferry Salty used to bring us over from Ellis Island," Moshe said, as the men boarded their boat.

"Salty is working with Nick the Stick." Shoshi blinked back tears.

"You're not gonna cry, are you?" Ziggy said to her with disgust.

"No!" she sniffed. Then she noticed the door in the sidewalk was still open. "Quick, let's go." She climbed into the hole and down the metal stairs, ending up inside a dark room. The boys followed behind her. When they all reached the bottom, they heard footsteps above them.

"Hide!" Moshe hissed.

The children scrambled behind a stack of crates. Shoshi peered around the edge and saw Igor and another man climb down the ladder, closing the door behind them. Igor had a flashlight in his hands. "We can check this stuff out later. Let's tell the boss it's here."

"He'll be real happy with the loot. That sailor sure did come through for us," said Igor's friend.

The children heard the two men walk up a set of stairs and through a door. When the children were sure the men were gone, they crawled out from behind the crates. The room was pitch-dark.

"I don't believe it," said Shoshi.

"You don't want to believe it," said Ziggy. "Just remember why you're here."

"Ah choo!" Moshe sneezed. "It's filthy down here."

"Eeeek!" Something soft and furry brushed Shoshi's leg and she jumped. "I hate rats!"

"Girls," Ziggy grumbled. He dug into his pants pocket and pulled out a box of matches. He struck one, and a small flame sputtered to life. They spotted a door at the top of the staircase on the other side of the room.

The match sputtered out and Ziggy lit another. "Hurry up. This is my last match."

"I liked it better in the dark." Shoshi gasped.

Silently, the children crept up the stairs and through the door, which lead to a deserted hallway on the main floor.

At the end of the hall was a room with a door made of frosted glass and emblazoned with a bright red rose. Shoshi tried the knob and, to her surprise, it swung open. It was a small room, and in the middle was a table, piled high with wooden baseball bats. A collection of carpentry tools hung on the wall. A man in a white smock was seated on a stool. He held a pointy knife and was carving a piece of wood. On his head was an old black hat, and he had a curly beard. Shoshi conjured up memories from when she was a little girl. The man looked up from his work. When Shoshi saw him, all her doubts disappeared. "Papa!"

The man squinted. "Shoshi? No." He shook his head. "It is not possible. I am dreaming."

"It's not a dream." Shoshi reached out and touched his sleeve. "See, I'm real. And so is Moshe," she said, as her brother and Ziggy walked shyly over. "Oh, and that's Ziggy. He's our friend."

"Pleased to meet you," Ziggy said.

"No, no. This is not happening. It *is* a dream. I must wake up and finish carving the bats for the baseball game." He waved his hands. "Go, go, evil spirits, go away and leave me in peace."

"Papa, we're real." Shoshi pulled out her amber charm.

Tears streamed down their father's cheeks. He hugged his children tightly. "But how can this be? You are dead. You were all killed in a pogrom in Russia."

"Who told you that?" asked Shoshi.

"My letters, they came back with black writing on the front. And your mother stopped writing."

"Mama wrote you a letter every week. But we never heard from *you*."

"I wrote to you, too. I gave my letters to Igor to mail. He said you were all dead." He slapped his forehead. "He told me lies. It *is* you, *mein kinderlach*." He rocked back and forth with them locked in his arms. When he released them, their father asked, "And how is your mother?"

"Mama is well. She's running the restaurant now. Aunt Sadie and Uncle Mendel stole our money and ran off to California. Oh, and one more thing," Shoshi said, pausing for breath. "Our new American name is Kaputnik."

"Kaputnik? What's a Kaputnik?"

"It's a long story, Papa," Moshe said.

"Then maybe we should all sit down, and you will tell it to me." He pulled three stools up to the table and motioned for them all to sit.

"Well, you see, it all started on Passover, just before the first seder," Moshe began.

Ziggy listened to the first few minutes of the story. But he soon became restless. No one saw him slip off the stool and head out the door. They didn't know he had gone until they heard a loud cry and footsteps racing down the hall. And by that time, it was already too late.

CHAPTER 22

Escape from a Bat Factory

Ziggy hated family stuff. His mother was always trying to hug him, and when his Aunt Clara visited, she couldn't stop pinching his cheeks. So when the mushy talk began with Shoshi, Moshe, and their father, he decided to explore the building. Ziggy was impressed – it was an interesting place. The long metal stairway that they had come up stretched upward to a second floor. Ziggy wanted to see what was at the top.

As he climbed, the only sound was the clumping of his shoes on the metal rungs. Close to the top, he heard a noise, as if someone were rattling the bars of a cage. Curious, Ziggy climbed higher. At the top, he saw another door, but this one was solid steel.

From inside came a low growl. Ziggy was intrigued. He tried the doorknob, but it was locked. He spied a rusty metal key hanging from a hook on the wall. He grabbed the key and inserted it into the lock. *Click.* Ziggy swung the door open and poked his head into the room. An enormous black dog guarded a pile of bats. The dog had on a collar attached to a chain with a peg that was bolted to the floor. Every time it lunged, the chain pulled the collar tight around its neck.

Ziggy moved closer. He saw letters etched into the dog's collar. "Fang? Is that your name?" The dog growled louder and bared its teeth. It began to bark. Startled, Ziggy tripped on the peg and fell into the pile of bats.

For a moment he lay stunned, but as his vision cleared, he saw the dog lunge toward him. Ziggy screamed and rolled over onto his stomach, protecting his face. When he looked up, the dog was just inches away, but the chain held him in place. Ziggy noticed that one of the bats had broken in half. Rising to his knees, he reached for it. To his surprise, he saw that the two pieces were designed to snap together and the inside of the bat was hollow. That's when he heard footsteps running up the stairs and toward the room. The dog heard them too. Its ears perked up, and it began to whimper. The closer the footsteps got, the louder the dog's whimper grew until it turned into a full-fledged howl.

Igor walked into the room. "How did you get in here?"

"I'm, I'm . . ." Ziggy stuttered.

Igor noticed the bat in Ziggy's hands. "Drop it," he said. He lunged at Ziggy, but the boy dodged his grasp.

This must be one important piece of wood, Ziggy thought, as he ran out the door and clambered down the metal stairs, with Fang and Igor close on his heels. Ziggy reached the ground floor and stopped. Which way had he come? He looked over his shoulder. Fang was galloping toward him, teeth bared, drool leaking from the corners of his mouth. Ziggy saw a door at the end of the hallway. Taking a deep breath, he sprinted toward it. His shoe got caught on a loose floor board that sent him tumbling to his knees. He struggled to get back up. Fang pounced.

"Papa, why does Nick the Stick keep you here?" asked Shoshi.

"Nick the Stick keeps me here so I will continue to make his baseball bats," said their father. "But that's not important; right now, we must find a way to escape."

"Can't we just walk out?" asked Shoshi.

"It's not that simple. Mr. Stick keeps this place well guarded. And now he has a strange animal that breathes fire guarding the entrance."

"That's Snigger!" Shoshi and Moshe said at the same time.

They heard a bloodcurdling howl and the door crashed open. Ziggy fell into the room. An enormous black dog bounded across the floor after him, its upper lip curled back to reveal razor-sharp teeth.

"We gotta get outta here!" said Ziggy, as footsteps pounded down the hall.

"How?" said Moshe. They were trapped. The only exit was the door, and the footsteps were headed straight for it.

"Stop! All of you." Igor rushed into the room, carrying a shotgun. The dog backed up to its master, and Igor patted its head. "Good boy, Fang." He faced Mr. Kapustin. "Where do you think you're going? Have you forgotten your deal with Nick?"

Mr. Kapustin pulled himself up to his full height. "We have no deal. You have lied to me for five years. My wife and children are not dead. You did not mail my letters. I do not owe you a thing."

Shoshi signaled to Moshe. He reached into his pocket, and his fingers closed around the dimpled surface of a matzo ball. He pulled it out and quickly threw it at Igor. It struck Igor's arm and sent his gun clattering to the floor. Moshe threw a second matzo ball, and it hit Igor in the head, stunning him.

"Quick," Moshe commanded. "Follow me." He dashed into the hallway. The others followed.

"Help!" It was Ziggy. Fang had Ziggy's trousers between his teeth. They all ran back to help him.

"*ROAR!*" Suddenly, the room was engulfed in a cloud of smoke.

"SNIGGER!" Shoshi shouted. Since they had last seen Snigger, he had grown immensely. He loomed over the dog. Fang shrank away from the children. Snigger blew out another cloud of smoke.

"I can't see!" yelled Igor.

"Let's go," said Ziggy.

"Follow me, children! I know this building like my own hand." The kids followed Mr. Kapustin, with a group of Nick's people right behind them. Mr. Kapustin lead the children through the hallway and ushered them up a staircase that had a wide door at its top. The children climbed higher and higher, past the second and third floors. When they finally reached the top, they pulled open the door and went through to the other side. They were on the roof of the building. Snigger bounded through the door after them.

Shoshi and Moshe stood beside their father gasping for air. Ziggy walked to the edge of the roof, looked down, and whistled. "Now what?" he asked, turning to his friends.

"I don't know," Shoshi gasped. Her lungs hurt from the climb. Her dress was torn, her hair had come loose, and she was weak with fear and exhaustion. Beside her, Moshe tried to look brave, but she could tell he was terrified too. And then there was Papa, who was so dazed by all that had happened that he seemed to be in a trance. The street was a long way down, and there was no fire escape on the side of the building. They were trapped. "Snigger," she said. "If only you could fly." Snigger looked down, snorted, and backed away from the edge. "It's okay." Shoshi wrapped her arms around his neck. "We love you anyway."

Igor, holding his gun, and two men wielding clubs barged onto the roof. The door opened again, and a shadow fell across the rooftop. Shoshi's knees buckled as Nick the Stick approached them.

"Leave the children out of this." Mr. Kapustin stepped in front of Shoshi, Moshe, and Ziggy. "Your quarrel is with me, not with them."

"It was. Until now," said Nick the Stick. "Igor, I want the dragon. Get rid of the rest of them."

Shoshi inched closer to Snigger. The dragon lowered his head and with a swift movement, picked up Shoshi and put her on his back. Then he did the same with Moshe and Ziggy.

"Papa, come too," yelled Moshe.

Igor aimed his gun.

Shoshi rubbed the dragon's head. "*Please*. You *can* fly. You *can* fly!"

The boys took up the chant. *"Fly, Snigger, fly."*

Snigger spewed flames.

"Shoot!" said Nick.

Mr. Kapustin lowered his head and rammed Igor in the stomach. "Go," he waved at Snigger. "Go, get out of here."

"Papa, come with us!" Shoshi reached for her father's hand. He stumbled, and the children pulled him onto Snigger's back. Snigger pawed at the edge of the roof.

Another step and they would fall down to the street. Shoshi clutched Snigger's neck with trembling hands. "Snigger, *fly!*"

Igor regained his balance, lifted the gun, and squeezed the trigger.

And then Snigger jumped.

Shoshi screamed and closed her eyes as they tumbled off the rooftop.

"Hold tight," said her father, as the building's windows whizzed by their noses.

"We're going to be killed!" Ziggy cried.

"No, we're not," shouted Moshe. "Look!"

Shoshi opened her eyes and gasped. "Snigger's wings are open! Snigger, your wings are open!"

Snigger lifted his head. As he did, his body soared higher and higher, toward the sky.

"Snigger, you're flying!" Shoshi laughed.

"I don't believe it!" said Ziggy.

"Is this how you got to America?" their father asked.

"No, Papa. We came on a ship," said Shoshi.

"We sailed in over there." Moshe pointed beyond the Statue of Liberty to Ellis Island.

They gazed in wonder at the panorama of the New York landscape beneath them. Shoshi wrapped her arms around Snigger's neck. Her tears dripped onto his scales "Oh, Snigger, you saved us again."

CHAPTER 23

A Rough Landing

Snigger circled the city for the third time. It had been a nice tour, but they wanted to be back on the ground.

"We'd better land soon," said Moshe. The sky was darkening, and the clouds let off a low rumble. "It's going to rain."

"I don't think he knows how to land," said Shoshi.

"I want to get off," said Ziggy.

Shoshi felt a raindrop. A strong wind blew thick clouds across the gray sky. "Snigger, I know you're having fun, but please take us down." The dragon listened. They flew over Hester Street. The children held on tight as Snigger hurtled toward the ground.

"Hold on!" shouted Mr. Kapustin.

"Yahoo!" said Ziggy. The dragon swooped down, skimmed the road, bounced up, and dropped down again, settling on a patch of sidewalk in front of Mrs. Kaputnik's Pool Hall and Matzo Ball Emporium.

Shoshi slid off the dragon's back. Her knees trembled, and she leaned against Snigger.

The dragon sank to the ground and rested his head on his paws.

"Good work," said Moshe.

Mrs. Kaputnik ran outside. "Shoshi! Moshe!" Once she had realized the children were missing, Mrs. Kaputnik had been angry; then panicked. But when she saw them swoop down from the sky on Snigger's back, she was just glad to have them home safe. "Are you hurt?" she asked them.

"No, but Mama, look, we found Papa *and* Snigger!" said Shoshi.

"Saul? Is it really you?" Mrs. Kaputnik took her husband's face in her hands. "Thank God you are safe. So, tell me," she said, "*where have you been all this time, and why didn't you write?*"

The news of Mrs. Kaputnik's husband's return spread through Hester Street like sparks from Snigger's breath. Safely in the restaurant, with the Kaputniks' regular customers by the family's side, their father told his story of being Nick the Stick's prisoner for five years.

"You never suspected he was lying?" asked Mr. Shmuel.

"No, he had shown me a letter that said my wife and children had been killed in a pogrom."

"*Oy, yoi, yoi.* Such a crook. Such a liar," said Mrs. Shmuel.

"He said if I did not do his work, he would harm the family I had left here in America," Mr. Kapustin continued.

"And of course, he never told you that those *no-goodniks* left for California when your wife and children arrived," said Mr. Seltzer. "Nick the Stick has been holding all of us for ransom for years."

"His henchman even tried to kidnap Misha once," said the organ-grinder. "But Misha bit him." The man chuckled. "Igor's hand turned red as a pomegranate. After that, he left us alone."

The restaurant door opened and a draft of warm air swept into the room. "What have we here?" It was Aloysius P. Thornswaddle. "I see that you have found your dragon," he said to Shoshi and Moshe.

"Yes, and we found our father. He's been Nick the Stick's prisoner for five years," said Shoshi. "Papa, this is Aloysius P. Thornswaddle, circus barker extraordinaire. He brought us the pool table and taught us how to sell the matzo balls."

"I see. It's good to meet you, Mr. Thornswaddle," said Mr. Kapustin.

"It is a pleasure, sir," Thornswaddle replied. "This is a most joyous occasion." Then he addressed the crowd:

"Everyone in this room has felt the sting and the intimidation of Nick the Stick's villainous cane." Mr. Shmuel lifted his violin and began to play. "You have all been threatened, teased, terrorized, and taunted by this vermin and his gang of bandits." Thornswaddle was on a roll. The faster he talked, the faster Mr. Shmuel played. "Today, I am happy to say, is the beginning of the end of your troubles. We," Mr. Thornswaddle waved at the children, "have a plan."

"We do?" said Ziggy.

"Tonight, we celebrate," Mr. Thornswaddle declared. "Tomorrow, we take action."

"So what is our plan?" Shoshi asked Mr. Thornswaddle, after the restaurant had cleared. The children were sitting at a table with their father, their mother, and the circus barker. Snigger, tuckered out from the day, was fast asleep in the kitchen. He was now so big that he took up almost half the room.

"Mr. Thornswaddle," Shoshi said. "What's your plan to get rid of Nick the Stick?"

"Mr. Kaputnik – may I call you that?" said Mr. Thornswaddle

"Why not? This has been a very strange day. So, who am I to question a new name?" replied Mr. Kaputnik.

"When we got married in Vrod," said Mrs. Kaputnik,

"I took your name. Now, in this new world, you can take mine."

Mr. Thornswaddle leaned across the table. "Mr. Kaputnik, did you bring a souvenir from the bat factory?"

"A souvenir?" Mr. Kaputnik looked back at him in confusion.

"He didn't, but Ziggy did." Shoshi went into the kitchen and came back with the bat that Ziggy had carried from the factory. "Is this what everyone is looking for? It's Nick the Stick's baseball bat; the source of the Yoinkles' power. Am I right, Papa?"

"Yes, Shoshi, you are right," said Mr. Kaputnik. Shoshi had grown into a smart young girl, and he was filled with pride.

"Is this why Dingle Hinglehoffer can never win a game?" Moshe asked.

"Are you trying to tell us that this is a magic baseball bat?" said Ziggy.

"It's not magic, but it is ingenious," said Mr. Kaputnik.

"Nick the Stick runs what they call a numbers racket. He would have asked this of you, too, Mrs. Kaputnik," Thornswaddle said. "He forces shop owners to sell bets on the ball games. No one ever refuses him because a gangster like Nick is very dangerous."

"Mr. Stick gets people to bet on the Slobbers. Then he fixes the games so that the Yoinkles win," said Mr. Kaputnik.

"Precisely," said Mr. Thornswaddle. "Then he keeps their money."

"Why would people bet on the Slobbers if they always lose?" asked Shoshi.

"Because Nick's men patrol the shops and force people to place their bets on every team but the Yoinkles. They scare people into betting against the Yoinkles. And you, Mr. Kaputnik, made the bats that allowed the Yoinkles to always win."

"What would happen if the Yoinkles lost their next game?" said Moshe.

"Now you are beginning to think like our enemy," said Mr. Thornswaddle.

"But what makes this bat special?" Ziggy asked.

"Two things." He turned the top half of the bat until it separated into two pieces. He held out the pieces for everyone to see.

"It's hollow," said Moshe.

"Yes. Because it is hollow, it is lighter than other bats. That means that Yicky Stickyfingers and the other Yoinkles can hit their balls further and faster than anyone else. But there is another secret to its value." Mr. Kaputnik turned to his children. "I believe my children know what it is."

Shoshi looked puzzled. "We do?"

"Yes, you do. You're both wearing it."

Shoshi looked down at her cotton dress, black shoes, and stockings. Then she snapped her fingers. "Do you mean our amber charms?" she asked, pulling her charm out from under her dress.

Shoshi took off her charm and handed the disk to Mr. Kaputnik. He held it up to the light. "Yes. For thousands of years, amber has been treasured. Some believe that it has magical powers. Especially those pieces that have inclusions."

"What are inclusions, Papa?" asked Moshe.

"Amber is liquid or sap from a tree. Over thousands, even millions of years, sap hardens. Sometimes plants or small animals become trapped in the liquid." He pointed to a small dark spot in the center. "That is a tiny spider that lived hundreds of thousands of years ago. Perhaps there is none like it on Earth today. In Russia, a tradesman from the city of Kiev visited our village. He was a strange man, with one blue eye and one black eye."

"Count Vladimeer," said Moshe.

"I was already a carpenter, making things out of wood, and this stranger took a liking to me. He would guide me through the forest and help me find the best wood for my carvings. One day we came upon a different type of prize. It was amber. This material was so valuable that it was illegal for anyone but the czar's people to own it. This man and I struck a bargain. I carved hollow walking sticks in which he hid the amber. What he did with it, I never asked. You two were very young. I wanted to bring you and your mother to America so I sold the sticks to him for money to pay for my passage here. The stranger rewarded me with two pieces of amber, which I carved into good luck charms for you. For centuries," he continued, "people have thought that amber is good luck, especially for children. I was leaving for America and I wanted you both to be safe."

Suddenly, Moshe remembered something. "When the stranger gave me Snigger's egg, he wanted my wood, but he also wanted my amber disk."

"Of course," said his father. "He was looking for the pieces that he had given to me. They were especially valuable because each had an ancient inclusion."

"The count found Snigger in the amber forest. Does that mean Snigger is magical too?" asked Moshe.

"I do not want to end this fascinating conversation," said Mr. Thornswaddle, "but what does all this have to do with Nick the Stick's baseball bats?"

Mr. Kaputnik picked up the bat and held it out. "Look inside," he instructed.

Everyone peered into the hollow opening.

"*Whew,*" said Ziggy.

"Nick the Stick is lining his baseball bats with amber sap," said Shoshi.

"The wood is strong because it is from the amber forest. And the sap gives the bat magic," said Moshe.

"At least Yicky Stickyfingers and the other Yoinkles think it's magic," said Shoshi. "I know how we can help the Slobbers win tomorrow's baseball game.

Mama, can you make us a batch of your very hardest matzo balls?"

"Of course," said Mrs. Kaputnik.

Shoshi told them her plan.

Shoshi sat on the fire escape looking down at the street. Moshe climbed through the window and joined her.

"Mama's giving Papa an earful about how Uncle Mendel stole our money."

"It's wonderful having him back," Shoshi said to her brother. "Moshe, I can't believe that Salty works for Nick the Stick. And we still can't trust Mr. Thornswaddle because he lied about knowing Salty. And how does Count Vladimeer fit into all this? Why would he steal Snigger? And how did Snigger end up at Nick the Stick's warehouse? There must be a connection." With a determined look, Shoshi said, "First we'll help Dingle Hinglehoffer win the baseball game. Then, we'll confront Mr. Thornswaddle and find out what is really going on."

CHAPTER 24

The Longest Baseball Game

Shoshi could hardly stand still. It was the top of the ninth inning, and the baseball game was tied at two for the Yoinkles and two for the Slobbers. Dingle Hinglehoffer was pitching, and Yicky Stickyfingers was at bat. For the first time, the Slobbers had a chance to win. The Yoinkles had missed many balls and the Slobbers had actually gotten two hits. But there was a problem. No one knew what had happened to the amber bat. To win this game, they needed it. Time was running out.

"It was gone when we got up this morning," Shoshi said to Mr. Thornswaddle. "Moshe had hidden it in the icebox. But when Papa went to get it, it wasn't there."

"It sounds to me like there is skulduggery here," said Mr. Thornswaddle. He looked out at the field. The matzo balls were working.

In the Yoinkles' dugout, Nick the Stick paced back

and forth. His white shirt was damp with sweat, and his gray hat was pulled down low over his forehead. "Whadda ya bums think yer doin'? I ain't payin' ya to lose." He waved his stick with its razor-sharp tip.

Out in the field, the Slobbers stood at their positions. "We might just win this thing," Dizzy Dan, the Slobbers' shortstop, said to their second baseman, Lefty Larue. He had earned his nickname by losing two fingers on his left hand to Nick the Stick the only other time the Slobbers had almost beaten the Yoinkles.

Dingle raised his right hand to get ready to pitch. He turned his body to home plate and threw the ball.

Yicky Stickyfingers swung . . . and missed.

"*Stee-rike* one," shouted the umpire.

"What're ya doin' ya stupid ballplayer?" shouted Nick the Stick. He poked Yicky Stickyfingers' backside with his cane.

"Youch!" Yicky Stickyfingers lowered the bat and, with a venomous look at Nick the Stick, crouched over home plate. This time the pitch was a low curveball that flew off the tip of his bat and behind him into the grandstand.

"Foul ball. *Stee-rike* two!"

A young boy reached out, plucked it from the air, and waved it over his head like a trophy. "*Ycch*," he made a face. "What kind of baseball is this?"

"A special one, young man," said Aloysius P. Thornswaddle, taking the matzo ball from the boy's hand. "Here, have a box of Cracker Jack instead. You'll get a prize."

"*Slobbers, Slobbers, Slobbers!*" the crowd chanted, as Dingle Hinglehoffer prepared to pitch again.

The Kaputniks and Ziggy watched the game from the Slobbers' dugout. In front of them, Snigger pranced up and down, entertaining the crowd by shooting showers of sparks into the air.

"What a great costume! It looks like a real dragon!" someone yelled from the stands.

"What a great light show – what d'ya think they used? Firecrackers?" yelled another.

Dingle Hinglehoffer wound up for the third pitch. The crowd was on their feet. The cry of "*Slobbers, Slobbers, Slobbers*" rose from the grandstand like a hot wind.

"Show them how a real pitcher pitches, Hinglehoffer!" a fan called out.

Dingle Hinglehoffer threw the ball. Shoshi watched as it left his hand, arced through the air, and whizzed past Yicky Stickyfingers' nose.

"*Stee-rike* three; OUT!" called the umpire.

Yicky Stickyfingers threw down his bat. "Yer blind as a bat!"

"I know a *stee-rike* when I see a *stee-rike*, and that was a *stee-rike*." The umpire waved his fist under Yicky Stickyfingers' nose. "*Three stee-rikes* and yer o-u-t, *OUT!*"

———

"Listen, everyone," Mr. Thornswaddle said, when the Slobbers gathered in the dugout. "Mrs. Kaputnik's matzo balls have brought us to this point. We are now tied with the Yoinkles. This is a very exciting moment!"

"Thornswaddle, we ain't got all day," said Lefty. "Where's the magic baseball bat?"

Aloysius P. Thornswaddle wiped his face with a hand-kerchief. His mustache ends twitched like exclamation marks above his mouth. "Trust me. It's coming."

"When? It's the bottom of the ninth," said the shortstop.

"Play ball," yelled the umpire.

The Slobbers were now at bat. They were three up and three down. Now they were back out in the field.

The Yoinkles repeated their pattern.

"This game is going into extra innings," the announcer shouted through a megaphone.

"Where is the bat?" said Mr. Kaputnik.

"I have my people working on it," said Mr. Thornswaddle.

"What people?"

"People." Thornswaddle stomped off the field.

"This game is going into extra innings," the announcer shouted through a megaphone. It was the top of the seventeenth inning. The score was still three to three. The Slobbers were on the field. And then Thumbs Magee, the Yoinkles' shortstop scored a run.

"We are doomed," said Mr. Thornswaddle. "Unless we score in the bottom of this inning, they have won."

"Is this what you are looking for?" Count Vladimeer appeared with a swoosh of his black cape. In his hands, he held Mr. Kaputnik's amber bat.

The Yoinkles took to the field, with Yicky Stickyfingers on the pitcher's mound. Excitement fizzed through the crowd like bubbles in a seltzer bottle.

Dizzy Dan was first at bat. Yicky Stickyfingers threw the ball.

Whoosh! Dizzy missed and the ball sliced across the center of home plate.

"*Stee- rike* one," called the umpire.

Dizzy hit the next ball, but it flew into the stands behind him.

"*Foul ball – stee-rike two!*" shouted the umpire.

Dizzy held up his hand for timeout. He turned to Dingle Hinglehoffer, who handed him another bat. Dizzy ran back to home plate.

Whoosh, came the pitch. *Thwack!* The ball flew past Yicky Stickyfingers and landed far out in left field. The crowd went wild as Dizzy raced to first base.

Next up was the Slobbers' catcher. Yicky Stickyfingers faced home plate. He squinted, windmilled his arm, and spat on the ball. Then he threw it.

Crrrack! The Slobbers' catcher hit a two-base run, and now Dizzy was on third base. The third batter struck out and the fourth batter hit a single and was tagged out at first base. Then the next batter hit a single and loaded the bases. Next up was Hinglehoffer.

"*Dingle, Dingle, Dingle,*" chanted the crowd.

In the Slobbers' dugout, the team held their breath. Dingle Hinglehoffer clutched the bat. The game depended on him.

Yicky Stickyfingers pitched.

Thwack! Up, up, up went the ball, over the infield, across the outfield, above the peanut gallery, and over the stadium walls. *Splash!* It landed in the East River.

People jumped from the stands onto the field. The Slobbers pounded each other on the back. Such was the excitement that no one took notice of Nick the Stick. He flipped open the knife on his cane, raced onto the field, and lunged at Dingle Hinglehoffer. "Yer gonna be minus one pitcher," he growled.

Out of nowhere, Snigger swooped in and grabbed him by the seat of his pants. With the gangster in his mouth, the dragon flew higher and higher until it seemed to Shoshi that his wings were touching the clouds. Then he nosedived and dropped the gangster, head first, into a pail of water in the Yoinkles' dugout. Mr. Thornswaddle and three policemen raced over to the dugout. "Officers, arrest this man! He attacked our pitcher with a knife!" said Thornswaddle. The policemen pulled Nick out of the pail and handcuffed him. To the roar of the crowd, they led a very wet and dizzy Nick the Stick off the field.

CHAPTER 25

Victory!

The whole neighborhood had crowded into Mrs. Kaputnik's Pool Hall and Matzo Ball Emporium for a party. But there were no matzo balls in sight.

"We used them all for the baseball game," said Mrs. Kaputnik.

No one cared. The Slobbers had defeated the Yoinkles, and Nick the Stick was in jail.

Mr. Shmuel played his violin. Mr. Seltzer pumped his accordion. The organ-grinder ground out a tune and Misha danced. Mrs. Shmuel passed out freshly baked cookies, and children held hands, circled around Dingle Hinglehoffer, and sang:

Nick the Stick has gone to jail, gone to jail, gone
   to jail,
Stuck his head into a pail,

My fair lady-O.

This is such a happy day, happy day, happy day,
Nick the Stick has gone away,
My fair lady-O.

The Brooklyn Slobbers won their game, won their
    game, won their game,
The Brooklyn Slobbers love their fame,
My fair lady-O.

A woman entered the restaurant with her husband.
"See, Zoltan, I told you this is the best place in New
York. And, look, they're having a party."

"Yes, dear," said the man.

Shoshi recognized the woman instantly. "It's Mrs.
Finklestein! How did she find us?"

The couple walked up to Mrs. Shmuel, and Mrs.
Finklestein said, "You, lady, we want a table."

"A table?" Mrs. Shmuel looked around the crowded
room.

Mrs. Kaputnik came out of the kitchen, and Mrs.
Finklestein's face turned purple. "You!" the woman
screamed. Everyone in the room froze. Mr. Shmuel
stopped playing his violin. Mr. Seltzer put down his
accordion. The organ-grinder stopped grinding and
Misha stopped dancing. "The *meshuganah* lady with the
dybbuk!" Mrs. Finklestein shrieked.

"I thought they locked you up at Ellis Island!" said Mrs. Kaputnik.

"It is you they should lock up – you and that, that *thing!* Is it here?" She looked around anxiously.

"Hello, Mrs. Finklestein." Shoshi sidled over and smiled up at the woman. "Did you bring any sausages for Snigger?"

"*Ayeee!*" Mrs. Finklestein grabbed her husband's arm. "Let's get out of here!" And without another word, she pulled him out the door.

Shoshi, Moshe, and Ziggy sat on the stoop of their tenement building. They were laughing so hard that Shoshi thought her sides would split. "If only Snigger had been here to really scare her." After depositing Nick the Stick in the pail, Snigger had flown out of the baseball stadium and hadn't returned. Her smile faded. "Where do you think he is this time?"

"*Hee, hee, hee.* Ye would no' by chance be lookin' fer a green animal, would yer?"

"Salty!" The children jumped to their feet. "What are you doing here?"

"A friend brought me," he said, pointing to Snigger, who was cooling off in the water from a fire hydrant. "I found 'im gallopin' up Houston Street."

Shoshi remembered Salty's betrayal. "You're a crook. You were working with Nick the Stick."

"We saw you carrying wooden crates from the ship into his warehouse," said Moshe.

"Now calm down, both of ye. Yes, I was workin' with Nick the Stick but it's not what ye think."

The Kaputniks, Aloysius P. Thornswaddle, and Salty sat around a table in the now empty restaurant. Salty launched into his story.

"Mr. Stick and 'is gang 'as been terrorizin' our ship's crew fer years. They pay crew members to steal cargo and deliver it to 'em so they can resell it. If someone refuses . . ." He ran his finger across his throat. "Last year, their goon Igor strong-armed me. 'E told me if I didn't cooperate 'e'd make sure I was arrested. Said 'e had 'is sources with the police, and I'd spend the rest 'o me life in jail." Salty paused for breath. He looked around the table at his audience and grinned. "Thought 'e 'ad me, 'e did. But I fooled 'im."

"How?" said Shoshi. "What did you do?"

"I met this 'ere gent." He nodded at Mr. Thornswaddle.

Mr. Thornswaddle hooked his fingers through his suspenders. "I, dear friends, am a private detective. I was hired by the steamship line to break up a ring of thieves. I had been working on the case for two years with nary a break, until I met Salty. And, you children helped."

"We did?" Moshe said with surprise.

"You gave Snigger to Salty, who was working for me from inside the ship. Salty was my spy."

Salty took over the narrative. "When Snigger came down into the boiler room, I saw an opportunity. I could 'elp you two and, at the same time, Snigger could 'elp me by scarin' me shipmates into lettin' me in on their operation."

"Our biggest problem," said Mr. Thornswaddle, "was to find out how they were getting the stuff off the ship, and where they were taking it. Once Salty was involved, we were able to track them. I didn't know about your father until after you rescued him. While we were at the baseball game, the police raided the factory and arrested Igor and the whole motley crew."

"As fer me shipmates," Salty piped up, "they were apprehended on the ship. So, you see children, by leadin' us to Nick the Stick, you are heroes, and so is Snigger."

The dragon raised his head and roared. Everyone laughed.

"Mr. Thornswaddle," said Shoshi. "Where does Count Vladimeer fit into all this?"

"You see, I really *am* a circus barker extraordinaire. It is what I did before becoming a detective, and it is now my cover operation. The count and I work together and travel the world seeking ancient treasure and mystical creatures that evil people sell on the black market. We want to keep these treasures from being destroyed."

The count suddenly appeared in the doorway. "Did I hear my name?" he said, crossing the floor.

"Ah, the very person I want to see." Mr. Thornswaddle greeted him. "I was just telling these good people about our partnership. But first, dear Vlad, pray tell us, how did you find the amber bat?"

Before he could answer, Salty leapt from his seat. "You!" He turned to the others. "This man tried to kill me and steal Snigger."

"My dear man, you exaggerate. I wasn't going to harm you; I only wanted to scare you into parting with the dragon. You see, it's very important that we keep the dragon safe from harm. I was surveying your apartment and saw Dingle Hinglehoffer take the dragon, so I seized the opportunity to liberate the pet. I had gotten him as far as our circus, but what I didn't know was that I, too, was being followed – by Igor. When I stepped out of the wagon, my back was turned, and he knocked me on the noggin. When I came to, the dragon was gone. As for the bat, Igor also took that. Moshe saw him sneaking out of the kitchen with it last night."

"I wanted to go after him myself," Moshe explained, "but Thornswaddle said I should let him handle it."

The count reached into his pocket and pulled out a giant egg. "I found Igor at the factory, and I traded him one of these for the bat."

Everyone gasped.

"Is it another dragon?" said Moshe.

The count winked his blue eye. "Let us just say that by Thanksgiving Day, Mr. Igor will have the biggest turkey in New York."

"And 'e'll be eatin' it in jail," said Salty.

Shoshi and Moshe were back on the stoop, hoping to catch whatever cool nighttime breeze drifted in from the river. Snigger, exhausted from the excitement, slept on the sidewalk. Salty and Mr. Thornswaddle joined them.

"Mr. Thornswaddle," said Moshe, "is the amber bat really magic?"

"It is if you want it to be. Nick the Stick used your father's hollow bats to hide the jewelry they stole from the ship's passengers. One day, Yicky Stickyfingers picked up a bat filled with amber, instead of his real one. He hit five home runs in that game and decided it was his lucky bat. Who knows?" He shrugged. "Maybe it was magic. It certainly helped Dingle Hinglehoffer in today's game."

"Of course it's magic." The count loomed above them. "Magic," he said to the children, "is what you believe it to be."

Salty stood and held out his hand. "Well, children," he said. "I'd best be on me way."

"Where are you going?" Shoshi asked.

"I don't know, but it won't be back to the sea. I've 'ad enough of boiler rooms and thievery."

"Why don't you stay here? You can work in the restaurant," said Shoshi.

"Thank ye," Salty said. "Ye are very kind, but I don't think I'm cut out to stay in one place for very long."

"Why don't you join the count and me in our work?" Mr. Thornswaddle said. "We are going to use our circus to continue our quest."

"I'd be honored," said Salty.

Aloysius P. Thornswaddle turned to Shoshi and Moshe. "Children, the dragon is an endangered animal. He is too big to remain in your restaurant. Besides, he is not safe here. More and more people will find out about him, and they'll want to exploit him; possibly use him to terrorize the good people in this neighborhood – even the world."

"But Snigger is *ours*," the children said in unison.

Snigger lifted his head and roared. Then Shoshi remembered the villagers of Vrod and how afraid they were of Snigger. "Moshe, they're right," she said. "We can't keep Snigger safe. He needs to go someplace where no one can hurt him."

"Where would you take him?" Moshe asked Mr. Thornswaddle.

"Why to our circus, of course." Mr. Thornswaddle placed a hand on Snigger's head. "Snigger will be the star of our show. He will delight audiences all over the world. And you, dear children, will see him whenever we return to New York."

"How often will that be?" Shoshi asked tearfully.

"Once every year. When the snow melts and trees burst into bloom, the . . ." Mr. Thornswaddle looked at the count.

"*The Flying Dragon Circus,*" was the Count's reply.

"Of course, *The Flying Dragon Circus* shall return, and Snigger shall be the main attraction."

As if on cue, the dragon rose to his feet, stretched his paws, and bowed.

Shoshi and Moshe applauded. "Snigger, you are going to be a star," said Shoshi.

"Then you will let us take him?" said Mr. Thornswaddle.

The children looked at each other and nodded. "Yes," they both said.

"We'll miss him," said Moshe.

"But we want him to be safe and happy." Shoshi wiped away her tears.

"Who knows," said Mr. Thornswaddle. "When you two are grown, you may join us and travel the world too."

Shoshi walked over to Snigger and put her arms around his neck. "Good-bye, Snigger. We love you."

Snigger rested his head against her shoulder. He blew out sparks.

Moshe patted his side. "You be a good circus star, okay?"

"Well, good-bye children. For now." Mr. Thornswaddle, the count, and Salty climbed on the dragon's back.

"Bye Snigger!" said the children together. "We'll see you in the circus!"

Snigger spread his wings and leapt into the air. He circled Hester Street three times and dipped his wings, as if waving good-bye. Shoshi and Moshe watched him soar up into the sky, his fiery breath lighting up the night. Then he disappeared among the clouds and was gone.

FAMILY LIVING IN PASTORAL PERSPECTIVE

REGARDING CHILDREN

A NEW RESPECT FOR CHILDHOOD AND FAMILIES

HERBERT ANDERSON AND SUSAN B. W. JOHNSON

WESTMINSTER JOHN KNOX PRESS
LOUISVILLE, KENTUCKY

Scripture quotations from the New Revised Standard Version of the Bible are copyright © 1989 by the Division of Christian Education of the National Council of the Churches of Christ in the U.S.A., and are used by permission.

Grateful acknowledgment is made to the *New York Times* for permission to reprint an excerpt from "Off on an Adventure: Not Observing Life, But Simply Living It" in *Life in the 30's* by Anna Quindlen. Copyright © 1988 by the New York Times Company.

Book design by Drew Stevens
Cover design by Jeff Tull, Fearless Designs

First edition

Published by Westminster John Knox Press
Louisville, Kentucky

This book is printed on acid-free paper that meets the American National Standards Institute Z39.48 standard. ∞

PRINTED IN THE UNITED STATES OF AMERICA

94 95 96 97 98 99 00 01 02 03 — 10 9 8 7 6 5 4 3 2 1

Library of Congress Cataloging-in-Publication Data

Anderson, Herbert, date.
    Regarding children : a new respect for childhood and families /
  Herbert Anderson and Susan B.W. Johnson. — 1st ed.
       p.   cm. — (Family living in pastoral perspective)
  Includes bibliographical references.
  ISBN 0-664-25125-0 (alk. paper)
    1. Children—United States. 2. Family—United States. 3. Child
  rearing—United States.   I. Johnson, Susan B. W.
  II. Title.   III. Series: Anderson, Herbert. Family living in
  pastoral perspective.
HQ792.U5A63   1994   94-21287
649'.1—dc20

CONTENTS

INTRODUCTION

THIS IS THE THIRD in a series of books on Family Living in
Pastoral Perspective. The first, *Leaving Home*, addresses the
need for children and parents alike to find ways of leaving
and letting go that are liberating and confirming. Clarity about the
process of leaving home is necessary for responsible autonomy. It is also
essential for those who choose to become married. The second book, *Becoming Married*, suggests that preparation for the wedding adds cleaving to the process of leaving. Individuals anticipating marriage need to
understand how the legacy of roles, rules, and rituals they bring from
their home of origin will affect their process of forming a marital bond.

In this third book, we examine what is ordinarily the next family
life-cycle task: raising children. Our aim is to identify what children
need, what families must provide for the sake of children, how families struggle with their childrearing tasks, and what society and the
church must do to support families in their care of children. This reflection on the needs of children and families is one way to enhance
our care for them, but it is not enough. We need to understand why
families and societies fail to provide what children need. We believe
that our children are in trouble partly because adults disdain childhood.
This book is therefore also about the need to transform the ways we
think about children and childhood. For that reason, this book is about
regarding children. It is about the need to transform the way we think
about children and childhood.

> When my children were very young, they often stopped at my office as they walked home from school. Eventually, it didn't matter
> to them whether I was there or not; they came to see Mrs.

O'Connell, the faculty secretary. She always referred to them as her "walking people." Her response was a wonderful recognition of their full humanity and a validation of their worth. She treated my children with respect and dignity, and they responded to her with affection. I remember Mrs. O'Connell with gratitude for what she taught me through her relationship with my children.

(Herbert)

The lesson Mrs. O'Connell taught is a simple one: *children are people*. Families, therefore, are made up of people. Some of the people in families have the role of parent; others the role of child. Because we are not defined by our roles, we can say that both children and parents are fully human. Families and societies are able to fulfill their child-rearing tasks when they respect the full humanity of children. When they do not, children suffer and the future of humanity is put in jeopardy. This simple lesson, that children are people deserving of our full respect, does not seem easy for us to grasp or put into practice.

Our Children Are in Trouble

The evidence is widespread that we do not regard children as fully human or at least worthy of the honor we give to adults. We may respect them for their potential, but by our actions we seem to be saying that the full humanity of children is not yet actual. If we do not regard children as fully human, we are more likely to treat them with indifference or even contempt in our families and in our societies. Underneath the public debate about family values or alarm about the plight of our families or the inability to establish a family-friendly society is a more troubling reality. We have fostered a *culture of indifference* toward our children.

During the year this book was written, the *Chicago Tribune* ran a series titled "Killing Our Children," for which it has since received a Pulitzer prize. Every day for an entire year, Susan, who is an urban pastor, and I read stories about violence of one kind or another against children in our city. The series was born in anguish and outrage and generated a similar response in its readers. As we probed deeper into everyone's anxieties, however, we concluded that children are not only endangered in cities like Chicago but in many other settings as well. For that reason, we have used the phrase "culture of indifference" to identify the ways in which children are at risk everywhere in this society.

Some years ago, a national magazine ran a story under the heading "Do We Hate Our Children?" The question still lingers with me. Most of the time I have been able to answer *no*. Then another story appears of a child being punched in the stomach or stuffed in a trash can or abandoned at McDonald's or pacified with toys and videos. Those stories prompt me to wonder again whether we may indeed hate our children or at least regard them with indifference. For too many nations of the world, military spending continues to use up limited resources. Children are the first victims of absolute poverty and are now regular casualties of war and exploitation. Indifference is a global dilemma.

Most of the time the consequences of our indifference are unintended and the damage is emotional and hidden. For some parents, however, annoyance or contempt ends in violence. Carmelita was only fourteen when she was killed by her stepfather. One year before she died, she wrote the following poem for her school yearbook:

> I live my life in shadows of darkness
> Behind the light, and full of sadness.
> Where owls would howl, and stars would shine,
> I worked all day from 9 to 9.
> Sent to accomplish forbidden deeds
> None of which I could succeed.
> At night I sleep on cold, hard floors,
> With thin paper blankets near opened doors.
> Each day I pray to the Lord above
> To give me faith, hope and love.
> And someday he shall set me free
> From all the pain that lives in me.[1]

The pictures in this poem reveal a child's life most of us would rather not see. Both in her living and in her premature, violent death, Carmelita was treated with contempt. If, however, hate or contempt are not attitudes that are readily identifiable, we all know biological parents for whom children are an inconvenience. We agree with those who observe that the indifference and neglect that result in the poverty of children is the greatest threat to the future of this or any society.

Although violence toward children is not always blatant or frequent, it is becoming increasingly common everywhere in our society. Children most clearly suffer from this contempt or indifference when they are addicted from birth or are sexually, physically, or emotionally abused by parents or others they trust. Our indifference is evident whenever people oppose a school bond issue because their children are grown. Parents live out this indifference when they are emotionally absent from their children or unwilling to walk at a child's pace. The injustices we inflict on children are visible manifestations of problematic attitudes toward childhood that are largely hidden from our view. That conviction has prompted us to write with some urgency about the need for transforming adult attitudes regarding children.

This indifference of society toward children is in stark contrast to a growing awareness expressed by an African proverb that "it takes a village to raise a child." Raising children is a communal activity. Families do not and cannot do it alone. We as a society need to recognize that families and the society are interdependent realities in childrearing. As this book has evolved, we have come to recognize how crucial it is that we foster the transformation from the *indifference that prevails* to the *respect that ought to characterize* our attitudes toward children and families in society.

Aim of the Book

Everyone agrees that we must make the world safer for our children. We need to do what we can to stabilize families and make them safe for children. We also need to develop social policies that support the work of parents and maintain nurturing environments for children. We certainly need economic programs that will enable people to earn enough to support their families. Each of these alternatives is beneficial and urgently needed. Most of all, however, we need to transform our attitude toward children. *The future of human communities depends on changing the dominant attitude toward children and childhood from contempt to respect.* Such a transformation begins with the recognition that in becoming adults, we do not lose our childhood.

Our argument in this book begins with a theology of childhood that rests upon the conviction that there is nothing greater than a child. In chapter 2, the focus is on how families change unavoidably when children are added. Both there and in the third chapter on the purpose of families, we have sought to acknowledge that families are not always as they ought to be. In chapter 4 we propose a theology *for* family living that presents a vision informed by the Judeo-Christian tradition. Finally, in the last two chapters, we examine the roles of society and church in enabling families to provide for the needs of children. As a response to the indifference regarding children in our culture, we propose in the final chapter that the church must become a "*sanctuary for childhood.*"

We have written this book for parents and other caregivers of children in the hope that everyone might come to regard children with greater respect. We have written this book also for pastors and other church professionals whose ministry includes planning programs for children and parents. We hope those who work in day care centers will find this a useful resource to rethink their work from a theological perspective. Teachers and other family advocates should be able to find support for their concerns about children in this volume. We also hope children will read this book. It is for children as well as about them.

Looking at Family from a Life-Cycle Perspective

Each of the five volumes in this series on Family Living in Pastoral Perspective examines one of the changes that can be expected in the ordinary life cycle of a family: leaving home, becoming married, raising children, promising again, and living alone. The particular, intimate, often conflicted human crucible that we call the family begins to shape us even before birth. Our families hand us a legacy—their sense of what is right and wrong, their rituals, their peculiar rules—all with the same sense that these are not peculiar at all, but universal rules by which human beings live. It is often a shock to discover that our family's way is only one of many ways, and that the way we thought was universal might not even be the best way. The legacy we have received from our family of origin is nonetheless the first and most powerful resource we have to negotiate the transitions and changes that mark a family's history.

The family as a social system changes according to its own history of evolving tasks. Each major transition in its life cycle offers a family the possibility to become something new. Such a moment of transition creates a crisis in the ordinary sense of that word because it is a turning point at which things will either get better or get worse. It is not really possible to have change without crisis or without grief. A family's capacity to grieve anticipated as well as unanticipated losses will in large measure determine its ability to live through the crises of change. If marriage preparation, for example, ignores the changes and contradictions in becoming married that evoke grief and sadness, it will impede rather than enhance the possibility that God is doing a new thing in forming this new family.

The addition of children inevitably changes things further. New roles are added. Families expand emotionally in order to make room for the gifts that a child brings. Patterns of interaction within a family are fundamentally altered whenever a new person is added. Sacrifice becomes a normative value because there are more needs to accommodate. The capacity of a family to make these changes will in large measure determine whether it becomes a safe environment for nurture and growth of its members. The more a family is able to think of itself as a changing context, the more it will be able to provide a context for change of children and adults alike as they grow up and grow older.

In an earlier discussion on the family, I had envisioned a life cycle of five epochs. The emphasis on epochs presumed a notion of family history that was much too static. It had the advantage, however, of having one epoch that addressed the needs of a family with young children under the rubric of "forming a family" and the needs of a family with older children under the heading "expanding the family." The assumption of the latter epoch was that the family as a system needed "to create an expanded context in order to accommodate the new ideas, feelings, and roles that accompany the individual growth of children and parents."[2] Because this book is about raising children from birth to leaving home, it must address the different and particular needs of children and families at different stages in their development in very general ways.

Emphasis on the family life cycle is the most practical and effective way of helping people understand the family as a social unit with a life and history of its own. It also provides a framework for thinking about how ordinary pastoral interventions related to the church's ritual life correspond to critical moments of transition in the family's history. The church's ministry with families often requires a delicate balance between attending to the needs of children throughout their stages of development and the needs of the family as a whole, which is itself experiencing change.

Paradox in Family Living

If change is central to the vitality of a family's life over time, paradox is what gives shape to its meaning and sustains its well-being in time. Paradox remains even when change occurs. We have to leave home in order to make a home. Becoming married requires a balance between community and individual autonomy, between self-determination and sacrifice, between private and public realities, and between continuity and discontinuity with one's past. Families are likely to get in trouble when they do not keep alive both dimensions of the paradox. On the other hand, families remain vital if they can stay in the contradictions that finally only God can resolve.

The first paradox is this: *the child is fully human although what is present in the child is yet to be realized.* Children are not human because of what they will become; they are human because of what they are. And yet what they are is still to be. The second paradox is that *in becoming adults, we do not lose childhood.* The transformation of adult attitudes toward children begins with the recognition that childhood is an inevitable dimension of being human. The third paradox has to do with our response to the full humanity of children. *Adults need to understand from the beginning of every life that loving means letting go.* If we honor our children as fully human from birth, we will protect them, love them, nurture them, but we will also let them go. This is one instance of the paradox of continuity and discontinuity in family living. Our children are ours and not ours from the beginning. Because children are small, weak, and needy, we need to nurture and protect them. Because they are a unique gift from God, we respect the story they will unfold. We are therefore *both* loving them *and* letting them go from birth.

Our ministry with families may in fact require that we intensify the creative tensions by "saying the other side." It is our pastoral task to intend paradox precisely because the contradictions in our lives that cannot be resolved often become the occasion for transformation. We believe that paradox is not just a therapeutic tool or a means to effect some new resolution, but an end in itself and a normal state. The helper's task is to assist people to live in the paradoxes of existence that are central to family well-being throughout the cycles of life.

This introduction was written on the Epiphany of our Lord. Epiphany is a celebration of the manifestation of the light of Jesus Christ in the darkness of the world. It is also the celebration of a child. Eastern sages who had followed the light of a remarkable star, the writer of Matthew reports, found a baby whom they honored as the child-king they sought (Matt. 2:1–12). With the birth of this child, God entered human history. Those who follow this child as the Christ are called to honor all humanity's children.

Acknowledgments

This series, Family Living in Pastoral Perspective, is the outcome of years of collaboration with Kenneth R. Mitchell. Unfortunately, Ken died suddenly of a heart attack on February 18, 1991, before this project could be completed. Although this volume has been written with Susan Johnson, the spirit of Ken Mitchell is very much present. We hope we have honored his memory by what we have written. I am grateful to the friends (new and old) who have agreed to join with me in completing this endeavor: *Becoming Married* with Robert Cotton Fite; *Promising Again* with David Hogue and Marie McCarthy, S.P.; and *Living Alone* with Freda Gardner. The collaboration with each of these authors has enriched the project as a whole.

We are indebted to many people whose stories have shaped our thinking about childhood. They are, for the most part, stories by adults about childhood because we believe that changing attitudes about children is the first agenda for our time. While their real names do not appear, these people who have shared the joys and sorrows of childhood and raising children have become internal conversation partners with us in writing this volume. The stories ascribed to Herbert or Susan are, however, the actual stories of the authors.

There are specific people we want to thank who have offered a suggestion or listened to a paragraph or ventured a critique that has shaped the development of this book. Joy Anderson, Phyllis Anderson, Susan Art, Tanya Chapman, Linda D. Even, Linda Feil, Freda Gardner, Larry Haverkamp, Richard Jensen, Maretta Jeuland, Dennis Johnson, James Jones, Sokoni Karanja, Michael Kerr, Jack McClure, C.P.P.S., and Deb Rossbach. Karen Speerstra continues to be a support for me about writing clearly and directly. And last, but not least, Harold Twiss. It has been a gift to us that he is a patient but persistent man as well as a wise editor.

This book is born in the hope that it might contribute to changing how we view childhood for the sake of our children. We do not intend to add to the stress of parents who are already beleaguered. The task of raising children does not seem to get any easier, no matter how hard parents try. If, however, we can begin to see childhood differently, more just and compassionate ways of childrearing will follow.

HERBERT ANDERSON

Epiphany 1994

1

NOTHING GREATER
THAN A CHILD

A NEWBORN CHILD is a mystery. It is amazing how something so tiny and vulnerable survives the ordeal of birth.
We wonder at the delicate hands and small gestures and
the loud sounds that come from such small bodies. There is also a
fierce dignity of the newly born that sometimes startles us. Every newborn is a new creation, and the unique personality of each infant child
is beyond human reckoning.

When we regard a child in this way, each new life becomes a
miracle, a unique gift to be protected and nourished. Yet the greatest
wonder of all is that *every newly born child possesses already the fullness of being human.* Children are not simply incomplete adults. From
birth, we are as fully human as we will ever become. Childhood is not
merely the prelude to adulthood; the child already has the value and
depth of full humanity.

> I look at him now at fourteen, and I see in my son qualities which
> were present at birth, even before he was born! I assume I will
> see these things about him again, and be surprised again, when
> he is nineteen or thirty. Now, as I watch him assert his adolescent
> self, I see him as he was when he was new in the world, and
> again at two, and again at six and ten. Some of it seems good,
> some of it I have anguished over every step of the way. Still, I
> could not have known who he would be at fourteen, though I've
> looked upon him, and fought with him every day of his life. Every
> day he unfolds before me in a way I never could have anticipated,
> and yet his path is illuminated behind him for me to see.   (Beth)

There is a second and equally amazing aspect of new life that

Beth understands very well: *what is fully present in the child is still to be realized.* We need to become what we already are. While we mature and develop as adults, we are still never more human than we are as a child. At the same time, we are always becoming what we already are. The vulnerability of being a child and the autonomy of adulthood are therefore paradoxically related. From that perspective, the aim of religious and psychological maturity is the same: to both become an adult and yet remain a child to an ever-increasing extent.

The "Childness" of Adulthood

Two assumptions follow from this declaration of the full humanity of children. The first is self-evident. *Children are people.* At every point throughout the life cycle, the person is a subject, whole and complete. The newly born infant, however undeveloped, is a comprehensive biological and psychological system of actions and reactions, of sensations and feelings, of potentials and limitations, of memories and projections. The second assumption is harder to embrace. *All people are children.* We do not lose childhood when we become adults. It endures as a quality of being that must be lived through and accepted as part of our humanity.

The term "childlikeness" does not adequately distinguish this human quality in adults from the developmental stage of childhood. What we mean is more than being "like a child." It is an enduring way of experiencing the world that continues to emerge as we move toward maturity. We will use the metaphor "childness" to identify qualities of being a child that continue in adult life: vulnerability, openness, immediacy, and neediness. We do not intend to suggest that these qualities exhaust what it means to be human. They are, however, necessary dimensions of an anthropology that is inclusive of children.

The mystery and vulnerability of "childness" is something we never outgrow. Robert Coles has made a similar observation. We are all children who "struggle toward childhood and never forget it or outlive it."[1] If becoming an adult is a struggle toward childhood and if part of that struggle is embracing the childness that endures, then it is clear that our regard for children depends on respecting "childness." *More than any other factor, our response to children and consequent practices of childrearing are shaped by our attitude toward the childhood that endures into adulthood as "childness" within.*

Most every Sunday, I gather with the children on the chancel steps for a brief conversation. One Sunday each year we talk about the stained-glass window in our sanctuary of Jesus with the little children. I remind them that Jesus said "to such belongs the kingdom of heaven." And I often ask them why Jesus said everyone must become like a child. On one occasion, nine-year-old Barry responded very quickly to that question. "I know, I know!" he said. "Because if everyone was a child, then no one would hurt children anymore." I don't remember what I said after that, but it really didn't matter. Barry had spoken a truth.   (Susan)

The little boy is right. Our attitude toward children is shaped by our understanding of being a child. If we hold that childhood is merely a stage we must pass through on our way to becoming fully human, that is, an adult, then it is difficult to honor the child with respect. We wrongly measure the worth of all persons, including children, according to adult standards. If we could believe, however, that every adult is "struggling toward childhood," that we never fully outgrow "childness," then perhaps, as Barry said it, "no one would hurt children anymore."

The Igbu people of Nigeria express this essential respect for children with the word *ginekanwa*, which means "What is greater than a child?" The question implies its answer: There is nothing greater than a child. Our aim throughout this volume is to embody and amplify the meaning of *ginekanwa*. We regard children by respecting them. Our respect for children begins with the recognition of their full humanity. In order to strengthen our resolve to regard children with respect, we will develop a theology of childhood. But first it is necessary to identify some early forms of indifference toward children that are repeated in modern expressions of contempt.

The Invention of Childhood

According to Philippe Aries in his book *Centuries of Childhood*,[2] the recognition of childhood as a stage of human development did not emerge in the Western world until the seventeenth century. Prior to that time, people who survived infancy became adults. What today we might refer to as young children were simply small adults. Once they reached the age of seven or eight, they were often apprenticed to another household for work. The needs of these small people were attended to for the sake of physical and economic survival because they were already valued laborers, not out of emotional attachment or out of commitment to the child's spiritual or psychological growth. The practice of abandoning children that was common in Europe even as late as the eighteenth century was based in part on the principle that the needs of parents outweighed the rights of the child. There was the expectation, as historian John Boswell concludes, that abandoned children would be taken in by "the kindness of strangers" who would provide for them in ways that their biological parents could not.[3]

In the sixteenth and seventeenth centuries, the patterns of work changed in most developed societies. Education became increasingly more significant. As a result, the time of being a child was extended and a definition of childhood began to emerge. Children were not simply a physically immature work force, but "fragile creatures of God who needed to be both safeguarded and reformed."[4] In this sense, children and childhood are both social inventions. The terms usually refer to a population and a period of time between infancy and adulthood. As societies became more complex and demanding, childhood became a necessary period of time in which to protect and instruct children. This early conception of childhood also had an effect on family living. It became the moral and spiritual obligation of the family to reform and transform children into socialized adults. That obligation remains to the present, even though institutions other than the family have assumed some of the socializing tasks.

Respect for children was not enhanced significantly by the invention of childhood. Being a child remains provisional and subordinate to adulthood. Nor are children regularly regarded as fully human. We are inclined to think their reasoning is limited and their emotions not always under control. Moreover, we presume that the kind of immediacy that characterizes a child's perception of the world must be muted later in life by what is prudent. We interpret children's inability to protect themselves simply as another sign that children are incomplete. And because children are defenseless, they are vulnerable.

Given this picture of children as provisional, subordinate, and vulnerable, it is not surprising that people often try to ignore their childhood when they grow older. That is one of the themes in a provocative short novel by Marie Luise Kaschnitz titled *The House of Childhood*. The central character has accidentally happened upon a museum that is referred to as the "House of Childhood." When she finally decides to enter it, she is drawn into a process of remembering her childhood. "It's amazing how little I remember from my childhood and how much I dislike being reminded of that time by others. . . . Time and again I meet people now whose faces grow dark at the thought of their childhoods although they apparently neither went hungry nor were mistreated as children."[5] If the time of being a child is something that adults are eager to forget in themselves, we begin to understand why children are easily overlooked and sometimes held in contempt.

A History of Indifference Toward Children

The struggle to establish and maintain appropriate attitudes toward children is not new. Every generation has had to find a way to raise its young. Sociologist Floyd M. Martinson offers a framework around which to organize some of the attitudes toward children.[6] He suggests that there are three dominant expressions of indifference: children as property, as depraved, and as incomplete. While some of these perspectives were more dominant at another time in human history, or are more common today in only a few cultures, residues of these perspectives linger and have negative consequences for children in most modern societies.

Children as Private Property

The idea that children are private property "precedes any notion of children as a special category or as a group entitled to special protection and instruction."[7] According to this perspective, children are the possession of parents, who have sovereign rule over them. Children are dependent and should be compliant. Only adults have rights. Parents, and particularly fathers, have the full authority to shape and control children's values and behavior. The abuse of power with children must be linked in part to this view that they are the property of parents and other adults. Adults assume they have power over what they possess.

The idea that children belong to their parents has shaped attitudes and actions toward children from early times. Selling children as laborers, or determining who their spouse would be, or even the practice of the father giving the bride away in a wedding, all illustrate this assumption that children are property. The practice of child sacrifice presupposed that parents even had the power of life and death over their children. The story of Abraham and Isaac (Gen. 22:1–18) is a challenge to the view that children are property. Parents are no longer required to sacrifice children, even to appease the gods.[8] Although ritual child sacrifice is foreign to modern society, as long as parents regard children as property who are thereby subject to parental power and wishes, children will be "sacrificed" informally. Parents jeopardize the well-being of children whenever children are prematurely preoccupied with performance at baseball or hockey games, with violin lessons, or in the classroom.

Parents who believe they have dominion over their children consider it a right to raise their children as they wish. They will defend the physical punishment of children on the basis of property rights. According to this view, children are not only the personal possession of their parents; the family is a private domain of those possessions that must not be violated. This angle on the relation between children and parents continues to influence legal decisions. It is the perspective used to support the rights of biological parents to the custody of their own children. The battle between divorcing parents over custody rights is often a painful illustration of viewing children as property. It is certainly an instance of indifference when the well-being of children becomes incidental to who wins the battle.

To regard children as property is a fundamental error with damaging consequences. Parents are not likely to respect the full humanity of their children as long as they can possess them. The human impulse is to control what we possess and ignore what we cannot control. Therefore, we need to modify the natural possessiveness of parents in order to transform our attitude toward children. Parents need to be reminded frequently that their children are not *their* children. They do not come from us nor do they belong to us. The Christian practice of infant baptism or child dedication is one reminder to parents that our children belong not to us but to God. The Protestant Reformers presumed this perspective in what they taught about parenting. "The only authority that parents, teachers, or magistrates had over children was that which derived from the responsibility to rear them in accordance with God's law and discipline."9 Parenthood is a trust, not a right. Children are a gift, not a possession.

Children as Depraved

The emphasis on discipline and the need to control children has often been based on the belief that children are sinful from birth. Regarding children as depraved has been the basis for justifying severe discipline or harsh punishment. In a broad sense, any emphasis on socialization presumes that children need to be taught or trained how to be human. We will spoil the child if we spare the rod. The dark side of this emphasis on disciplining children against their natural depravity is that it has sometimes led to physical violence. Proponents of harsh punishment of children may justify their views on religious grounds. Sinfulness must be beaten out of the child. Consider this remembrance:

My father took Matthew 5:48 literally and seriously: "Be ye therefore perfect, even as your Father which is in heaven is perfect."
To implement this requirement, he made sure we never sinned
and when we did, he cleansed us with his belt or a stick or elec-
tric wires, an umbrella, his fist, his feet, whatever was close to
him. We were beaten until his arm got tired and we were beaten
daily in the name of God because we sinned daily. The words
evildoer, carnal, daughter or son of the devil, were yelled at us
along with stupid, idiot, good for nothing, dummy, empty brain
and others. Very often we were beaten two or three times a day.
I ran away twice when I was six.   (Isabella)

What Isabella remembers did not happen long ago. It is a painful
illustration of the conclusion of social historian Philip Greven in his
book *Spare the Child*. "For centuries, Protestant Christians have been
among the most ardent advocates of corporal punishment. The Bible
has provided fundamental texts that have served successive generations as primary guides to childrearing and to discipline."[10] The discipline of a child's sinfulness does not, however, justify violence. All
forms of physical punishment are hurtful and harmful. They leave
scars, as Isabella knows well, that do not easily heal.

Phillipe Aries contends that this creation of a severe disciplinary
system for children within school and family also created a new ob-
sessive love of children in place of society's previous indifference toward them. He also maintains that even though this new attitude
pervaded society, it was housed in the exclusive privacy of the modern
family.[11] This obsession with producing well-trained children has dominated family living. According to the historian Steven Ozment, the
"willful indulgence of children" was identified as the common flaw of
parents at the time of the Reformation.[12] In order to make sure that parents produced well-disciplined Christian children, their authority was
increased.

Respecting the gifts of childhood should not be confused with
romanticizing the child as the embodiment of human innocence. All
creation suffers because of human sinfulness. Children are no exception. Children participate fully in the reality of sin because they are
creatures of God. Therefore, it is indeed the responsibility of parents to
train children in self-discipline so that they might serve and survive in
the world. This need to provide a disciplined framework for children is
not itself a problem. The dilemma is rather that the preoccupation with
producing proper children becomes another form of indifference when

children are physically abused or when the unique humanity of each child is ignored.

Children Are Incomplete

The great humanist philosopher Erasmus once observed that "human beings are not born, but formed."[13] According to this view, a child is obviously not fully human at birth. Rather, the child is regarded as a creature in search of humanity. Rational and moral self-control does not come with birth. The qualities of maturity that raised humans above animals must be created by "hard, persistent exercise under vigilant parental and tutorial discipline."[14] One could not even assume that children would simply grow to be adults; they needed to learn how to be adults.

As a consequence of this perspective, children needed first of all to be protected *from* society in order to be prepared to function *in* society. The development of childhood was a way to exclude them from much of life as lived by adults. It was believed that children needed a world designed for them in which it was safe for them to play and learn. During this time, nothing was expected of children. Responsible behavior came later, when they were prepared to take their places in adult society.

Families were often indifferent toward children in earlier times because of the frequency of infant mortality, or because children were sent away to work at an early age. When we began thinking about childhood as a stage of human development, the earlier indifference did not disappear altogether. It simply took a different form. In order to ready them for the adult world, parents subjected children to special treatment, which included a kind of quarantine from both the pressures and rewards of society. Severe punishment of children continued, however, because parents believed it was their responsibility to mold the children's souls and bodies into adulthood.

This perspective gives the appearance of valuing children by creating environments to protect and train them. In fact, however, it overlooks the present needs of children by focusing on preparing them for their future in society. And the more dangerous, complex, and adult-oriented society becomes, the more it is necessary to prolong childhood into adolescence and even into young adulthood in order to provide enough time for preparation. This model is expensive for society and it diminishes children. What is presumably aimed at protecting children becomes a way of oppressing them.

Contemporary Expressions of Indifference

It is not easy to understand the depth of indifference to or even contempt against the well-being of children in our society. We have been helped to understand the depth of this contempt by the work of Janet Pais, who has been both an attorney and a parish director of religious education. She suggests that adults have contempt for children precisely because they are small, weak, and needful. In a book entitled *Suffer the Children*, she links the avoidance of vulnerability in adults with our attitudes toward children. "Adults define themselves as strong, children as weak, and adults have no use for weakness."[15] They are indifferent toward children because adults cannot accept their own childness (what Pais calls "the child-self").

This attitude of contempt for the weakness and vulnerability of childhood, Pais suggests, underlies the various forms of physical, sexual, and psychological abuse of children. The abuse of anyone less powerful is a way of continuing to repress what we fear in ourselves. The issue obviously goes beyond children. In a society that glorifies size, strength, and self-sufficiency, anyone who is small, weak, or needful is treated with contempt. This contempt for what is powerless or vulnerable leads to the abuse of children as well as the oppression of the disadvantaged and weak.

Most people agree that children and families are in trouble in our time. Signs of what we have labeled the "culture of indifference" are still present. Variations on all these three perspectives continue to permit and even encourage violence toward children. It is indifference when parents are emotionally absent or when they invade a child's world with adult expectations or when they verbally taunt or humiliate a child. It is indifference when our children can buy guns more easily than pencils. It is indifference when we compel them to see more than they can bear to see or carry prematurely the pressures and demands of adult living. It is indifference when children are killed accidentally in the crossfire of gang warfare while playing on the front steps of their home. It is indifference when children are expected to fulfill expectations of success or achievement because it preserves the family's status or reputation. Too many of our children are underfed and homeless or suffer from emotional impoverishment as well as physical abuse.

There is an ongoing debate regarding the current crisis in the family. The decline of the two-parent family is frequently identified as the primary factor eroding the well-being of children. In particular, the absence of many fathers from family living is often cited as a major cause of this crisis. The solution, according to this view, is to strengthen two-parent families as the normative setting for raising healthy children. We fully concur with the need to strengthen the family for the sake of our children. We believe, however, that there are a variety of family structures that can nurture children effectively if there is sufficient personal commitment and environmental support. More on this later.

The deterioration of supporting environments like neighborhoods, nurturing schools, and religious communities is another reason given for the family crisis. This is particularly critical if one holds the view, as we do, that it takes *more* than two parents to raise children. When we say that "it takes a village to raise a child," we mean that two competent parents are not enough for the task of childrearing; we also need to develop supportive environments that are economically viable. While government and the business sector of society are not responsible for the nurture of children, they contribute significantly to the kind of environment in which families might successfully raise children.

The structural causes and solutions for the present crisis of children and family are critical issues to explore but they are not our focus here. The aim is, rather, to examine attitudes about childhood itself. Our children are being victimized by the indifference of societies. As we have noted, the present attitudes toward children, toward childhood, and toward families are a reflection of our ideas about the human condition and the function of family in society. *The transformation of our attitude toward being a child is one of the fundamental and urgent agendas for our time*. Our future depends on it. While we are aware that it is impossible to legislate respect toward children by making new laws or writing new policy, we also believe that it is unlikely children will thrive without both respect and legislation.

Children as Citizens: A Positive Alternative

Transforming our attitude toward children is a process that must occur at many levels and in many ways. The way a family welcomes a child is a significant factor in changing how we think about childhood. If a family embodies justice and compassion in its life together, it creates a community that respects both children and the childness of adults. Chapter 6 proposes that the church must become a "sanctuary for childhood" in order to counter the widespread contempt in our culture toward those who are small, weak, and needful. For the transformation of our attitude toward children to endure, the changes need to be reflected in laws and policies as well.

If we regard children as people from birth, they have the status of full humanity in our families. We must accord them the status of citizens in society as well. Such a structural change would have wide-ranging consequences. Rather than just creating separate environments that are safe for children, we would seek to find ways of integrating them as citizens into society. This is an improbable ideal and a necessary dream. It is improbable because modern societies have become increasingly adult-centered. It is necessary because we will otherwise allow the technical, industrial, computerized worlds we inhabit to become more impersonal and dangerous for children and adults alike.

The sociologist Floyd M. Martinson has said it very well. "Children's rights as society's citizens [are] on a par with those of adults, even with those of parents, though the interests of children and parents are not synonymous."[16] Children and adults are of equal worth. In order for adults to regard children as fully human beings of equal worth, they must be willing to prioritize children's needs as highly as they do their own in all culture-creating activities. In a word, *the rights of children will modify the rights of adults.*

In order to dream this dream in which children and adults are regarded equally, we need to make fundamental changes in the ordering of society. Regarding children as citizens provides an even plane for considering their needs in relation to adult needs. Some radical reordering may be necessary because many societies are ill-equipped to accommodate children's needs and interests. We have assumed their subordination as a given and created social structures that continue the dominance of adults and the subordinate position of children.

Establishing the full citizenship of children will make it more difficult to regard them as property. They are neither the property of parents nor the wards of the state. They are full members of the human community and therefore citizens of its societies to be given the respect due all its members. Regarding children as citizens makes it mandatory that we reorder society in order to care for anyone who is small, weak, or needy. Such regard is the beginning of a new attitude of respect toward being a child, but it will not automatically settle issues related to possession or eliminate the subtle forms of indifference pervasive in our society. Because our indifference is so deep, it is even possible to rearrange who is responsible for childrearing without changing our attitude toward childhood. For that deeper transformation, we need to incorporate childhood into our definitions of what it means to be human.

A Theology of Childhood

The central Christian story begins with the birth of a child. In the birth of the Christ child, God took on all the powerlessness, weakness, and neediness of human childhood for the sake of our salvation. What is remarkable about that story is that the truth of God is embodied in a child. It is the Child who carries in himself the hope for the world. The consequences of that event are twofold: (1) childhood, not just our humanity, is capable of bearing transcendence; (2) we cannot know the fullness of God without understanding what it is to be a child.

Two images from the teachings of Jesus contribute to our rethinking the place of children and the meaning of childhood in human life. The first is the familiar picture in which Jesus welcomes children in order to touch them and bless them in a loving and healing way. In the second, Jesus places children in the center in order to transform the present with the future that God makes new. When we welcome children, we welcome the divine in our midst. These stories of children should not be understood merely as examples of the compassion of Jesus or as support for the practice of infant baptism. They illustrate how the teaching of Jesus turns upside down all earthly expectations: the last will be first, the meek will inherit the earth, and children have full membership in the realm of God.

Treating Children with Equal Regard

The disciples were acting in accord with the customary practice of the time when they sought to keep the children from Jesus. In the household codes and in other social practices, children were regarded as a threat to orderliness in the household because they were prone to stubbornness and impetuous behavior. Moreover, children were thought to be incapable of rational discourse and action. They were to be obedient to the will of parents while in training for their valued *future* role as adult citizens. In the meantime, children were not welcome.

> People were bringing little children to him in order that he might touch them; and the disciples spoke sternly to them. But when Jesus saw this, he was indignant and said to them, "Let the little children come to me; do not stop them; for it is to such as these

that the kingdom of God belongs. Truly I tell you, whoever does not receive the kingdom of God as a little child will never enter it." And he took them up in his arms, laid his hands on them, and blessed them. (Mark 10:13–16)

The picture of Jesus welcoming the children presents a radically new and more inclusive vision of the human community. This action of Jesus continues to challenge our assumptions of anthropology and expands the norms for discipleship. From the perspective of the Christian gospel, we are not to lord it over any who are weaker. We dare not rule over children; rather we grant them dignity and worth in the middle of the community. The sayings of Jesus about children and discipleship compel us to respond to the child in our midst as fully human and worthy of respect. Jesus welcomed children in order to bless them. We are to do the same.

While the focus of this saying of Jesus is on discipleship and living under the reign of God, it has implications for our rethinking childhood. A child's worth is neither derivative nor conditional. Children and adults are of equal worth and childhood is valuable in itself. The word from the Igbu people has it right: there is nothing greater than a child. As Janet Pais has observed, it is the "deeper truth of the gospel of God the Child which requires us to place the highest value on children and to treat them with ultimate seriousness and respect."[17]

The sayings of Jesus also invite us to see adulthood in a new way. "Then he took a little child and put it among them; and taking it in his arms, he said to them, 'Whoever welcomes one such child in my name welcomes me, and whoever welcomes me welcomes not me but the one who sent me'" (Mark 9:36–37). The full identification of Jesus with the child ("whoever welcomes one such . . . welcomes me") is the foundation for our conviction that childhood is not something we outgrow. We learn from children about being human *and* about being disciples of Jesus. Being a child is a model for humanity in its fullness because it includes dependency and the freedom to live with the vulnerability.

The Child Is the Future of the Story

The biblical story of Jesus and the children shifts our focus by demonstrating that the child is the link to the future. The child carries his or her past into a future that is yet to be formed. In that sense the child symbolizes the link between past and future in the narrative of the family. The child is not only in the midst of the community;

the child is in the middle of the story. Rethinking childhood therefore includes a reaffirmation of the future that God continues to make new.

One of the constant themes throughout this series of books on family has been the importance of recognizing the power of the past to shape the narratives of our lives. The child is the convergence of several family narratives and the origin of a narrative that is yet to be expanded. In the child the parents look ahead to the generosity of life that first called them together to form a family. That way of thinking is not meant to locate the worth of the child in the future. Rather it is a recognition that the power of God, to be discovered anew in the future, comes to meet us in the child.

In the end, children and adults face the same dilemma: it is difficult to be vulnerable and dependent if we are not recognized as uniquely separate persons of worth. For that reason, the biblical mandate has it right: we must honor our children or our childness if we want to participate in the realm of God. Whoever wants to live under the reign of God must do so in the way of a child. Regarding children with respect and recognizing the childhood in us all is not only essential for vital human community, it is fundamental for our salvation. If childness dies, we will never see God.

The Qualities of Childness in Adulthood

The idea that we never outlive childhood illumines our understanding of being human in four ways. Each of these four images of childness is true of children and adults alike. We must embrace and respect childness as an inevitable dimension of human life. (1) We never outgrow the vulnerability of childhood, even when we are no longer obviously small, weak, and needful. (2) The infinite openness of childhood is already an expression of mature religious existence. (3) The immediacy of being a child is what makes direct speech possible. (4) Children teach us about dependency and neediness as inescapable dimensions of being human.

> We had spent a relaxing evening with friends who have children about seven and nine. After dinner, we went to the living room to enjoy jazz on the stereo, fire in the fireplace, and conversation. We talked late into the night about everything and nothing. The children brought me clay and I made small dinosaurs, pieces of fruit, grotesque figures of witches and trolls, watches and rings

while we talked. My friend's youngest child curled up next to me on the sofa, dug a place for his head in my rib cage, and asked: "Are you a grown-up or a child?" "A grown-up," I said. "Are you sure?" he asked.

(Susan)

The question from Susan's young friend suggests that the answer is either/or. Not so. As adults, we are always both. Learning how to live with that paradox is one of the keys to psychological and spiritual maturity. It is also necessary for effective family living. Our response to children will be greatly enhanced if adults are able to acknowledge their childhood that endures.

The Vulnerability of Childhood

Human beings are creatures without a built-in physical defense. We do not have tusks or fangs. The length of time the child is dependent on the care and protection of others is a distinguishing characteristic of being human. Children, therefore, are particularly vulnerable in the literal sense of that word. They are susceptible to being wounded because they are small, weak, and needful. Eventually, we all learn to walk and run and get our own food and protect ourselves a little bit. But we never outgrow vulnerability.

It is not easy, however, for adults to acknowledge their vulnerability. We spend a great deal of time and money and energy building tusks and fangs of one kind or another to defend ourselves. It has been a particularly masculine fantasy to be the strongest and hence invulnerable to attack. As Janet Pais has observed, adults have contempt for children because we do not like reminders of weakness. Our intent in this section is not to promote weakness or infantilize children forever or excuse the violence toward others that often comes from unacknowledged vulnerability. It is, rather, to heighten our awareness of a simple reality: all people, including children, are vulnerable.

Sometimes we are so intent on eliminating all windows of vulnerability that we lose connection with our childness. Here is how Robert Coles says it:

All this talk about being "mature" and growing up and progressing through stages and phases misses the point of how important it is to retain that *connection*—not to "the inner child" but to the sense of vulnerability and yearning that childhood is about. That's a big part of ourselves. Or it ought to be.[18]

Learning from children the art of being vulnerable is necessary in order to be fully human as an adult. Autonomy in adulthood without vulnerability is a thin veneer of bravado.

We know about the vulnerability of God from the suffering of Jesus. In a fundamental sense, God's suffering, and human suffering as well, is the result of risking love. Until they learn otherwise, children risk loving. And because there is sin and evil in the world, the risk of loving is that eventually we will suffer because of it. If children are people and all people are becoming children in the sense of retaining childness, then we also need to keep the child's willingness to engage the world with yearning and unashamed vulnerability as we mature. It is part of being human. Being comfortable with vulnerability also strengthens family living. The family that can grieve together, for instance, has a better chance of staying together.

The Openness of Childhood

One of the most disarming characteristics of children is how quickly they learn to trust. From the beginning of life, children are held by strangers, submit to the control of others, follow paths they have not walked before, believe what they are told as true. In their seemingly boundless trust, children already have what is regarded as the ultimate quality of religious life. Stranger wariness is also a dimension of human development, but some people never let go of mistrust they have learned as children. It is an indication of the fragility of childhood openness.

We are indebted to Roman Catholic theologian Karl Rahner for his theological observations regarding childhood. Rahner has argued eloquently that the human adventure is to become a child to an ever-increasing extent. He regards childhood as the basic human condition, which is always appropriate for the life that is rightly lived. The spiritual qualities of openness to what is new or untested, the willingness to be surprised, and the courage for fresh horizons are already present in the openness of childhood.

> The mature childhood of the adult is the attitude in which we bravely and trustfully maintain an infinite openness in all circumstances and despite the experiences of life which seem to invite us to close ourselves. Such openness, infinite and maintained in all circumstances, yet put into practice in the actual manner in which we live our lives, is the expression of religious existence.[19]

Rahner's vision of the openness of childhood is a challenge to adult beliefs that the world is not to be trusted. We must be prudent, that is sure. But the openness of childhood is hope not yet disillusioned and receptivity not covered with fear. In that sense, childhood is a gift given and preserved in the promise of God's enduring love.

The Immediacy of Childhood

Almost every parent can remember a time when a child's response was direct and spontaneous and profoundly embarrassing because of its truthfulness. Every parent dreads those moments when the candor and spontaneity of children lead them to say things that adults have learned to mute.

A small group of friends and members of the congregation had gathered for a service of promise and blessing for Linnea and Beth. As the presiding minister, I allowed time for those in attendance to offer their thoughts and prayers. After a very short silence, Beth's five-year-old daughter began: "Well, I have a thought. I was thinking about pulling out this tooth because it is very loose, but I don't want to get blood on my dress." Not to be outdone, her nine-year-old brother added this: "I want to congratulate my mom on finishing my sister's dress so we could enjoy the afternoon." (Carlton)

Human life is relational. From birth, we are sustained and stretched by our interactions with others. The ability to respond to another is what makes it possible to develop the delicate patterns of mutuality between children and their caregivers. In the beginning, the child's response to others is unfiltered. As children mature, however, they learn when and to whom things can or cannot be said. We have included immediacy because we believe it is a quality of being a child that adults need as well. Imagination, play, and celebration are variations of immediacy that enrich all human life. So is wonder.

The Neediness of Childhood

Children need tender touch as well as food and shelter in order to survive the fragility of infancy. By smiling, they can invite someone to hold them, but they are wholly dependent on the response and care of others for nurturance and protection. Although eventually adults nurture and protect themselves, we never outgrow our dependence. The fundamental and inescapable truth about being human is our finitude. Being dependent is a consequence of being finite creatures. The sociologist Martinson puts it this way: "If children in all their dependency are recognized as of equal worth with adults, it means that dependency can no longer be seen as something negative but must be taken into the model of what it means to be human."[20] If we recognize this quality of dependence as a dimension of being human, then mutuality and interdependence will be the norm for living in families and communities and between nations.

Parents who hurry the independence of their children are often eager for them to be less needy. And if they are less needy, they will limit the freedom of adult caregivers less. A two-year-old on a plastic two-wheeler or a formal dinner party for an eight-year-old and her friends are more than signs of independence. Hurrying children to grow up is a form of indifference that is helped by affluence and modern technology. It is also another indication of the discomfort of adults about the dependency of childhood. It is an irony of our time that infants in less-developed countries, where neediness and dependency are the norms of living and modern conveniences are less available, often have a better chance of growing up healthy.

This vision of dependence as a norm for human life is given particular form and content in the teachings of Jesus. In the new kind of identity that Jesus brings, we are constantly receiving and never holding or possessing. Human life, as the theologian Arthur C. McGill once observed, is a *resting-in-neediness*. "In the kingdom of Jesus we always begin with neediness, we always live outward toward *neediness*, and we always end in neediness."[21] If the Christian life is marked by living in neediness, then it is not surprising that being like a child is a prerequisite for faithful living. Children teach us about dependency and neediness. Preserving dependence as a quality of childness enriches and deepens living as an adult.

Honoring Childhood and Respecting Children

The transformation of our attitudes toward children and childhood will not be effected quickly or without struggle. Nor will it always be easy to measure the change when it occurs. Nor will our actions on behalf of children always correspond to a change in attitude. For example, providing nursery and day care facilities that are informed by Christian compassion and respect is a good thing for children, but it does not necessarily change the attitude of parents. It is not enough to focus on teaching values to our children if we do not value our children themselves. If, however, we begin to act with the assumption that children are fully human from birth and worthy of our deepest respect and that adults never outgrow childhood, we believe there will be consequences for our behavior toward children.

1. *If we honor childhood as full humanity, we will learn to "go at the pace of our children."* If we honor childhood as full humanity, we will not go so fast or expect too much, lest we leave a child behind. What we see too often are parents or adults walking ahead and either dragging a child or yelling at the child to catch up. It is not easy for adults to go at a slower pace. "Going at the pace of the children" suggests a way of responding to anyone who is not able to go as fast or do as much as we would like. Among other things, it is a way of honoring the reality of childhood.

This image comes from the meeting of Esau and Jacob after years of fear and conflict. After they reconciled with each other, Esau invited Jacob to go with him. But Jacob had many children and young animals in his company. So he said: "Let my lord pass on ahead of his servant, and I will lead on slowly, according to the pace of the cattle that are before me and according to the pace of the children, until I come to my lord in Seir" (Gen. 33:14). This is a splendid picture of gentleness toward the young. It is a metaphor for childrearing for parents who are in a hurry. It is also a declaration of justice. The young will not survive if we go too fast. Jacob knew that and so do we.

2. *When adults are comfortable with the vulnerability of their own enduring childhood, it is easier for them to be empathic with a child's experience of the world.* The capacity for empathy is enhanced when there is recognition of some common experience or of an openness to remembering. If adults are willing to acknowledge that they never fully outgrow childhood, they may be able to be more empathic with the child's experience of being small and powerless. It is said that violence toward children is often the result of frustration born out of a lack of empathy. When children cannot tell us why they cry, we have to imagine what hurts. At the same time, being empathic toward children will remind adults of their own vulnerabilities. Being empathic with children is therefore even more emotionally demanding than slowing our pace or rearranging our schedules. If we can be empathic with the world of the child, we will not see the world of adults in the same way again.

Empathy has four parts. It begins with careful listening to the other's story. It includes setting aside what we think or what we think the other should do or feel so that we can hear a child's story from the child's point of view. The second part of empathy involves communicating to another what we have heard with enough accuracy so that the "other" feels heard *and* understood. The third aspect of empathy is the recognition, at a deep level, of our common humanity. Adults who are split off from their own childness will have a difficult time empathizing with the less powerful, including children. The fourth aspect of empathy is imagination. Beyond noting our common humanity, understanding each particular child as "other" requires the capacity to imagine a world different from our own. The willingness to imagine the world of a child as other than my own *and* worthy of my knowing it leads to a recognition that is gracious.

3. *If parents understand childhood as full humanity, it will be easier to respect and honor children without indulging them.* The alternative to a "culture of indifference" is not childcenteredness. Children are in the center; that is inevitable. There is always a danger that parents will understand care only in terms of overinvolvement in their children's lives. In reality, we do dishonor to children when we invade their world excessively. When their lives are controlled by the well-intended expectations of parents, children have very little to call their own. Respect is not the same as control. Nor is it the same as expecting our children to be like adults.

> I often wonder why we micromanage our children's schooling so obsessively. I don't remember my parents being as involved in what we did in school. I worry a lot that something bad will happen to them. Many of my efforts to control the lives of my children are motivated by this nagging fear of the future or some other malignant anxiety. My own diminished expectations of the future make me so afraid of the world that awaits our children that I doubt their ability to succeed on their own. Both my wife and I are over-involved in our children's lives but I don't know how to get out. (Michael)

It is an ongoing struggle for parents to keep a balance between too much and too little involvement in the lives of their children. In the first volume in this series, *Leaving Home*, it was noted that it is easier for children to leave home if their uniqueness has been respected from the beginning of life. It was suggested in the second volume, *Becoming Married*, that parents of sons and daughters who are marrying will continue that respect if they *stay close, but stay out* of the lives of their children. Although it is necessary to stay close while children are young, the paradox remains. The most loving thing parents can do for their children is to respect the integrity of their full humanity from birth. For that reason, it matters a great deal how a family responds when a child is added.

2
CHILDREN CHANGE THINGS

THE ADDITION of a child is both a gift and a challenge. It is a gift of new life. The unpredictable and creative energies of infants and children revitalize families and human communities even though the task of caring for the young is often exhausting. The arrival of a child is a gift of hope that reaffirms our belief in the future that God continues to make new. A child is a sign that hope overcomes despair. The coming of a child is a gift of love because the spontaneous affection of a child reminds us over and over again that transcending love is never conditional. Children are ultimately a gift of God's self for the sake of creation and a sign of God's continuing commitment to the future of humanity.

The coming of a child is also a challenge to our reluctance to change because it requires that the family and other communities to which the child belongs must modify previously determined and sometimes fixed patterns of interaction. It is a challenge to our inclinations toward selfishness and short-range thinking because an infant always calls us out of ourselves into ever-widening environments. The arrival of a child is a challenge to any sense of security in sameness because each child is a new creation of God with unique gifts to give to the world. The birth of a child is a regular sign that the world is constantly changing.[1]

Children change things. I should have that embroidered on a pillow or stamped on my forehead. Perhaps our first child, Quin, changed things most. Before he was born, we were two people struggling with a relationship, sometimes flying off with our own personal demons, sometimes cleaving together, assuming a future but fearing for it, too.

Then, inadequately prepared and uninformed—which made us just like everyone else, I suppose—we created an indelible future and watched it grow, first inside me, then in a cradle next to our bed, then in the crib upstairs followed by the big-boy bed with the side rail. We took on new identities: Mom. Dad. Some days it seemed we would never be Anna and Gerry again. Some days it seemed like the hardest thing we had ever done. Most days it seemed like the best.

Christopher came next. I hate to write it that way. I don't want him ever to feel second string. I suspect the danger of that is small. He is Monday's child, "fair of face." He is his brother's closest friend, and the light of my life. He made us a family, and made me realize that I had a commitment to my children's father that I had never quite had to my husband.[2]

Anna Quindlen's observations about the addition of children illustrate the aim of this chapter. Children change things. That is unavoidable. What changes and how much changes varies with the circumstances of a family, of course, but some change is unavoidable.

The change that children bring to a family is an invitation to experience the mystery of life in everyday events of care. Children reveal vulnerabilities and neediness common to us all. They teach us to play and smell the flowers. They also tax our endurance and flexibility. Caring for children, as Bonnie J. Miller-McLemore has observed, "requires deep reserves of energy, extended periods of patience, and a heightened intellectual activity that seldom has been recognized as such."[3] When we let them, children change our definition of what it means to be human.

Making the Transition to Parenthood

Families cannot prepare fully for all the changes children generate, and the addition of a child is only the first challenge to a family's ability to adapt. Although most couples make the transition to parenthood relatively well, such a change—even when desired and anticipated—is stressful. Successful adaptation to the addition of a child depends not only on the psychological health of both parents as individuals, but on the health of their relationship and its capacity for change. Not surprisingly, unresolved issues from one's family of origin may return to affect one's own acceptance of and competence in parenting.

The arrival of a child makes visible the fundamental paradox of autonomy in community that governs all family living. From the beginning, the task of the family and other significant communities related to the child is to support the development of each unique self in a social context that is committed to maintaining its life together. The process by which an infant is incorporated into a family and other communal contexts requires a delicate balancing between the needs of the individual infant and the needs of the family as a whole. When the paradox of autonomy in community is not maintained, children are the first to suffer.

Throughout this chapter, words like "arrival" or "addition" are used as a reminder that birth and adoption are not the only ways by which a child comes to a family. Children may accompany a parent to a new marriage and family configuration. Sometimes children are cared for by grandparents or some other relative instead of a parent, a constellation of family more common in nonwhite family settings. This arrangement, referred to as "relative [foster] care" by social workers, is recognized as a more successful option than customary foster care for many children.

As families of all backgrounds are challenged by the stresses of modern life, informal relative care is also increasing. "Extended" families that actually incorporate friends into the ranks of the family care system are also growing. Often children are spearheading such movements, modifying and rearranging their own circle of adults and peers in new familylike configurations that reflect their needs. Although we cannot do justice in these pages to all the permutations of family, we regard the diversity of caregiving patterns as a sign of vitality. Despite the challenges of each unique situation, two things are universally true: *we need to welcome the child into an existing family,* and *the existing family needs to change to accommodate the new situation.*

Welcoming the Child

Welcoming begins long before the child is born and continues long after birth or the arrival in a family. A pregnant mother welcomes her child when she refrains from drinking or smoking during the pregnancy. A man and a woman welcome a new child when they anticipate changes in their relationship that make room for a child. Older children are welcoming when they change rooms in order to make space for the new baby to sleep. The aim of all these preparations is to make the emotional as well as physical space for the new child as hospitable as possible. A family must revise its patterns of interacting and modify its understanding of membership in order to make room for a new arrival.

Children are seldom born into an open space. Parents often have multiple commitments that precede and may even supersede the needs of a child. Sometimes the family space into which a child is born is filled with hidden expectations or cluttered with occupational commitments. When there are already other children in the family, the expectations and the ambiguities are multiplied. Even when the family provides a welcoming space, it is not necessarily free. There may be spoken and unspoken expectations that set conditions on what a child is to become.

> It was the day for the baby to be born. Everyone was present; but the grandfathers, J.O. and Bert, were somehow the actors. Due in mid-May, the baby had delayed until now. But it was to be so, they said. On the day before, Louise had taken a big dose of castor oil to start the labor process. Now in the small hours of the morning, she was at work. Today must be the day. It was Minnie's birthday, and her son Ernest's too. So of course the baby would be born to celebrate Ernest's thirty-third birthday and his mother's fifty-fifth. The baby owed it to them. He—it would be a boy; no girls' names had been considered—would surely arrive now. And he did. His world was gathered to welcome him, to tell him who he was to be, to predict, to adore, to demand, to celebrate, to love, to define. (Kenneth)[4]

There is little doubt that Kenneth was welcomed by a family that had long awaited his coming. From before he was born, this child had a special place in that family. There was room enough, despite the great company of adults who shared the same space. There were, however, obligations embedded in the family's anticipations. It was not insignificant for this child's life that he was born on the birthday of his father and his paternal grandmother. He would mark out the years of his life according to already established dates. He would eventually know the strings that were attached to his welcome, but they were already at work from the beginning.

Even when a child is not welcome, however, membership in the system changes. The inability of a family to be a welcoming community not only damages one child; it diminishes the possibilities for every family member. Enduring hostilities or resistance toward a new family member are reasons for concern. The incapacity of a family to welcome its own members is an immediate concern and, as the family continues to change, a warning of issues yet to come.

When the Welcoming Is Painful

Hidden or unacknowledged grief is one of the strongest impediments to hospitality within the family. Sometimes the birth of a child is expected to fill an empty space in the lives of the parents. That empty space may have resulted from the recent death of a parent or significantly supportive relative, the loss of employment outside the home, a husband's emotional absence, or a long-standing personal emptiness in one of the parents. The void may be the loneliness of an adolescent who has a baby to provide meaning or find a friend. Some couples hope that having a baby will save a troubled marriage by making a bridge between the marital pair. When the child is unable to fill up a parent's emptiness, the disappointment has serious consequences. If the space into which a child is born is a vacuum, the child is almost always a victim.

The birth of a child with a handicap intensifies the challenge to a family's capacity for hospitality. Such a child may need special services, a unique learning environment, and additional health care. Other children's needs, or the couple's needs, may be squeezed out by the overwhelming special and appropriate demands of one member of the family. The care of a handicapped child is financially as well as emotionally draining. Our society recognizes, to some degree, the need for a community response to such extraordinary need, but the coordination of and payment for such services still rests primarily with the family, and the emotional burden of real hospitality is not shared.

All parents dream in anticipation of the birth of a child, and our children rarely match our dreams. The birth of a child with a handicap shatters expectations and dreams, but the welcome of a dreamed-about child may be difficult even when the child is healthy or normal. Some parents have unrealistic dreams for their children; normal is not good enough. The child may not match an earlier child's achievements, or may burst a dream by exceeding the achievements of an earlier child. A child may be born the "wrong" sex, or may possess an undesirable feature or family trait. A child may not share a parent's interests or talents and thus frustrate the kind of hospitality the parent is ready to offer. Letting go of dreams and myths is a profound loss for which people must grieve in order to welcome a child.

A special kind of sadness occurs when a child is born after a significant death. When, for example, a child is born shortly after the death of a parent, welcoming the child is complicated by conflicting agendas.

The desire to celebrate the birth of a child limits the freedom to grieve fully the loss of a parent. On the other hand, the grief for a parent or close relative may be so intense that the child is hardly welcomed. If the child resembles a beloved family member who has died recently, the child's own uniqueness is overlooked in favor of the resemblance. The birth of any child elicits both sadness and joy. It is important for the sake of the child that we grieve in the midst of the celebration.

The Changes Children Evoke

The history of a family may be marked out according to role changes that accompany changes in its membership. In the first volume in this series, *Leaving Home*, it was suggested that a change in status in relation to one's family of origin is part of the differentiating process. The one leaving has a new sense of autonomy in making choices about his or her life. Ideally, the family participates in the process of leaving home by granting the leaver a new status as adult son or daughter with all the "rights and privileges thereto appertaining." The process of leaving home is often incomplete until that role shift occurs. Sometimes, as in Pablo's story, achieving a new status does not occur until well into adulthood.

> My mother and father came to visit one Christmas when my children were very small. My mother's sister Carmen and her husband Raphael were also there. My mother asked me what I wanted for Christmas. When I told her I would like a power saw, she was horrified. She made several attempts to get me to say I wanted something else, but I would not. Finally I told her to get me whatever she wanted. She kept insisting that I stop wanting a power saw. Her solution was to give me a check for the approximate amount of money it would take to purchase a power saw but only on the condition that I not buy a power saw with the money. When she handed me the check on Christmas morning with her conditions, I handed it back saying, "In that case, I don't want it." My father and uncle Raphael spent the rest of Christmas day delivering the same message: "Don't you care how deeply you have hurt your mother?"   (Pablo)

Becoming married entails another role shift. Sons become husbands and daughters become wives. The process of becoming married will obviously be impeded if that role shift is not made. The role shift points to a change in primary commitment and loyalty as well as the redirection of energy to the task of bonding as a marital pair. That bonding process gives shape and form to the family that is being created. The couple are architects of their family as they establish clear boundaries of separation and negotiate new loyalties.

What happens when a child enters a family is not always what should happen. There are some changes that occur in families when a child is added that are not useful for either the child or the family as a whole. There are other changes, like sleeping schedules, that are necessary but temporary. Still other changes in family patterns are both necessary and permanent in order for children to flourish. We suggest that there are four inescapable changes that occur when a child is added: adults who become parents add to their identity the *social role of father or mother*; the *freedom of parents is limited* in order to accommodate freedom for the child; the *need for shifting loyalties* becomes a permanent reality; and the *worldview of adults is transformed* by parenting. Parents who do not acknowledge these changes in their lives diminish, sometimes severely, the environment and relationships in which their children will grow.

Becoming Fathers and Mothers: The Role Change

When a child is added to a family, another fundamental role transition must take place. In a biological sense, the change is automatic when a child is born. Ready or not, people become fathers and mothers when they bring a child into the world. Even if they are not married, they become parents. Being a biological parent does not automatically translate into an acceptance of the ongoing role of mother or father. For married couples, this transition to the parenting role increases the need for a clear separation from the homes of their origin and enough modification of the marital bond to make time and space for the child.

> Sheldon and I had been married for five years before we decided to have a child. We did Lamaze together and shared equally in preparing the baby's room. We had decided before the child was born that Sheldon would take two weeks off work so that we could share the first moments with our child. The day he went back to work, the partnership was over. He was late getting home from work three days in a row. It was, I discovered, a brief partnership in parenting. Even though I was very glad my maternity leave allowed me to be home with our daughter for three months, I had expected Sheldon to share fully in the responsibilities of parenting.
>
> (Lisa)

What Lisa experienced is common. The first eighteen months after a child is added to a family is often characterized by an increase in marital dissatisfaction, loss of intimacy, and even a loss of self-esteem. The stress in the first years of parenthood is not due just to the inequitable distribution of labor between new mothers and fathers. There may be serious disappointment when the child care arrangements between well-intentioned people like Sheldon and Lisa are less equitable than they had expected them to be. Most couples plan to share the child-rearing more than they actually do.

Balancing Parenting and Working

Although both women and men in this society are guaranteed twelve weeks of unpaid, job-protected leave for the birth of a child, change in patterns of parenting will be slow for a variety of reasons. The culture of the workplace continues to expect that women/mothers will be the ones to stay home when a child is born. A man worries, and with some justification, that if he takes a long paternity leave, he will be perceived as someone who is not serious about his work. Moreover, as long as the salaries of men continue to be larger than women's, even for the same work, couples may decide simply on prudent grounds that the husband should continue and maybe even intensify his normal work schedule in order to ensure sufficient income for the family while there is only one income, with usually more expenses.

> Although I work in a reasonably progressive office, four years ago, as the birth of our first child neared, no one in authority came to me and said, "We hope you'll feel comfortable taking a few weeks off." I asked about a paternal leave policy; there was none. So I arranged to take two weeks vacation. It was a good thing I did, because our daughter ended up back in the hospital twice in the first 10 days of her life.
>
> When we had our second child I was in a better position to argue for a formal, unpaid leave, and had I asked I would probably have been granted it. But I didn't ask. In fact, two days after our son was born, I slipped back into the office to "look at the mail" and soon resumed full-time work.   (Colin)[5]

Colin's story illustrates how difficult it will be to effect the transformation of attitudes among men about childrearing that couples increasingly expect. The culture of the workplace and the economic necessity for someone to be the primary family wage earner prompt men like Colin to keep doing it and in fact working more. There is also profound, lingering ambivalence about changing patterns of being men and husbands and fathers. The workplace, for all its pressures, offers established roles and predictable patterns. A newborn child is much more mysterious and unpredictable than the workplace, and therefore more unsettling. Involving more fathers in childrearing is a necessary agenda for our time. Our efforts to get fathers to spend time with their families are complicated by an ambivalence in them about becoming equal partners in childrearing. Envisioning a new relationship between work and family for both men and women is the major thrust of Bonnie J. Miller-McLemore's book *Also a Mother: Work and Family as a Theological Dilemma.*[6]

Ironically, the mystery of childhood's unfolding requires not only openness and flexibility, but patience and routine. An adult tires of peekaboo and retrieving the dropped toy long before the child does; the parent does not look forward to the clockwork of nap time, snack time, and story time, while the child thrives on such routines. For adults who are accustomed to making their way in the workplace, it is not only the unpredictability of childrearing but its sameness that is trying. Even the best marital bond cannot ensure the kind of balance between parenting and working that egalitarian relationships hope to create.

Impediments to Becoming Parents

Preparations for the addition of a child are sometimes seriously complicated if the prospective parents have not satisfactorily separated themselves emotionally from the families of their origin. The interventions of well-meaning grandparents—always in the interest of the child—often undercut the fragile sense of competence of new parents. Differing approaches to parenting may force husbands and wives to make choices for each other that violate presuppositions about loyalty to their families of origin.

We had only been married a short time before our first child was born. Neither of our parents were happy about our marriage or that we had chosen to live "so far from home." Some of their opposition melted away when we announced that I was pregnant. Both grandmothers were determined to have equal access to their first grandchild.

Cliff's mother was a fastidious homemaker who kept her modern fourth-floor apartment spotlessly clean. It had been that way, Cliff remembered, even when they had been poor. My mother was more casual. I grew up in a warm climate. Most of the time when we were kids we wore very little at all. My mother thought that clothes were more for pretense than protection.

When our baby daughter was born, Cliff's mother showered her with clothes she had been sewing for months. She was so pleased to have found an androgynous pattern book for baby clothes. I did not use them. Four months after our daughter was born and after his mother had visited us, Cliff and I had a huge fight. He admitted that he resented his mother's fussiness when he was a child but he still thought our daughter should wear more clothes. It took us several fights and a consultation with our pastor to realize that our conflict was about loyalty to the families we came from. Finding our own pattern of childrearing required more compromising than either of us had expected of marriage.   (Rosinda)

The birth of a child is often a test of family loyalty, as it was for Rosinda and Cliff. Couples who find it easy to establish their own unique patterns of having breakfast or making love or writing checks discover that raising children is a new test of family loyalty. When grandparents are geographically removed from their grandchildren, insisting on maintaining their family traditions of childrearing becomes a way of ensuring quality care from afar. New parents who are not sure what to do may welcome advice from their own parents until that advice becomes something more. If, however, sons and daughters have established clear boundaries with their own parents, then they will be able to make appropriate use of family wisdom in early childrearing without destabilizing the marital bond.

Family Freedom Is Changed

The arrival of a child limits family freedom. Especially when the first child is born, there is an awareness of how many patterns of eating and sleeping and working and making love must be modified. The changes that subsequent children require may not be as dramatic but they are still necessary. Even in those families in which one person is designated to set aside time and limit mobility to care for a small child, there is inevitably less freedom for everyone in the family.

The addition of a child demands that the family rearrange its space and alter its use of time so that there is room enough and attention enough for the child to grow in safety and without fear of abandonment. Caring for a small child limits everyone's freedom to manage time and mobility. In order to "go at the pace of the children," everyone needs to go a little slower. However, a family may designate a mother or father or grandparent or an older child, or it may hire a professional child care worker, to be the one to give up time and mobility in order to be near enough to nurture and protect a small child. When only one person slows down or limits her or his freedom, the family as a whole is diminished because it does not change.

The issue of loss of control of one's own time and mobility illustrates the fact that, despite our deep joy in children and our powerful desire to bring children into the world, the entry of a baby into a family always involves a kind of loss. As a rule, the gain we experience far outweighs the loss, but the loss is there nonetheless. Whole patterns of life shift. Wardrobes change. The family as a system, even if that system is only the marital pair, must absorb the change and adapt to it at the same time. The family may require one person to make all or most of the sacrifices or it may distribute the burden more equitably. But the deeper truth is that the arrival of a child puts new limits on every member's life, and therefore everyone must share in the sacrifice.

> We were able to make two visits to see our first grandchild in the first year of his life. When he was eighteen months old, Benjamin Walter came with his mother to visit his grandmother and me. Before he arrived, we scoured the house for things that might hurt Benjamin or that he might hurt. Small breakable items came off the coffee table in the living room; three large potted plants went upstairs; antiques came off the lowest shelf of the baker's rack; several electric-light sockets were covered with plastic covers. We made external changes in how our house was arranged and organized in order to make it safe for Benjamin. We wanted visiting his grandparents to be an experience of freedom to explore without danger. (Grandpa Walter)

The experience of Grandpa Walter is familiar to anyone who has responsibility to care for a small child. Because children are vulnerable, they need to be protected from possible harm without being prohibited from exploring their world. In order to create an environment in which it is safe for the child to exercise freedom to explore, parents and other caregivers will need to limit their own freedom to manage time and mobility. The alternative is to put a child in a playpen, attach her to a bungee cord, or tie him in front of a television set, putting limits on the child for the sake of the caregiver's freedom. It is a struggle to establish appropriate childrearing patterns that fall between strategies in which parents do all the adapting and those in which parents change their living patterns hardly at all.

Managing time and mobility is a major dilemma for parents because it is impossible to raise children without sacrifice. Even when the aim is to establish a marriage relationship that is sustained by a mutuality in which each one's needs and desires count as equal to the needs and desires of the other, sacrifice is still necessary. The complexity of modern life in the home as well as the workplace requires sacrifice in order to establish and maintain an egalitarian marriage. What makes a marriage just is that the sacrifice is mutual, both in who makes it and in who benefits by it.

We live in a culture that seems to favor families with children. More and more fine restaurants feature children's menus and child seats to attract upwardly mobile young families with children. It is possible to purchase a special "running" stroller so that a parent may take his or her small child jogging without diminishing the pace. Portable cribs, disposable diapers and bottles, and collapsible strollers may give the appearance of being child-oriented. These inventions, valuable as they may be, extend the illusion that children do not change the pace or priorities of adult life and that parental freedom need not be curtailed by children's needs. None of these inventions or conveniences is evil in itself, but together they provide a slippery slope by which adult convenience determines what is good for children.

As a soccer coach for a neighborhood league, I wait after practice with the children whose parents are late. Children feel awful, feel guilty and ashamed, when their parents are late to pick them up. Almost every week I wait with one particular girl. Her father and mother are divorced; this sometimes leads to confusion about rides. Both parents have professional careers with complicated schedules, and a child custody arrangement overlaid on top of these. I tell their daughter that I understand, but she says that I don't. Neither of her parents really want her living with them, she says. "I'm terribly inconvenient," she says with an air of artificial maturity and defiant tears in her eyes.   (Alan)

In a variety of subtle ways, we are defining children and childhood to fit adult needs and conveniences. It has been said that toddlers were not old enough to adjust to strangers and strange situations. Now, however, parents who cannot miss a day of work may drop their child off at the "Sniffles and Sneezes" clinic of the local hospital when their children are too sick for their regular day care center. We once thought that five hours of class time was about all elementary children could tolerate. Now, however, to accommodate the work schedules of parents, children need to manage eleven hours at school. It may very well be that children are more resilient than we once thought they were. But that misses the point. Children are expected to tolerate more so that parents are limited less.

The capacity to accommodate and willingness to sacrifice to establish a just marriage will become a prelude to the demands of parenting. Having a child is rewarding, watching a child grow is very satisfying, receiving the spontaneous love of a child is very fulfilling, but raising children cannot first of all be an exercise in self-interest. Parents give more than they get back, accommodate their desires for the sake of the child's needs, and set aside their freedom in order to create an environment in which children are able to explore in safety. The attitude of parents toward infant children in particular must be characterized by sacrifice more than self-interest.

Shifting Loyalties in the Family

When children are added to a family, they enter a system already in existence with established patterns of interaction. The kind of environment that a couple has begun to create during the process of becoming married is therefore crucial for the addition of children. Ideally, they will have established an environment in which there is freedom for new family intimacies to form and new loyalties to be established without threatening the marital bond. The arrival of a baby destabilizes old or new and fragile loyalties.

With the addition of a child, it is natural and inevitable for triangles to develop because there are now at least three in the family. Triangles are inevitable in all human relationships. Triangles become problematic when they are paths for coercion or secrecy. A triangle is made up of three points that are connected and ideally in constant motion. Triangles vary in families according to their number, intensity, composition, complexity, and healthiness. The standard family triangle that is first created with the arrival of a child will look like figure 1.

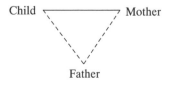

FIG. 1. Family triangle after arrival of a child

Part of the task of welcoming a child is to establish a process of shifting alliances so that no one, including the father, becomes a permanent outsider. Triangles become a problem when relationships are fixed or alliances are secret in such a way that it is difficult for loyalties to shift. An emotional triangle occurs, as family therapist Edwin Friedman describes it, when "any two parts of a system become uncomfortable with one another, they will 'triangle in' or focus upon a third person, or issue, as a way of stabilizing their relationship with one another."[7]

My father's business travels often postponed family decisions. When I was five, I learned the word "unilateral." I asked my mother for something and she said she would talk to my dad because she did not make "unilateral decisions." In my mind I envisioned a ladder with one side to hold on to [uni-ladder-al], and I always assumed my mother made this rule so that my brothers and I could not coerce her into siding against dad in some way. Now that I have children, and my husband travels, I realize my mother was also using her prohibition on unilateral decisions to draw my dad back into the family whenever he came home.   (Brenda)

Brenda's story is a good illustration of the value of keeping alliances clear but mobile in order to stabilize any system that has three parts. Her mother naturally had an ongoing bond with her children that was intensified by the father's absence. When she insisted on including the father in major decisions, she not only established the mother-father alliance but also linked the father with the children. If, however, he was only the "heavy" who said no, then the mother's avoiding the hard decisions would in fact enhance her primary bond with the children and further isolate the father as the third point on the triangle.

The addition of a child has a destabilizing effect on the marital bond. The mother's preoccupations during pregnancy and the initial intimacy between mother and child after birth may cause the husband/father to feel neglected or like an outsider to this new relationship. For couples whose bond is more like fusion than intimacy, the arrival of a child may threaten marital closeness with new demands for more authentic intimacy. For couples who are more distant than close, an unstable triangle may be formed in order that the child might meet one or both parents' needs for closeness. The ability of both parents to create a three-party system with the child in which closeness is always shifting will help to determine the happiness and well-being of a family.

From the moment we brought Josh home, Claire was totally devoted to him. I thought I was prepared for this, but I was stunned by its impact on our intimacy. First, we no longer had a quiet time together before dinner because she was breast feeding. Josh's lack of predictable sleeping and eating patterns interrupted other moments too, but I was pretty understanding. One night, Claire and I were finally alone and all was quiet. I began to touch her and kiss her and her breasts began to leak. In a strange way, I found this charming and even powerful. I wanted her attention and affection so much. But Claire jumped off the sofa, and shouted at me accusingly: "You can't do that! I need that for the baby." For the first few years, really until Josh was mobile and began getting into things, I was an intruder in my own marriage. It was frustrating. (Jim)

It is common that husbands and new fathers feel like intruders, as Jim did, in their own family because of the primacy of the maternal bond. Learning to shift loyalties is not easy but gains new urgency when the first child is added. *The key to effective family living is a system in which alliances shift and togetherness always moves around.*

A primary impediment to shifting alliances occurs when love is confused with possession. The impulse to possess our children may be present already at the birth of a child. It is revealed when one parent always refers to a child as "my son" or "my daughter," even when speaking in the presence of the spouse. Such language usually suggests that one spouse regards his or her relationship to the child as primary. When there is more than one child, parents sometimes each take one child as theirs. One of the most destructive emotional triangles occurs when parents fight with each other through a child for the affections of that child. It is a battle without winners or losers.

In my family of origin, I was my mother's primary friend and ally for as long as I can remember. I was her helper in the kitchen when I was young. I filled in the empty spaces that were created by my father's preoccupation with his pastoral work. His preoccupation with pastoral work was sustained by being an outsider in the primary family triangle. Not long after my mother died, my father told me that when I left home for college the light went out of my mother's life. To this day, I am sorry that I was not more understanding with my father about what that might have meant for him. It helped me understand the power of the bond I had with my mother, from as early as I can remember. I also understand better why it was so hard for me to make friends with my father. My mother could only understand making friends with my father as a threat to her alliance with me. (Herbert)

When parents need their children, for whatever reason, they are likely to establish a possessive bond. The intense bond between Herbert and his mother was born in such need and maintained out of desperation. What she lost in the end, however, by keeping father and son apart was greater than what she won.

Keeping a balance between autonomy and community, between separateness and togetherness, is the central paradox of this entire series of books on family living. Perhaps the most fundamental expression of that paradox is the relationship between parents and children: we love them *and* let them go from birth. Even when children are small and vulnerable and needing our protection, we hold them without holding on. The religious practice of baptism or child dedication is a strong corrective to the parental inclination to possess children. From the beginning, they are ours and not ours, because they belong to God. When parents understand that their children are a loan from God, they are less likely to possess or control or abuse their children in order to satisfy their own needs.

Our Worldview Changes

In his novel *Anna Karenina*, Leo Tolstoy writes about the anxiety of a father at the birth of a child. "His feelings for this little creature were not at all what he had expected. There was not an atom of pride or joy in them; on the contrary, he was oppressed by a new sense of apprehension—the consciousness of another vulnerable region."[8] Despite the pride and joy that many parents feel, the anxiety that Tolstoy relates is real as well. The world is filled with danger, imperfection, intrigue, and evil. If it is a dangerous place for adults, it is certainly not safe for children. The urge to protect one's child from the world, or to clean up the world they will inhabit, brings parents into a new relationship with the world. Whatever one's politics or worldview, children present us with the consciousness of "another vulnerable region" that we must protect.

The less broken or vulnerable must take care of the more broken and vulnerable. That is the lesson about the world we learn from our children. The birth of a child brings about a new sense of responsibility that carries along with it a new anxiety.

In the quiet of the early morning on the day scheduled for my Caesarean, I sat on porch swing with my baby and my thoughts and my fears in a mild state of panic. I was not ready to give up this baby inside of me. The motion of the swing back and forth was soothing and Brendan kicked his approval as he moved about in his cramped space. I just sat, swinging and sharing the last few attached heartbeats with my child, rubbing my abdomen as though to soothe a fussy baby, and telling my baby of my fears about motherhood. Would I be a good mother? Would I be able to balance woman, wife, and mother? Would I be able to make the world safe for him? Then, without knowing what time it was, I knew it was time. Somehow, in that quiet hour on the porch swing, Brendan "told" me that he was ready to be born, ready to test my mothering abilities and his father's fierce love, ready to shake the balance of our family. And I felt ready, too. My panic was gone, replaced by a sense of anticipation, eager to meet this little person face to face. (Dayna Ann)

As Dayna Ann's story helps us see, the bonds of affection and care begin to develop between parent and child even before the child is born. Her fears anticipate the changes in a parent's worldview that accompany that birth. Our view of ourselves changes, but so does our view of the world. The utter helplessness of the infant child stamps a new responsibility on a parent's soul and changes forever a parent's bond to the world. Our children expect so much from us; we are all they have. Although our care is temporary, it is essential and irrevocable. It is not surprising that the birth of a child into a world that is not safe may evoke a crisis of faith.

It takes faith to have a child. It takes faith, when one is pregnant, to follow the pregnancy as it unfolds, to realize the new life that grows within one's own. It takes faith to imagine the new child, the new personality, the new demands, the otherness that new life brings. It takes faith to be a parent, to risk being a parent like one's own parents and to risk new ways of parenting. It takes faith to parent as a mother-father team, to accept the assistance (wanted and unwanted) of parents, let alone pediatricians, baby-sitters, teachers, counselors, neighbors, friends.

There were several of us who had babies at the same time. Later on, we laughed together about how we all wanted to quit labor, get up from the delivery table, and walk away before the baby came. We laughed among ourselves about how we imagined grabbing our men by their throats during labor and screaming into their faces, "You did this to me!" We laughed about the silly things we said or did at that time but we did not joke about the inexorable struggle of giving birth to a child. Nor did we joke about the inexpressible power, wonder, and sheer joy we possessed in that moment when we brought someone into our circle and into the world. The terror and the joy are sacred to us, just as the new life is sacred in our eyes. (Susan)

The infant is not the only one who must trust. It may take a village to raise a child, but it takes faith to welcome a child into one's family and world. It is faith that empowers parents—new parents and parents at every stage—to meet the unknown that new life brings. What is required is more than faith in the goodness of the world or even faith in one's own capacities. In the face of present levels of violence around the globe and the potential for widespread environmental destruction, having a child requires faith in the promise of God's providential care. It takes faith in the future of God to have a child.

The Old Testament theologian Walter Brueggemann has used this awareness of the planet's fragility to ask whether our faith will have children. "Is there a future, given the precarious reality of our human community in a nuclear age, for in that context the crucial question is not even the survival of faith, but the survival of children."[9] The possibility of planetary disaster because of our abuse of the environment or from a nuclear holocaust makes faithful childrearing even more crucial for our time.

After Jon and I were engaged, a large part of our discussions centered on whether or not to have children. I wanted them. He was willing to adopt (maybe) but didn't want any of his own because of his concerns about environmental destruction and the possibilities of war. Here was a man who recycled, who walked whenever possible, who conserved energy and reduced waste products, but had little hope for the future. He did not consider himself to be a Christian, which I think shaped his view of the future. When the bombs dropped in Baghdad, they dropped right into the middle of our relationship. They confirmed his vision of the future and the end of our engagement. (Evon)

For Jon and Evon, as for many couples today, Brueggemann's question is just right: Will our faith have children? The faith that makes it possible to bring children into a world with a precarious future must be centered in the possibility of God's future. Theologian Ted Peters has written about the future this way: "It is the power of God's grace calling us forward and empowering us to center our existence through trust in the future that will be God's."[10] Our hope is in the future that God promises to make new. It is this faith in God's future that enables us to decide to have children today.

In the meantime, we also need to be making choices in the present that will create a sustainable future for our children and their children. The family calls for our deepest ecological passions and our best political wisdom in order to ensure a future that will be safe for our children and so that our children will be safe for their future as well. It is even more than what our children ask of us; it is what our faithfulness to God and God's creation demand.

3
WHAT ARE FAMILIES FOR?

CHILDREN ARRIVE with needs attached that demand attention. The physical needs of the child for nutrition, affection, and a clean diaper are impossible to postpone and difficult to ignore. That is why it is inevitable that children change things. The arrival of children with their needs in tow also generates new questions for parents. Some of those questions are practical:

> How do we stop the baby from crying?
> What should be done about diarrhea?
> When will the umbilical cord fall off?
> Why does our baby spit up so much?
> Shouldn't the baby be sitting up by now?
> Should the baby be awakened to be fed?

New parents will find answers to most of these questions from their own parents or other relatives or friends who "have been through it" or from a host of baby books that promise to answer all the questions parents ask. This book will not replicate the practical wisdom that is available from a variety of sources on infant and early child care.[1]

Other questions raised by the arrival of a child are not so easily answered, however. These are questions of family purpose or meaning. A child is a sign of transcendence that prompts parents to think beyond themselves. After four consecutive sleepless nights, the purpose of the family becomes an existential question. Sometimes, when parents wonder what went wrong, the questions of meaning or purpose are born of fear that they have failed. When new parents are overwhelmed by the amount of work it takes to care for such a small person, they also want to know what families *must do*.

Couples becoming married are not usually preoccupied with questions about purpose. They have work schedules to coordinate, hidden expectations to reconcile, mutual needs to recognize, rituals of intimacy to establish, checkbooks to balance, and unexpected differences to accommodate as they seek to form a marital bond and make a home. Even couples who understand their marriage as a sacramental sign of Christ's love for the church may take the *purpose* of their life together for granted. The arrival of a child, however, makes such questions unavoidable.

The question of family purpose has become both more complex and more crucial in recent times. It is more complex because many of the tasks performed by families in preindustrial societies are now performed by other agents in society. The urgency of questions of purpose follows from that change. What *can* or *must* families do that no other institution can do as well? And for whom? Because the childrearing years are an increasingly smaller portion of a family's life history, and because we now believe that adults continue changing throughout life, we no longer regard families as just a place for growing children. The next volume in this series, *Promising Again*, will explore the issues of family living beyond the childrearing years. This book, however, is about the family's role in raising children.

Considering the purpose of the family also introduces questions about the relationship between family form and function. The family has endured in part because it has adapted to changing needs and circumstances. Moreover, structures of the family have changed over centuries and will continue to change while its purposes have remained more constant. We assume that a family is what it does. This idea that form follows function is a theological reality as well as an architectural principle. *Christian teaching has more to say about what families must do than what they should look like.*

The Lengthy Neediness of Children

Human infants are vulnerable from birth. They are more dependent and needy for a longer time than any other newly born creature. A two-day-old giraffe walks independently on wobbly legs but a two-day-old human infant depends on the nurturing of others to survive. Ordinarily, as the poet W. H. Auden writes in "Mundus et Infans," it is the role of the mother to "supply and deliver [the infant's] raw materials free."[2]

Children suffer when they are not provided with the free "raw materials" needed for growth. They will not endure without the nurture and protection of caring adults who anticipate their needs. Ordinarily those caring adults are parents. The lengthy fragility of infancy is in fact the first and most obvious reason why human beings need something like a family.

There are times when the ability to protect and nurture children is beyond the control of families because of war or famine or some other catastrophe. Often, however, when children die of malnutrition or suffer abuse or go to school hungry, it is a sign that adults have failed to provide for their minimal needs. Children need to be fed and protected in order to grow. That need is basic. We will return to this theme in chapter 5, when we consider the relationship between family and society. What appears to be neglect may instead be the inability of families to earn enough income to provide the "raw materials" their children need. What children need beyond mother's milk to survive and grow is neither free nor cheap.

The second basic need of children is safety. We noted earlier how important it is to make a child's environment safe, whether by "child-proofing" closets and stairways and wall sockets or checking the lead content of paints. The goal, however, is not just safety. The aim is to make the child's space safe without minimizing freedom. In order to ensure the safety of children without limiting their mobility, the freedom of parents or some other caregiver must be curtailed. The child's protection and the freedom of parents are inextricably linked.

The family also embodies safety as a sign that shelter is possible, to instill courage so that children and adults can endure unfriendly or hostile environments. It is difficult for a family to become a safe haven when the world is violent. Moreover, we live in a society that presumes a high level of violence as normal. The sexual and physical abuse of children and violence toward women are among the residues of patriarchy. Fear and suspicion and the perception of constant danger are awful companions for children. The failure of a family to be a shelter of safety sometimes, in fact, mirrors the wider society. Still we must admit that families fail when children are afraid to grow up.

Establishing a home that is emotionally safe is an even more complicated task. Chapter 4 will describe four very basic qualities of family living from a Christian perspective: hospitality, compassion, justice, reconciliation. These themes articulate a theological vision for family living that is also most likely to foster human growth. They provide the foundation for family life that is emotionally safe. A child who is emotionally safe is free to act like a child, think like a child, talk like a child. The growing awareness of verbal and physical and sexual abuse of children has increased our determination to provide for their emotional and physical safety. Interrupting abusive situations is a necessary intervention on behalf of children. Attention to providing that which "befits" a child's development is even better because it endures.

Beyond Basic Needs: Attentions Befitting Each Age

Beyond the minimal needs for protection and nurture, as Auden reminds us again in "Mundus et Infans," it is the obligation of adults to "show [the infant] all such attentions as befit his [or her] age."[3] These "attentions" are not as self-evident as the physical needs for food and shelter. Nor are they as universal. Developmental needs vary according to cultural definitions of being human. Each culture has a unique vision of what it is to be human that will influence how the needs of the young are organized. Every family, and sometimes even each parent, has a catalog of what it believes must be provided in order that children will grow and flourish. Moreover, it is not possible to say exactly when adults stop needing what children need. What we have identified as the lingering childness of adulthood is a reminder that the needs of children are the needs of people.

The following list of "attentions" befitting children is focused on *needs*. There are social or cultural opportunities beneficial to children that are not basic necessities. The presence of two parents in a stable marriage is certainly desirable but not necessary in order to create a dependable and nurturing environment. The kind of love that children need to foster self-esteem is generally not gender-specific. Nor is there only one family form that can provide what children need to grow. There are, however, certain "attentions" (beyond basic survival) that children need in order to thrive.

1. *A child needs the enduring, irrational involvement of at least one adult in care and joint activity with the child.* What this means for the sociologist Urie Bronfenbrenner is that somebody has to be "crazy about kids."[4] The irrational commitment of parents toward their own children enables parents to overlook the lingering smell of baby powder in the house or sleepless nights or mashed peas on the TV screen. Sometimes the "crazy about kids" role is filled by grandparents who have the freedom to dote on their grandchildren without the daily responsibility of rearing them. Other times it may be an uncle or aunt, or

a neighbor or a teacher or a pastor, who delights in the activities of a child. Though it need not be one person throughout the child's entire life, this role does not tolerate much proxy. In order that young people will receive attention and praise enough to develop a sense of self-worth, they need at least one adult who is "irrationally" committed to their well-being.

This attitude of "craziness about kids" is essential for the development of a child's sense of well-being. It begins with an unconditional recognition of the child's uniqueness in what is sometimes referred to as mirroring.[5] That process provides a psychological nutriment as necessary as food to sustain the beginning of life. Recent infant studies have concluded quite convincingly that human infants develop an active willingness to produce the kind of affectional bonds they need. People of all ages (and children are no exception!) need to be recognized in order to be valued and in order to sort out their perceptions of the world. When parents, whether single or married, must limit their attention to a child because of the press of daily routines and obligations, the child will suffer unless someone who is "crazy about kids" fills the void.

2. *A child needs developmentally appropriate expectations and behavior.* The family is an environment in which it should be possible for children to play and to learn, to be happy and silly and carefree and vulnerable. It is important for children to be expected to behave in ways that correspond to their stage of development. The child who is not made appropriately responsible (for her room, for things he breaks, for setting the table) does not easily mature into greater responsibilities. We may say that such a child is favored or spoiled, but a child without expectations is in fact a *neglected child*. Children are also neglected when they are regarded as appendages to the inner workings of family and are not incorporated into household decisions or routines or are ignored at the dinner table. There are times when the neglect is more like abandonment. It is as much a matter of neglect to expect too little of a child as it is to expect him to act beyond his years.

Sometimes children are given roles in the family or in relation to one or both of the parents that makes them prematurely responsible. The child whose purview is too broad or demanding for her age or his ability, the *parental child*, appears to be very mature and responsible. Sometimes that role requires that an individual give up childhood prematurely and become a "little adult" by age nine or eleven. When there is only one parent in the family, there is a special temptation to expect a child to function as surrogate spouse, or a parent's best friend, or the parent for younger siblings. Because they learn the new language first, children of immigrant families become translators or spokespersons too early in life. Even when there are two parents in the family, a child may prematurely become the confidant of one spouse or the permanent family peacemaker.

> When I was nine, my mother woke me up and took me with her to the hospital where my father, an alcoholic, had been brought following a traffic accident. We left my older brother and the dog home in bed. In the emergency room, my mother's hands rested firmly on my shoulders as she guided me through the maze of desks and doctors to my father's room. My mother's hands positioned me in front of her everywhere. I was ashamed; I could feel the contempt of the doctors and nurses for my father, a drunk who had injured himself and other people. I will never forget the moment that night when I realized that my mother had taken me along to protect her from their anger and her own.   (Nancy)

Children need freedom to be children. Children like Nancy can be deceptively perceptive under stress and nimble beyond their years in handling difficult situations. When they are grown, however, parental children will often return to their families with great sadness, conflict, and resentment because of the early loss of innocence. The premature urgency to be competent has the effect of terrorizing self-esteem and denying feelings.

It is often a characteristic of urban families that children become streetwise like adults much too early. In a book with the compelling title *No Place to Be a Child*, James Garbarino and others have described the ways in which children under the stress of dangerous environments—war, poverty, racism, famine, violence—must give up their childhood in order to survive.[6] Yet even when children are better off economically, childhood is in jeopardy. Some child custody and visitation schedules, though workable for adults, are harrowing for children to keep. Some carry pocket calendars in order to keep track of their complicated schedules.

The phenomenon that child psychologist David Elkind has identified as the *hurried child*[7] is played out in a variety of ways in both privileged and underprivileged social settings. In either instance, the child does not have freedom to engage in age-appropriate behavior. Helping children form good habits like brushing teeth and doing homework depends on age-appropriate expectations of what they can do.

Within the crucible of family, children learn to observe rules like taking turns and not hitting and respecting the property or space of others. Children also need to develop empathy for others without assuming responsibility for their well-being. That is the basis for compassion and hospitality without conditions later in life.

Families fail whenever parents abdicate or negotiate away their authority. This kind of failure is evident when children seem more like adults than the adults themselves. Some adults in families are so chaotic and inconsistent that children must learn strategies of passivity and overcompensation in order to survive. Families fail when children are responsible for raising themselves or their siblings or for cleaning up after a drunken parent or measuring up to adult standards of behavior.

> I used to dread coming home from school in the afternoon, just opening the door. If my mother was lying on the sofa in the living room, arm across her face, covering her eyes, then it was a "bad day." My dad used to say to me, "Don't bother your mother. She's resting. This is just a bad day." On bad days, we tiptoed past her; sometimes I kissed her lightly on the forehead, not because she wanted me to, but because it made her seem less dead to me. We couldn't turn on the lights, the radio, the TV, so on my mother's "bad days" I cleaned the kitchen. The harder I worked, the better I began to feel. My mother always seemed to perk up when she saw the kitchen clean. But I was always afraid to have a friend over, and as a child I also felt anxious in other people's houses.   (Amy)

Amy learned how to cope with her mother's neediness, but at the expense of her own childhood. She had learned what to do in order to survive. Amy's family failed her, because it did not seek help to cope with the emotional absence of her mother. *Whenever the success or well-being of a family depends on the competency of its children, the family fails.* Children like Amy are amazing, but they are usually amazing at a price. Unaddressed mental or physical illness, self-abuse, or addiction in a parent, especially when children are left to cope or compensate on their own, are situations in which families fail.

3. *A child needs role models for being an adult and for belonging to a family.* While an infant may relate to a number of adults throughout the early years of development, no one has more emotional influence than a parent on images of adult behavior. Since most children do not see their parents at work, they are more likely to regard behavior in the home as normative. For that reason, parents need to practice at home the virtues they expect their children to develop. It is

never enough for parents to insist that their children do what they say rather than what they do. Children are keen observers and discriminating judges of the marriages, friendships, dating patterns, and civic relationships of parents. Parents are primary models of adult behavior for their children.

Parents are also the first teachers about parenting. What parents hand on to their children is very often an extension of the legacy they have received first from their own parents. The fact that parents today have to be taught how to be parents is an indication that the learning sequence is no longer adequate. Our parents failed to teach us what we needed to know in order to raise our own children. Sometimes, however, the lessons we learned from our own parents are simply outmoded.

Because changes in living are happening so quickly and dramatically, parents face very different issues today than their own parents did. Since that pattern is likely to continue, a skill-oriented approach to parenting is not enough. *Parents need to learn principles of human relationships and develop attitudes toward children that will endure the quixotic shifts of modern family living.* The anxiety of parents today is an understandable response to the double task of learning and passing on that learning simultaneously.

> When Kendall and I married, we anticipated sharing both housekeeping and childrearing much more than either of our parents had. We both worked, but neither of our mothers had worked outside the home. Seventeen years and three sons later, we are still married but that is about all I can say. We have argued and argued and negotiated and negotiated, and in the end the family tasks were still divided according to traditional lines. I still get furious when our children refer to their father as the "baby-sitter." What I am afraid we have taught our children is that intimacy is a set of negotiated details.   (Shanda)

Shanda's fear that her sons would have learned lessons about intimacy she did not want to teach is well founded. Children are great imitators. Whether they intend to or not, adults are always modeling adult behavior and gender identity for children, even for children who are not their own.

In order to counter the powerful images of women and men that are promoted through the media, parents need to be clear and consistent and intentional about what they want their children to imitate. When parents are uncertain themselves about who they are or what they value, images from the broader culture will have a stronger influence. Most lessons in adult living are not gender specific. Children can discover the meaning of compassion or hospitality or justice or forgiveness from parents or adults of the same or opposite gender. Being a single parent is demanding in this area, however, because one person must represent all the ways of being adult.

There are specific lessons best learned from an adult who is the same gender as the child. For that purpose, two parents are better than one. Because so many children grow up without a father regularly present in the home, we need to develop alternative systems of role modeling that are gender specific for boys. And even when there are two parents in a family it is possible for boys to grow up not knowing their fathers. The stories that Harvard psychologist Sam Osherman tells about sons in search of their fathers are overwhelming testimony to the fact that being an absent father is not a role model that men consciously want to repeat.[8]

4. *A child needs respect for personal boundaries.* Children learn how to respect by being respected as unique persons of worth. While this may appear to be the opposite of "craziness about kids," it is not. Once the umbilical cord is severed, the infant is a separate and distinct being. From that time on, a child needs to be respected as a separate person with distinct thoughts and feelings and a story to write. If parents and adult caregivers begin with that assumption about the worth of each infant person, it will change how they respond.

It is not easy for parents to respect the boundaries of their children. They will talk about their children to teachers; they must explain special needs to baby-sitters; they consult with neighbors or relatives when they are worried; sometimes they brag about their children to strangers and friends alike. In order to gather information about a child's behavior, parents may believe that they are entitled to violate the privacy of a child by reading a diary or going through pockets. Each of these covert inquiries must be weighed and measured as a breach of a child's autonomy.

As children grow older, respect of parents for a child's boundaries means allowing them their own friendships and relationships, their own failures as well as successes. For parents who are overly invested in their children, honoring their freedom to fail is painful. The success of their children may be equally problematic for overinvested parents because it fosters autonomy and independence. Parents need to be reminded again and again that they can house the bodies of children but not their souls, because their souls "dwell in a place of tomorrow you [parents] cannot go, not even in your dreams."[9] Stories of fathers who thrive on their sons' athletic careers, and mothers who are jealous of their daughters' boyfriends, are extreme versions of a deeper struggle of all parents to regard their children with respect and celebrate their journey toward separate personhood.

Children who are respected by their parents from the beginning of life are most likely to gain self-respect. In order that children might find their identity and realize their worth, the family needs to be an environment in which there is enough warmth and unconditional love that the child is recognized as a separate person. The following words from the *Apostolic Exhortation on the Family* of Pope John Paul II convey a message for all parents: "In the family, which is a community of persons, special attention must be devoted to the children by developing a profound esteem for their personal dignity and a great respect and generous concern for their rights."[10] This respect for the rights and dignity of a child is a translation of the image of children as citizens into arenas of family living.

There are several ways to organize a list of what children need. In the end, however, the exact themes or phrases are not really important. It *is* important that we begin discussing family purpose by asking questions about what children need. If family can be a place that attends to the needs befitting children at each age, then it is more likely to be a place that respects the needs of adults as well. Unfortunately, that does not always happen. Some families fail to provide what children and adults need to endure the ordinary and extraordinary crises of growing and living.

When Families Fail to Provide What Children Need

All families have problems, face crises, cope with stress, struggle with illness, manage complicated situations. They may even have to endure tragedy. In a society that understands success as the absence of negativity of any kind, a family may appear to fail even when it has not. A family does not fail because there are deprivations or even difficult problems. Coping effectively with a crisis, or assisting a family member during a time of upheaval, is, in fact, what it means to be family. Even when outside help is needed, the family may still be a *crucible of coping*. A family's success or failure is measured by its ability to cope.

Most families have some regrets that they did not do as well as they could have. Every parent has "What ifs" and "If onlys." Every child, every adolescent, every adult who looks back sees not only what was good, but also what was hard, what was unfair, what was frightening, what was awful in his or her family. No family is perfect. Although most families are good enough, some are damaging or even dangerous to their members. Families risk failure when the conditions for family living make it unsafe or inappropriate for children to be children. When a child cannot be vulnerable while becoming strong, or dependent in the midst of growing autonomy, the family has failed. Such families are usually not very safe for adults either.

The health and welfare of families hinges on a delicate interdependence between family and larger community. Families not only fail when parents or something internal to the family is disturbed or incomplete; families fail because too much is expected of them with too little support. Families alone cannot change the environment in which children are raised. In families where there is chronic illness in the context of inadequate health care or child care, families are at unreasonable risk of failure. In an economy that leaves families in situations of chronic unemployment and underemployment, the family alone cannot struggle successfully against the effects of poverty or financial insecurity. Even families that have enough financial resources at present to support a comfortable lifestyle worry that they are one salary check away from disaster.

Families that are able to shield their children from the effects of a violent culture are lucky more than successful; violence is so pervasive and random that no one family can neutralize it. No one blames parents who want to keep their children safe, but we have not counted the cost of raising children in a state of perpetual hypervigilance. Making our homes armed fortresses will not stop the cycle of violence. It simply domesticates it. Families fail when children are physically injured, threatened with violence, or made witnesses to violence and threat within the family. Families also fail their children and the future of humanity when they do not or cannot help children reject the violence they see.

Our discussion of the failure of families is not meant to blame the family for all that is ailing in society. Nor does it aim to blame parents that their children are troubled. The intent is to examine the failure of families in order to identify the resources they need to succeed. Some of those resources must come from within the family even though external intervention may be necessary to mobilize them. Some resources must come from the society itself and from religious communities that respond to families in ways that will strengthen their sense of well-being and worth. And some of those resources come from children themselves who develop their own strategies for survival.

What Children Need to Survive Their Families

Everyone has at one time or another wondered whether he or she can continue to cope with family living. As we said above, most families are good enough, but some families are dangerous to the well-being of those who live in them. In those families, what children need is not available or is regularly violated. Sometimes the most children can hope for is to survive their families without too much personal damage. Children may survive, even thrive, in family settings that are labeled dysfunctional because they have found sources of strength within themselves. For many children it is enough to know that they are loved by God. The promise that God will not abandon them even when their families do is both sustaining and encouraging. Children also survive destructive or dangerous families if they have advocates on their behalf outside the system. Those advocates help children endure a difficult or even destructive family setting in several ways.

Advocates help a child establish a source of self-esteem outside the family. If the only messages that a child receives in the family are negative, it is necessary to find a source of affirmation outside the home in order to foster self-esteem in the child. Families that insist on conformity as the way of ensuring stability also damage their children by prohibiting difference. Children in those families need to find an outside source that will validate their uniqueness.

Advocates maintain protected channels through which children can make complaints. In families where there is very little freedom to differ or criticize, children need to establish an appropriate way to be critical or simply to make complaints. In the country of Norway, there is a government person whose job it is to hear the complaints of children. Along with providing safe channels for complaint, adults also need to be able to hear the screams of children. Children who know how to scream, literally and figuratively, will not be silent victims.

I was having breakfast one spring morning after retirement when I heard a child screaming. A six-year-old girl was being terrorized by a stray dog and her mother was immobile. Once the dog was on his way and I had been thanked, the mother chided the child for screaming so loudly. I gently reminded the mother that if it had not been for her daughter's good screams, I would still be eating my breakfast and her daughter might have been injured by the dog. (Stanley)

Advocates know the reporting mechanisms and institutional interventions available in a community when there is abuse. This form of advocacy assumes that we are responsible for other people's children. We cannot be of service to a child in need if we do not know the resources of our own communities. The publication of a neighborhood directory of resources could mean the difference between safety and threat for a child.

When there are no advocates on their behalf, children develop their own defenses against violence or abuse within the family. These coping strategies may have a long-term negative effect on the child but they remain a saving grace in the short term. We include them in this chapter not as recommendations for how children should be made to cope, but in recognition of the heroic resilience, adaptability, and strength that childhood possesses.

Children survive because of a capacity to know the implicit rules before breaking them. Children are literalists. They believe what they are told. Children who can anticipate the unspoken rules are less likely to get in trouble. (We will say more about family rules in the next chapter.)

Children are tireless seekers. They search the environment for love and affirmation. They move with determined wonder into other families and relationships in an intuitive search for affection and meaning. Children will cling tenaciously to a memory of how life "could be."

When I was eight, I went on my first overnight to a girlfriend's house. We lived on the same street, and our families were very close. In the morning, after breakfast, I sat watching cartoons with my friend and her two sisters on the sofa in the family room. As their father prepared to leave for work, he came in and kissed them all on the forehead to say goodbye for the day. I was at the end of the line on the sofa and he kissed me too. In my own family there was no kissing or hugging or holding of each other. I held onto that kiss like a treasure, like a tangible sign that families could be places of safe affection. (Wanda)

Despite grave misgivings about and sometimes even fear of their parents, children still love them and want to give their parents freedom to fail. This love and need for love may, of course, make a child vulnerable to abuse or to a willingness to blame himself for what goes wrong in the family. It may also be a window of hope for reconciliation. If children can eventually give their parents freedom to fail, there is a chance that everyone in a family will have new freedom to fail and still belong.

Children come with their needs attached. It is the family's responsibility to respond to those needs in a manner that is appropriate to each age. Families fail when they do not respond to the fundamental needs of children. Regarding the needs of children with respect is a central purpose of the family. There are other meanings for family living that relate primarily to adult needs. They are secondary, however, to the family's task of providing a framework in which children are recognized as fully human and encouraged to discover their own unique gifts as they move toward responsible adulthood.

We have lingered over the needs of children because they are primary. We do not mean to imply that children should get whatever they want. Parents and other caregivers need to be clear about the difference between needs and wants. Children usually confuse them. The needs of children are not static. They change as children mature. Moreover, it is important to recognize that a fourteen-year-old child has different needs than a child of three. Parents have needs as well, and they change. The needs of small children are often not negotiable. The obligation of parents is to accommodate to those needs. As children grow older, the needs of parents and children gain greater parity. Developing just ways of responding to the competing needs of children and parents is one of the themes in the next chapter.

Responding to the Needs of Children

There are three ways to examine family living in response to the needs of children. We must ask first about purpose. What must families do for the sake of children that cannot or should not be done elsewhere? Secondly, we must ask about family form or structure. Does one family structure provide more effectively than any other for the needs of children? This question is linked to purpose in the same way that architects like to suggest that form follows function. If we lose sight of this connection, we are likely to absolutize certain family forms to the exclusion of others at a time when we need greater diversity of structures to accommodate the emerging needs of families. Finally, we ask about what families believe. Beliefs determine the behavior of members or the family as a whole even more than do purposes or structures.

What Should Families Do?

The challenge of a family is to foster the identity and unique worth of each individual member while at the same time preparing children for responsible citizenship in the world. Forming an identity and training for citizenship can never be separated without jeopardizing either the individual or society. The following quote from the United Nations World Summit on Children in 1990 is an articulation of the parallel purposes of individuation and socialization common to all families:

> All children must be given the chance to find their identity and re-alize their worth in a safe and supportive environment, through families and other care-givers committed to their welfare. They must be prepared for responsible life in a free society. They should, from their early years, be encouraged to participate in the cultural life of their societies.[11]

We have chosen to frame our discussion about family purpose with this statement from the United Nations for two reasons: it was written with a global context in mind, and it reflects the paradox of autonomy in community that is basic in this series on family living in pastoral perspective. The goal of individuation is the formation of individuals with enough autonomy to be together in community with other separate and particular persons. The goal of socialization is the creation of communities stable enough to encourage individuation for the sake of autonomy. The twin purposes of socialization and individuation are inextricably linked.

According to ethicist Gilbert Meilaender, the family is in trouble precisely because of confusion about its purpose. The family is failing in its purpose to nurture the next generation "because we have too little commitment to or sense of a story that we might pass on."[12] Meilaender's stress on the family as a historical as well as a biological community leads him to emphasize the socializing purpose of family. Parents commit themselves to "shape, mold, and civilize their children" into a particular understanding of being in the world. Even though other agencies contribute to the socialization of our young, *the family is still the first socializing force.*

> In the nursery school where I teach, I am constantly amazed by the ways in which children imitate what they learn at home. Not long ago, I observed several four-year-olds playing house. Marissa does not look up from making dinner on her pretend

stove when she says, "Don't even think of coming in here with shoes like that. Wash your hands and call your brothers." In the doll corner, Tiffany and Danny were fussing over a doll. "I think it's another ear infection," Danny says, cradling the doll. "I'll call the clinic," sighs five-year-old Tiffany, shaking her head as she picks up the phone. Sara is at the closet and mirror, holding a phone and calling up an invisible staircase. "Do you have the check-book? [Silence.] Check in your pants pocket. I have to go to the store." Back in the play kitchen, a four-year-old father, seated at the table, is saying to the first child: "Wash your hands; you've been playing with the dog."

(Barbara)

As this story illustrates, families socialize even when they do not intend to. The children in Barbara's class had learned their lines at home. It is crucial for the sake of individuals and for the sake of society that the family continue to "prepare children for responsible life in a free society."

When parents fail to attend to this task, schoolteachers spend time teaching children how to blow their noses instead of how to read or write, and then children become adults who have difficulties relating. Schools, both public and private, decry the fact that they must stop instruction in order to teach basic hygiene, personal care, and the fundamentals of community behavior. Parents, on the other side, are often quick to say that the forces socializing children come from outside the home. While there are undoubtedly major socializing factors from outside the home influencing the behavior of children today, the family is still the first place where we are taught how to live with others.

Socialization is not its only purpose, however. The family must also provide an environment safe enough for children to "find their identity and realize their worth." *This process of self-definition or claiming one's own personhood is generally called individuation.* It has to do with developing autonomy, becoming free to differ, valuing one's worth. Forming a separate person capable of participation with others is a family task. That is the focus of the first book in this series, *Leaving Home.* Cutting loose from the emotional moorings of our infancy is a lifelong process that is in the interest of self-definition. The family is the primary context in which and from which this separation occurs.

Family purpose is therefore a paradox. Individuation, as the process of forming a separate self, and socialization, as the way of preparing people to live together responsibly, are *both* necessary purposes of a family that seeks to prepare people to live together responsibly. As we have noted again and again in this series, the vitality of family living depends on keeping that paradox alive. At minimum, the family is responsible for raising up individuals capable of living together in order that another generation will be prepared for the ongoing care and nurture of humankind.

From most religious perspectives, the family has another purpose. It is to be the school for virtue, a domestic church in which daily family living nurtures faithfulness and strengthens its members for service in the world. It is a believing and evangelizing community—a sign and a meeting place of the covenant between God and humankind. *The Apostolic Exhortation on the Family* of Pope John Paul II expresses the view that the family is an evangelizing agent on behalf of building up the reign of God:

> The Christian family, in fact, is the first community called to announce the Gospel to the human person during growth and to bring him or her, through a progressive education and catechesis, to full human and Christian maturity . . . . In fact, as an educating community, the family must help people discern their vocation and accept greater responsibility in the search for greater justice, educating them from the beginning in interpersonal relationships, rich in justice and in love.[13]

While not all religious traditions would understand the family's role in this way, *there is general agreement that the family is a school for virtue.* Martin Luther said it this way: "The greatest good in married life, that which makes all suffering and labor worthwhile, is that God grants offspring and commands that they be brought up to worship and serve him. In all the world this is the noblest and most precious work on earth."[14] The family is a sphere in which God is at work, building on the love that we experience naturally in family relationships and extending that love beyond the family into wider communities of concern.

What Family Structures Work Best?

Two parents are generally better than one. Four eyes see more than two. Two voices can be more authoritative than one. Two genders involved in parenting expand the possibilities for adult modeling. Decisions by two parents (who agree) are more likely to be sustained. For all these reasons, we concur with the common sentiment that a healthy mother-father partnership is most likely to create a financially secure and emotionally stable environment for childrearing. Although the two-parent family may be the optimum context for childrearing, we hold that the single-parent family and other enduring forms of family may also provide what children need. Even two parents are not enough without the support of wider environments. That is what we understand to be the meaning of the popular aphorism "It takes a village to raise a child." We will return to this relationship between the family and its social contexts in chapter 5.

The principles about family structure that undergird this approach to raising children were first articulated by Herbert Anderson in *The Family and Pastoral Care*.[15] In that book, Anderson identified three themes at the center of a theology for family living:

1. *Change and adaptability are indispensable aspects of all life and a sign that God is always making something new.* The capacity of the family to adapt to change is not only one of the reasons the family has endured through human history; it is also a characteristic of each family's life history that encourages the development of individuals. The present diversity in family structure may be experienced as a crisis, but it may also be understood as an instance of God's constant re-creation.

2. *The commitment to interdependence is essential both for the family as an organism in the world and for each particular family unit.* Each family is within itself a mysterious and complex ecosystem that balances autonomy and mutuality. Each family, whatever structure it takes, is linked to a larger environment in a parallel interdependent way.

3. *The pluralism of family structure in our time is not so much an instance of decline as it is an extension of the diversity inherent in the creation that God has labeled good.* The diversity of family structures over history is not just an accommodation to necessity; it is the result of physical, social, and psychological changes that are built into the process of human growth toward maturity. The celebration of diversity within a family is finally for the sake of freedom and creativity.

The focus of this volume is not primarily on structure. In the ongoing debate about form and function, we have chosen to emphasize what families do more than what they look like. For the future, the need is for more rather than less attention to the family in the social and economic contexts of our lives. People say contradictory things about families. For example, we believe that parents know what is best, but they should be arrested if they do not buckle a child's seat belt. The government should not interfere in family life, but unwed fathers should be arrested if they do not pay child support. The family is what the family does. What the family does or at least needs to do is build and maintain a community that fosters human growth. There is a growing consensus that shifts the focus of our attention from structure to function.

We need to keeping asking what characteristics of family living are most likely to enable children and other family members to thrive and grow. We also need to be attentive to the ways in which the form of a family will enhance the fulfillment of its purpose. While having both a father and a mother involved in the childrearing process remains the ideal, a variety of family structures can fulfill the needs that children have for a supportive and protective environment in which they can grow to their full potential as unique individuals and as responsible citizens. In the end, however, neither purpose nor structure is primary. What matters most is what families believe and seek to transmit to the next generation. Helping families discern what it is that they believe is a primary pastoral agenda.

What Do Families Believe?

Every family has a belief system that shapes how it functions as an organism within itself and in relation to its larger social world. In that sense, every family is a believing community. Some of those belief systems are informed by traditional religious teaching. Others are not. Family beliefs are like an assumptive world or operational theology that provides a framework for determining how a family functions and how it evaluates the external forces that act on it. What families believe is important because it affects the choices the families make regarding ways of interacting in the present or goals for the future, the allocation of responsibility and power, and the accumulation and distribution of wealth.

Beliefs that have the most power to affect family choices or patterns of interaction are seldom expressed explicitly and thus affect a family's life in an unchallenged way. Most families have sayings or maxims instead that become bearers of their belief system. These sayings may be unique to a family's mythology or they may have their origin in common usage, but they have become "family maxims" by functioning within the system to reinforce a belief or a rule.

My father had a number of sayings that were against pride. He would remind us often that "pride goeth before a fall." And if that didn't work, he would remind us—and mostly me—that all praise goes to the Lord. And then when someone would fall from a pedestal of any kind, he would say with some satisfaction, "*Sic transit gloria mundi*" [so passes the glory of this world]. The rule in the family was clear. Don't be proud. The myth was equally obvious. We were not to be a prideful family. The power of family sayings is illustrated by the fact that to this day, it is still difficult for me to take appropriate pride in what I do.   (Herbert)

The beliefs and rules in Herbert's family are quite clear—do not be proud. When the values of the system are so transparent, they may even be carried in rules posted on the refrigerator door or sustained by the rituals but never debated.

A maxim or saying is, however, the most direct window into a family's system of beliefs about itself and its world. Consider some of these maxims, for example, as bearers of family beliefs:

> If wishes were horses, then beggars would ride.
> It costs only a little more to go first class.
> If you can't pay cash for it, you don't need it.
> You can laugh your way to hell, but you can't laugh your way out.
> You are either part of the problem or part of the solution.
> Halitosis is better than no breath at all.
> Things without all remedy must be without regard.
> Talk is cheap, but it takes money to buy whiskey.
> Every tub must sit on its own bottom.

This last saying is attributed to a Norwegian grandmother who has been fiercely independent all her life. Now, at ninety-eight, she lives alone and cannot understand why her grandchildren are not independent as well. Self-sufficiency is a belief that is frequently promoted by family sayings. The problem with self-sufficiency, as Pamela Couture has reminded us in her book *Blessed Are the Poor?*, is that it covers over the interconnection between individuals, families, social institutions and the government necessary to foster human life.[16]

The "self-protecting family" is another pattern, like self-sufficiency, that is isolating and does not promote interdependence. Sayings like "Don't hang out your dirty laundry" or "Whatever happens in this family stays in this family" or "Outside this house it's a dog-eat-dog world" or "Always wear underwear" promote caution and diminish trust in anyone or anything outside the family. The negative consequences of these family belief systems are the same: they foster isolation and discourage interaction between the family and its environment.

Maxims are frequently used to remind members not to bring shame on the family. After all, it is often said, "What will the neighbors think?" Children are taught through these sayings that hard work and good behavior are rewarded. They are also reminded to stay in their place: "Little pitchers have big ears," or they are humiliated, "An empty wagon makes the most noise," as a means of control. It is alarming how many family sayings seek control by diminishing the self-esteem of children or others.

Not all family beliefs promote self-sufficiency or isolation or diminish self-esteem. A saying like "Have you ever seen a hearse with a U-Haul trailer?" discourages greed. One might assume that a family with a saying like "You can eat with only one spoon at a time" would not only discourage greed but encourage charity. "He'd bring home a stray elephant if it looked hungry" celebrates generosity in an odd sort of way. Other family sayings like "If you can't say something good about someone, don't say anything at all" promote such values as fairness or kindness.

Most families (and other human systems) are unaware of the implicit beliefs or values that govern their operations. Sometimes it is enough that families make explicit the beliefs that have been implicit in maxims. The family will make its own changes in what it believes. In other circumstances, it may be necessary to help families discover the deeper truths of their lives. Those who care for families may need to insist on "saying the other side" in order to initiate changing family beliefs. Helping families discern their beliefs is an exercise in theological reflection. That process of reflection evaluates operational family beliefs according to some vision of Christian living in families. In the next chapter, we will consider hospitality, compassion, justice, and reconciliation as elements in one expression of a normative Christian vision for family living.

4

CHRISTIAN THEMES FOR FAMILY LIVING

EVERYONE HAS some kind of picture of what we would like families to be. It may be a family picnic in a park or an elderly couple holding hands or parents cuddling their kids in a church pew or people working quietly at separate tasks in safety and comfort under the same roof. Perhaps it is a picture of relatives gathered for a barbecue by the lake or children coming home for the holidays or the smell of gumbo cooking in Mama's kitchen.

> I have been divorced for ten years but I still have in my head a picture of a man and a woman and their two children seated at a dinner table. The man is never more than 35 and tall. The woman not more than 33 and small. The children are clean and the roast chicken with gravy is not dried out. In the picture, they never speak, so there is no possibility of conflict.   (Luanda)

There is considerable power in the myths we hold about what families ought to be or what we would like them to be. We want our homes to be happy and well-functioning. We would like our families to be attentive to our needs without asking too much in return. We hope that they will be supportive but not confining. And we are frequently disappointed because the families in which we live seldom match the pictures in our heads.

Our intent throughout this book is to encourage families who are struggling to do the best they know how to do. In so doing, we have tried to strike a middle way between families as they are and families as they ought to be. Some families, it is true, are seriously dysfunctional and dangerous for the people who live in them. It is possible, though not probable, that a few families are nearly perfect even for those living in them. Most families, however, muddle through, hoping not to do too much harm and maybe even some good. They are neither impoverished nor flawless. They are simply good enough. While such families regularly fall short of their ideal, they are still able to honor childhood and provide support good enough to nurture the people who live in them.

What Makes a Family "Good Enough"?

It is difficult in human matters to keep a balance between things as they are and things as they ought to be. If we emphasize "things as they are" in order to be understanding, we may unwittingly reinforce the status quo by undermining the possibility of imagining change. On the other hand, too much stress on the normative may discourage people by mandating possibilities beyond their imagination. When this struggle between the "is" and "ought" is applied to family living, the metaphor of "the good enough family" is a gracious word. We introduce it here as a reminder that most families are neither dysfunctional nor perfect. They are simply good enough.[1]

Each family develops in ways that are shaped by the legacies it has received from its own origins. Each family is also influenced by its own cultural particularity, its moment in the life cycle, and its image of an ideal family. A "good enough family" is less than its own ideal and yet competent enough to raise reasonably adequate children. In order to do that, a family needs to fulfill two basic tasks: nurture its children into psychologically healthy adults, who then leave the family to make commitments of their own; and strengthen the personalities of the parents, encouraging them in their continued growth as individuals and in their relationship.

The family is a constantly evolving reality. Change is the norm. Sometimes the structure of a family changes. At other times, the roles or rules or rituals that regulate interaction are modified. In that sense, the family is always becoming good enough. Our use of the "good enough" metaphor is meant not to foster complacency about family incompetence or destructiveness or undercut the necessity of norms. It is, rather, a reminder that when we stop expecting perfection, we may discover that more families are good enough after all.

Our insistence that most families are good enough does not eliminate the necessity for a normative vision. We need some kind of moral map or ideal in order to engage in critical reflection about any experience of living. Without a route, Joel Anderson has observed, "there is no getting lost; but if there is no possibility of being lost, one isn't really anywhere at all."[2] That observation is not far from the biblical axiom "Where there is no vision, the people perish" (Prov. 29:18, KJV). Family living is no exception. We do not sketch maps in order to roll them up and beat ourselves with them. Rather, we use maps to discover where we are and whether where we are is good enough. A Christian vision for family living should not add to the powerlessness or guilt people feel already for having failed to achieve their ideal picture. It should rather empower families to move toward a new future.

A Theology for Family Living

Our intent in this chapter is to develop a theology for the family that might be such a vision for living in our times. We begin by asking what Christians bring from their tradition as a whole that is of relevance for living in a family. We do not, therefore, limit our exploration to what the Bible says specifically about family life or what the church has taught concerning family problems. Rather, we are free to develop themes from the Christian tradition in general that might be beneficial for family living in particular. This is what we mean by a theology *for* the family rather than a theology *of* the family.[3] We have selected hospitality, compassion, justice, and reconciliation as four themes from the tradition that have relevance for family living today. These qualities are not exhaustive of the resources of the tradition nor are they uniquely Christian, but they are distinctively enriched by the Judeo-Christian vision of living with others.

The vision for family living we propose is not limited to one particular structure. It applies to families without children, single-parent families, and families of second marriages, as well as more traditional nuclear and extended families. We believe this diversity of family form is inevitable because needs vary and because creation is unfinished. We celebrate the diversity of family patterns, not because difference is easy, but because it is real. Diversity is the consequence of freedom and creativity. No one form of the family will meet all our needs for a place to discover our gifts and prepare for responsible citizenship in society. But every family, in order to be good enough, needs a vision.

In articulating this vision, we hope to identify the qualities of family living that honor the full humanity of children and the childness of adulthood. Because it is impossible in one chapter or even in one book to do justice to the ways families must be and become in order to attend to the changing needs of children, we can only suggest in broad strokes what families must make concrete and particular. Moreover, the disrespect toward children we have already identified is rooted in and sustained by social patterns of injustice, hostility, and disrespect. The transformation of society's attitude toward children will affect the family most deeply when it is a fundamental human agenda. What the church contributes to this transformation is a vision of family living that is shaped by the Christian understanding of hospitality, compassion, justice, and reconciliation.

The Family Is a Hospitable Community

In many parts of the ancient world, showing hospitality to strangers was a law of the land. Wayside inns were scarce. It was more than a courtesy to welcome the stranger at your gate; it was a sacred obligation and a matter of survival. Not surprisingly, therefore, the biblical writers include hospitality when they list the virtues of faithful living. Along with loving in a genuine way, outdoing one another in showing honor, and being patient in suffering, the apostle Paul admonishes the Christians in Rome to "extend hospitality to strangers" (Rom. 12:13). The writer of the letter to the Hebrews adds a bonus to this admonition. Sometimes those who have shown hospitality to strangers have "entertained angels without knowing it" (Heb. 13:2).

We mostly think of the stranger as a "foreigner" or "alien" or "sojourner" from another country. Such strangers in our lives evoke fear or fascination because of their difference. If the difference is too great, however, we may determine that the stranger is also dangerous. Sometimes the stranger is an enemy. In a wider sense, though, the stranger is anyone who is not me. Therefore, the stranger who is "other to me" could be child or spouse or neighbor. Hospitality to the stranger is any act by which we honor the "otherness" of another human being. For that reason, ethicist Thomas W. Ogeltree has put welcoming the stranger at the center of the moral life.[4]

When we offer hospitality to a stranger, Ogeltree suggests, we welcome something new, unfamiliar, and unknown into our lives that has the potential to expand our world. The process of welcoming the stranger begins by recognizing his or her "otherness." The stranger has a story to tell that may transform our world of meaning. This attitude toward the "other" has global consequences. The theologian Kosuke Koyama has observed that "the only way open to us to stop the violence of genocide in our world is by 'extending hospitality to strangers.'"[5] Doing so is the essence of the Christian gospel. It may also be necessary for survival in a pluralistic age. If everyone is a stranger in the sense of being an "other," then no one is a stranger anymore. It is the same for childhood. As young Barry said to his pastor, "If everyone is a child, then no one would hurt children anymore."

When the Stranger Is Our Child

The infant born into a family is "flesh of flesh" and therefore does not seem alien. Particularly for the mother, the infant hardly seems a stranger as it moves from being "my body" to "child of me." Even so, mothers often admit they do not know the child they are nursing. In the early process of development, regardless, the child must become an "other" and so a stranger, even to the mother. What Ogeltree says about regard for strangers must therefore be applied to our attitude toward children. "Regard for strangers in their vulnerability and delight in their novel offerings presupposes that we perceive them as equals, as persons who share our common humanity in its myriad variations."[6] When we think of our children as strangers in this sense, we have yet another reason to respect their full humanity.

If we begin with the assumption that adults and children share a common humanity with myriad variations, then we will honor the "otherness" of our child from the beginning. We will welcome that child who is "stranger" because we believe that he or she has a story to tell we have not yet heard. Regarding our child as stranger is a prelude to recognizing his or her uniqueness. This perspective is essential if we are to create a space in which children are free to grow. Honoring the child as a person of equal worth who has a story to tell is a necessary precondition for developing autonomy and fostering self-esteem.

The characteristics of hospitality essential for welcoming a child continue throughout a family's history. Providing space in which children grow and flourish is very much like showing hospitality to strangers. When children bring home friends who are different or ideas that are strange, the limits of family hospitality are tested. When families are unable to welcome or at least receive new people and ideas, adolescent children may need to leave home in order to find a context hospitable enough to do the kind of personal exploration that is part of forming an identity. When children who have left home return for a visit, they may bring with them strange ideas or persons to whom they are attached. Eventually, they may marry persons who are more different than parents expect, and bring grandchildren to visit who are wonderful strangers.

In order to be hospitable, a family needs to be open to change. No family is infinitely flexible, however. Every family has a limit to its tolerance of diversity. Families that regard difference as dangerous will have more difficulty welcoming strangers. Families are also likely to struggle with being a hospitable community if they regard diversity as antithetical to community. It is certain that families need to have standards about behaviors and beliefs, about what they will "let into the house" and what they will not. *One of the beliefs that determines how well families function, however, is about "showing hospitality to strangers."*

> When he was 13, my brother Jeff would wear only two shirts. And he only liked one kind of pants. My mother simply told him he'd have to do his own laundry. When he refused to cut his hair and wore a ponytail, she said as long as it was clean, she didn't care. He put posters of rock groups on the walls in his room and his mattress on the floor. He had Christmas lights around his window all year long, but all my mother said was: "You need a place to do your homework. It's your room." When Jeff's weird friends would come over, they would look in his room and say, "Your mom is really cool," and Jeff would shrug and say, "She's all right, I guess."
>
> (Liz)

Jeff was fortunate and, we suspect, eventually so was Liz. Their mother was able to "entertain" different and (probably to her) weird behavior and at the same time maintain standards of conduct that were essential. In this instance, the biblical admonition to "show hospitality to strangers" confirms one of the common characteristics of effective family living: *recognize difference and honor diversity.*

As a vision for family living, hospitality is likely to be increasingly important *and* difficult as societies become more pluralistic. Neighbors are no longer ethnic kin or religious companions. They are strangers in many senses of the word. The diversity that is part of the larger society is experienced in families also as interracial and interfaith marriages become more common. Children will adopt ways of thinking and acting very different from what they were taught. Because pluralism is likely to increase in almost every society, hospitality is no longer just a religious ideal—it is a human necessity. In a paradoxical way, the family's ability to be hospitable to difference depends on having clear but permeable boundaries.

Boundaries That Are Clear but Permeable

A cohesive family identity is established by clear but permeable boundaries that mark its particular membership but do not close off interaction among members within the system or between the family system and its environments. *A boundary is not a wall but an invisible separation that distinguishes between the parts or members of a system or among the units of a larger ecosystem.* Good boundaries are necessary for roles and functions within a family to be both specialized and interdependent. Clear and permeable boundaries also make it possible for families to entertain diverse ideas and to make room for the stranger without feeling (or being) overwhelmed. Without clear boundaries, it is difficult for a family to foster enough autonomy among its members so that they are comfortable with diversity.

> My sister Julie and I were born ten months apart. We were soul mates who shared clothes, books, friends, and a bedroom. When we went to art classes at the local community center, my work was noticed by the teachers. Although Julie was not artistic at all, my parents told everyone we were both talented. I decided to go away to art school while Julie lived at home and commuted to college. It was not easy for anyone in our family. Fortunately, I met Richard. He liked me and he liked my artwork. One weekend he turned his apartment into a makeshift gallery and had a mock "opening show" for me. Eventually I was able to become a person separate from my sister and my mother. What is sad for me today is that no one in my family has seen what I have painted or what I have become. (Jennifer)

A family without boundaries, like the one Jennifer came from, may appear to be close-knit. Its members may think alike, enjoy being together often, share closets and sweaters and bathrooms easily, and hold emotions in common. If someone in a family without boundaries is depressed, everyone is depressed. Unanimity is synonymous with love and happiness. However, when the boundaries are unclear, freedom to be separate or different is limited. So is hospitality. The environment of a family without clear boundaries is neither free nor hospitable. It is a private place closed to the world outside.

There is another kind of family, in which the boundaries within the system are rigidly defined in order to ensure the independence of all members. This is a family with a "closed-door" policy on almost anything. Each individual's own ideas, thoughts, emotions, "emotional space," or jars of peanut butter are fiercely protected within the system.

Within the family, the boundaries are more like impenetrable walls. Family members lack the kind of emotional closeness that is necessary to sustain a community and nourish individual growth in community. Yet, in relation to the outside world, the family gives every appearance of being a welcoming place. Sometimes, in fact, the boundaries between the family and its outside environment are so porous it is difficult to maintain a sense of identity for the family as a system. The family becomes a public place without identity. It may welcome the world, but internally children are neglected and its members are isolated from one another.

Hospitality in Inhospitable Worlds

Boundaries create a space in which it is safe to be intimate. It is crucial that we accept that role of boundaries in our lives as good law. Nevertheless, because the worlds in which we live are not always safe, we are sometimes tempted to make boundaries into walls that separate the family from its environment. When that happens, hospitality suffers. Children must be told not to take candy from strangers and not to speak to people they do not know. They need to know that hospitality *from* strangers may be a dangerous thing. Because the world has become a frightening place for adults as well as children, some families are prompted to pull the shades, unplug the TV, screen carefully who or what comes into the family and control where people go when they leave, and make home into a well-defended cocoon, isolated from its environment.

Because of developments in communicative technology, it is increasingly difficult to make boundaries around our homes that are impermeable to outside influence. For that reason, families need to create an environment that is able to entertain a wide variety of beliefs and behavior, but in a critical fashion. When children are young, it is obviously necessary to do whatever is possible to limit their exposure to material that they are not yet cognitively able to process. However, children need to learn how to discern differences in beliefs and conflicts in values earlier than we once thought they could. The practice of talking things through and thinking aloud about material that violates a family's system of values becomes an essential aspect of a family that is a hospitable community.

Sometimes the world outside is not the only place of danger. We are increasingly aware that our homes are not always safe for women and children. Boundaries are violated whenever children are emotionally *or* sexually *or* physically abused. Boundaries are violated when women are forced to engage in sexual intercourse against their will. Boundaries are also violated when sons and daughters alike are expected to function in ways inappropriate to their age and vulnerability. We need boundaries to protect ourselves from people inside and outside the family. We cannot do without them.

Boundaries may prevent violence but they do not generate the respect needed to sustain enduring relationships. Learning to "show hospitality to the stranger" is necessary to transform our attitudes toward the "other" from indifference or neglect to respect. Boundaries are a structural necessity, but hospitality is a moral mandate. When we welcome a child, we not only honor an "other" who comes as a vulnerable gift with a story to tell; we enter into a reciprocal relationship in which the child who is "stranger" and guest will also be friend and host and the parent the guest. It is this quality of reciprocity that transforms the family from a company of strangers to a community of shared meanings.

The Family Is a Compassionate Community

A family shaped by Christian principles will not only honor the uniqueness of every "other" within its system. It will also be characterized by mutual compassion. If boundaries keep the parts of a family system separate, compassion reminds us that we belong to one another in enduring ways. Compassion is therefore an essential component of a Christian vision for family living because it recognizes the interdependence of all living things. The family is a compassionate community because it cares for the most vulnerable ones in our midst—children, persons who are handicapped, and the elderly. No quality of family living is any more important for building a community than learning how to suffer with one another.

> We had so much trouble becoming a family. Doug and I knew we had our work cut out for us when we adopted a brother and sister who had been in foster care. They lived with us for two years without trusting us. Whenever I offered Anita a gift or even a cookie, her eyes would check with her brother, Jason, to see if it was OK. Whenever we put her to bed, Jason would tuck Anita in all over again. Jason hid food so that he would never have to ask us for anything for himself. Then, one day, he fell off his bicycle. I saw him fall from the kitchen window. He came running into the house and into my arms. I cleaned up his skinned knees and elbows. Even the tip of his nose was scuffed. Later that evening,

> and for two more days, Jason milked his injuries for all they were worth. He sat on our laps to watch television and demanded ice cream. He pretended to fall asleep on the sofa so that Doug would carry him to bed. Jason trusted us to be compassionate when he was vulnerable and we did not fail him. That's when we became a family. (Mellicent)

A family is a compassionate community when it responds with tenderness to the least fortunate or most vulnerable in its membership without blaming them, humiliating them, or diminishing their identity. The compassion of Mellicent and Doug preceded and followed Jason's trust when he was vulnerable. Compassion is essential for effective family living. It is also a reflection and extension of God's care.

The Womb of God

Compassion has many meanings in the Hebrew tradition. It conveys a sense of cherishing or soothing as well as pity and a gentle attitude of mind. The same word is used to describe the tender love of God toward humankind *and* the love of parents toward their children. "As a father has compassion for his children, so the Lord has compassion for those who fear him" (Ps. 103:13). God's compassion is like a mother's as well as a father's: "Can a woman forget her nursing child, or show no compassion for the child of her womb? Even these may forget, yet I will not forget you" (Isa. 49:15). For Old Testament theologian Dianne Bergant, God's compassion is more than emotion. "As the womb brings to birth life with all of its possibilities, so divine compassion brings to rebirth life that was threatened or perhaps even lost."[7] God's compassion is creative as well as comforting, intimate as well as protecting.

Jesus exemplified God's compassion as he moved among those who suffered from illness, pain, poverty, loss, and disability. *Compassion* is the word used often in the New Testament to describe the deep-seated emotion evoked in Jesus by the desperate plight of the people who came to him. He listened to them, sometimes silencing the harshness of others. He touched them, even those like the lepers, who had been deemed untouchable. He was moved by compassion to heal them. The compassion of Jesus is a sign of the reign of God. Compassion is therefore not an optional virtue for the Christian or for a vision of Christians living in families.

The compassion of God provides a pattern for Christians to follow and a standard against which to measure their lives. To have compassion as Jesus did is to feel intensely the pain, the hurt, the sorrow, the brokenness of another. To show compassion is "to cry out with those in misery, to mourn with those who are lonely, to weep with those in tears. . . . Compassion means full immersion in the condition of being human."[8] We are drawn back to Bergant's image of the womb of God. Compassion is the unifying dynamic of God's love that reminds us we have all come from the same womb. In turn, we are challenged to a way of living that is as compassionate as God is compassionate.

Compassionate Empathy

The biblical understanding of compassion is particularly important for developing a vision of family living that is sensitive to human vulnerability. We have already noted that our inability to acknowledge the childness that continues in adulthood is one source of indifference toward children. When we enter into the world of other family members, we will feel their pain and share their joy. A family is a compassionate community when all aspects of the human situation are dignified by kind and gentle care.

Compassion should not be confused with the desire to fix the trouble or eliminate the pain. Empathy with another's sorrow is itself a gift. Compassion may lead to impatience or an unhealthy sense of grief if our desire to relieve pain becomes primary. Gentle hearing of one another is enough. Nonetheless, we will not overlook the struggles of those we love. Nor are we free to ignore the effects of our actions on others. Each one is affected by the actions of the other, and by the woundedness of the other. In such a context, our suffering is never simply a private, individual matter. It is systemic in its origins and in its consequences. We are never alone in our pain.

The family respects the uniqueness of each member and it suffers with each one who suffers. This is the paradox of compassionate empathy. It is important for the sake of family living that compassion begin with recognizing the uniqueness of the "other." Otherwise compassion is easy sympathy or even pity that is condescending. We use the language of empathy to describe our efforts to respect the uniqueness of another person. We use the language of compassion to articulate a vision of the family as a "community of the suffering ones." Our willingness to suffer with others makes concrete the admonition of the apostle Paul that "those who live might live no longer for themselves, but for him who died and was raised for them" (2 Cor. 5:15). This is the mystery of being a compassionate community. Because we share in

God's compassion, we live with one another as fully and intimately as God lives with us.

The Needs for Compassion throughout the Life Cycle

The family as a compassionate community is a place of abiding solidarity in which each one has a sympathetic awareness of the vulnerabilities of the other and a commitment to care for the other. Like hospitality, compassion is a quality necessary for family living throughout its history. The following moments in a family's life illustrate the ongoing need for compassion.

The first test of compassion in a family ordinarily occurs *when a newborn cries through the night* or through the day for reasons unknown to the parents or caretakers. The growing number of children who are killed in order to stop their crying is an alarming sign of the absence of both empathy and compassion.

The birth of a child with a severe handicap is the source of deep sadness and it evokes abiding compassion. The child born handicapped is permanently vulnerable. Sometimes, however, the care of a child who is developmentally disabled mandates more affection and compassion than parents have to give.

A pregnant teenage daughter needs the compassion of her parents. It is too late for discipline or even lectures on being careful. Gentle listening and compassionate empathy are needed to understand the daughter's plight without condemnation.

Mothers and fathers feel intensely the pain and struggle of children as they grow up in a very complex world. *A teenager's suicide attempt* is so terrifying for everyone in the family that sometimes compassion is covered over by feelings of guilt or anger.

Husbands and wives are moved by the anguish each feels in *the world of work*. When the work that one does is corroded by a dehumanizing environment, it becomes a matter of survival for the family to be a compassionate haven. Sometimes, however, there is not enough compassion for all the pain people feel.

No situation challenges a family's capacity to be compassionate more than to have *a loved one dying of AIDS*. When families have become a place of care for a person with AIDS, they have often discovered a depth of compassion in their life together theretofore untouched.

When grown children have trouble in their marriages, parents worry. Even if they determine wisely not to interfere in the marital conflict, a parent's heart still aches when a daughter or son suffers and grandchildren have divided loyalties.

To have a spouse or a parent with Alzheimer's disease is an awkward and agonizing struggle for middle-aged sons and daughters. It is difficult to continue being compassionate toward a parent who has become a stranger.

Several of the situations described above press the edges of our compassion. Empathy is essential for family living, but compassion without limits can be problematic. The nuclear family is a finite community with limits. The needs of one child, no matter how genuine, cannot indefinitely supersede the care of other children in the family. When families ignore the necessary limits of compassion or provide indiscriminate compassion, they may unwittingly foster unhealthy patterns of dependency in everyone. In contexts where the extended family is a functioning reality, the resources may be greater but the need for compassion with common sense and prudence is no less. As with hospitality, compassion must respect the boundaries we give each other; one person's compassion may compromise another person's dignity.

The Family Is a Just Community

It is justice, in the Christian tradition, that preserves the integrity of the individual and community by modifying compassion and hospitality. When justice is embodied within a family, it affects the way such a community functions in three particular ways.

1. *A family is a just community when all members, including children, are given equal respect and consideration.* This is the logical consequence of regarding children as fully human. Because children have full citizenship in the family, the respect for privacy adult family members expect is granted to children as well. If the family is a just community, the rules about hitting or interrupting or lying are applied to adults and children equally. When families are governed by the principles of justice, everyone is entitled to the information necessary to make responsible decisions; therefore secrecy erodes justice in the family. Power is distributed differently in a family in which there is a commitment to justice for everyone. If a family is just, it will be a community in which there is mutual respect, in which expectations are explicit, in which no individual's needs and desires dominate, and in which authority is not arbitrary.

2. *The just family is a community of moral inquiry.* This is the second consequence of being committed to making families just communities. It is true that a family teaches justice by being just. Parents teach children values by the way they value children. They also teach values by how they decide to spend money or participate in recycling projects.

But there is more. It is increasingly difficult for children and adults alike to make moral decisions because our choices are more and more ambiguous. The family becomes a community of moral inquiry when everyone old enough to participate is included in a decision that has ethical weight. The principle of reciprocity that is part of hospitality provides a helpful reminder that children may also teach parents about what is just. A child's sense of justice is a voice that needs to be heard in family deliberations.[9]

3. *The family is a just community when it acts as a moral agent.* It has been said that the ultimate reason why people live together is so that they might do something together. It may be something as simple as the daily sorting of bottles and cans and paper for recycling. Or it may be a family activity that takes the needs of other families as seriously as one's own. Families are more likely to commit themselves to projects in society or in the world if they regard the needs and desires of other families as equal to their own.[10]

> I have spent the last three Thanksgivings serving turkey at a homeless shelter because it is too far for me to go home. Some friends had me over one Thanksgiving, but it wasn't the same. As long as I can remember, my mother and father would invite every lost soul at church to our home for Thanksgiving. When we were teenagers, my brother and I called it "Losers Day," which always evoked a speech from my mother (seconded by my father). Sometimes I think my brother and I complained just to hear our parents explain to us again how this was not our table, it was God's table and we just happened to be sitting at it. Now it seems that the only Thanksgiving table that is right for me is the kind my parents always set: God's table with whomever happens to sit down at it.   (Martin)

If we are to maintain families in which fathers and mothers and children alike have opportunities to develop their gifts and pursue their dreams, in which moral dilemmas are openly debated, and in which acting justly is a family activity, then everyone will need to learn the art of accommodation for the sake of justice. It requires personal sacrifice in order to be a just parent *and* a just child. If the family is to be a community in which care is justly provided, then it must also be a place where criticism is evenly offered and rules are enforced equally.

Understanding What It Means to Do Justice

The prophet Micah reminds us, in a passage that by itself provides a vision for family living, that justice is something we do because it is what God does.

> He has told you, O mortal, what is good;
> and what does the Lord require of you
> but to do justice, and to love kindness,
> and to walk humbly with your God?
> (Mic. 6:8)

The context of this passage is a time in Israel's history when power was being centralized in the urban, military, industrial establishment in Jerusalem. Micah was a voice *from below* on behalf of those who had become voiceless. He has identified the distortions and abuse of power and then here proposes this splendid summary of faithful living: love kindness, do justice, and walk humbly with God.

The Old Testament theologian Walter Brueggemann understands a biblical view of justice in this way: "Justice is to sort out what belongs to whom, and to return it to them."[11] There is therefore a dynamic, transformative quality to justice. Those who work for justice cause things to change and expect things to change so that people might live abundantly. When anything is alienated from those to whom it belongs, there is trouble. Because there is trouble and injustice in the world and things are not always where they belong, change for the sake of redemption means "giving things back."

The ethicist Karen Lebacqz has argued in a similar way that justice is a process of restoration. It is, therefore, an ongoing human necessity. Underlying justice as an act of restoration is a particular vision that incorporates for Lebacqz "the exodus image of liberation, the rainbow image of covenant, the jubilee image of new beginnings, and the christological image of identification with the poor and the oppressed."[12] The image of covenant reflects the expectation that people and things will be where they belong. Giving things back is a way of redeeming or restoring the covenants in which we live.

This image of justice as restoration has immediate implications for our understanding of the family as a just community. It presupposes the necessity of boundaries in order to establish and maintain "what belongs to whom." It assumes the mutual recognition of "otherness" that is fundamental for being hospitable. And it builds on an abiding solidarity of relationships held together ultimately in the womb of God's compassion. When justice is added to a Christian vision for family living, we are summoned to give back what does not belong to us, cancel debts, honor each gift, and redistribute power.

When Family Rules and Roles Are Just

There are many aspects of family interaction for which justice is an essential virtue. (1) Children need discipline that is consistent and expectations that are age-appropriate. (2) The distribution and redistribution of power in a balanced way is an ongoing need. (3) Especially at the beginning of marriage, couples are sorting out which family of origin has the most influence. (4) The more options individuals have from which to choose, the more critical it is that some process be in place to ensure justice for everyone. We have chosen rules and roles as two aspects of family living to illustrate the need for justice.

The rules that govern a family's interaction need to be explicit and unambiguous enough to minimize the effects of human sinfulness and wrongdoing, but also flexible enough not to violate the integrity of individuals or the needs of the system. Such rules will have bonding power as well as governing power. The power of family rules to reinforce the family's bonds is dependent on the following factors. The rules must be (1) flexible enough to take into account the differing circumstances and changing needs of persons as they grow older; (2) visible enough so that everyone knows there *are* rules and that *these* are what they are; and (3) consistent enough in their application for both parents and children. It is difficult to insist on the importance of keeping rules that parents continue to break.

One of the ways in which families maintain arbitrary, and therefore unjust, authority is to keep rules hidden. Covert rules, like covert belief systems, have excessive power because they are not subject to critique or available for negotiation. Making explicit family rules that have been hidden or implicit becomes an act of restorative justice by taking back for the family as a whole what has been kept in private by the rulekeeper.

My brother and sister and I would fight a lot. And whenever we would fight, my mother would make up a new rule. We had rules about sharing all toys, rules about television, rules about Dad's favorite chair, rules about doors to bedrooms, rules about almost everything. But I don't remember a single rule we actually had to obey. Except this unspoken one: you must not make Mother cry. When we were squabbling, she would walk through the room with her hand over her face, saying, "I just can't stand it. I try so hard to raise a nice family." Sometimes she would cry on the phone to Dad at work, but whenever she cried, as soon as she started to cry, we would stop fighting. The first time my wife cried after we

> were married, I got in the car and drove away for two hours. I
> hated it when my mother would cry. (DeQuan)

Rules that are just are developmentally determined. They change as the needs change. Rules that are aimed at ensuring the safety of children are necessary in the beginning but less significant as children grow older. Sometimes the needs of children require personal sacrifice on the part of parents for the sake of justice. Sometimes children need to learn to wait while the needs or desires of parents are satisfied. In the end, however, we believe that families would be better off with fewer rules more consistently enforced. Too often families seek to resolve a crisis, as DeQuan's mother did, with another rule. Whenever we consider family rules, it is important to remember one theological truth: neither individuals nor families are saved by rules.

Families function best when the roles are clear and flexible and there is general awareness that the roles are never more important than the people who fill them. Every human system has assigned parts or roles. Some of these roles are structural. Some have to do with presumed gender-specific behavior. Families that seek for justice will work toward redefining family roles in such a way that all the members have freedom to develop their gifts and pursue their dreams. Other roles are more dynamic or emotional and have to do with the parts people play to keep the family system functioning as a human community. Generally, these emotional roles are assigned in ways that are not easily identified. A family is not likely to be a just community if emotional roles are fixed and not evenly distributed.

These emotional, or dynamic, family roles belong to the system as a whole. Therefore it is an act of restorative justice in a family if a role such as "the responsible one" or "the peacemaker" is taken from one individual and given back to the family as a whole. A family that seeks justice will work for an equal and flexible distribution of emotional roles in which everyone will have a turn at being naughty or righteous or klutzy or playful or even a little crazy. When a family locks people into particular emotional roles, it acts unjustly and may even sacrifice one of its members to keep things as they are. Such was the case for Marybeth and her family.

> Because my father traveled a lot, much of my childhood was
> spent taking care of my alcoholic mother. It was actually better
> when my father was away because he was very domineering.
> When I was a sophomore in high school, I began worrying about

what would happen to my mother when I went away to college. She refused all requests to get help. So did my father. I was so desperate that I took an overdose of sleeping pills and then called the therapist I had been seeing secretly. The police arrived along with an ambulance just in time to break up another fight between my parents. I recall feeling extremely guilty, not because I had tried to harm myself but because I had exposed a family secret. My outburst did little to change anything except to make my isolation worse. (Marybeth)

Families that seek justice regularly struggle to keep in balanced proportion the needs of the community and the needs of individuals. The roles that are necessary in order to maintain the organism as a whole (which often limit individual choice or personal autonomy) must be kept in paradoxical tension with the freedom for self-determination of family members (which may conflict with the organism's needs). Keeping alive the paradoxes of family living is one expression of restorative justice.

Our best efforts to establish the family as a just community will not fully succeed. The family is a flawed institution. Most parents are good enough, not perfect. It is important to realize that parents need only to be adequate to the task of training and nurturing in order to raise reasonably adequate children. Sometimes we cannot give back to children and women what is taken from them through abuse in the family. Most of the time, however, the mistakes that parents make can be remedied, even when we think they cannot.

Justice must therefore be coupled with reconciliation in families shaped by the Christian tradition, even as justice itself is nourished by compassion and hospitality. It is easy to forget the gospel vision of new beginnings in the daily routine of bills and dirty dishes and leaky faucets, nosy neighbors, cranky children, aging parents. Therefore, families should endeavor to find ways to imagine a peaceable kingdom in which the lion and the lamb can lie down together, where children do not bicker, parents do not fight. Many families do that imaginative, re-creative work only rarely, packing it into the expectations of a vacation or holiday. A regular pattern of worship as a family, family meetings, or being together for simple evenings at home are appropriate and manageable ways for families to imagine how they would like to be.

The Family Is a Reconciling Community

It has been said that the family is where we are most clearly known to be sinners "in the particular." In a family it is known when one member is painfully fastidious, hopelessly messy, crabby when overtired, or perpetually late. It is also known when one has been abusive or manipulative, cowardly or mean-spirited, careless or selfish, violent, untrustworthy, or just plain lazy. Family is not only the place that has to take one in; it is also the place where it is known full well who it is that is coming through the door.

Because it is so difficult to hide our sinfulness in the family, it is a community where forgiveness and reconciliation are both longed for and resisted. We long to be understood and accepted by those whom we love despite our faults and transgressions. We long to feel love for them despite their faults which have divided us from them. Yet, because family bonds are so emotionally intense, because they are so formative of us at our best and at our worst, because family is not only a sanctuary from the world but also a crucible in which we probe and prepare our relationship to the world, the family is a hard place to find forgiveness and to be forgiving.

As a result of the forces that pull us toward one another and the forces that cause us to push away, families are the first places where we experience not only unconditional love but also buried anger, unresolved conflict, and unforgiven violations of intimate trust and understanding. We are reluctant to do the hard work essential for reconciliation, even though we long to be reconciled. Old habits are resistant to change and stress retrieves things from our past. We also misunderstand what reconciliation is and are sometimes suspicious of its place in life.

It is imperative for a number of reasons that the family become a reconciling community. Lingering anger, guilt, and sorrow undermine community within the family and disrupt the future possibility of community more broadly defined. Family therapy literature has made us aware of the destructive power of secrets kept by a family.[13] Moreover, the continuing reality of divorce means that both parents and children live with painful separations that are not always reconciled. The pluralism in families and in the culture makes it essential to be reconciled in the midst of differences that rub against one another. The more we recognize the uniqueness of the "other," the greater the likelihood that we will experience ordinary conflicts in any setting, even (or especially) the family. Finally, because weapons of destruction are more available now than ever before in our homes and our societies, we need to learn how to practice reconciliation for the sake of a human future.

The suffering caused by violence, whether toward individuals, families, or whole societies, is the most difficult element in the process of reconciliation today. The indifference toward childhood in our culture, and the particular violence toward children in our homes and neighborhoods, are pressing reasons why the family must be a reconciling community. Violence is both the cause of vulnerability, as people become victims, and its consequence, as fear blurs the boundaries between victims and perpetrators. Even when we are not attacked directly, we may not feel safe in our homes or our communities. At an even deeper level, violence destroys the narratives that sustain communities and form human identity. It is an act of justice to restore order where violence has been committed. It is an act of reconciliation when we begin to reconstruct memory in order to hope and trust again.

Reconciliation is most clearly associated with the writings of the apostle Paul, though it is supported by countless interwoven images of repentance, faithfulness, forgiveness, and grace throughout the Bible. For Paul, it is God who does the work of reconciliation:

> All this is from God, who reconciled us to himself through Christ, and has given us the ministry of reconciliation; that is, in Christ God was reconciling the world to himself, not counting their trespasses against them, and entrusting the message of reconciliation to us. (2 Cor. 5:18–19)

From its biblical usage, the Roman Catholic theologian Robert J. Schreiter has identified several characteristics of reconciliation. Foremost, it is something God does. Therefore, reconciliation is something we discover or come to know, rather than something we make or achieve for ourselves.[14] For this reason the Christian understanding reverses the usual expectation that repentance precedes reconciliation.

First, it takes time to repair a life that has been violated or a trust that has been broken. Reconciliation is not a hasty peace. Insisting on premature forgiveness for a serious offense is not a solution but part of the problem. Sometimes in our efforts to get children reunited or to make them give and receive apologies, we have overlooked a child's intuitive sense of time. It takes time to make peace, and reconciliation keeps its own timetables.

Second, reconciliation is more than acquiescence. In this sense there is no reconciliation without liberation. Schreiter reminds us that "if the sources of conflict are not named, examined, and taken away, reconciliation will not come about. What we will have is a truce, not a peace."[15] Forgiveness reopens a victim to the possibility of trust and new life, but only justice and liberation will keep a victimizer from abusing again. When churches have counseled women to suffer quietly with ongoing domestic violence, they have promoted the sickness of secrecy rather than a ministry of reconciliation.

Third, reconciliation does not just right wrongs. It brings us to a place we have not been before. In that sense, it is more than putting things back where they belong. With reconciliation, both the victim and the oppressor are re-created. That conviction is rooted in the paradoxical connection between the crucifixion and the resurrection. In God's reconciliation, one who has been offended is brought by God's grace to forgive the offender, who in turn is prompted to repent by having been forgiven.

Finally, reconciliation is not a rational strategy. Nor is it a process with definable tasks and measurable outcomes. It is, rather, a way of being in the world that recognizes and responds to God's work of reconciliation within and among us. Divine faithfulness is unfathomable. We practice reconciliation not by being faithful in a perfect sense, but by being faithful in a returning sense. Reconciliation is the fruit of fidelity; it is the quiet development of new life where there was only death, of new love where there was only hatred and fear, of new hope where there was only despair. We practice reconciliation when we listen and when we wait attentively. Robert Schreiter has linked reconciliation with compassion in a way that helps us understand the meaning of broken fidelity in family living.

> Attention must be restored if reconciliation is to take place. . . . Just as any spirituality cannot hope to grow without turning its attention constantly to God, so too attention to the healing of painful memories is of the essence in the ministry of reconciliation. Attention, in turn, is the basis of compassion, of an ability to wait and to be with, to walk alongside a victim at the victim's pace. . . . What we lack in empathy or parallel experience we can make up in attention, an attention that does not impale the victim but creates an environment of trust and safety.[16]

Learning how to be attentive, to walk at the pace of the children, and to wait for the healing of painful memories will not eliminate all the suffering in families today. Neither will it eliminate the conflicts that are the inevitable consequence of honoring difference. Nor will it end sibling rivalry or the neglect of aging parents or flagrant disregard of parental authority. It will not bring an end to lingering patriarchal assumptions that continue to be a source of violence toward women and children both in the family and in the society. But if we can understand that forgiveness is not something to be earned, then perhaps we might also discover that being a reconciling community can bring a family to a place it has not been before.

We have considered four Christian themes that have implications for family living: hospitality, compassion, justice, and reconciliation. Because these themes are not exclusively Christian, all people who are struggling to do their best in families should find their own experiences reflected in this vision. Because these themes are at the same time filled with Christian meaning, they not only imply what is good enough; they form a Christian vision of what the family could be. Such a vision invites families to be more than they are. It also challenges the church and society alike to work toward creating the kind of environment that would make it possible for families to approximate this vision. Our discussion turns next to the responsibilities of society regarding children and families.

5

IT TAKES A VILLAGE TO
RAISE A CHILD

IT TAKES more than loving, caring parents and more than
family to raise children. It takes a community committed
to their well-being. That is the meaning behind the African
proverb "It takes a village to raise a child." Together with other families and individuals we create an environment in which pregnancy and
birth are filled with promise, in which nurture and discipline are possible, in which children are valued and families protected for the sake
of every individual and for the sake of the community. We call this
context a "village" because people are linked together by mutual need
and a common covenant. In such a setting, families are no less responsible for their children, but they rely on one another and the institutions
they create and sustain to participate in the process of raising children.
The image of the village affirms a fundamental truth about the interdependence of all of life.

We may all nod pensively in recognition or even smile in agreement with the proverb "It takes a village to raise a child," but "village"
means different and sometimes conflicting things. There is controversy
about what the village should look like; there is disagreement about
how much the village should be involved in the task of raising children. Too much involvement is called *paternalism* if the government is
the village. Too little response from the larger social context means that
both children and families are victims of indifference. The disagreement and confusion behind the proverb are reflected in this comment
by a single parent:

> Where I grew up, if I misbehaved I could be reprimanded by any-
> one in town and I knew that my parents would stand behind

whatever was said. Neighbors and shopkeepers and teachers and ministers had a kind of covenant to work together to help bring children up right. I moved away from that town, grateful to be out from under too many ears and eyes and noses. Even though I was glad for the freedom, I have often said I was raised by my community. Today, I don't know my neighbors and I don't dare criticize my children's friends. The covenant has been broken, and we are not better off. I am tired of hearing about what families and parents are doing or not doing for their children as if every social ill were all our fault. We have to figure out a way to get the covenant back and make neighborhoods into villages. I don't want to lose my freedom, though.   (Kent)

Kent is right. Families should not be blamed for what they cannot do alone. We have lost an essential but unspoken covenant that seemed to sustain a common commitment to the well-being of children. Yet we do not want to give up the freedom of individual fulfillment that is one of the elements that has eroded that covenant. The struggle to establish a relationship of interdependence between the individual and the community of the family is therefore replicated in the relationship between the family and the larger society. The battle between "me" (whether as individual or family) and "we" (whether as family or social community) must end in a tie—in the paradox of interdependence and mutual responsibility.

The relationship between the family and its wider society is organic and always changing. Despite the nostalgia that many of us may share with Kent, we cannot turn back the clock, even though we might like to retrieve something of the covenant that has been lost. What worked for hunter-gatherers was changed in agricultural societies. The relationship of family and society changed again under industrialization and it is changing yet again in our postindustrial society. The way ahead for the family in the social context is neither clear nor simple. What is certainly true about the "village" proverb, however, is that families have not raised and do not and cannot raise children alone.

This chapter will examine the fundamental interdependence of family and society and explore both what families need from their communities and what they contribute to society. Because we intend to honor the diverse local contexts in which the relationships between family and society must be worked out, our comments will be more impressionistic than prescriptive. Nonetheless, two questions emerge from the many ordinary decisions we must make: (1) What does society do for the family that the family cannot do for itself? (2) How can we define the relationship between family and society in a way that keeps interdependence alive?

The Interdependence of Family and Society

Society is a broad term which encompasses public and private institutions as well as the informal structures and networks of a local community. We acknowledge not only historical changes in the relationship between family and society but regional and cultural differences as well. A family in rural Africa, a family in a small town in Iowa, a family in a suburb of London, and a family in the south Bronx may want many divergent things, but they also all need a few essential things. They must seek from the larger society what they need to survive that they cannot produce in isolation.

A commitment to interdependence is essential for families and societies because it is essential to life itself. Teilhard de Chardin has observed that "the farther and more deeply we penetrate into matter, by increasingly powerful methods, the more we are confounded by the interdependence of its parts."[1] Christian theology also teaches that the world, as created by God, is knit together at every level in a wonderful complexity which, though sin unravels it, testifies to the wisdom of God and the interrelatedness of all things.[2] It is the way in which God's care moves into our future with us.

The survival of the human community, and all of creation together, hinges on the belief that interdependence in society, like reconciliation in the family, is a necessary ideal even though it often eludes us. Part of what makes it difficult to understand interdependence is its paradoxical nature. We are aware that we act in interdependent ways when we perform *separate* tasks in *mutual* responsibility and accountability at all levels of community. We remain *separate* and *unique* even when we are *linked together* through our common goals and experiences. Even so, we are more inclined to say that things are one or the other than to think paradoxically.

The relationship of family and society, though the family's needs are absolute, is complex and interdependent in part because the same people who are part of families make up the "village." Sometimes people are complacent about their role in forming and reforming society for the sake of a common future. At other times, the relationship of family and society is sufficiently unclear that appropriate roles are hard to find. As a result, families in particular feel alienated from society or powerless and dependent in relation to it. There are many layers or concentric circles making up our social fabric. Power at the local level does not always translate into power at the level where decisions are actually made. Even so, we need to remember that while there are tiers to society, the social structure is people all the way up. For this reason, a society never graduates from its need for or obligation to all the people, even the children, who comprise it.

The first network of relationships beyond family most often includes our friends and neighbors, our children's friends and their families, and—increasingly—the people with whom we work. These people overlap with or comprise the network of local public and private institutions, such as schools, churches, libraries, recreational facilities, and day care centers. Governments and agencies at the municipal, state, and national levels and a host of national professional and trade unions, associations, and multinational corporations and interests make up society. The health of these relationships is assessed by the clarity of purpose *within* each of them, the effectiveness of communication *among* them, and their responsiveness or mutuality to one another.

It is clear from public rhetoric and private suffering that the relationship between family and society is changing fundamentally. Some believe that society is not doing enough to support children and families; others are determined that government and social agencies should not interfere with family life. There is concern over the self-sufficiency and freedom of families to raise children their own way. There are misgivings among some about models of family assistance that might establish patterns of chronic dependence on the larger community. Society cannot and should not be a substitute for families, even when critical relationships and resources for children are lacking. These disagreements about the relationship between society and family have become part of public policy debates. They are also poignantly revealed at every level of family and community relations—from school dress codes to child pornography laws, from crossing guards to welfare reform.

> David was devastated the first time the fictional city he created in a computer game was destroyed by fire. Here he was, born and raised in Chicago, having studied the Great Chicago Fire in school, and yet he had not thought to provide his community with a fire department. His next city was cautiously service-oriented, complete with hospitals, schools, day care. The city's water supply became

undrinkable. "Man," he said after the second game, "it's always
something." From then on, with all the appetite of a sixth-grade
boy, he concentrated on causing his cities to blow up or crash in
more and more dramatic ways.   (Dennis)

What David discovered in his computer game is a social reality:
everything is related to everything else. We are increasingly aware that
when families fail in large numbers, their environment contributes to
that failure. That is to say, where there is trouble in families, there is
likely to be a crisis in the "village" itself. Therefore, we cannot to do the
urgent work of rehabilitating families without at the same time addressing problems in education, transportation, health care, employment, race and class and sex discrimination, conspicuous consumerism,
and the exploitation of the land, all of which contaminate the "village"
environment in which families attempt to survive. It is true that a civi-
lization is only as strong as its families because its future lies in the
health and welfare of its children. However, the converse is also true:
families can only thrive in healthy communities.

Social systems theorists Jaime Inclan and Ernesto Ferran, Jr.,
help us to understand what is at stake in the controversy about family
failure versus social failure. In their study of poverty in the United
States, they refuse to blame one culprit for the fate of poor families.
They claim that present social thought has been driven by the need to
allocate blame rather than locate responsibility. Instead of blaming the
system *or* the family, they describe a new kind of thinking which recognizes "multiple realities and therefore multiple responsibilities."
About families in poverty, they suggest:

> Within [this] framework, we can simultaneously stress that the
> system is 100 percent responsible for the problem of poverty and
> its consequences and that the family is 100 percent responsible
> for the problem. Each will have to do something different if there
> is to be an overall change. And the responsibility of both, each at
> its contextual level, is to operate to achieve change within its field
> of operations.[3]

The paradoxical and systemic perspective that Inclan and Ferran
bring to the issue of responsibility can encompass many issues. The
strength of this integrative approach is that it not only calls for responsibility to be shared, but also prompts all parties involved to see how
their futures are intertwined. It is based on the inescapable interdependence of the human community. We will return later in this chapter to

consider ways in which we might keep the paradoxical interdependence of family and society in a balanced tension. First, we need to identify the essentials that a society *must* provide for families and children that they cannot provide for themselves. When we understand what a society must provide, we are more clearly aware how perilous indifference toward children in a society can be.

The Essentials That Society Provides

The United Nations World Summit for Children recognized a crisis in the protection and nurture of children around the world. It also recognized that the fate of children cannot be separated from the fate of societies. The final report of the Summit proposed to improve the welfare of the world's children by enhancing the health and nutrition of all children, developing basic schooling, ensuring the rights of children, eliminating preventable diseases, protecting children from the ravages of war, diminishing poverty, strengthening the role of women, and fostering sustained and sustainable growth and development in all countries of the world.[4] Those promises are more easily made by politicians than kept by governments. Nonetheless, they are an articulation from a global perspective of the basic support all children and families need from the societies in which they live. Let us focus here on six essentials that, from a global perspective, must be provided by societies for the sake of all our children: a sustainable environment, basic health care, safety from harm, the human rights of children, a viable economy, and adequate education.

A Sustainable Environment

Our children need clean water to drink and clean air to breathe. While these may not seem like much to ask, every nation in the world struggles with serious environmental issues. Some communities face a loss of natural resources; some have become the dumping grounds for the disposal of hazardous waste. Like other issues, the environment is a communitywide issue which also depends on significant changes in the behavior of individuals and families. Recycling, for instance, can be supported and legislated at the societal level, but it will only succeed as individuals and families change their personal behavior. Corporations can and must be constrained to deal with industrial pollution, but, as consumers, individuals and families must deal with those issues as well.

Today we learned that for every family there needs [to be] seven trees so we can have air to breathe. I know out my window we already got no trees. How come we ain't dead?   (Danny)

Children like Danny are often made aware of the environment at an early age. They are made anxious not only about their immediate health but also about an environment that is truly endangered and unsafe. Danny is a nine-year-old boy with asthma who lives in a housing project in the inner city. There is very little he can do to make sure his environment is unpolluted. If Danny lived on a farm, he might insist that his father not deposit pesticide cans in a sinkhole near the stream where he fishes. Danny's insistence would change the situation a little but it would not change much. *A family that is not able to protect its own children cannot be expected by itself to protect the environment.*

The task of providing a safe environment for our children's future is the responsibility of everyone at all levels in a society. The achievement of environmentally sound and sustainable development will require the action of citizens and families as well as nations and corporations. The environmental agenda for the sake of our children's future is international and intergenerational. Justice for children and for all future generations can be gained only through a global alliance. If we ignore this responsibility, our children are in peril.

Basic Health Care

Many of the recommendations coming from the World Summit for Children focused on the health needs of mothers and children around the globe.[5] Poverty, malnutrition, diarrhea, the traumas of unskilled deliveries, lack of safe water, inadequate primary health care, and injuries or starvation due to war are among the factors responsible for death and disease among children around the globe. The United States continues to have the greatest percentage of children living in poverty of any industrialized nation. The infant mortality rates in our major cities exceed those of many developing nations. Pockets of our population have lower immunization rates than nations that were targeted by the World Health Organization for immunization drives in the '80s. It is, however, technically possible for children everywhere to be free from preventable diseases. What we lack is the will to do it.

A document written by the United States Conference of Catholic Bishops on "Putting Children and Families First: A Challenge for Our Church, Nation and World," makes the following statement about the need for health care for the children of this society:

> Our nation's continuing failure to guarantee access to quality health care for all people exacts its most painful toll in the preventable sickness, disability and deaths of our infants and children. Beginning with our children and their mothers, we must extend access to quality health care to all our people.[6]

The lack of basic health care is a particularly tragic reality for poor children. They are twice as likely as other children to have physical or mental disabilities or other chronic health conditions that impair daily activity. It is therefore difficult to attend to the health needs of many of our children without at the same time addressing the issue of poverty.

Most families have something like a medicine box or cabinet where adhesive bandages and other emergency medical resources are kept. Some families foster good health in their members (including children) by the kind of food they provide. But health care is more than a family affair. It must be the responsibility of society as well, because of the professional and technical services involved. Even if we could agree, however, that everyone in a society should have access to basic health care, the problem would not be solved for children. Infants and small children do not take themselves to a doctor. Parents and other adults need to be committed to the health of children to make a difference.

Safety from Harm

It has been said that one can the measure the quality of a society by the protection it gives its most vulnerable members. If that is true, no one is safe when our children are at risk. *A society that tolerates or cannot control violence in the streets and violence in the home is particularly dangerous for children.* A *New Yorker* magazine cover brought this point home in a shocking way with a cartoon depicting children getting off the school bus loaded down with book bags, gym shoes, and automatic weapons. There is something desperately wrong with a society when a child cannot go to school or a slumber party at a friend's house or ride a bicycle in a quiet park without the fear of being killed. It is the responsibility of society to make sure that a child can go outside to play without great personal risk. Families cannot do this alone. The protection of children by society happens at all its levels. A society works best when parents both take responsibility *for* the community in which they live and receive *from* community institutions, government, and businesses a responsiveness on behalf of the needs of children.

Children need from families and from the larger society freedom to be children. That is not easy to accomplish when a society becomes violent because children are as much aware of trouble in a society as they are of trouble in their parents' marriage. Nonetheless, it is important that our children not be expected to absorb the anxiety of an entire society. At the same time, a community that hides from its deepest problems and concerns endangers children all the more because it promotes fear and hopelessness and powerlessness in unspoken ways.

> On a recent community hunger walk to raise money for local food pantries, participants were asked by passers-by what they were doing. One very excited six-year-old kept answering for the group: "Don't worry! We're feeding the hungry!"   (Roland)

Our children are looking for a reason to hope. They wait expectantly to see evidence of hope in the adults who care for them. It is important for the sake of children that communities remain hopeful without denying their struggles to survive or be safe.

The quality of life within any community can be judged by the effectiveness of its safety net for people who are in harm's way. Sometimes that safety net includes food, clothing, and shelter for any person or family in immediate need.

> I was twenty-five and married before I had my three children, and it was not until I was divorced that I began to work. I could (barely) make ends meet by working, but I was losing my mind. My children were too young to be left for long hours and I was too stressed to manage my job, my home, and my babies. I didn't have family to call upon; finally I had to quit my job. I am not ashamed to say that we became homeless. We lived in a women's and children's shelter while I worked my way through the maze of public aid. As the children grew older, I got involved in advocacy for women on public aid. That is how I eventually found my next job as a secretary for a private foundation. I disliked the shelter and I disliked public aid, but because of them I was able to be a mother to my children when they needed me.   (Tanya)

At other times safe homes for neglected or abused children will be needed. And at times psychological counseling, job training, or spiritual care are what is needed by those who have been harmed by life. When the foster care system of a community does not work, it has failed to provide a safety net for those who are most vulnerable. The failure of a society to provide a safety net for its children is another illustration of "the culture of indifference."

The Human Rights of Children

The World Summit for Children set forth a principle for regarding the rights of children that is applicable in every society: "*The principle of first call for children complements the historic Convention on the Rights of the Child that seeks to ensure that children under 18 years of age develop to their full potential free from hunger, want, neglect, exploitation, and other abuses.*"[7] In order to achieve the aim of this principle, children should have a high priority in the allocation of resources in bad times as well as good times, at the national and international levels as well as at the level of local communities and the family. Commitment to this principle means that the best interests of children are first priority.

The image of "children as citizens" points to their right to participate in family and society. "*Participation rights include the freedom to express opinions and to have influence in matters affecting one's own life, as well as the right to play an active role in society at large.*"[8] As we have already noted, the right to citizenship is a logical consequence of regarding the full humanity of children. It has implications for the participation of children in the life of the Christian community. It means the opinion of children shall be given due regard in the family. At minimum, it means the voice of children must be heard.

> When our daughter Molly was just two, we moved to California. My parents often took care of her while we worked, so they were understandably annoyed about our move. It was three years before we visited them again. I expected that the visit would be difficult for me but I did not anticipate Molly's response. The moment we entered my parents' home, she was terrified. I could not understand her response because she had not seen them since she was two. When I pressed her for some explanation for her response, Molly said: "It happened before I had a voice." (Jeffrey)

Children have the right to childhood. The denial of childhood through premature expectations of adult behavior is another form of exploitation. A child may grow up prematurely in cases of extreme hardship within the family. An older child may raise younger siblings in the event of the death or disability of a parent; a hearing child of deaf parents may act as interpreter. These challenges are true hardships for a child. Beyond these extreme circumstances, however, there are other, more pernicious expectations of premature adulthood that a culture may place on a child. They are reflected in the toleration of child pornography, the lack of sufficient child labor laws, the peddling of dangerous substances or behaviors to a child audience, or the exploitation of children for political gain. There are those who would harm children if the society is not vigilant. Protecting freedom of expression for adults should not be at the expense of safeguarding children from exploitation and abuse.

The World Summit for Children explicitly links the rights of women to the rights of children. In all societies, more women and children live in poverty than men; in families where one parent is absent, the vast majority of childrearing is done by women. It is also true that in developing nations where women do not have the same property rights as men, women are very likely to be the principle provider for their families as well as primary caretaker of children. When a society strengthens the role and voice of women, legally and economically, it addresses the agenda of the family.

A Viable Economy

Poverty is not just the absence of adequate financial resources. "It often entails a more profound kind of deprivation, a denial of full participation in the economic, social, and political life of society and an inability to influence decisions that affect one's life."[9] All families need to have a way to provide for their members. They must have some goods or services to trade in order to participate in the larger economy. For the family to succeed, the society must have a viable economy, and individuals in that society must have access to sufficient education and training to enter that economy.

> I usually tell people that I can't really remember my father, but the fact is I remember two things. I remember how he used to come into my room after I was asleep to say good night to me. Sometimes he would fall asleep across the foot of my bed, and I would scrunch down in the covers so I could put the blanket over him, too. He was always gone before we got up in the morning. My father never graduated from sixth grade. He hauled garbage for a mill during the day, and at night he made deliveries; my mother took in laundry. The other thing I remember about him is the expression on his face after he died. My father died when I was five. He fell asleep at the wheel and his delivery truck went off the road. In the casket, he looked so peaceful; I remember he looked like he was sleeping.   (Alicia)

A viable economy is measured in part by the possibility of earning enough income to provide for the basic needs of a family. If it is not possible to support one's family by working full-time in the economy or it is not possible to train or retrain to do so, then the economy is not viable. When parents must work as much as Alicia's father worked, there is neither time nor energy left for them to attend to ordinary childrearing responsibilities. A viable economy is also measured by the proportion of its employable citizens who work. If there are jobs for only a portion of those who need to work to support their families, then the economy is not viable. If the holes of a society's safety net become too large, it also becomes more difficult for families to recover from temporary unemployment or large medical bills.

These measures of viability can refer to a large (even national) economy, but economic viability is also measured at a smaller, local level. A local economy is viable if family income is spent within the community at a level that supports other essentials of a particular community. If families in a cohesive community are forced to spend most of their income on basic necessities outside their community (or to entities whose assets are held outside the community and therefore not reinvested in it), then the national economy may be viable, but the local economy will deteriorate until the community itself is robbed of its capacity to provide for families.

Because of the chronic economic need of many families in this society, the public policy debate has centered around such critical issues as the minimum living wage, the question of equal women's wages for equal work, childcare and parental leave for parents who must work and who have young children at home. These public policy questions are important, but they beg an underlying question about the viability of our economy and the health of children and families. If the highly valued, maybe even overworked, ideal laborer in our economy is expected to be well educated, highly mobile, and preferably single, then the adjustments in work patterns required by men and women with children are in fundamental opposition to a family's needs.[10] An economy that makes it difficult or impossible for working parents to invest significant time, energy, and resources in raising their children is not viable. A viable economy will be sensitive to and accommodating of the needs of the family.

Sometimes the work ethic and the labor patterns of industrial and postindustrial societies have separated parents from their children in ways that make it difficult to pass on the value of work. As a result, children see how parents spend money more than how they make it. Parents certainly serve as role models, as teachers, as friends. But children need adults beyond their immediate family as well, adults who represent and invite them into the world, who provocatively yet safely invite them to explore the world and themselves. Children need the benefit of working side by side with competent adult labor, in jobs suited for their child-body and child-mind. They need the interest and forward gaze that only an adult can provide in order to imagine a future unfolding as they experience their capacities building and their sense of responsibility budding.

Adequate Education

"Basic education is a learning foundation for all citizens, in which the tools of reading, writing, and numerancy, as well as fundamental knowledge and skills of life, are acquired."[11] According to the World Summit for Children, it is essential that societies ensure that every citizen is equipped with the basic tools of learning and the basic knowledge and life skills relevant to his or her environment in order that every individual has a fair start in life and the capacity to participate fully in the economic and cultural aspects of a society.

The ongoing struggle to support an adequate education system is one of the troubling aspects of this society's indifference toward children. It illustrates the futility of trying to locate blame. The ability of children to succeed in school is largely dependent on early development in the home. The growing number of high-risk children entering our schools compromises the education of everyone. Because a child's critical learning years, at least in terms of language, are already over by age six, society can no longer assume that its responsibility for educating children begins when they start school. This conclusion intensifies the need for understanding interdependence between families and society for the sake of children.

In addition to basic education, a society that has space and time for a child's creative urge is a blessing not only to children but also to its future as a culture. Part of the freedom of being a child is the freedom to be creative, to explore, to invest, to take things apart and put them back together again. Such freedom is also a key to creativity and the future of culture. In that sense, the culture is at risk when children are too frightened or too hurried to play. Just as parents celebrate the first steps of their children, a society replenishes its culture as it recognizes the creativity and self-expression of children.

What is at stake in this consideration of the essentials that society must provide for children and families is a deeper question, namely: Are we responsible for other people's children? If the answer is no, then parents will continue to regard society as either friend or foe in the childrearing tasks. From that perspective, the work of society (including the church) is to support the family. Parents are responsible for raising children. If the answer is yes, if we understand that it takes a village to raise a child, then we need to redefine the roles and responsibilities of raising children in more interdependent ways. The transformation of our attitude toward children from indifference to respect is the beginning of that redefinition.

The Relationship Between Family and Society

It takes a village to raise a child but the creation and maintenance of the village also takes a citizenry. That simple declaration reflects some of the confusion about the interrelated functions of family and society. Society is, after all, made up of the same individuals who come from and make up families. For that reason, it is not easy to define the relationship between family and society. In order to keep alive the paradox of interdependence between family and society, we need to: (1) diminish the privatization of the family and other consequences of individualism, (2) foster an understanding of the family as a *crucible* in which both socialization and individuation occur, and (3) restore the family's voice as a critic of society in order at the same time to restore balance to the family-society paradox.

The Privatization of the Family

The privatization of the family has added to the confusion over the separate and related roles of family and community. Although certain socializing functions of childrearing, such as education and career preparation, have been carried out by the society, other aspects of family life, such as nutrition, personal hygiene, and moral training have become private matters within the family. This division of responsibility has genuinely lessened the interdependence of families. It has also meant that the holes in the safety net are wider, and families can sink or swim alone. The privatization of family life means that we care for one another's children less routinely. It has also meant that we cannot easily describe the ways in which the community cares for our children, nor can we articulate how the family relates to society.

In the book *Habits of the Heart*, Robert Bellah and others interpret the increasing precariousness of traditional families as the result of unchecked individualism in our culture.[12] Obligations to self have taken precedence over obligations to family or community. The authors portray the crisis of the family as part of a larger social change, which includes the decline of commitment to personal relationships and to such pivotal social institutions as church, neighborhood, and family. Finally, as individualism replaces social-connection commitment, they argue, people no longer possess even the conceptual framework through which to identify and desire the social bonds of community. Bellah's social critique steps beyond family-friendly public policies and examines the cultural patterns that have shaped such policy.

The German sociologist Ulrich Beck presents an argument similar to Bellah's regarding the crisis of the family in postindustrial modern society in his book *Risk Society*. He describes a social crisis affecting the family that is more than a shift in mores. The strains on the maintenance of social bonds, Beck argues, are built into the organization of marketplace societies. The tendency toward individualization is inherent in such a society. The constraints of traditional social structures like the family have been exchanged for the constraints of the labor market and the demands of consumption in a market-driven society. Beck concludes that the family does not possess a voice strong enough to contend with market forces even if it should choose to do so. Ultimately, "the market model of modernity presupposes a society without families or marriages. . . . The ultimate market society is a *childless* society—unless the children grow up with mobile, single, fathers and mothers."[13] The contradiction between the demands of a free-market economy and the requirements of family living remained hidden as long as families were supported by one wage earner who was free from domestic obligations. According to Beck, either the patterns of work or the models of family living will need to change in order for both men and women to be free to work.

The family is caught in the middle between conflicting values in a consumer culture. In an essay entitled "The American Family v. The American Dream," Barbara Ehrenreich has observed that our economy makes two absolutely contradictory psychological demands on its members.[14] On the one hand are the "puritanical" values that expect people to be good workers and lead orderly and law-abiding lives. On the other hand, people need to be "permissive" enough to be good consumers. The economic enterprise depends on enough hedonism to stimulate mass consumption and enough discipline to produce what we consume. It is an increasingly terrible trap for families with modest income.

Several models of the relationship between family and society emerge from and are expressions of our present confusion. In the first model, the family is *consumer*. The family is the central unit of human life and contracts with the community for goods and services it needs and cannot produce for itself. The family employs the services of schools, community centers, agencies of recreation, hospitals, and even law enforcement to serve its purposes. Although families may need to pay for services, the model essentially assumes that community exists in order to serve the family. A second model, the family as *cottage industry*, reverses the image of the first. In this model the family serves the demands of society. Families produce and nurture children to become productive consumers and useful citizens of the larger society. Both of these models assume one-way relationships between family and society.

A third model of the relationship between family and society presumes a basic indifference or even hostility of society toward the individual and the family. Here, society is a vortex of dangerous currents and forces, and the family, by contrast, is a *comfort station* for its members, away from the heartless world.[15] Families interact minimally with the wider community, because the primary purpose of family is to provide insulation from the insults and pain of life in the world.

The greatest limitation of these three models is that they fail to recognize that the family is, in fact, made up of the people who also make up the society, and that the health of each is dependent on the permeability and mutuality of both. To assume (1) that the purpose of society is to serve the family, or (2) that the purpose of the family is to serve society, or (3) that the family and society exist in a relationship of uncomfortable but stable hostility presumes that the family and the society are distinctly separate, that they are inhabited by different sets of people.

When the family is "consumer," the role of the family in shaping the future of society is overlooked. Such a society would be crippled by idiosyncratic individuals with little or no commitment to maintaining the community. When the family is "cottage industry," however, it is the creative liberty of the individual that is sacrificed; the individual and the family serve the social order above their own needs. The family as "comfort station" maintains thick walls of separation from the society. Relationships outside the family are characterized by a high level of suspicion and even a kind of "sectarian" self-sufficiency. Highly mobile, insulated, nuclear families behind wooden fences in a suburban community along a commuter line into a major city are an illustration of this sectarianism.

The Family as Crucible

A fourth model for the family's relationship with society presumes both public and private aspects of family living. In this model, the family is a *crucible* in which the needs of the individual and the needs of the community are negotiated and balanced. The boundary between the family and the society is not a thick wall of separation; rather, it is a permeable boundary. This model asserts that it takes a village to raise a child because we care for one another's children and because we receive care from other units in society. It also recognizes that the village is created and maintained by individuals and families. In the "crucible" model, the community never takes the place of parents and families, but it does encourage and undergird children and families. By the same token, families acknowledge what they receive from the community and contribute to it, in order to ensure its continued success. The relationship between the family and society is governed by the principle of interdependent responsibility.

It is important to understand this image of the family as *crucible* in relation to the purposes of the family. If the family is understood as the first and basic cell of society, then one real purpose of the family is to establish and maintain social stability. Families raise children to participate in the community in which they live, in its economy, its government, its culture. In that sense, the family works for society in its socializing purpose. It is undoubtedly true that the well-being of the family and the society are linked, but it is clearly only part of the goal in raising children to make them fit into society's mold. Families also raise children to be free and creative individuals who will leave their mark on the society. Thus it is important not to lose sight of the individuation purpose for families.

It is both unrealistic and dangerous to expect the family to be the sole anchor of society. It is in the best interests of the society to raise children who are intelligent, creative, independent, and mature people who will make their own way in the world and have their own impact on it. The expectation of citizenship must be one that weds the vision of sacrifice for the greater good of society with a healthy commitment to individual freedom and creativity. It is the role of family as *crucible* to be in cooperative tension with the wider community, to engender that balance of commitment and freedom through their raising of children.

The role of the community in relationship to the family is to provide an environment in which children are allowed to be children and families are supported in their childrearing.

Restoring the Voice of the Family

There are so many needs that are linked to the family, and so many forces working against its well-being, that the family is often unable to articulate its own agenda, unable to speak up for children and childhood. Conservative critics and social theorists call for the family to pull itself back together, lift itself up by its bootstraps. Sometimes the attitudes toward the family from the culture are like angry indifference. When we fail to understand the crisis of the family in interdependent ways, we cannot change our patterns of living as a society enough to make it better for families. It is necessary for the future of the family that it find a critical voice. There is a parallel between strengthening the voice of the family and developing a new regard for children. *Where there is no village, the family will fail.*

The family is often blamed, or scapegoated, for problems it did not cause in the larger society. It is therefore unrealistic to expect the family to manage privately a crisis that implicates the society in its public responsibility. The boundary between family and society is, in fact, permeable in only one direction. It is possible for the family to become committed to privatizing its life. The larger society, on the other hand, has demonstrated in a variety of ways that it is not terribly sensitive to the needs of the family. The logo of the Children's Defense Fund is appropriate to the relationship between family and society: "Dear Lord, be good to me. The sea is so wide and my boat is so small."

The resolution to the current crisis depends in part on giving families greater voice in economic and community planning. We cannot continue to encourage self-determination and creativity within the family when the family has no power for self-determination at the level of society. To a greater and greater degree, social workers, therapists, and community leaders recognize that families desire good things for their children and communities desire good things for their families, but they are powerless to enact them or to represent their demands to the governments and corporations that make decisions on public policy.

The insidious forces of racism, regionalism, and contempt for the poor conspire to choke the voice of the family even more. Individualism, privatism, and consumerism may be perilous forces in the lives of affluent members of modern society, but they are deathblows to low-income families. Low-income families contend with all the same pressures and dangers that more affluent families do, but live closer to economic peril should unemployment, illness, divorce, crime, or other crises strike. Beyond this, lower-income families are forced to live in communities plagued by business disinvestment, poor schools, bad or insufficient housing stock, industrial pollution, and deficient public services. The rhetoric of the free-market economy and the anxious accommodation of the middle class are outshouting the real cries of children and families.

Weaving an Interdependent Social Fabric

The family has proven itself durable but not powerful in industrialized societies. We have witnessed, even applauded, an accommodating flexibility in the family that has contributed to the economic vitality of our nation. However, we are also witnessing the repercussions of its accommodation, especially for the least powerful members of society—women, children, racial and ethnic minorities, low-income families—which eventually incapacitate them. No social program can effectively replace family life; likewise, the family by itself cannot reform society. What is called for is a vision of a more just social order that is large enough to transcend compromise and deep enough to empower and support the present constellation of families in building communities that are life-enhancing.

The crisis of the family cannot be separated from a host of other social institutions, cultural assumptions, and philosophical and religious commitments that affect and are affected by the family. These are also in crisis. They hang together like an intricately woven fabric that is unraveling before our eyes. We cannot fix one without fixing the others. Robert Bellah is correct when he suggests in *The Good Society* that "the task of restoring family life, whatever form the family may take, cannot be the family's alone."[16] Nor does the family, as Ulrich Beck suggests, have the clout to demand what it needs in the face of current economic pressures and realities. What is required is a fundamental shift in the agenda of a society.

Because the family is interdependent with other elements of society, the vision of a society good to families needs to be much more deeply and genuinely collaborative. At present, the level of trust is so lacking, the systems for blaming and powerlessness so entrenched in the society and the family alike, that cooperation and dialogue cannot be assumed, even where interventions intend to aid the family. Partnership, collaboration, interdependence, and self-determination are requisite in a more just society in which families can thrive. What is called for is the development of a focused purpose for the family, a reformation of the cultural attitudes toward children that undergird and surround it, and sufficient public policy to allow family members security, self-determination, and creativity in their lives.

In order to become the village we seek, it is essential that we rediscover how to care for other people's children and that we reclaim in our present society a public and private regard for all children. We have lost our ease with interdependence between family and society, and we live in a time when we only reclaim relationship and responsibility with wrenching negotiation. In this chapter the voice of families has been promoted with the knowledge that families are only learning what and how to speak. The church is unique among institutions in its capacity to help families discover their voice and vision in a community of honesty, hope, and reconciliation. In the next and final chapter, we focus on the church's mandate for the sake of children and families.

6

THE CHURCH
AS A SANCTUARY
FOR CHILDHOOD

IN ITS THEOLOGY, the church is committed to welcoming
children and honoring childhood. The invitation of Jesus
to "let the children come" permanently expanded the
membership of the people of God. The church today is called to do
what Jesus did: to welcome children in order to bless them. Similarly,
Jesus revolutionized our understanding of being human when he suggested that childness is a criterion for Christian discipleship. As Christians, we experience humanity in its fullness when we honor what is
vulnerable, open, and always emerging and unfolding. Our childness,
in that sense, is not something we ever outgrow. The church bears witness to a mystery in children that adults can hope to embrace: the mystery of how the present and future are fused in the child, fused yet
unknown, already present and yet always becoming.

In its practice, the church has been a witness on behalf of children, but at the same time it has failed to embody the vision of the new
human community it proclaims. Children are often excluded by theological definitions and ecclesiastical rules from full practicing membership in the church community. The church has been reluctant to
rectify church teachings that unwittingly promote the abuse of power
over the less powerful—whether children, women, minorities, the
poor, the handicapped, the oppressed. Most graphically, the church has
participated in the "culture of indifference" toward childhood through
its silence and complicity in instances of child sexual abuse. The vio-
lation of children is not mentioned often enough in the chronicle of
human sinfulness when Christian people gather. The church is therefore both an agent of change regarding our attitudes toward children

and itself in need of transformation. The prophetic voice of the church is weakened by its inability to practice what it proclaims.

A Sanctuary for Childhood

One of the ways the church fulfills its purpose is by articulating clearly the vision of a new humanity incarnated in Jesus Christ. It is urgent that the church be a clear, prophetic voice for anyone who is small, weak, and needy, not only because our children are in danger, but also because our response to them is the measure of our regard for all humanity. Proclaiming a vision, however, is not enough. The church must also embody the vision of a new humanity that Jesus proclaimed. A church that practices to be a community where children are welcomed and honored as fully human and where there is compassion and justice for all persons will become a *sanctuary for childhood*.

In ancient Israel, a sanctuary was a place of special holiness where people worshiped. It was a place apart. In the Middle Ages, a church could also be a sanctuary where people who were vulnerable for a variety of reasons would be safe. For example, anyone who touched the door knocker of the cathedral in Durham, England, was protected. The image of sanctuary is used here in these two ways. Because church is a place that signifies the presence of God, it must also be a place of safety for people.

> In our church we have a quiet, furnished parlor off the main social hall where coffee hour is held. On Sunday mornings it serves as a place to read to small children, change a diaper, or unobtrusively breast-feed after the worship service. One week, the five-year-old son of visitors emerged from the parlor and announced to his unassuming parents and to the entire coffee hour, with deafening clarity, "Mom, you gotta see this. They're nursing in here!" The child's enthusiasm amused us briefly, not as a disturbance, but as a true aspect of our gathering.   (Susan)

The church that is a sanctuary is a place where mothers are free to nurse their babies. It is also a safe haven for children and adults who know the vulnerability of childhood in their lives. In many communities, the church is already known as a place with a telephone, a bathroom, and caring adults for children who are lost or lonely or locked out or confused about custody arrangements that day, who have had a bicycle stolen, who are being threatened by a gang, or who are thinking about running away. It is also a haven for young people who are not at home anywhere else. Unfortunately, children have also been violated in the church by people they trusted.

Recently, churches have publicly declared themselves to be an "Open and Affirming Community" (or "Reconciled in Christ") for everyone, including homosexual persons, or a "Nuclear Free Zone" for the sake of the environment. In both instances, the declaration has been aimed at rectifying any misunderstanding concerning the inclusivity of a church or its commitment to a sustainable future for the earth. We believe that a church needs to be equally public about its commitment to children by declaring itself to be a "Sanctuary for Childhood." Such a community will provide the kind of protection that fosters freedom for everyone, children and adults alike, to be vulnerable and needy as well as strong and self-sufficient.

The church ministers to children and families at ordinary and extraordinary moments throughout their lives. This special access derives from the correspondence between faith formation and human development. As a consequence, the church is often a partner with families in the ordinary crises in childrearing: the day-to-day joys and concerns; the developmental steps, hurdles, and milestones; the ordinary and wonderful process of life and the unfolding of sustaining relationships. The church also ministers to families in extraordinary crises, where that very unfolding of life is threatened for a child or an adult. The burdens of illness or an accident, the griefs of loss, the anguish of economic instability or poverty, all threaten the childhood of children and adults alike. In all this, the church has a privileged access to people in families that is not available to other helping agencies of society.

If a church transforms its attitude toward children in order to be a *sanctuary for childhood*, it will deepen the sacred trust of its access to families. What the church has ordinarily done for children and families will take on new significance. It will welcome children as full participants in the life of God's people; it will support the vocation of being a parent throughout its ever-changing roles; the formation of faithful children will have new direction and urgency; the church will continue to intervene when children or families experience extraordinary problems and needs as well as advocate for systemic change where families are endangered by social conditions; and it will challenge individuals, families, and society to a deepening regard for childhood as the measure of God's justice and mercy in the world.

Each of these areas of ministry is an essential component in a Christian vision of a just society that the church embodies as a *sanctuary for childhood.* No one church can do them all, however. The needs and expectations of children and families regularly outstrip the resources available in particular parishes to respond to those needs. The privileged access of the church becomes a burden when these needs cannot be met. We have sought throughout this book not to undermine the fragile self-esteem of families who are trying to accomplish the difficult task of childrearing with limited resources. Most congregations have limited resources as well. They will need to join with others in order that the whole ministry of the Christian church includes *welcoming* children, *supporting* parents, *forming* faithful Christians, *caring* for families effectively, and *challenging* all persons to regard childhood with a new respect.

Welcoming Children

Christian communities expand and deepen the welcome to a child through prayers and symbolic activity and the community's hospitality. The local faith community that gathers in the name of Jesus is a place of hospitality for all God's people. Welcoming children as full participants in the life of God's people is one expression of hospitality that every particular religious community can and must do. The initiation of children by baptism or by dedication establishes the church as a communion in which oneness leads to equality. "There is no longer Jew or Greek, there is no longer slave or free, there is no longer male and female; for all of you are one in Christ Jesus" (Gal. 3:28). The ritual of initiation is, therefore, a sign of the catholicity of the church and the future of God.[1] It is a public declaration that children are people with full membership in the family of God. It is also ritual that begins the lifelong process of forming faithful Christians (see figure 2).

Because birth continues to be a complex process in most human communities and because of the lingering vulnerability of children, it is essential that there be a ritual of initiation in infancy that both incorporates and individuates. As Margaret L. Hammer has observed in

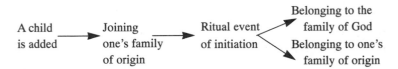

FIG. 2. The process of welcoming a child

her book *Giving Birth*, families who are not church members "still turn to the church and its rituals to mark the birth of a child."[2] The parallel processes by which an infant is incorporated into a family and a believing community is another paradox in family living. We need to maintain a delicate balance between autonomy and community, between the needs of the child and the needs of the family and community. The event of birth and the ritual of baptism or child dedication mediate this fundamental paradox of individual in community.

Initiation as Incorporation

The addition of a child changes communities. We have already noted in chapter 2 how families are changed when a child is added. For Christian communities, a new child member is a sign of hope that the name of Jesus will be remembered and the grace of God proclaimed for another generation. Children are also a gift to the church because they challenge spurious faith and self-delusions by pressing straightforwardly for a deeper understanding of the mystery of God's grace and the ambiguities of human living. They can be relentless ambassadors for God. When children cry or talk out loud during worship or in other ways disrupt things in unpredictable ways, their spontaneity is regarded understandably more as an annoyance than as a gift. Nonetheless, children evoke a spirit of wonder and benediction and sometimes provide surprising and unsolicited consolation.

Children know when they have been excluded from the church's life. Such exclusion causes bewilderment, confusion, and hurt for the child. On the other hand, the inclusion of children as full participants in the life of a religious community is a regular reminder to adults that they are experiencing more than they know when they take part in the sacramental liturgies of the church. "All this is merely to suggest that in their own way children in fact play an extremely active, even prophetic, role in the household of faith."[3] These changes are most likely to occur when religious communities recognize the full humanity of children. When child membership is only provisional, however, the catholicity of the believing community is diminished and its witness to a new view of childhood is muffled, because being human is still defined by criteria of adulthood.

Christian rituals of initiation are more than a celebration of birth for the communities that surround the child. They are a divine act of adoption by which a child is claimed by God. Every ritual of initiation is the beginning of an individual's lifelong journey of dying and rising in Christ. The ritual is thus a sobering occasion for parents because it recognizes that this child will be confronted by evil that inhabits the world. This understanding of initiation is also a reminder for the parents that they hold their child as a sacred trust from God. This understanding of initiation can be a source of strength for people later in life who wonder if they were ever welcomed into their families of origin.

The spirit of Christian hospitality transforms the rituals of initiation into signs of the providential care of God. Both infant baptism and child dedication remind us, in spite of the reality of evil in the world, that the child will be held in the care of God and sustained by the prayers of the faith community. Because all life is sacred even when it is fragile, weakness and wobbliness have their protected and loving place—not only in the bosom of the family and in religious sanctuaries, but always and ultimately in the love of God.

> When our son was born I received a well-meaning and yet deeply disturbing letter from an older family friend. It conveyed her impressions of the violent, turbulent, and volatile world into which we had brought our child. She was not wrong. Within his first three months of life the President of the United States and Jim Brady were shot, the pope died, two passenger planes went down in accidents which killed everyone on board, John Lennon was murdered, and the Middle East erupted in renewed turmoil. I had not made the world such a terrible place, and yet I found my older friend's mournful letter disturbing. Our child's dedication in church came two weeks after the letter. In a wonderfully strange way, I was reassured that our son would be safe. I felt that the faithfulness of the church would treasure his frail existence in the midst of an imperfect world. (Stephanie)

Although it is essential that parents fulfill their nurturing and protecting responsibilities toward their children, God's trustworthiness ultimately transcends their own efforts to be dependable. Trust, faith, and hope are born in a child through the reciprocity of parental care and God's faithfulness. Because she believed that her son was held safe in the promises of God, Stephanie was free to care for him without being overly protective or anxious. When parents can rest in the promise of God's care, the ritual of initiation transforms a particular family's acceptance into global belonging.

Initiation as Individuation

The child who is initiated into a community and a life of faithful struggle is also particularized as a unique gift of God. To be baptized means to be chosen and named by God as a distinct individual and at the same time to be incorporated into a community that transcends all human particularity. *The ritual of initiation into Christian community is at the same time a reminder to parents that the child in their home is "theirs and not theirs" because the child belongs to God.* Parents bring life into the world only to give it away.

For the sake of the child parents need to understand that the ritual of welcome is at once also the ritual of releasing or letting go. Each child begins a new story that is uniquely his or her own. Infant baptism and child dedication are public acknowledgment that parents understand their role as an interim arrangement. The parents promise on behalf of a child who will someday stand alone before God. Parents and others in the believing community promise to tell the stories of faith and to impart by their life together the joy and meaning of the gospel. They also promise to speak freely of life's brokenness, evil, and pain. They do this not only because they love the child and want to be good parents, but also because they recognize that ultimately the child belongs not to them but to God. That is the paradox of parenthood from a Christian perspective.

Becoming a separate person capable of being in community with others is a lifelong process. It begins with the physical severing of the umbilical cord that sustained the unborn child. The process continues when the infant child begins to move away from the emotional womb that has been protecting and nurturing it from birth. Infant baptism or child dedication is another moment in the formation of a separate self. When Martin Luther suggested that the infant has faith, he was pointing to an unprovable truth that is central for the perspective we are developing: the child is an agent in his or her life process from birth. Baptism is the beginning of a discipleship that demands ultimate loyalty. In that sense, the psychological hatching of the baptized for the sake of autonomy is never an end in itself. It is always for the sake of discipleship.

Supporting Parents and Others in Their Care of Children

Support for parents begins before the child is born. The process of becoming married is itself preparation for being a parent. That process needs to accomplish two things essential to creating an environment hospitable to children: it needs to clarify relationships with the couple's families of origin while at the same time working toward building a relationship grounded in love and respect and marked by a willingness to sacrifice. Solidifying their marital bond is the most significant preparation expectant parents can make for the arrival of a child. Insofar as the church is engaged in an ongoing ministry with a newly married couple after the wedding, it is helping to establish a home that will be able to make emotional space for a child. (See *Becoming Married* in this Family Living in Pastoral Perspective series.)

The church is a community of support for everyone who has childrearing responsibilities. Most of the time, those people are parents, but there are others who also need support in their care of children. The nonparental wife or husband in a second marriage often struggles to establish a working relationship with children of a spouse. Sometimes the people needing support are distant grandparents, who are too far away to be of any direct help but close enough to the situation to feel a genuine concern for their grandchildren. Adult caregivers whose occupation is childcare in a hospital or a day care center or who serve as foster parents also need support. Much of the church's support for all people in these circumstances happens informally. There are also structured ways to support parents in their vocation of childrearing.

Preparation for Parenting

For churches that practice infant baptism, preparation of the parents for the sacrament has two foci: to review the meaning of baptism in the Christian's life, and to explore with the parents how the addition of this child has changed and will change their family's life. The intersection of the stories of the newborn, parents, and faith community is the soil in which baptismal rituals are planted. Infant dedication also begins an exploration that leads to the development of faith in the human life cycle.[4]

Preparation for the ritual moment of initiation is preparation for parenting. The story of the birth, the process of naming, the early fears and joys of having a child, the delight of grandparents who have waited so long for a grandchild, the struggle to find just ways of dividing the childcare responsibilities, the relationships that need healing, the other children who need a blessing are all appropriate topics to consider with new parents. The purpose of these questions is to help families understand the meaning of baptism or dedication in the midst of human growth and spiritual development. It is also an occasion to help families make explicit the beliefs that are often implicit in their daily living.

Religious communities have often responded to the struggles of daily family living by providing seminars on parenting skills. Teaching skills can be a helpful resource for developing a sense of competence in people who are overwhelmed by the demands of being a parent. Teaching childrearing skills in the church must always be done carefully so that it does not unwittingly undermine the fragile self-confidence that many parents have about their childrearing responsibilities. If our assessment of the crisis in parenting is accurate, the church would help by encouraging the qualities of hospitality, compassion, justice, and reconciliation that were described in chapter 4. The church provides an accepting atmosphere for parents to explore their values and beliefs as well as their fears and frustrations.

If the church is to be engaged in the process of effecting a transformation of our attitudes about children, it also needs to enhance the self-esteem of parents. One way this is accomplished is by affirming the *vocation of being a parent* as a Christian ministry through preaching and teaching and symbolic activity. It also means affirming the personal gifts of people who are parents. We began this book by noting that our children arc in trouble partly because adults disdain childhood. If the church is a sanctuary in which we are all struggling toward childhood, then it will care for its children by helping adults to honor the childness that endures in themselves and one another.

Abuse Prevention and the Church

The church cannot be silent on child abuse in our time. It is our sacred trust to create sanctuaries of healing for those who have been abused and for those who are abusers. The intent is not to promote forgiveness as a hasty peace but to recognize that every Christian community is a fellowship of reconciliation. The church also has the obligation to seek to prevent further child abuse by empowering people to ask questions, validate feelings, acknowledge the rights of children, and continue to struggle with the questions that experiences of abuse raise.[5] The church, more than any other community in society, understands with both clarity and compassion the depth of the individual and social evil of child abuse.

The sexual abuse of children is invasive and terrible, yet it exists on a continuum with other damaging patterns of physical, verbal, and psychological abuse. Sometimes the distinctions between contempt and abuse are too fine to distinguish. The transformation of attitude toward children implies more than the avoidance of violence; it requires an end to indifference or contempt toward children. Regard for their full humanity is the beginning of any program that seeks to prevent the emotional or physical or sexual abuse of children. The church is in a position to be a center for prevention by distributing information and fostering attentiveness regarding all forms of abuse. If a church is to work for the prevention of abuse, it will need to explore some of following questions:

1. *Is there sufficient information available?* Is there material on church bulletin boards or tract tables or in general publications about child abuse and the sexual abuse of children? What resources are available in your community to help both abusers and those abused?

2. *Does your Sunday school curriculum perpetuate male/female stereotypes?* Does it promote unquestioning obedience of parents? Does the teaching about marriage promote an understanding of mutual respect between women and men?

3. *What are the laws about confidentiality and the obligation to report signs of abuse?* Is it clear what people are to do if they suspect that children are being abused?

4. *What are the ways in which sexuality is considered as a positive gift in your community of faith?* Is the church at least a place in which parents are free to discuss their awkwardness in talking to children about sexuality? What is taught about sexuality and/or violence that might be confusing to children?

5. *Is your church a place where children and adults alike are free to go when they are hurt or hurting?* Is it a place where people are encouraged to ask hard questions of one another about how we live? Is it a community where personal sin is acknowledged and social evil is confronted?

Because the church is a *sanctuary for childhood*, it is a place that recognizes the vulnerability of adults as well as children. As such, the church needs to be a place that is safe enough for persons who abuse children to make confession *and* a place that protects children from harm. The church is always a voice for justice with reconciliation and compassion with challenge. Nonetheless, the primary advocacy of the church is for the most vulnerable—whoever is small, weak, and needy.

Churches and Families in Partnership: Forming Faithful Christians

The church and the family share an increasingly complex task in forming children into mature, sensitive, and faithful adults. That partnership is one manifestation of our belief that "it takes a village to raise a child." Neither church nor family can form faithful Christians alone. What is required is a shift away from a larger phenomenon called "the socialization of reproduction" in which childrearing functions were gradually transferred from the family to such social agencies as school, church, and recreation groups. Teaching the faith to children, once the responsibility of the family, has come to be regarded by too many families as a service the church provides. Churches today are finding it more and more difficult to fulfill that expectation because of declining personal and financial resources.

Families are themselves overwhelmed with the responsibility for fostering meaningful and encompassing values in their maturing children. Without the supportive network of other family members, without a shared set of values in the community, parents often articulate a feeling of inadequacy and confusion over what or how to teach their children, when and how to correct behavior, even what maturity is. Increasingly, parents of high school, middle school, and even elementary school children find that values and parenting strategies differ so greatly from one household to the next that it is also difficult to form the networks or alliances that once made parenting effective and decreased parental anxiety.

> When our daughter was fourteen, she ran away from home and was taken in by another family in our neighborhood. No one called me or my wife; they did not call the school or even the police. We were frantic. Finally, one of my daughter's friends told a favorite teacher where she was staying. We were furious with the parents who hid her from us. Their response stunned even more. "I didn't even want your daughter here," the mother said, "but my daughter demanded that she be allowed to stay. If I had called you, my daughter would have run away from me. I couldn't risk that. My daughter and I have a delicate trust." We felt so alone, as if there were no shared values, no common rules, nothing.   (Darrin)

What Darrin and his wife discovered is what all too frequently undermines even the best efforts at childrearing today: *the isolation of parents*. While the church cannot eliminate all differences of values or parenting strategies, it can provide a forum for sharing common struggles and a framework for exploring deeper values and common hopes while still honoring diversity.

It is important that parents pass on to the next generation what they believe and the biblical stories and other stories of faith that sustain those beliefs. The process of telling those stories and articulating that faith has, however, become more complex as society has become more pluralistic, secular, and open-ended. More and more people hold belief systems that are highly individualized and idiosyncratic, with relatively few roots in any organized or historic tradition. *The church and families need to be partners in forming mature and faithful individuals* who know the stories of faith but also understand how to resolve conflicts without violence, who are committed to mutual understanding, and who are comfortable with diversity without closing off the search for consensus or shared meanings.[6]

Learning by Participating

Children are sensitive about their "place" in any setting. It is therefore important that a church arrange and use its space in ways hospitable to children. For example, whenever there are special celebrations, such as baptisms, dedications, or confirmations, or when there are special instruments in worship, children need to be where they can see. Booster chairs for children would enable them to see more. Having a youth room that the "kids can mess up if they want" is useful, but it may convey that the rest of the church building belongs to the adults. If too many places in a building are off-limits to children, it should not be surprising when children conclude with some accuracy that they do not belong in the church.

A worship service is not aimed only at a child's level of perception or interest. Even so, a child's response can tell us a great deal about who we are and what we do. Children may be our least subtle warning to examine patterns of worship. They bring a naturalness to worship that raises questions about formalized routines. A child's response to worship can range from boredom or rebellion to confusion or fear. It is worth noting when a child observes, "My grandmother's church is all the same color—dark." Children may help us discover that worship need not be what it often is—overly intellectual and passive. A child's openness to gesture, touch, movement may be a reminder for everyone that we bring our bodies with us to worship.

I will always remember a library book on the Pilgrims, in which a pen-and-ink drawing portrayed the place of children in their churches. A deacon patrolled the church aisle during worship with a long pole in his hand. On one end was a feather for tickling the noses of adults who fell asleep; on the other end, a brass ball for rapping children on the head who talked or squirmed. When I was a child, my grandmother gave us cherry-flavored Life Savers in

church, whether we were good or bad, which I considered a sign of
our cultural advancement over the Pilgrims.   (Kyle)

A weekly children's sermon is another way to communicate with
children their place in worship. The children's sermon is a moment for
storytelling. Well-told stories from scripture and the history of Christian faithfulness enrich a child's imagination. What is most important,
however, is that children feel included and valued and loved by the
community of faith. It is the children's time in an assembly otherwise
mostly designed for adults.[7] The "children's time" also provides an opportunity for a public conversation that builds a pastoral relationship
with them. Like the closeness and respect and humor children often develop with special teachers, the relationship between children and their
pastor contributes to the sense of belonging and trust which are the
building blocks of faith.

This time with children in the Sunday liturgy is an opportunity
often misused. In order to diminish the abuse of children under the
guise of welcoming them, we need to be very clear about why and for
whom we do children's sermons. When children are asked questions
that even adults find difficult to answer, an event aimed at including
children furthers indifference by disregarding the world of the child.
What we say to children must begin inside their world. Even when
children are spontaneous and immediate and say cute things, bringing
laughter to churches, it is abusive to enjoy them at the expense of their
dignity.

As children grow in the church, hands-on participation furthers
their understanding and belonging. Responsibilities vary with age and
competence, and range from group singing and acting as acolyte to
scripture reading or ushering. It is always important that instructions
and expectations are clear. Children do not like to fail, especially in
public. The worship service holds such power and mystery for a child
that the issues of "being invited" and "messing up" are both significantly enhanced. By giving children meaningful and appropriate roles,
constructive behavior and hard questions are encouraged.

I have taken very enthusiastic and hardworking work-campers to
the Arkansas ranch of the ecumenical agricultural and livestock
mission Heifer Project International. There they have done everything from fence repair and painting to slopping pigs and vaccinat-
ing lambs. In one session, they began the week by pounding white
wooden crosses into the ground to represent the infant mortality

> rates in various parts of the world. At the end of their work week,
> they triumphantly removed crosses from the ground. Infant mor-
> tality was still a world challenge, they were told, but they were
> now a part of the solution.   (Susan)

There comes the moment when children, as with the group that
went to Arkansas, begin to claim the status and power of the adult
world of faith. They need real jobs to do that will help them see themselves as part of the solution. They need freedom to be fearless and
relentless investigators in preparation for their own adult baptism or
confirmation of baptism. Their questions, sometimes perceived by
adults as a mixture of doubt, protest, and genuine inquiry, spring from
their budding intellect and ego *and* from a deepening insecurity regarding their competence as persons in a complex world. If we regard
our children and their questions with respect, it is more likely that they
will experience the church as a community of committed inquiry as
well as of faith.

Interpreting the World with Children

Children live with more fears than most adults realize. Not so
long ago, we were aware of the effects of the threat of nuclear war on
children; now our children worry whether our devastation of the environment will leave a planet for them to inhabit when they grow up.
Parents who respect the full humanity of their children know how
much their children worry. Concern about issues like the use of drugs,
crime, teenage pregnancy, and AIDS is overwhelming to children and
adults. When children and adults do not have a context in which to
speak about these worries, the result is isolation and fear rather than
community and compassionate understanding.

> An eight-year-old child in our community was hit and killed by a
> drunk driver. The family belonged to another local church and
> was well known in school and community affairs. Three weeks
> after the funeral, I was giving my children's sermon on a Sunday
> morning. I don't remember what I was talking about, but as I was
> finishing, Annie, also eight, raised her hand. "Next week, will you
> talk about drunk driving?" she asked.   (Susan)

It is impossible to shield children from all the suffering and concerns of the world. It is also difficult to interpret danger, evil, and
tragedy to children. The task of churches and families is not just to
protect children, but to make them feel safe and empower them with

a sense of agency in a world whose menace is overwhelming for everyone. The church has both the theological capacity and the mandate to help children and families cope with the jarring realities to which children are exposed without creating new fear. It does this by helping them interpret *their* experience of the world with an awareness that God is present.

Forming Children for Faithful Living

In order to be strengthened to face the jarring realities of living in today's world, children need to know the stories of faith that sustain all Christians and shape their identity. Children also need to be formed by a spirituality appropriate to their age—to be faithful in Christian living when they are eight or twelve or fifteen years old. The five traits that follow are only suggestive of faithful Christian living for children. What is finally most important is the recognition that children have their own spirituality and that they struggle to remain faithful to the way they were formed.[8]

1. *Becoming respectful of differences.* Parents intentionally and unintentionally pass on their own attitudes about people and ideas that are different. Those attitudes may or may not be tolerant. Being formed as a person who is respectful of difference is more than being tolerant. It begins with the conviction that difference is respected because the uniqueness or specialness of each person is to be honored. Children are formed into respectful persons by being respected. Helping children learn how to consider the stranger as someone who has gifts to give that will enhance life is a delicate and yet essential task for our time. Children who are respectful of difference will be hospitable to differences in their already diverse and complex world.

2. *Becoming persons of courage.* We teach young children to be brave. We do not want them to be afraid of the dark or of new challenges or unfamiliar surroundings. We often assume that if we can teach children not to be afraid, they will be brave. So we tell children stories of bravery they love to hear. The courage we want our children to discover is beyond bravery. It is born in community. It is the courage we discover when we are held and we know that we are no longer alone. To be alone and frightened is a terrible thing for adults as well as children. Hopefulness is one response to all the calamities of life children see. Courage is another. Courage is not the lack of fear but the resolve to act in spite of fear. It is a way of being in the world sustained by the promise of God's presence that transcends fear without eliminating it.

Our children need to know the courage that comes from being loved by God even in the midst of being afraid.

3. *Practicing generosity*. Teaching children how to share is an early socializing task. It is an essential skill for living with others, which counters the impulse to be possessive of what is mine or even what is not mine. When children share toys, they do not give away what they possess. Hence being generous is beyond sharing. It is the willingness to give away what I have because another's needs are greater. The spirit of generosity in children is built upon two other characteristics: one is imagination; the other is the belief that a child has gifts to give. We are reminded again how essential it is for the personal and spiritual well-being of children that they be regarded as fully human with gifts to give from the beginning.

4. *Becoming grateful.* Gratitude is the essence of Christian living. Parents try to teach their children to say thank you even before they know what it means. If they are given something, the parental litany is usually something like "What do you say?" and the expected response is some variation of thank you. Adults will need to be prepared to be surprised by what children include when they are encouraged to be thankful.

> My children's sermon on Thanksgiving always begins by asking them what they are thankful for. On one occasion, a little girl was quick to say, "I am thankful for my baby sister." I knew there was no newborn child in that household. The mother had been divorced for five years and took care of her children alone. No one else volunteered any thankfulness, so I finally asked, "What baby sister?" "The one my dad and his new wife had," she said. About all I could say was something like "A baby is something to be thankful for." (Susan)

The quality of gratitude is, however, more than saying thank you. It is rooted in the awareness that all of life is gift. We hope our children will grow to understand that everything we have is from God. Possessing things is not the same as being grateful for them. Parents who respond to their children as gifts will be likely to foster this attitude of gratitude.

5. *Learning to lament*. We hold babies when they cry. Unfortunately, we eventually stifle the natural capacity to lament by encouraging children not to cry. As children get older and more private, parents worry when their children are sad and will not say why. If our children are to be prepared to be attentive to the pain they see without being

overwhelmed, we will need to teach them to lament. The alternative to lamentation is apathy. When people become apathetic, nothing matters. Apathy is a common malady of our time, which children learn too well. It is a way of coping with pain and suffering by not feeling.

> I had sent my seven-year-old daughter to the little grocery store in our neighborhood, partly because we needed bread and partly because she was being a pest. I began to worry and then felt guilty when she was gone longer than she should have been. Just as I was about to look for her, Carly waltzed in the door without the bread. When I scolded her about being late, she said firmly: "Bonnie's doll broke its arm. I had to help her." I said some foolish parental thing like "You don't know how to fix a doll." "I could help her cry" was all Carly said, with considerable dignity, and walked away.   (Velma)

Jeremiah lamented over the people of Judah because "death has come up into our windows" and the children have been cut off from the streets (Jer. 9:21). In response to the ruin of the land, the prophet encouraged women to "teach . . . your daughters a dirge, and each to her neighbor a lament" (9:20). In order to live with suffering and injustice without apathy, we will need to teach our children to lament. Carly already knew that helping Bonnie cry was something she could do. What Carly will learn later is that we need to lament so that reconciliation is honest and justice real.

Caring for Families in Crisis

The term "family crisis" is used here in two ways. The first crisis is in the family itself. The family is an institution under siege. Even ordinary events like starting school, going to birthday parties, managing adolescence, and leaving home are potential crises for families or individuals who are vulnerable because of economic insecurity or emotional poverty or perplexing diversity or random violence. The second family crisis is in the society. Forces we have identified as the "culture of indifference" continue to disempower the family in its relation to society. The agendas for the family and the society in response to this crisis are therefore the same.

The church has been and continues to be a resource for families at the time of personal catastrophe. Sometimes, the church and its clergy are even expected to intervene in situations where social services and government agencies may have evaluated the intervention as too dangerous or costly, or where they may not be welcome. The church is also called to articulate a vision of societies and families in which the full humanity of children is honored. A third response of the church to the family crises today is a less familiar one. The church must help to mobilize and strategize for change within neighborhoods and corporations and in government in order to refashion social structures in ways more hospitable to children and families. Even though particular congregations may not be able to respond to family crises in all three ways, the church as a whole must keep all three responses in balance.

Extraordinary Crises

People still expect support from the church when a child is arrested for possessing drugs or a father is laid off from his six-figure management job or when the mother's father has a stroke or when a marriage ends in divorce. There are some times, however, when the family crisis is beyond the competency of the church's ministry. The growing acceptance of the practice of family therapy makes it a very helpful resource for families when the conflict is old and the destructive patterns of interaction are complex. Because helping families change requires more time and skill than they usually possess, clergy need to be familiar with therapeutic sources that work with families from a systemic perspective.

One of the most difficult and important tasks in the pastoral care of families is to help them see that the problem they have defined in relation to a child or some other individual is in fact a problem for the system as a whole. As with any good care, this intervention must begin by acknowledging how the family has defined its dilemma. Responding to this phenomenon of scapegoating in families in this way is a ministry for the sake of justice, because we are seeking to take back the problem from one person and give it to the whole family, where it belongs. Because families have often invested a great deal in their definition, pastoral efforts at reframing are likely to meet with resistance.

In some situations it is neither possible nor necessary to make a referral. What families may need is a third and neutral ear to help them seek out an answer to an emotional and/or ethical muddle. They may need support through the grief of an unexpected and traumatic loss. Sometimes families simply need a referee to ensure that people fight fair, keep the conflict contained, and return to their own corners when the struggle is over. Very often, the trouble in a family that prompts them to seek help, or for which they need help they do not seek, is that

things are out of balance. In order to restore things to proper paradoxical balance, it may be necessary for the pastor to "say the other side."
In order to provide that resource, pastors need to stay close and stay
differentiated from families in their care.

Strategies for Change

Our privatism about pain often impairs the church's ability to
make accurate assessments for the sake of helpful interventions in response to the issues in our families, our communities, and our society.
We have already noted how the churches have participated in the culture
of indifference by remaining silent on abuse in the family. It is also an
indictment of the church that it has not led the way in seeking a public
policy on the family. In order to develop appropriate strategies for social
change on behalf of children and families, we need to speak freely in the
church about what is not working. If we *see clearly* the anguish of many
of our children and families, we will widen the horizons of our care. Seeing clearly is the first task for the sake of change. Unfortunately, families who want to hide their pain create churches that do the same.

If communities of faith are able to transcend their fears of dis-
closure and make an honest assessment of the state of childhood in
their midst, families may not need to hide their pain so much. However, as long as every family suffers alone, the underlying culture of indifference toward children will continue unchallenged. If, however,
every church were to become a sanctuary in which families and individuals struggle together, the indifference toward children in the culture would change. If every church determined to do one thing,
however modest, for children in its neighborhood, it would be a sign to
children that they have not been forgotten.[9]

Churches are unique social organizations because they are volun-
tary and most often community-based. Social workers and family therapists are increasingly convinced that services that work must be
community-based in order to empower families to solve their own problems. Beyond this, in situations that demand organized community advocacy to address basic community needs, the church plays an
important role in bringing people together to solve their own problems,
in articulating a vision and in selecting safe, effective, and morally de-
fensible strategies.

In the meantime, interim strategies will continue to be needed.
The church has provided and still needs to provide a safety net for
families by distributing clothes, running soup kitchens and shelters for the

homeless, sponsoring day care centers, and providing programs in literacy. Churches have helped to advocate for and sponsor blood pressure clinics, inoculation drives, and WIC (Women, Infants, and Children's Supplemental Food) programs. Where community needs are not being met, churches have provided effective mediation between the individuals and families in a community and the community's service institutions and professional social services networks. It is critical, however, for the sake of more fundamental change in the social order, that churches and clergy continue to ask to what extent these interim strategies support the status quo through effective but short-term crisis management.

It is clear that a major reformation of the social order is necessary in order to maintain the family as a viable social unit in modern American society. The role of the church and its clergy in this reformation is both pivotal and daunting. If the church is to be an integrative force in society, it must simultaneously help families in crisis *and* contribute to the reformation of the social context. Churches will continue to sustain families through ordinary and extraordinary crises even though the resources of the churches are dwindling because of decreased volunteer hours and greater financial constraints. For the sake of all children, the church must also participate in the unfamiliar work of social reform and community development. In order to be a credible catalyst for change, churches must also consider how they have participated in the culture of indifference.

Challenging the Indifference Toward Children

We end where we began. The fundamental challenge of our time is the transformation of our attitude toward children and childhood from indifference to respect. It is a challenge for which the church is uniquely qualified. Government may pass laws requiring fathers to pay child support. Corporations and small businesses may decide it is in their interest to provide day care centers and generous family leave time. Neighborhoods may mobilize organized vigilance against crime or add playgrounds and park benches. All these actions will enhance the environment for children. Yet in order for these changes to endure, we need to honor the full humanity of children.

The church is the voice of conscience in the social order. It exercises this prophetic task by articulating a vision of justice and peacefulness for all persons in society. The church is also a sanctuary for childhood, which welcomes and guides children, nourishes parents, and intervenes in ordinary and extraordinary family crises. Local communities of faith regularly make difficult choices regarding the allocation of their increasingly limited resources. Even so, churches are called to embody the vision they proclaim. In that sense, congregations witness to the larger society by the way they welcome children and support families who are struggling to do the best they can.

The troubling reality for many churches is that they have more tasks to do than resources with which to do them. Families and churches are alike in that matter. More and more is being asked of fewer and fewer. Churches regularly struggle with responding to the ordinary and extraordinary crises among children and families while still articulating a compelling vision in response to the larger cultural and social issues of our day. Both of these roles are pivotal and are linked together in the promise that God continues to make all things new. The church and the family and larger social structures like neighborhoods and government also share a common agenda. Unless the larger social environments begin to change, not even the church—with all its charity and compassion—will be able to meet the desperate needs of families and children today.

The role of the church in this common agenda is not only to continue to articulate a vision of a new social order in which those who are small, weak, or needy are always safe. The church is also to embody countercultural community that lives according to the paradoxical belief that the fullness of humanity is to be found in struggling toward childhood. The corollary to that belief is also inescapable: if childhood dies, we will never see God. The church has an obligation to speak out for all people, especially for the poor and oppressed and most vulnerable among us, in order that our children will be safe. In that sense, the care of children itself is a window on what we believe.

Jesus placed a child at the center of the circle. The faithfulness of the church's witness to Jesus is measured by how it regards the weakest and most vulnerable in our midst. When a society understands and is in sympathy with childhood, it will not wield power over others, valorize violence, practice discrimination, teach hate, destroy the environment, or preach materialism or indifference toward anyone. A church that is a sanctuary for childhood will not lose its theological focus, although a variety of issues may emerge and recede over time. Children are not more important than the poor, the sick, the elderly, the environment, or other causes; but our compassion for childhood (and thus for children) is a life-sign. With it we take our pulse as humanity.

NOTES

Introduction

1. *New York Times*, April 6, 1992, Sec. B, p. 3.

2. Herbert Anderson, *The Family and Pastoral Care* (Philadelphia: Fortress Press, 1984), 37.

Chapter 1. Nothing Greater Than a Child

1. Robert Coles, "Struggling toward Childhood: An Interview with Robert Coles," *Second Opinion* 18, 4 (April 1993): 58–71.

2. Philippe Aries (trans. Robert Baldick), *Centuries of Childhood: A Social History of Family Life* (New York: Vintage Books, 1962).

3. John Boswell, *The Kindness of Strangers: The Abandonment of Children in Western Europe from Late Antiquity to the Renaissance* (New York: Pantheon Books, 1988) According to Boswell, abandonment was not always a sign of indifference. Parents abandoned their children because of poverty and shame or when domestic resources would be compromised by another mouth. They hoped the child would be found and cared for by someone else. "Society relied on the kindness of strangers to protect its extra children, a kindness much admired and prominent in the public consciousness" (433). Eventually, however, what had been a relatively effective system of transferring child-rearing responsibility in ancient and medieval Europe became a simple technique of disposal.

4. Aries, *Centuries of Childhood*, 133.

5. Marie Luise Kaschnitz, *The House of Childhood*, trans. Anni Whissen (Lincoln, Neb.: University of Nebraska Press, 1991), 3, 5.

6. Floyd M. Martinson, *Growing Up in Norway, 800 to 1990* (Carbondale, Ill.: Southern Illinois University Press, 1992).

7. Ibid., 2.

8. Jon D. Levenson, *The Death and Resurrection of the Beloved Son: The Transformation of Child Sacrifice in Judaism and Christianity* (New Haven, Conn.: Yale University Press, 1993).

9. Steven Ozment, *When Fathers Rule: Family Life in Reformation Europe* (Cambridge, Mass.: Harvard University Press, 1983), 153.

10. Philip Greven, *Spare the Child: The Religious Roots of Punishment and the Psychological Impact of Physical Abuse* (New York: Alfred A. Knopf, 1990), 46.

11. Aries, *Centuries of Childhood*, 413.

12. Ozment, *When Fathers Rule*, 133.

13. Quoted in ibid, 136. It is common from an African perspective to regard the child as not yet a person. "To say that a small child is 'water' is equivalent to saying that he is not yet a person, that he has no social meaning yet. He is not solid yet. Belonging still to the cosmos, he must grow tough before he asserts himself as a social being, and this process involves many dangers." From Pierre Erny, *Childhood and Cosmos: The Social Psychology of the Black African Child,* quoted in Thomas A. Nairn, "The Use of Zairian Children in HIV Vaccine Experimentation," *The Annual of the Society of Christian Ethics,* 1993, 238.

14. Ozment, *When Fathers Rule*, 139.

15. Janet Pais, *Suffer the Children: A Theology of Liberation by a Victim of Child Abuse* (Mahwah, N.J.: Paulist Press, 1991), 9.

16. Martinson, *Growing Up in Norway*, 10.

17. Pais, *Suffer the Children*, 16.

18. Coles, "Struggling toward Childhood," 71.

19. Karl Rahner, *Theological Investigations 8* (New York: Herder & Herder, 1971), 48–49.

20. Martinson, *Growing Up in Norway*, 11.

21. Arthur C. McGill, *Death and Life: An American Theology* (Philadelphia: Fortress Press, 1987), 83.

Chapter 2. Children Change Things

1. Some of these themes were first developed in Herbert Anderson, "Pastoral Care in the Process of Initiation," in *Alternative Futures for Worship: Baptism and Confirmation*, vol. 2, ed. Mark Searle (Collegeville, Minn.: Liturgical Press, 1987), 103–136.

2. Anna Quindlen, "Off on an Adventure: Not Observing Life, But Simply Living It," *New York Times*, December 1, 1988. For an empirical assessment of the impact of the addition of a child, see Jerry M. Lewis, M.D., *The Birth of the Family: An Empirical Inquiry*, (New York: Brunner/Mazel, 1989). We have taken for granted that parents affect children and that children must be taken care of, but we have overlooked the fact that children can also affect their parents in a wide spectrum of ways. See Anne-Marie Ambert, *The Effect of Children on Parents* (New York: Haworth Press, 1992).

3. Bonnie J. Miller-McLemore, *Also a Mother: Work and Family as Theological Dilemma* (Nashville: Abingdon Press, 1994), 158. We agree with Miller-McLemore when she suggests that "a theology that begins to listen more attentively to its mothers and children will gain insight into the demands and dynamics of nurture, the creation of personhood, the blessings of mutuality, and the values of the gift of life" (40). Her aim is to redefine the roles of

mothers and fathers in order to enhance the practice of childrearing; our focus on developing a new respect for childhood seeks to accomplish the same aim.

4. Kenneth R. Mitchell, personal correspondence.

5. Colin Harrison, editorial, *New York Times*, August 31, 1993. See Philip and Carolyn Cowan, *When Partners Become Parents* (New York: Harper-Collins, 1992). In a ten-year study that followed the lives of seventy-two couples and their firstborn children, the Cowans document carefully the decrease in marital satisfaction during the first months of parenthood. The loss of intimacy and the loss of self-esteem are common and not surprising. What was most disappointing to the couples that the Cowans studied was that the egalitarian ideas of shared childrearing did not materialize as expected.

6. Miller-McLemore, *Also a Mother*.

7. Edwin Friedman, *Generation to Generation* (New York: Guilford Press, 1985), 35.

8. Leo Tolstoy, *Anna Karenina,* quoted in *The Oxford Book of Marriage* (New York: Oxford University Press, 1990), 169.

9. Walter Brueggemann, "Will Our Faith Have Children?" *Word and World* 3, 3 (1983): 272–83.

10. Ted Peters, *God—the World's Future: Systematic Theology for a Postmodern Era* (Minneapolis: Fortress Press, 1992), 170.

Chapter 3. What Are Families For?

1. There are many books on parents. Some cover particular developmental tasks, others address major agendas in the childrearing process. Still others are concerned with particular roles in raising children. We hope that this book will give a framework for evaluating these books from the perspective of Christian theology. In his revised edition of *On Becoming a Family: The Growth of Attachment Before and After Birth*, T. Berry Brazelton, M.D., has effectively incorporated new studies on the early development of attachment between infants and parents (New York: Delta/Seymour Lawrence, 1992). See also James Comer, M.D., and Alvin Poussaint, M.D., *Raising Black Children* (New York: Penguin Books, 1992).

2. W. H. Auden, "Mundus et Infans," from *Selected Poetry of W. H. Auden* (New York: Modern Library, 1958), 76.

3. Ibid.

4. Urie Bronfenbrenner, "Discover What Families Do," in *Rebuilding the Nest: A New Commitment to the American Family,* ed. David Blankenhorn et al. (Milwaukee: Families International, 1990), 27–38. (The phrase "crazy about kids" appeared in an earlier version of this essay.)

5. "*Mirroring needs*: a need to feel affirmed, confirmed, recognized; to be feeling accepted and appreciated, especially when able to show oneself," from Ernest S. Wolf, M.D., *Treating the Self* (New York: Guilford Press, 1988), 55.

6. James Garbarino, Kathleen Kostelny, and Nancy Dudrow, *No Place to Be a Child: Growing Up in a War Zone* (Lexington, Mass.: D. C. Heath & Co., 1991).

7. David Elkind, *The Hurried Child: Growing Up Too Fast Too Soon*, rev. ed. (Reading, Mass.: Addison-Wesley Publishing Co., 1988).

8. Samuel Osherman, *Finding Our Fathers: How a Man's Life Is Shaped by His Relationship with His Father* (New York: Fawcett Book Group, Columbine, 1986).

9. Kahlil Gibran, *The Prophet* (New York: Alfred A. Knopf, 1923), 18.

10. John Paul II, "Apostolic Exhortation on the Family," *Origins* 11, 28–29 (December 24, 1981).

11. Quoted in *New York Times*, October 1, 1990, sec. A, 10.

12. Gilbert Meilaender, "What Are Families For?" *First Things*, no. 6 (October 1990), 39.

13. John Paul II, "Apostolic Exhortation on the Family," 439.

14. Martin Luther, "The Estate of Marriage," in *Luther's Works*, ed. Walther I. Brandt, vol. 45 (Philadelphia: Muhlenberg Press, 1962), 46.

15. Herbert Anderson, *The Family and Pastoral Care* (Philadelphia: Fortress Press, 1984), 21–79.

16. Pamela Couture, *Blessed Are the Poor?: Women's Poverty, Family Poverty, and Practical Theology* (Nashville: Abingdon Press, 1991).

Chapter 4. Christian Themes for Family Living

1. It was Donald W. Winnicott who is identified with the phrase "the good enough mother," from *The Maturational Processes and the Facilitating Environment: Studies in the Theory of Emotional Development* (London: Hogarth Press and the Institute for Psychoanalysis, 1965), see 37–55. Bruno Bettelheim expanded the metaphor in *A Good Enough Parent: A Book on Child-Rearing* (New York: Random House, 1987). Our use of this metaphor is a continuation of Bettelheim's intent. "My title suggests that in order to raise a child well one ought not to try to be a perfect parent, as much as one should not expect one's child to be, or to become, a perfect individual. . . . But it is quite possible to be a good enough parent—that is, a parent who raises his [or her] child well," xi.

2. Joel H. Anderson, "Self-reflection, Intersubjective Critique, and Ethical Autonomy," trans. Joel H. Anderson, *Deutsche Zeitschrift für Philosophie* 42, 1 (1994): 97.

3. This distinction between a theology *for* the family and a theology *of* the family was first developed in Herbert Anderson, *The Family and Pastoral Care* (Philadelphia: Fortress Press, 1984), 9–18.

4. Thomas W. Ogeltree, *Hospitality to the Stranger: Dimensions of Moral Understanding* (Philadelphia: Fortress Press, 1985.

5. Kosuke Koyama, "Extending Hospitality to Strangers: A Missiology of *Theologia Crucis*," *Currents* 20, 3 (June 1993): 169.

6. Ogeltree, *Hospitality to the Stranger*, 3.

7. Dianne Bergant, "Compassion in the Bible," in *Compassionate Ministry*, ed. Gary L. Sapp (Birmingham, Ala.: Religious Education Press, 1993), 25.

8. Donald P. McNeill, Douglas A. Morrison, and Henri J.M. Nouwen, *Compassion: A Reflection on the Christian Life* (Garden City, N. Y.: Doubleday & Co., 1983), 4. For a comprehensive treatment of the need for parental compassion, see *Compassionate Child-Rearing: An In-Depth Approach to Optimal Parenting,* by Robert W. Firestone (New York: Plenum Press, 1990).

9. Larry L. Rasmussen, *Moral Fragments & Moral Community: A Proposal for Church and Society* (Minneapolis: Fortress Press, 1993). In his chapter entitled "The Ecology of Moral Community," Rasmussen reinforces the importance of the family as a community of moral inquiry: "Our most basic moral learning is prior to the 'reason' with which we might eventually question, clarify, and extend it, and the communities of intimate others first work this crucial moral work. . . . There simply is no substitute for small-scale communities of moral generation" (124, 135).

10. The pioneer work of Kathleen and James McGinnis promoting the family as a school for peace and justice is reflected in their book *Parenting for Peace and Justice* (Maryknoll, N. Y.: Orbis Books, 1988). For a more general consideration of this theme, see *Bringing Up a Moral Child: A New Approach for Teaching Your Child to Be Kind, Just, and Responsible,* by Michael Schulman and Eva Mekler (Reading, Mass.: Addison-Wesley Publishing Co., 1985).

11. Walter Brueggemann, Sharon Parks, Thomas H. Groome, *To Act Justly, Love Tenderly, Walk Humbly: An Agenda for Ministers* (Mahwah, N.J.: Paulist Press, 1986), 5.

12. Karen Lebacqz, *Justice in an Unjust World: Foundations for a Christian Approach to Justice* (Minneapolis: Augsburg Publishing House, 1987), 153.

13. Evan Imber-Black, ed., *Secrets in Families and Family Therapy* (New York: W.W. Norton & Co., 1993).

14. Robert J. Schreiter, *Reconciliation: Mission and Ministry in a Changing Social Order* (Maryknoll, N. Y.: Orbis Books, 1992). The theme of forgiveness/reconciliation in the family is not important only as a religious perspective. See Terry D. Hargrave, *Families and Forgiveness: Healing Wounds in the Intergenerational Family* (New York: Brunner/Mazel Publishers, 1994).

15. Schreiter, *Reconciliation*, 23.

16. Ibid., 72.

Chapter 5. It Takes a Village to Raise a Child

1. Pierre Teilhard de Chardin, *The Phenomenon of Man*, trans. Bernard Wall (New York: Harper & Brothers, 1959), 48.

2. A more complete exploration of the theme of interdependence is found in Herbert Anderson, *The Family and Pastoral Care* (Philadelphia: Fortress Press, 1984), 50–58.

3. Jaime Inclan and Ernesto Ferran, Jr., "Poverty, Politics, and Family Therapy: A Role for Systems Theory," in *The Social and Political Contexts of Family Therapy*, ed. Marsha Pravder Mirkin (Needham Heights, Mass.: Allyn & Bacon, 1990), 209.

4. *Children and Development in the 1990's: A UNICEF Sourcebook,* on the occasion of the World Summit for Children, September 29–30, 1990, (New York: United Nations).

5. Ibid., 47–131.

6. U.S. Catholic Conference of Bishops, "Putting Children and Families First," *Origins* 21, 25 (November 28, 1991).

7. *Children and Development in the 1990s*, 7, (italics added), The Convention on the Rights of the Child was adopted by consensus on November 20,

1989. It is the "Magna Carta" for children, detailing "the individual rights of any person under 18 years of age to develop to his or her full potential, free from hunger, want, neglect, exploitation, and other abuses" (8). For a philosophical consideration of the rights of a child, see Loren E. Lomasky, *Persons, Rights, and the Moral Community* (New York: Oxford University Press, 1987). Children's rights, Lomasky argues, "rest on precisely the same ground as those of adults: creation by a God who endows them with rights. . . . Respect within the family for the individuality of each of its members is the precursor of a rights-regarding community" (170–71).

8. *Children and Development in the 1990s*, 9.

9. U.S. Catholic Conference of Bishops, "Putting Children and Families First," 9.

10. Ulrich Beck, *Risk Society: Towards a New Modernity*, trans. Mark Ritter (Newbury Park, Calif.; Sage Publications, 1992). "The market subject is ultimately the single individual, 'unhindered' by a relationship, marriage, or family" (116). It is not surprising that the family is often a constant juggling act of disparate, multiple ambitions requiring maximum mobility, with the obligations of being married and raising children.

11. *Children and Development in the 1990s*, 154.

12. Robert N. Bellah et al., *Habits of the Heart: Individualism and Commitment in American Life* (Berkeley: University of California Press, 1985). Privatization of the family is an extension of the individualism that is pervasive in our society. "Taking care of one's own," Bellah observes, is an admirable motive. "But when it combines with suspicion of, and withdrawal from, the public world, it is one of the conditions of the despotism Tocqueville feared" (112).

13. Beck, *Risk Society*, 116.

14. Barbara Ehrenreich, "The American Family v. The American Dream," *Family Networker* 16, 5 (September-October 1992): 55–60.

15. Christopher Lasch, *Haven in a Heartless World: The Family Besieged* (New York: Basic Books, 1977)

16. Robert N. Bellah, *The Good Society* (New York: Alfred A. Knopf, 1991), 260.

Chapter 6. The Church as a Sanctuary for Childhood

1. Ted Peters, *God—the World's Future: Systematic Theology for a Postmodern Era* (Minneapolis: Fortress Press, 1992), 297.

2. Margaret L. Hammer, *Giving Birth: Reclaiming Biblical Metaphor for Pastoral Practice* (Louisville, Ky.: Westminster/John Knox Press, 1994), 4.

3. Ibid., 50. A very useful discussion of the place of children in the church may be found in *Children in the Assembly of the Church*, ed. Eleanor Bernstein, C.S.J., and John Brooks-Leonard (Chicago: Liturgy Training Publications, 1992).

4. Herbert Anderson and Ed Foley, Capuchin, "The Birth of a Story," *New Theology Review* 4, 4 (November 1991): 46–61.

5. We are indebted to Deb Rossbach of Cleveland, Ohio, for her help on the issue of abuse, her insights on the ways in which the church continues to ignore or belittle the issue of family abuse, and her passion regarding the role of the church in the prevention of child abuse. For a particular resource for

congregations, see Jade C. Angelica, *A Moral Emergency: Breaking the Cycle of Child Abuse* (Kansas City, Mo.: Sheed & Ward, 1993). See also Mary D. Pellauer, Barbara Chester, Jan Boyajian, *Sexual Assault and Abuse: A Handbook for Clergy and Religious Professionals* (San Francisco: Harper & Row, 1987). For in-depth theological examination of the issue, see James Newton Poling, *The Abuse of Power: A Theological Problem* (Nashville: Abingdon Pres, 1991). Information on particular issues can be found by contacting the Center for the Prevention of Sexual and Domestic Violence, 1914 North 34th, Suite 105, Seattle, WA 98103.

6. David W. Anderson called for this kind of partnership in a brief essay "Home and Congregation—Partners," in *The Lutheran*, vol. 6, 2 (February 1993): 23. For a general discussion of this partnership, see Diana S. Richmond Garland and Diane L. Pancoast, *The Church's Ministry with Families* (Waco: Word Books, 1990).

7. Jerry Schmalenberger, *Plane Thoughts on Pastoral Ministry* (Lima, Ohio: CSS Publishing Company, 1994), 91–93. For a more thorough consideration of children's sermons, see Gerard A. Pottebaum, *To Walk with a Child: Homiletics for Children* (Loveland, Ohio: Treehaus Communications, 1993).

8. No one has captured the voices of the children of our age better than Robert Coles. See *The Spiritual Life of Children* (Boston: Houghton Mifflin Co., 1990). Susanne Johnson has proposed that the church's educational task should be understood in terms of Christian spiritual formation. Her emphasis on participation as the theological foundation of formation is a significant advance in the direction of developing an approach that presumes the full humanity of the child. What is missing from her approach is sufficient attention to the reciprocity between church *and* family in that formation process. See Susanne Johnson, *Christian Spiritual Formation in the Church and Classroom* (Nashville: Abingdon Press, 1989).

9. One of the best resources for the church's ministry of advocacy is put out by the Children's Defense Fund. Kathleen A. Guy, *Welcome the Child: A Child Advocacy Guide for Churches* (Washington, D.C.: Children's Defense Fund, 1991). This book is an effort to add another voice to the movement of advocacy for children. For a summary of some of the issues of advocacy, see "Child Advocacy: Let's Get the Job Done," by Nancy Amidei, in *Dissent*, Spring 1993. Her words reinforce the conclusion of this book: "Progress toward securing basic health, education, and income support will not come easily, but it would make a dramatic difference in children's lives. Done right, the effort would strengthen our sense of community and mutual responsibility for the vulnerable among us. . . . Meanwhile, year after year children die. To paraphrase the president, *in the depth of winter, we must force the spring*" (220).